FICTION FACTORY INCORPORATED

Published/Created: Knoxville, KY: Fiction Factory
Incorporated, 2016.

Edited by R.M. Collins & A. D. Cox

Front and back cover design by James Grea

Library of Congress Cataloging-in-Publication Data

Incorporated, Fiction Factory.

The Forgotten Federation by Fiction Factory Incorporated:

1st ed.

p.   cm.

Summary: A gifted geneticist battling a tyrannical world
government struggles to locate and edify a new generation of
superheroes to save a crumbling world.

ISBN-10: 1535171782   ISBN-13: 978-1535171786

1   2   3   4   5   6   7   8   9

[1. Superheroes — Fiction.   2. Aliens — Fiction]

DEDICATION

For Robert...who over the years has shown me exactly what it takes to be a superhero.

Other books by **FICTION FACTORY INCORPORATED**

VICKIE VAN HELSING

Haunting Thelma Thimblewhistle

The Chronicles of Dead Anna

CONTENTS

RESURRECTION

Hudson couldn't help but smile at the drawing. Sure, it was creative. He propped his elbows onto the lunch table and examined it closer. He sat there chewing on his favorite pencil, the one he always gnawed on, the one that was most likely killing him by lead poisoning. The Harland University newspaper highlighted the headline: NEAR-MISS AT GENETICS LAB. Below the caption was a photo of broken, singed equipment scattered around the lab area. Hudson was clearly in the photo standing to the left, speaking with the insurance company about the incident. One of his coworkers had drawn soot all over him, hair standing on end, little riddles of flame dancing around his head.

In reality, he didn't need to teach. Sometimes, he couldn't comprehend why he did it. It wasn't for the money, that was for sure. Since Parliament had passed new education regulations, a professor's salary wasn't what it was in the old days, the *good* old days. They called it "lowering cost/increasing efficiency." Hudson called it "screwing the teachers." Fortunately, with taking the Vice President position at Inron Genetics ten years before, he didn't worry so much about his financial situation. He was the all-star scientist, the genius playboy, the kid who had solved the enigmatic equation that allowed HRV-

EST to come to life. It was all part of control, but control didn't begin with HRV-EST.

Control started with Ophelia Keating.

After the death of President Collins, Keating's rise to power was swift. Her popularity with the frightened and weak propelled her to the top of the election ballot. She emerged a hero from a war she never fought, at least that's what Hudson suspected. And Keating had ideas—many ideas—concepts that made the world a safer, better place. The first thing to cause rumblings through society was the intention to join the world's governments into a single working body called *Parliament*. There would no longer be an America, or a Canada, or a United Kingdom, but a collective, unified body. The currencies of the world would be combined into a single measure known as *Centicoin* for ease of use and the good of all. The newfound intercontinental peace easily sold the illusion of planetary unity to the people of Earth.

Next in the line of novelties, the Biotic Scan Chip, or BSC. All citizens underwent implantation, and all children received them at birth. Contained in one's right wrist, the chip contained all information about a person—medical and dental records, school history, working resume, and financial data. BSC was the only method of payment to purchase any goods, and wages were loaded twice each month. Parliament denied the chips carried the ability track or monitor citizens, but most secretly suspected otherwise.

Even those in favor of earlier changes admitted surprise with the introduction of *Global Population Control*. Parliament partnered with Evolution Service Technologies to begin the worldwide initiative called the *Human Reproductive Vector* intended to regulate the birthrate, referred to as HRV-EST. The world's citizens reported to be "immunized" against free reproduction. To qualify for children, applicants completed an examination to obtain a proper birthing license. Parliament said the program was a means of ensuring those who had children could take care of them, a platform where children were not born but grown. It would control the financial crisis for abandoned children and limit the growing number of abuse cases across the globe. "All children would have a happy home."

Yes, that's what Parliament said.

HRV-EST encountered much difficulty getting off the ground. The young Hudson received a call from his Director instructing him to host a weeklong brainstorming session to uncover the missing equation causing the embryos generated to die mere weeks after genetic conception. After over three days of calculation, a total of fifty hours, Hudson found the missing key himself, an accomplishment he lived to regret. And though Parliament delivered the HRV-EST program to the planet in a positive light, like most things that involved the government, it soon became corrupted. Those with the most *coin* got the best offspring. HRV-EST became an embryonic "chop-shop" where parents genetically engineered the perfect child. They paid to custom-tailor children with preferred intellect, look, and physical ability. Those without the funds to do so received the lesser genomes. And it was all thanks to the young and talented Doctor Andre Hudson, who became affluent from his repentant accomplishment.

To Hudson, though, life was more than wealth, more than Centicoin, more than the material. That's why teaching was so important. He continued education because being around the students kept him young; and now in his mid-forties, he needed as much rejuvenation as he could collect. There was nothing worse than getting older while aimlessly adrift in a sea of regret. Long ago, when he was younger, he had been something much more than a genius. He possessed something far more valuable than Centicoin, greater than attractiveness, grander than repute. He was part of something bigger, and he owed his existence to a man named *Steve Sutherland.*

Hudson could recall it so vividly. He was fourteen and in the gutter. He was an orphan brat who listened to no one, too smart for his own good. The only things he knew how to do were fight and steal, and he did both admirably. He invented the most creative ways to avoid responsibility. Escaping from a broken home, he learned early on to depend on himself. He had survived on the streets since

3

he was nine years old. He fell in with the wrong crowd and became part of the ACE Gang, a young group of thieves organized by the very shady, Evelyn Karns, better known as *the Madame*. Evelyn was quite an industrious woman. In her mid-fifties, she had a plethora of employees who worked in her organization stealing and selling everything from cars, to drugs, to sex, even human organs.

While Evelyn was evil, she was not without integrity. She never allowed the kids to be associated with employees who pushed drugs or flesh. If you completed a hit around a child, you'd soon go missing yourself. Cursing around the children could get your knuckles broken. Kids ate first, and sometimes best. If you were one of Evelyn's children, you were indeed one of Evelyn's children. All children got cake for their birthday, a stocking at Christmas, and a chocolate rabbit for Easter. If a kid betrayed her, they received the most horrific punishment of all—banishment from the underground. And if you knew what was good for you, you would skip town altogether. If you were irresponsible enough to remain in Seventh City, you would become a target when you came of age. After all, adults were fair game. However, as long as you were young, you were safe—in most ways, at least.

The ACE Gang was her little band of car thieves, her ratty pickpockets who would break your fingers to steal your wallet, and Andre Hudson was one of her favorites. One fateful night Hudson attempted to pick the pocket of a wealthy young doctor leaving one of the most exorbitant hotels in the city. The guy looked familiar, though Andre didn't realize why. The man left the hotel and walked down the block, most likely on his way to dinner with a gorgeous woman. And Andre followed the man. He looked to be around his early to mid-twenties, tall, handsome, and rather surreptitious. Andre transformed into the man's little shadow that night, lurking mere feet from him, yet miles away. He watched the man take out a thick, black leather wallet and throw money around as if it meant nothing at all. Andre was sure to score big; wouldn't Evelyn be pleased?

As the two made their way down busy 9th Avenue, Andre saw his window of opportunity. The surrounding crowd would make it easy for him to snatch that thick leather wallet from the man's coat pocket before he could realize what happened. Andre remained close to him, but far enough away to go unnoticed. It was an old trick performed by many thieves, one Andre mastered. As they rounded the corner, if Andre could get close enough to the man he could snatch the wallet and scurry into the darkness undetected. Making their way to the intersection of Avenue C, Andre knew he would have his chance. He stretched out his hand to snatch his prize, grasping nothing, falling deep into the darkness.

When Andre opened his heavy eyes, he found himself bound to an elegant wooden chair in a dark library with books lining shelves to the vaulted ceiling. The only light in the room was a fireplace that roared before him. A chemical odor saturated his sinuses. He shook his head, trying to throw the grogginess from his mind.

"It'll wear off," said someone from the shadows. The stranger picked up a large crystal bottle of bourbon and poured himself a drink. Then, he poured a glass of ice water. "It's a concoction I made—a combination of chloroform on an ether base, but not as heavy." He sat the pitcher down. "I'm a doctor—I can deal with blood and guts. But for some reason I just can't stand to see people puke. Depending upon what they've eaten it can be a bitch to get out of the carpet."

Andre didn't respond to the stranger. Through the fading haze, he saw a man step into the firelight, his suave gentleman from the street. "Who are you?"

"Dr. Steve B. Sutherland," the man said as he reached to shake Andre's hand. "Oh, sorry." Steve winked and unbound the boy's arms. It happened so quickly that he could barely see Andre, who bolted from the room with cat-like reflexes. Still disoriented, Andre muddled through the maze of the mansion, knocking over vases, shelves, and running into walls. His mind felt foggy, disconnected, separated from the rest of his body, but he had to get away. As he fumbled down the steps, he ran headfirst into an older woman carrying a wide, silver tray that just happened to smell fantastic. He stumbled backwards and braced himself on the railing of the grand staircase.

"Mister Hudson!" the woman exclaimed, causing Andre to stop cold. "Child! You need to calm down before you break a bone or something."

"Or his neck. This vase was three grand, Martha," Steve called from the top of the stairs.

Andre stood there bewildered. Why weren't they rushing him? Why didn't they try to stop him? How did they know his name?

"Here, honey, you need to eat something. I made you some spaghetti."

Andre didn't say a word.

Steve began to stroll slowly down the stairs with a defeated look in his eyes. He sighed. "At least eat before you go, Mr. Hudson."

Andre couldn't deny that the food smelled delicious, and he hadn't eaten all day. Cautiously, he followed Martha and Steve down the stairs and through the large dining room to the kitchen where the three of them took a seat. He examined the spaghetti for a moment, eyeing it with suspicious evaluation, combing through it with the heavy silver fork.

"Kid, it's fine. Eat," Steve chuckled.

Martha sat there waiting for Andre to give her food a taste, wanting to see the boy's face. It was always the "first-bite expression" that Martha loved. It was an unspoken gratitude, validation for her hard work at the oven. Without a doubt, it had to be the best spaghetti Andre had ever eaten.

"Well… how is it?" she asked with a smile, already knowing the answer.

"Goodff," mumbled Andre through his stuffed mouth.

Martha patted Andre's hand, smiled, and then stood up to begin straightening the kitchen. Steve then took the seat across from him. "That's my main woman, Martha." Andre looked at Steve with suspicion and then back down his plate. "Why were you going to steal from me?"

"I wasn't. And this is kidnapping," Andre lied. *Just call the damn cops, already*, he thought.

"Brother, come on. Get over it. I know who you are, and I know who you work for. So, don't give me that innocent shi…"

"Steve!" Martha hissed from the kitchen.

"… stuff."

Andre sat back, his stomach full. It was obvious this Steve fellow was onto him. There was no point in continuing the charade. "Okay. Fine! You got me. Call the police and let's get this over with."

"But I don't want to call the police."

"Then, what do you want?"

Steve sat for a moment, thumbing the dark soul patch under his bottom lip. "I need your help."

"And why would I help you?" Andre said with a snort.

"Because you're too smart to be a hoodlum for the rest of your life and too stupid to realize it."

Andre sat there for a moment staring into Steve's eyes. "So, what kind of help do you need from a boy? You some kinda freak?"

"Don't flatter yourself, kid. Consider it…a *job*, if you will."

Andre thought for a moment. "And just how much does this job pay?"

Steve smiled. "Nothing." He leaned forward, placing his elbows on the table. "I thought you would just do it out of the goodness of your heart."

Andre laughed. "So, a 'good deed.'"

"Affirmative," said Steve with a smile.

Affirmative. The word would prove to be Steve's favorite term, his slogan. Everyone came to realize that a simple "yes" wasn't in Steve Sutherland's vocabulary.

Andre took a sip of his milk. "And what do I need to do?"

Steve leaned in. "I want you to help me take down the Madame."

Andre gave him a blank look and then spat out a boisterous laugh. "Man, you're freakin' nuts. Look, it was nice to meet you and all, but I think you need to show me the way out of this place."

"Look, she's going down regardless."

"Then, you can do it without me."

"Affirmative, but I could do it sooner *with* you."

Andre got up from the table and shook his head. "Like I said. I need to go."

"To what? What do you need to go to?" Steve said as he sat back.

"My life? Hello?"

"What life?"

And as Andre began to open his mouth to shout one of a hundred possible snarky remarks, he wasn't so certain of his life anymore. What was he to say, that he was going back to his glamorous life of petty thievery? To no family—no mother, father, education, and no real home? Andre shrugged. "Listen, just who the hell are you anyway, man?" he barked as he put his coat around his shoulders. "Are you, like, FBI or something?"

"No."

"Then, why don't you let the cops do the bang-up job they're doing already and leave it alone? Who do you think you are?" Andre turned and began to march away.

"Are you leaving, honey?" Martha said walking back into the main kitchen.

"Affirmative," Andre spat with snide indignation.

Steve smiled and sighed. He rubbed the weariness from his face and said, "Fine... okay. But, before you go I want to show you something."

Andre smiled in a dismissive fashion and nodded his head. If it would get him out of that house, he was all for it. He followed Steve back to the upstairs library, the place where the adventure began. Steve walked to the far bookshelf and took hold of a large black book that lit up with life, scanning his palm.

"Access granted," said the reverberating systemic voice as the bulky shelf moved forward and slid open. Inside was a large room that appeared to be some high-tech, scientific laboratory full of computers and gadgets of every make and model. They stepped in to see a glass display case rising from the floor. As the case turned, Andre saw something inside, like a suit or uniform. It looked like a cross between a robotic android and a suit of armor. It had a steel-clad vest, and in its center was an emblem—a red letter F atop a blue star, surrounded by a grayish-white circle. One gauntlet was a complete mechanical glove, and the other was a large cuff that extended up the forearm. The massive legs and boots of the suit possessed gears and hydraulic levers. The whole outfit was bright chrome with red adornments. Andre knew of just one person who wore a suite like that.

"Dude," he said in awe. "*You* are Wrath…?"

"I think they did a good job, don't you?"

The voice shook Hudson from his daydream. He turned around to see Sheila Copeland, one of the lead lab technicians, standing beside him. "What?"

"Your fifteen minutes of fame, there," she replied pointing to the newspaper article of the university lab accident.

"Oh! Oh, yeah. Jimmy's handiwork, I presume?"

"I was sworn to secrecy… but, yeah, it was Jim."

Hudson leaned back in the chair and rubbed his eyes. "I am ready for Friday." He looked at the television hanging on the wall in the lunchroom. The news was aglow with coverage of the latest Scourge outbreak, the month's economic review, and the upcoming Parliamental World Summit scheduled to take place toward the end of the summer, the first one of its kind to occur in years.

"Me, too."

"Did we get the monthly EST report from the head office, yet?"

"On your desk."

"Awesome."

"Oh, and you have visitor."

Hudson looked at her questionably. "Who?"

"A Mr. Gunner? Some kid, I think maybe from your night class?"

Hudson rolled his eyes. *Oh yes, Damian Gunner…the inquisitive one.* He had overlooked Damian's request to speak to him after class. "Oh, God…I completely forgot." He checked his watch. "I have a meeting in five minutes I cannot be late for. Could you tell him to get with me tomorrow night after class? Tell him I promise!"

"Will do," Sheila replied. "But you're going to have to start keeping promises at some point, Andre."

Hudson gathered his things and began to dash from the lunchroom.

"Your pencil," Sheila said with a smile as she picked up the chew toy in disgust.

He ran back and took the pencil from her hand.

"Your notebook."

Hudson smiled, rolled his eyes, and grabbed his notebook. As he started on his way once again, the news shifted to a breaking story that pulled at his attention when he heard the words, "We're on site here are Alemede Component Company where fifty-two-year old Richard Lawrence was murdered this morning."

Buster? The only "Richard Lawrence" Hudson knew of was Buster from Alemede, one of the vendors where Inron got their genome mapping modules. As he stepped back and looked at the television, he saw firetrucks putting out residual flames that remained. Smoke bellowed from the upper doors and windows of Alemede. The reporter in the crisp gray suit held the microphone steady in front of a shaken young girl.

"The alleged perpetrator of the crime is said to be Ellen Braxton, who started working at the company only weeks before." The picture of a young, attractive girl with sandy-blonde hair appeared in the upper-left-hand corner of the screen. The reporter walked to another younger woman who was gnawing on a massive wad of gum. "We are here now with another employee of the company, Rosalie Miller. Rosalie, in your own words, what did you see?" asked the reporter.

"Well, Ellie had just got into trouble for ruining a bunch of equipment, and Buster took her to the back to talk with her. We all stayed on the main floor and kept working." The girl took the huge wad of gum from her mouth. "And then we heard this big ruckus. A group of us ran back to see what was going on and opened the door just in time to see her shocking the hell out of Buster. Just burnt him to a crisp right there... like popcorn."

The girl's nonchalant attitude toward the tragedy caused the reporter to shift with discomfort. "Yes, um...did you see what she used to attack him?"

"Not clearly, no. But it was electrical, whatever it was. It was almost like she was *made* of electricity or something. It was all over her—big, bright blue sparks and stuff. It was wild. Burnt him like toast right there in front of us."

"Why do you think she would have attacked Mr. Lawrence?"

Rosalie thought for a moment. "Well, some of the team thinks he was going to make her pay for the supply she ruined, so she took care of him." The girl looked at the camera with a deep expression of sarcasm. "But... if you ask me, girl? I'd say he tried to get in her panties, just like that old pervert did most of us girls, and she wasn't having any of that shit. Good for her! And I would have..."

The reporter turned sharply, dragging the microphone away from Rosalie, who just kept rambling and shaking her head with attitude. "And that's the story we have here so far. Richard 'Buster' Lawrence of Region H-64 was killed today in what some are calling an attempt to avoid liability, but what others are calling self-defense. Back to you, Edward."

Made of electricity. Hudson stood there unable to rip himself away from the floor. *Big, bright blue sparks.* Yes, he knew the blue sparks. He had witnessed them on numerous occasions. Could it be? "*Voltage—electrical goddess, nice to meet you.*" That's how Vickie introduced herself the first time Hudson had laid eyes on her. He heard Vickie's voice so clear it was as if she was standing right next to him whispering into his ear. He gave up hope a long time ago; a thick blanket of disillusionment and despair now covered all promise. But, if it were true—if the plan had worked—it meant the chance for revolution, for triumph... for *resurrection.*

.

ELLEN

Ellen cowered in the alleyway clutching her bloody wrist. Her mind was running at full speed, nearly overheating. The tears stung her eyes. She was afraid, and she was completely alone. Though she knew her day wouldn't overflow with delight, she thought it would at least be the typical day filled with mundane tasks and customary regret. She never thought it would end with culpability; she never thought it would end with murder. The day started just like any other day.

"Get up, lazy ass!"

Ellen lay still with her eyes closed tight, hoping he would simply disappear.

"Do her hear me, girl? Get up!" With a final bang at the door, Eddie, her mother's drunken slob of a boyfriend, staggered away. His was the last voice she wanted to hear during her perfect dream, that recurrent, magical dream, the one she experienced on regular occasion most of her life. In it, they were together, she and the mysterious boy, her prince with no face. She never saw his features, just his eyes, those big, ice-blue eyes. He was tall, and he was strong, so very strong. Her fingers always wound up buried in his wavy, sandy-blonde hair. Oh, how he loved her, and she loved him.

With a sigh, she tossed the musty blanket from her face and threw one leg to the floor. Though she barely recalled her father, she longed for him. She had been so young when he died, but without a doubt, things were better in those days, those days when blankets smelled fresh. She got up and looked at her reflection in the mirror. Her muddled hair would have to do. Her mother, Dahlia, had pressed her work uniform, which made Ellen smile. There it was hanging on the doorknob of her closet, fresh and clean. Dahlia was so proud that Ellen had landed such a prestigious job at Alemede Component Company, a notable technology corporation in Region H that designed and constructed lab equipment for Parliament.

Her mother would never allow Ellen to leave the house appearing unkempt. It was pride, plain and simple, a vanity that her mother no longer possessed. On the rare, joyful occasion where Eddie could bum enough Centicoins to visit one of the local pubs, the two of them would talk. How Ellen loved those moments, those rare instances where they were mother and daughter, not convicts serving sentence. The conversations never changed. How did they wind up at their destination? How would they escape? What they could do if they were part of the world's elite?

Ellen gathered her things and unlocked the large bolt on her bedroom door. Eddie was less prone to leering at her since the incident several months before. Ellen had awoken in the middle of the night to find him in her room half-naked, drunk, mumbling something about "getting it" from her "like her mother wouldn't" any longer. Things escalated at once. It was the one time her mother had threatened to call Regional Authority on him, which would not end well for him since there were several outstanding warrants for arrest. On the plus side, that event led to a more pleasant Eddie— no more black eyes for her mother, and a thick, shiny lock for Ellen's bedroom door.

At one time, years in the past, they had been a clean, respectable, middle-class family. Ellen was five years old then. Her father, Charles

Braxton, was a lawyer, a free-spirited, righteous man whose convictions would land him six-feet under the ground. Just like many of the time, he was not proud of the direction in which the world government headed. A "collective government," one-world currency, Biotic Scan Chips, population control—just a few of the many things that drove her father into panic. Ellen knew of how he pushed against the changes and tried to fight them. The more he pushed, the more matters became worse for them. He lost his job; they lost their home. Everything crumbled. Though her mother begged him to stop his crusade, he would not bow down, because it "wasn't right." Her mother said that sense of conviction led to his murder in a filthy alleyway, an apparent theft gone awry, and his death left them with the only scum who would give a widow branded a traitor a second glance.

Ellen shook herself from her thoughts and looked at the clock. She reached for her necklace and fastened it around her neck. The oblong silver pendant was a gift from her father, given to her the week he died. She stared at the stone in the middle, an iridescent red ruby. *Take good care of this for me, okay?* She could hear his voice. It was junk…silly costume jewelry that sometimes turned her skin green, but it was all she had left of him. She reached to turn on the small bedside lamp and saw a bright flash. The lamp popped and sizzled.

"Ow! Damn!" she yelled. And just like that, the lamp was dead—just like her hairdryer, just like her straightening iron. The mucky apartment was becoming more dangerous by the second. As she bent to pick up her socks, Eddie cleared his throat.

"What the hell, Eddie! Don't you knock?" she yelled.

He stood at the door thumbing at his crotch as if that was normal, acceptable behavior. "What difference does it make? Not like you're gonna open the door anyways, right? It was unlocked."

"So?" she said. "What do you do? Stand around and listen for the door to unlatch?"

He was disgusting—the thick hair that lined his shoulders always seemed damp with sweat. He was still wearing the same tank top he had worn the entire week, stained with ketchup and other mysterious fluids.

"And why do you have to lock it every damn time you come in here?" he added.

"There's a reason for that, pervert!"

"What? Who? Me?" he chuckled as he ran his hands into his tank top.

"Get out, Eddie," she said as she gathered her work uniform.

"Hey, girl, you don't have anything I ain't seen before."

"And I am sure that's true, perv. Have you checked the breaker box, yet?"

Eddie belched. "Not yet. I can't find my toolbox."

Ellen rolled her eyes. "Well, my lamp just tried to kill me, so you need to get it fixed before the apartment blows up."

"Fine, fine, fine. Whatever. Dahl has breakfast ready."

He mumbled other choice things to himself as be meandered through the hallway. She pulled her uniform on, noting the freshness of the fabric. She was wise enough to shower the night before, best to do so while Eddie was asleep. She already uncovered four peepholes he drilled in various places in the bathroom to watch at his leisure. Therefore, she found it best to bathe on nights he passed out from a day of indulgence. It made her skin crawl; the thought of his eyes on her flesh made her want to vomit.

She stepped into the kitchen where her mother sat. As was typical, the woman looked in shambles. Her mother smiled wide when she saw her in her uniform.

"What?" Ellen asked with a smirk.

"I just love those uniforms," Dahlia said through her smile. "They spare no expense at Alemede. You'll have such a good career there." She got up and walked over to Ellen, picking a piece of loose thread from her collar.

Ellen smiled back at her and took her hand. "You're so silly."

"Well, I can't help it. Now, eat up. You have to catch the train soon. You don't want to be late on your second week."

Ellen picked up her toast and walked to the refrigerator where messages where scribbled. "Linda called?"

"Oh, yeah!" Dahlia replied. "I forgot all about that. Last night after you went to bed. She was wondering how the new job was coming along. It was so nice of her mother to get you on there."

Alemede was preferable to other jobs forced on Ellen. No workplace in Region H was free of venality. To be honest, it made her rather nervous to work with the expensive equipment of Alemede, but it was far better than cleaning grimy toilets or working a corner like some of her other friends. Ellen got a small glass of juice. "Yeah, Betty is great. Is that all Linda said?"

"Well," her mother added with apprehension. "She also wanted to know if you were still coming to the graduation party. I told her I'd ask, but that you probably wouldn't want to go."

Ellen turned to her. "Why wouldn't I want to go? All my friends are going to be there."

Dahlia shifted in her seat. "Well… honey. Since you had to leave school I didn't think you would want to take part in…"

"I didn't *have* to leave school, mother," Ellen said with a frigid tone she regretted at once. Dahlia looked down, ashamed by the declaration.

Ellen realized she really couldn't have remained in school. Someone had to work. Centicoins didn't earn themselves. Her mother said that years ago the government used to offer help to those who qualified for need. Parliament offered no such relief to the poor. You worked, and if you didn't work, you didn't eat. Her mother was far too ill to work the long hours needed to live. Before Eddie's transition to full-time drunk, he had been a talented electrician. These days if he was lucky to find someone to hire him in spite of his questionable record, the job was lost in less than two weeks for a multitude of irresponsible reasons. In the deprived Regions of world, the government collected the starved bodies of the weak and disabled and hid them away from knowing eyes. Those who didn't die of starvation died of *Scourge*, an incurable, contagious pathogen that decimated the body fast. In only a few months after infection, the tissue cells of the body would begin to putrefy, leading to hemorrhaging and death. The disease originated in a new species of rat known scientifically as *Rati Conrumpere*. Most people called them *Rot Rats*.

The only other family was Dahlia's sister, Ellen's Aunt Janice. Every now and again, Janice secretly gave Ellen some Centicoins. Ellen would always intend to save the funds for rainy days, but it stormed so often. The coins bought much needed food, or satisfied rent that often went unpaid due to Eddie's consistent negligence. Even Ellen knew that Janice's help stopped at her front door. Like most of society, she refused to associate with the loathsome Eddie in any shape, form, or fashion. As long as her mother had Eddie, there was nothing for them. They had no one else, nowhere to turn. Eddie didn't make much, but what he did make from his electrical work was crucial to their survival.

Ellen walked over and hugged her mother. "I'll fix it, Mom."

Her mother looked up to her and fought back the tears glistening in her eyes. "I know you will, honey. I'm so proud of you."

Eddie belched as he walked into the kitchen. "Is there any left?"

Ellen rolled her eyes at her mother and walked past Eddie, patting him on the shoulder. "You are a prince among men, Eddie."

"Thank you for noticing!" he said. "Finally, someone sees the stud I am."

"You're a stud all right," her mother sighed. "Ellen, don't forget your lunch!"

Ellen hated riding the trains. They were old, rickety, and reeked of urine. As she grew closer to her destination, she chewed on her necklace, a nervous habit she couldn't break. She exited the train at Region H-70 and walked the final four blocks to the factory. The odor in H-70 always seemed odd to her—a marriage of bread, exhaust, and motor oil. The buildings stretched so high you could barely see the clouds in the sky. The city was teeming, so congested. Upward was the only direction left for the world to grow. Ellen had seen old photos from her grandmother's time, which showed a much different world—a world with space, grass, fresh air and flowers, far from the clogged, greasy society around her. She wondered what it would be like to be in that clean, open world.

Ellen entered the side door of the factory where all employees scanned themselves into clock control for time keeping.

"Hey, lady!" called a voice from behind her. Ellen turned to see Betty, Linda's mother, coming through the door.

"Hey, how are ya'?"

"I'm old, Ellen, honey. Just old." Betty passed her wrist under the clock scanner registering her arrival. The screen blinked green.

"I'm starting to feel that way myself," Ellen said with a smile.

"Oh, please," Betty said as they made their way into the building. "You're a young thing, girl. And now you have all *this* to look forward to." Betty stopped and ran her hands down her ample figure.

Ellen laughed. "Sexy."

"Yes, Ma'am."

They walked through the neutralizer, which Ellen hated. The alleged "tasteless, odorless" chemical it emitted to remove static electricity from the body actually tasted rancorous, no matter what the company said. If she didn't close her eyes and hold her breath, the bitterness permeated her senses most of the day, making her feel nauseous. *It's gonna give us all cancer...I know it.*

"So, did you get to talk to Linda last night?" Betty said as they walked into the construction arena.

"No, I fell asleep, but Mom gave me the message this morning."

"The party is next weekend, and it just won't be the same if you don't come, Ellie. Dahlia told Linda last night she didn't think you'd want to go."

Ellen pulled up her visor and turned on the chipset press. "Yeah, I know. But, really, I'm planning to come. I wouldn't miss it."

"Good! Linda would die if you weren't going to be there." Betty stopped and looked at Ellen with sympathetic gaze. "I am so sorry about graduation, Ellie. Your father would still be so proud of you."

Betty made her way up to the sequencing room where she and her team built the higher-end governmental components while Ellen got started with inspection. As she situated herself, Ellen felt a presence close behind her. When she noticed the aroma of cheap cologne, she discerned who it was.

"Hey, pretty girl," Buster said. Buster Lawrence was the lead supervisor in her area, a despicably creepy man who sniffed around her like a dog after a fresh slice of beef.

"Hi, Mr. Lawrence." She smiled trying to take solace in the fact that at least he wasn't Eddie. If Buster hadn't been old enough to be her grandfather, it wouldn't have felt quite so creepy.

"Oh, you don't have to call me Mister, pretty girl." Ellen tried to keep the forced grin. He patted her leg, allowing his hand to roam higher on her thigh. "If you need anything, you let old Buster know."

"Will do, Mr... uh, Buster."

As he walked away, Ellen turned to focus on her station. As the system spat out finished chip sets, her mind wandered. What would her father think of her? Would he be pleased to realize she had left her education to take a job working for the very government he despised? The press pieced together the small components used in embryo growth monitoring for the HRV-EST program. HRV-EST, pronounced *harvest*, was one of the many programs instituted by the government to make the world a better place. Her father believed it confined society, like all other "positive" programs. For the life of her, Ellen didn't understand the meaning behind the HRV-EST acronym. She knew that it was part of the company called Evolution Service Technologies, wherever that was. The EST logo covered everything in her area.

Sinking deeper into her thoughts, she suspected her father wouldn't be proud of what she was doing. She wondered if he would even speak to her, or her mother, seeing how they had devolved. She saw nothing on the horizon of her youth and only emptiness for her existence. And at that moment, she hated her life. She despised the prison in which she found herself, the cell with no windows, no doors, just filth, and the stench of urine.

As Ellen reached to place a finished gene monitor into the production pile, a small zap of blue electricity popped from her index finger. Burnt copper permeated her nose, and she felt sick. Others around her hadn't immediately noticed the gaffe. Realizing something was now wrong with the batch, Ellen hoped to close down the box and send it through the line as if nothing was wrong. Someone could wonder about it later.

"What in the hell is that stench?" Buster asked as he walked to her table. "Why am I smelling fried circuits?"

"I...I don't know," Ellen replied with a quiver in her voice.

Buster walked to the production batch and looked inside the box. He picked up one component and sniffed it. "You are friggin' kidding me!" His exclamation made others turn and look. "These are fried, little girl—absolutely fried!" He pitched the broken chipset into the box causing Ellen to flinch. "Did you go through the neutralizer?"

"Yes, she went through, Buster," said Betty, who had heard the ruckus. "We both did."

"Well, by God, someone didn't! Something fried these."

"Buster, that is a whole box of Gene VDUs. Do you think that a little static could fry a whole box of..."

"Shut the hell up, Betty! I didn't ask you!" The room fell quiet. Buster stood there for a moment. "Get back to work," he demanded. "You," he said, pointing to Ellen. "Come with me."

Ellen felt as if she would vomit. Betty patted Ellen's shoulder as Ellen followed Buster off the main work floor. He led her to the back of the factory to the molding room where machines shaped heated metal fixtures. The scalding metal hissed as it slid from the large conveyer belt into the icy water. Buster took a seat and then held out his hand, motioning for her to sit.

He sighed. "Look, Ellen, I really like you. I do. When Betty recommended you, I was against it at first, but after meeting you..."

I wanted to get in your pants, Ellen thought.

"... I thought you had potential. But, that's a whole lot of Centicoin in that box, a whole lot of cost."

"How... how much cost?" Ellen asked in an apprehensive manner.

"Umm... not sure. Maybe... five, six thousand Centicoin?"

That was a great deal of Centicoin, more than Ellen had in

savings altogether. "But, I don't have…"

"Shh… I know, I know. I mean, who does? Right?" Buster stood. He slowly paced for a moment, pondering. "But, I bet we could work something out, though."

Ellen shook her head. A knowing smirk crossed her face. She had been waiting on it. "Look, Buster, I don't think we need to go down that road, okay?"

"Now, now… look, we don't have to do anything harsh. Just a little help is all. It won't even mess up your pretty hair. I can write all that off… say it was the press that jacked it up. Just… lend me a hand." He leaned his crotch against her elbow.

It was sudden, so sudden she didn't have time to control it. All she saw was Eddie, sweaty, half-naked, in her room, talking about how he would give it to her, *give it to her good*. She pushed Buster away from her. "Stop! Now!"

His face twisted into a look of anger. "Look, bitch, you either cooperate, or you better be able to cough up six CC. Simple as that. You want your job? You better give me a job."

Ellen got up and sighed. "Fine. I quit then." She turned to make her way out of the room. All she could hear was her mother who would be so heartbroken Alemede didn't work out as expected.

Before she realized, he had her by the throat. "I'm gonna get a full day's work out of you." He dragged her over to the table by the cooling vat as she fought against his grip. He slung her on top of the table, knocking all the paper invoices and folders to the floor.

"Stop!" she screamed. "You won't get away with it!"

"The hell I won't, girl. No one is gonna care," he said as he unbuttoned his pants. "No one will even notice another…"

The vibration of the metal stung her hand as she smacked the heavy sheet against his skull. Ellen stiffened as Buster stumbled back, blood gushing from his head. A part of her wanted to run while she had the chance, but another part of her was in shock at the sight of blood. He held his head and looked at her with a furious anger.

"You *bitch! You little bitch!*" he roared as he tackled her and dragged her to the cooling bin.

22

As he shoved her head into the bitter water, the liquid filled her sinuses. The scent of metal flooded her nasal passages. She could feel part of her hair ripping from the roots as he tightened his grip. He shouted as he held her underneath the water, though she could not decipher his words. He plunged her into the vat repeatedly and ripped her backward giving her just enough time to gulp a deep breath. She swallowed more and more of the steel-littered water, and as she grew weak, she wondered what he would tell the others. How would he get rid of her body? Would anyone even care? She could envision her mother in her mind's eye, hysterical, weak, unable to get away from Eddie, doomed to die in the street around the filth and Rot Rats of Region H. She could see Eddie taking great pride in having the upper hand once again in the house, making her mother do whatever he wanted, whenever he wanted. There was her father's face, the disappointment in his eyes, knowing that if she hadn't tried to work for a government who had betrayed her family she wouldn't be in her predicament. Curiously, the next thing she saw was the color blue—a vivid, bright blue—like the color of sky in her grandmother's old photographs. She felt the electrical current stand up all around her, lift her, and fill her soul.

So, this is dying, she thought.

As Buster fell to the floor, Ellen jerked herself out of the water. The stench of burnt flesh and fried hair filled the room. She rubbed the thick water from her eyes and tried to untangle her surroundings through the smoke. For a moment, she thought the building had caught fire. Looking at her hands, she could see the blue electricity dance around her fingertips and make its way up her arms causing the fine hair to stand on end. That's when she noticed the scorched, charred remains of what used to be Buster Lawrence, flames smoldering in his eye sockets. His eyes, which had ruptured during the incident, were gooey pockets that drooled down his black cheeks. He had chewed his tongue completely in two. By the smell of it, he had lost all control of bodily functions. It appeared as if an electric chair had pumped millions of volts through his fat frame. She looked again at her hands as the electricity dissipated, a current that somehow flowed from within her flesh.

"Ellen…" Betty and several other workers stood in the glow of the red emergency lights, their faces locked in absolute horror. "Ellen, honey, what did you do?" Betty meekly asked.

The metal-soaked tears burnt Ellen's cheeks as she rushed through the building. Glass from the shattered lights littered the floor and crunched under her feet as she rushed past the traumatized crowd. The sirens grew more pronounced; she now had little time. She hailed a taxi and made her way home. Outside of asking for her destination, the dumbfounded driver didn't say a word to her.

Ellen busted through the door of the apartment in hysterics and rushed to her room.

"Ellen? Ellen? Come here! Betty just called me. What is going on?" Dahlia shouted entering the room behind her distraught daughter.

"Mom…I can't…I can't talk right now; I have to get out of here." Ellen began to pack everything she could fit in her old school backpack. "Where is Eddie?"

"He went to have beer with his buddies. Why? You better tell me what is going on!"

Ellen slammed her drawer shut and then took her mother by the shoulders. "Mom, listen close, okay? I don't know what happened, or wh-wh-what I did, or how I did it. But I have to get out of here. They're going to catch me." Ellen got her passcode book from the top drawer and handed it to her. "This is my passcode, okay? There is about three thousand CC in the account. Do *not* tell Eddie!"

"What? Where did you get this money? Did you steal it? Is that what this is about?"

"It's what I've saved plus some from Aunt Janice." Ellen ran into the bathroom with her mother in tow.

"Janice? Why would Janice give…"

Ellen picked up the scissors and took a deep breath. With a quick thrust, she stabbed the scissors into her right wrist. She cried out in agony as she dug into the bone.

"Oh, my God! Ellen! Stop it! Stop it!" her mother screamed.

"If I don't get it out, they'll track me!" With her forefinger, she dug the BSC out of her wrist and held it in her bloody hand. She walked to the toilet, flushed the chip, and then took her mother by the arm. Looking deeply into her mother's eyes she said, "Mom, listen to me. I don't know when I'll be back, but I *will* be back, and I'm going to get you out of here, okay? We will leave this hell hole, get away from Eddie. And no matter what you hear, it *wasn't* my fault, okay? Understand?"

Tears welled in Dahlia's eyes. All the woman could do was nod her head in agreement.

"I love you, Mom!" Ellen said as she wrapped her bloody wrist up in a spare hand towel.

And with that, Ellen kissed her mother goodbye and ran into the rain unaware of where she was going, what she would do, or who she was.

DAVID

David wiped the steam from the bathroom mirror, unable to shake the angel from the dream out of his mind. He gazed deeply at his reflection, unsure of who stared back. He had dreamt of the glowing figure for years, the extraordinary angel made of light. She often visited his nights, and together they talked for what seemed like an eternity. Hopes, dreams, fantasies—the subjects were limitless, the moments timeless. Somehow, the angel was changing him. Something inside of his deepest heart was transmuting; he didn't know why. Was it for the good? Maybe. Did he like it? Not at all. For some strange reason he couldn't quite explain, he was developing *integrity*—a *conscience* of all things! Not that he was self-centered by nature, but he was as close to a complete ass as one could get without actually being a complete ass.

It was his parent's fault, especially where his father came into play, the man who taught him from a very early age to look out for number one. *You are the only person you need to please, boy; remember that!* And his dad has stood by that fact with conviction. In David's structured world, everything was planned, well organized, calculated. When the Porters created a child, it was a large, drawn-out process, full of cost considerations, planning, and flowcharts. They detailed and documented everything about David before his birth. His looks were custom-tailored per his mother's request—sandy-blonde hair, blue eyes, tall, strong. She had even listed "strong chin" on the form. "Smart" was the last thing on the list which spoke a great deal to his mother's shallow nature. Yes, David Porter was the smartest, best-looking kid that money could buy, and he detested it.

As he got dressed, he reflected on the things he had worked hard for through his life, which equated to absolutely nothing. Everything he possessed was given freely without any effort on his part—everything. His car, his clothes, his computers, even his grades in college—all bought and paid for by his mother, who was lucky enough to be a rather important constituent in Parliamental Congress. For the life of him, he did not understand how the woman landed such a cushy seat in the global government—she was not intellectual and even less likable. When David was four years old, fortune shined upon his small family. Not that the Porters ever hurt for Centicoin, mind you, but adding congressional income to his father's lucrative (and sometimes illegal) medical practice boosted their status greatly.

David didn't understand why his general outlook about life was changing. He felt it had something to do with the death of Abernathy. Oscar Abernathy was a grunt—a nerdy, introverted kid who would do anything to become part of a fraternity, any fraternity. He visited every frat house on United Regional University campus and received nothing but rejection, even though on paper he made a fine addition to any house. The day Oscar first stumbled into Psi Rho Phi house, David was resting on the couch playing video games. At first glance, he believed the kid was there to sell tickets or candy for a fundraiser. The brothers gathered around Oscar asking silly questions that poked fun at him. Finally, the muffled snickering made David curious to the boy's real purpose there. With much reluctance, the house took Abernathy's application and told him they would "be in touch."

That evening, they all sat around laughing about the strange visit, making light of the boy's request, milking it for every petty insult and cruel taunt they could extract. It wasn't until David stopped Charlie from tossing Oscar's application that the conversation took a more serious turn, pushing the brothers into actual discussion on Oscar's enrollment in the house.

"Dude," Charlie began. "We ain't letting that freak in here. That's nuts."

"Agreed!" moaned Derek as he bounced his signature hacky sack on his knee.

"Wait, wait, now," David stopped. "Let's think this through, brothers." He smiled and stood. "How often do we fight about who's got the beer run?"

"A lot," Alex confirmed.

"Agreed," Derek said again.

Alex laughed. "As a matter of fact, it's your turn to night, Lenny!"

"Screw you in the ear, guys!" Lenny sang from the living room.

"Seriously, though," continued David. "My man Oscar could come in handy. He could do… practically all the crap we can't stand to do, right?" David could tell that his case was winning over the others.

"Agreed," chuckled Derek, nodding his head. As Derek bounced the bobbing hacky sack to his other knee, Alex reached over and snatched it out of the air. Derek glared at him, his face melting into a pathetic expression. He sniffed.

"Give that damn thing back to him, Alex! I swear," Alan said as he yanked the sack from Alex and tossed it back to Derek to bypass the nerve-wracking whine.

"Man, I don't know," William said. "Don't that seem a bit shitty? Bring him in to be a slave when he's thinking he will really be part of the frat?"

Derek's look turned somber. "Aw, agreed," he sighed.

Alan threw a wadded piece of paper at William's face. "Oh, cry about it, Will. The kid *would* be part of the frat… technically. I think it's a great idea, man."

"What do you think, Pete?" David asked.

Pete Roland was the drumline god of the URU band. Also, he was the official house representative, the one they sent to Dean Kidmon to explain why the house had once again landed on the evening news. The frat had appeared in the papers for a multitude of reasons, none of which were noble, so they definitely required a good PR person, and Pete was just that. "I say let's do it," Pete said as he drummed on the table with his tattered drumsticks. "First thing… he's cleaning the hall toilet. Ken dropped timber in there again this morning."

"Eww! Agreed!" Derek howled.

And they all laughed.

At first, it was fun, distracting even. Oscar was a willing participant for just about anything the brothers imagined. The entire semester, the boy ran errands, cleaned the house, did laundry, and grocery shopped, all while keeping up a 3.94 GPA, which made the house look pristine on paper. And over time, Oscar grew on them, especially David. It was difficult not to let the kid get under your skin. His good-natured goofiness was just the thing the guys needed to lighten the air.

All went well until spring semester when the brothers noticed Oscar was growing quiet and even more reserved than usual. Guys typically don't ask guys what's wrong, of course, so most of them ignored Oscar's sullen behavior. As the rush of the warm air heated the cool winter nights, spring fever set the campus alight, causing the house to forget all about Oscar's attitude. Spring Break was upon the university, which meant many, many raucous festivities. So other houses wouldn't outdo them, the brothers decided to throw an all-out bash on campus. It would be, as Alan put it, "epic." The house party kicked off at 8:00 that Friday night, and Oscar quickly became a main highlight. At moments, he was the lead of the joke; other times he was the butt of the joke, but he always in the joke, and he loved it. Well, David believed Oscar loved *most* of it. Around eleven that night that David noticed Oscar seemed to hover around this girl named Cindy Daniels, a cheerleader-type with a reputation for being snobbish and unequivocally rude.

"Hot, huh?" David said as he snuck up behind Oscar.

Oscar jumped with a start and then laughed. "Yeah, yeah... she sure is."

Cindy walked to the dance floor with two of her girlfriends. David pondered for a moment and smiled. "You know what, dude... you ought to go and dance with her."

Oscar contemplated for a moment and said, "You don't think she would be mad?"

"Mad? Oh, hell naw. Cindy? She's a cool lady. She'll dig you for sure." Even while David was telling Oscar the lie, he knew it was wrong. Cindy, being the prude he knew her to be, would take one look at poor Oscar and dismiss him. It would be nothing more than a joke, right? Something the brothers could get together and bash on later, all together, rumbling about what a *bitch* Cindy was.

Initially, Oscar started by dancing, or at least trying to, about ten feet from her. He continued to move closer and closer until he was right beside her. Noticing Oscar was eyeing her, Cindy gave a knowing wink to her girlfriends. To David's surprise, she turned right to Oscar and danced close. Closer and closer she moved until she was right on him. David and the other brothers began enjoying the spectacle, rooting for Oscar, laughing so hard they were about to choke on their chuckles. And for a moment, it seemed Cindy would be cool, play along, keep the crowd going. They all cheered for Oscar, who, by this time, sensed he was the biggest stud the campus had ever known.

Then, it happened.

Cindy shoved Oscar hard into the snack table, right into the large desert trays. The music went dead as the crowd tried to surmise the situation. Some laughed; others were caught completely by surprise. Poor Oscar looked up at Cindy with the most pitiful look the crowd had ever seen, his nose a bloody mess on his face, his eyes welling with tears.

"I hope that was as much fun for you as it was for me. Now, step the hell off, loser," she spat. To add insult to injury, she tossed her beer in his face. No one made a sound. Fortunately, since karma can be instant and swift, while Cindy walked away in triumph she slipped on the scattered deserts. Her friend caught her, but as she did, she exposed one of Cindy's misshapen breasts from her botched boob job. The crowd exploded in laughter as the two girls fell into the pool.

Alan ran forward with his cell phone, capturing the moment on film. "This is so going on the net!" he shouted. The crowd applauded. "Did you see that freaky booby, man?"

David couldn't help but feel moved by the fact that Cindy's cruelness had backfired instantaneously, that the party didn't view Oscar's mishap as humorous, but instead thought Cindy's googly boob was the funniest thing they had ever seen. It was hilarious to everyone except Oscar, who thought the crowd was laughing at his expense.

Two of the brothers helped Oscar to his feet. David approached Oscar and expressed a sincere apology for sending him over for slaughter, trying to make light of it, poking fun at Cindy. And for a while, Oscar tried to act as if the event didn't bother him, but Oscar's feelings were obvious to David. Later into the night, however, impromptu sex with Amy Lindermill rubbed Oscar out of David's mind.

No one saw Oscar for the remainder of the party. It wasn't until he didn't show up at the frat house the next morning to help clean that the brothers started to worry. Later that afternoon two girls from the nursing school found his body while walking through Richardson Park. There was poor Oscar in his small, beat-up sedan with duct tape lining the seats. Dried blood and bits of flesh littered the back windshield which had a single bullet hole in the center of the glass. He had been dead for over twelve hours. They said he had fired the gun at the wrong angle causing it to destroy part of his brain and rupture his left carotid artery, so he didn't die immediately. It was just Oscar's luck to have missed his target, laying there only to slowly bleed to death.

No one knew where he got the gun.

And that was the first time, possibly in his whole life, that David Porter felt the emotion known as guilt. He didn't know if his actions had caused Oscar's death, but he knew they hadn't helped. He knew Cindy's cold push was the final straw Oscar needed to end his own existence. It eventually came out that Oscar had been battling depression for years. After meeting Oscar's abusive father at the small, insignificant funeral, it didn't take long for David to piece the puzzle of Oscar's suicide together. It only added to his guilt when Oscar's mousey mother told him that being part of Psi Rho Phi was the biggest highlight of Oscar's life, that Oscar was so proud, that he "loved" the boys there "like brothers."

The words stung so much that they nearly brought blood to the surface.

After that, things changed for David, little by little, bit by bit. He could feel something budding within him, something essential, necessary. And he felt it was something good. It had to be. Becoming someone else, anyone else, would be better than the frigid prick he felt he had been. Now, eight months after Oscar put a bullet through his brain, David viewed things in a different light, clearer, seeing things for what they truly were.

"David," called his mother's shrill voice from downstairs. "Get down here now! We have to get things settled and get on the road."

David sighed and started down the steps. *Of course... get things settled... plan it out... get everything nice and neat.* "Yeah, yeah," he said in a flat tone.

"Now, we have to get you registered for fall classes. Senior year is big. They said your car would be done tomorrow morning. So, I will drop you off at the campus registry before heading to the meeting. Is that okay?"

"Affirmative," David said with a slight salute.

His mother looked at him. "And where have you picked that up? *Affirmative.* Just say 'yes' like a normal person."

"I don't know, mother. Must be one of those nasty habits from college you go on about." In fact, David had no idea from where that word had originated, or why he had begun to use it with such frequency. Somehow, it felt natural, like it must be said. It felt wrong not to say it.

"That's right. That's right indeed. Nasty habits. You've got too many of those. You better straighten up and fly right, young man. There is only so much Centicoin can do, and having to buy your grades this semester just isn't going to cut it anymore. Senior grades are too expensive."

"Why not just go ahead and buy my diploma? Save a little coin," he said with frigidness, so frigid his mother paused. He slumped down at the kitchen bar.

"David, you better watch it," she said as she situated her massive purse over her shoulder. "You've never complained about getting ahead before, you certainly didn't complain about it when I got you that car, so I don't know why you need to start now."

David chuckled. "Getting ahead? Really? That's what you call it? A better word for it may be 'cheating.'"

His mother cast him a defiant glance. "Listen here, son. I don't know what's got into you lately. Since you've been back, you've been off center. I don't know why. Maybe it was that little boy who blew his brains out."

Blew his brains out. She said it so cold, so crass. "His name was Oscar, Mother."

"I don't care what his name was. We have a reputation to uphold. You have a lot of eyes on you—big eyes—Parliament eyes. You always have. They want you in Parliament. I know it. I heard that President Keating herself asked about you last month. Everyone is expecting big things from you. We have just been making sure you achieve your full potential."

"So, what is wrong with a 3.0 average? I have been doing fine on my own. Why does it always have to be perfect with you guys?!"

"Because, by God, that is what we pa…" She stopped herself, but David understood what she was saying.

"Oh… oh, yeah. Because that's what you *paid for*, right, Mother? When you built me in the damned lab? Maybe 'smart' shouldn't have been last on your list, huh? Maybe when you stop bribing everyone at Parliament to give a damn about…"

She slapped him before she realized what she had done. David felt his fingers dig into the thick marble of the kitchen counter. He looked at her with anger, so much so he could tell she was frightened.

"Oh, honey," she quivered. "I am so sorry. You know I didn't mean that."

David stood, his six foot-five frame towering over her. "I think we better leave now, Mother. Go get in the car."

And she quickly did just as he instructed. He reached over and put his wallet in his back pocket. As he marched through the door, searing with anger, he didn't notice that during their altercation his crushing grip had left perfect finger impressions embedded deep into the three-inch thick marble counter top as if the rigid stone was warm putty.

CARSON

C arson finished polishing the canopy of his father's pride and joy, the plane of his father's own design, the *Cloak S-900*. He didn't know why his father called it that; it sounded a little too intense to Carson. His father made certain the craft had all the best augmentations—GPS tracking, long-range homing antenna, hover turbines, network link, and even the *Camouflage R18 Radar Muffler*, a banned device that prevented any GPS or targeting device from locking onto the jet. In actuality, he knew if the government recognized what the plane could do, he would be thrown in prison faster than he could say, *I didn't know it did that!*

He stepped back and took a long look at the craft. "Miss you, Pop," he said, patting the hull. He turned around and made his way back to the main hangar where he saw a very attractive young woman waiting for him. She wore a blue suit and held a notepad. The lanyard around her neck signaled she was yet another reporter. Still, he smiled.

"Hi, there. Could we get your name for the story?" she asked.

"Carson. Carson Quinley," he said, wiping his greasy hands on his jeans. He held out a welcoming hand.

"Sorry, I'm wearing white," she said with a pretentious tone, pulling the fresh pencil from behind her ear. "So, what's the name of this garage?"

"It's a hangar, and it's called Quinley Air Field," Carson said with a smile.

"Oh, you own it?"

"Yes, Ma'am. My father passed it to me and my sister when he died."

She appeared concerned. "Oh, I'm so sorry. Was it recent?"

"Hmm, I'd say about four years ago, when I was fourteen."

"Oh, so you're a young thing, huh?" she said with an air of flirtation.

With his polite southern drawl, ice-blue eyes, wavy hair, and grease-rat demeanor, he got these responses from women often. "I'm eighteen, Ma'am."

She smiled. "Ooh, well, you're the right age, I think." She leaned in closer.

Carson didn't let these types of flirtatious compliments go to his head, because he was a humble guy...but mostly because he was homosexual. Advances from women, while certainly appreciated, were more amusing to him than complimentary.

"Bubba!" Carson called. "Hey, man… come lend me a hand." A hulking brute emerged from the main office, bald, covered in tattoos, handsome, rough. He walked toward where Carson and the reporter stood.

The reporter touched Carson's hand. "I'm a Pisces," she said with a smile.

At that moment, the hulk called "Bubba" leaned in and kissed Carson on the mouth. He patted Carson with a firm hand on the behind, lifting Carson slightly from the ground. Then Bubba smiled at the reporter, and with a knowing wink walked to the tool center behind them.

"I'm a Virgo," Carson slyly replied to her. He could almost hear flies buzzing around inside the woman's gaping mouth.

"Uh," she began. "Um, do you mind if I, um," she struggled, pointing to the rest of the news teams gathered at the air field gate.

"Oh, no, not at all. Talk soon, now," and he tipped his baseball hat to her as she scurried away. He let out a hysterical laugh. "Oh, oh, I love it. I do."

"You need to quit calling me 'Bubba,' shithead."

"Oh, Dennis, but you look like a Bubba. Lisa! Don't you think he looks like a Bubba?" Carson said to the woman who was working the desk in the large office building that was lined with windows.

Lisa stepped out of the door and walked over to Dennis. "Honey, you look like a Bubba. And Carson, please quit kissing my husband."

"You're just mad because your little brother kisses better than you," Carson said.

Lisa shot a scowl to Dennis.

Dennis looked to Lisa, and then to Carson. "He does kiss pretty good," Dennis added.

"Ha!" blurted Carson with a triumphant shout.

"Oh, you two shut up," Lisa growled. "So, when is his highness supposed to get here again? I'm ready to get these people out of here."

"Ah… he's about a half hour late," Carson replied.

"Figures," Dennis added.

"You know how politicians can be," Carson said. "Don't make a crap to me; we got our money. It isn't like he's taking this thing in the air today, anyway. As long as it looks pretty for the pictures, we're good."

When General Arnold Esterburg of the Parliamental Skyforce retired, the world was grateful. One of the highest-ranking officials of Parliament, he had become somewhat of a wild card for Parliamental Congress, as well as the world at large. His antics were horrendous for public relations. The government experienced an onslaught of PR clean-up after he exposed the hidden tracking capabilities of the BSC chipset. He also bragged about how people with the right amount of Centicoin could practically "build their own baby." His sexual exploits were also nothing to ignore. Over his illustrious career, he entertained several ladies, which he referred to as his *professional staff*, some too young to even be named. Esterburg was all-around despicable. Discourteous, tactless, and offensive to about everyone, the world took a collective sigh of relief when he retired from his post.

While Parliament didn't miss him, the public ached to keep up with the latest Esterburg foolishness. After the public called his war record into question—namely his ability to start the engine of a jet, let alone fight a war in one—he decided he would show the world a thing or two. He soon purchased an antique Northrop T-38 Talon warplane, a two-seat, twin-engine supersonic trainer jet. And this led the General to Quinley Air Field. To the aviation public, Xavier Quinley, a war hero in his own right, was one of the most advanced Technical Science Engineers in Tactical Aircraft Maintenance. His young son, Carson, was an up-and-comer. Carson made a name for himself early on with his ability to work on advanced aviation mechanics with the precision of a physicist. He was the youngest recipient of the coveted Astronautics Aviation Award.

Carson knew the General sought him out specifically to work on his new purchase. The only problem was the geezer didn't tell Carson he bought a hunk of junk. Carson rebuilt the antiquated engine—twice. The aircraft itself was so outdated, regardless of whether it was on the ground or in the air, anyone who wanted to continue living needed to avoid it. Carson struggled to believe the plane once trained top-notch pilots. The business would have needed an additional 10,000 CC and three solid months' work to rebuild the contraption enough to get off the ground without incident. Notwithstanding, everyone realized the General loved to be in the public eye more than anything, be it for noble acts or embarrassing offenses. So, everyone assumed Esterburg's latest promotional tactic was to gather the media at the air field to show off and talk about his magnificent "war plane."

"When did these people get here?" Lisa asked.

Carson rubbed sweat out of his eye with his forearm. "I'd say about two hours ago? Said the General was going to be here to take pictures with this piece of shit at six. Who cares? More advertising for us."

"And dad always said…," Lisa began.

"Any publicity is good publicity," the siblings said in unison.

They noticed the reporters rumbling and buzzing.

"Oh, look who's here," Dennis said as the huge stretch limousine pulled into the area.

"Aww… well, it must be nice," said Carson with a snort. Carson closed the door of the old plane and wiped it down so it would appear spic and span.

A well-dressed service man from Esterburg's entourage walked toward the trio. "Hello there!"

"Howdy!" Carson said, tossing the stained work towel over his shoulder.

"So, does the landing strip face away from the sun? Or do you know where the best angle may be? We want to be able to really make out Esterburg in the cockpit when he takes off."

Carson and Lisa looked at each other in surprise.

"Oh," Carson laughed. "We don't need to do that. It can't fly today. We're just getting it ready for pictures, right?"

Perturbed at the notion, the official said, "Listen, kid… after all these weeks of lessons, he's flying the thing today. Why would we call all of these outlets to show up just to take his picture next to the plane? We need headlines."

"Look," Carson replied boldly. "We still have about three more months to get this thing aviation-ready. It's not *ready* to fly today. So, unless you guys want the headlines to read: ESTERBURG IN PIECES—OVER FIVE SQUARE MILES, you can go on back over there and tell all those people to come back in September."

Slighted, the service man stomped away and returned to the herd.

"What in the hell made them think we were flying today?" Lisa whispered to Carson.

"I don't freakin' know, but they need to get over that right now," he spat back.

"Be quiet," she shushed. "These are the wrong people to be pissing off, Carson."

"Better to be pissed off than dead, right?"

Three of the suited men gathered Esterburg and walked toward Carson. The sight made his stomach twitch.

"Oh, hell, Carson. Now be nice," Lisa said.

"Shh," he replied. "Can I help you gentlemen?" Esterburg approached him. Carson held out his hand. "General, it is so nice to finally meet..."

"Boy, get this piece a' shit plane in the air," Esterburg said in a flat voice.

"What?" replied Carson with surprise.

"Get it in the air. And get it in the air now," Esterburg hissed. "I didn't come all this way to get some damn portrait with a plane. If I wanted a picture, I'd take it myself. Get it done. Now."

"Sir, I don't think you realize..."

"Son, I said *now!*"

And that is when Carson, who commonly had trouble controlling his temper, slipped out of control. "Look... *Sir...* this thing isn't flying today. It needs a lot more work done on it. We told your people earlier this week. I told them directly that we wouldn't be ready for a flight test until the fall, and they were fine with that."

"Can it get in the air?" Esterburg asked.

"Maybe, but it won't stay there," Carson answered. "Now, I am sorry, General, but this just isn't going to happen. You aren't flying this plane today." Then, to add sympathy, he said, "Your safety means too much to us."

Esterburg huffed. He thought to himself and said, "You know what, son, you're right. I'm not flying this thing today."

Carson smiled. "Thank you, Sir. I appreciate..."

"*You* are. Suit up."

Carson's eyes widened. "What? You're out of your mind if you think I'm taking this thing up in the air."

Esterburg leaned close to him. "Son, you don't seem stupid to me. These good people just want to see it fly. We can always say I

42

was the pilot, right? No one is going to know any different or care. So, you have two choices: get this thing up in the air long enough to get it on tape… or I'm going to have you shot for assaulting me. Either way, there's going to be exposure for me today."

Carson didn't understand how to respond. What the man was saying to him seemed unfathomable. How could the man get away with it? "You can't do that," was all he could manage.

Esterburg laughed. "I've not gotten where I am by exactly playing by the rules, son. I can do just about anything I want in this god-forsaken world, and without recourse. I *made* it that way. Why, I could pull out my gun and blow your nasty, grease-covered head off right here and no one would blink twice. I have a whole crowd of people here who will believe anything I tell them." Esterburg glanced at Lisa. "Then, I'll shoot her and that goon over there for good measure. It's simple: I got here; you started haggling over coin you felt we owed to you. I said I wouldn't pay, and you attacked. Clear as that." He held a fat finger up to Carson's head. "Pow… goodbye, dipshit."

If looks could have torn Esterburg's neck in two, Carson's gaze would have blown him to pieces. He was so furious, it was almost worth the dying. If he moved with enough stealth, he could stab Esterburg in the throat with his screwdriver before they could stop him. Either way, they would both go down. He looked at Lisa noticing the petrified grimace on her face. He held his two fingers up to his eyes and pointed at her, showing they understood each other. They had shared that little gesture since childhood. It was their way of saying they saw each other, that they got it. Carson reached up and opened the door to the jet.

"Carson, don't!" Lisa called.

He motioned for her to be quiet and stared at Esterburg, who gave him a sick grin. "I'll be back for your ass," he threatened.

"Ha! That's if you make it back, son. Me and my *ass* will be here waiting for you." Esterburg's entourage laughed. "The good news is we don't need to see you land!"

Carson started the engine and taxied the plane through the field toward the runway while the enthusiastic camera crews rolled. He aligned the jet to the centerline on the runway. Two of the error indicators were already blinking. "I guess I'll be seeing you in a bit, Dad," he said with a choke in his throat. He applied the brake and set the flaps into zero degrees. The RPMs would never reach satisfactory arc, but he would have to overcompensate with the throttle. He positioned the rudder pedal to maintain as much of a balanced center as possible. Then, he started forward. Once he got around 20% below the rotation speed, he set the flaps to the lift position and tried to speed up. *Hell, I'm not even going to make it off the ground.* He had been pressing the RPMs enough for the heating indicator to illuminate with warning. Once he reached rotation speed, he pulled back on the yoke with cautious pressure and closed his eyes.

To his surprise, the jet lifted into the air with ease. He felt a sudden sense of liberation. Now, all he had to do was get high enough to turn around and land without overstepping the runway. He took a massive sigh of relief and relaxed. One of the alert indicators faded away, which was definitely a good sign. Plans formed while he was in the air, plans to get back at Esterburg. He snapped selfies of himself at the controls of the plane to make sure people knew the geezer wasn't the pilot at the controls. He caught the time and date stamp on the control panel, too, for added significance.

"There you go, you fat bastard," Carson said. "We'll see how the papers like this story when I give it to them." The only thing the public liked more than watching Esterburg was watching Esterburg become the fool.

It had been a long time since Carson had been in the air. There was peace in the skies that few comprehended. His father recognized the feeling; he gave it to Carson. And it was the greatest gift. It was different being the pilot than being the passenger—liberating, exhilarating, knowing you were in control. The wings of the plane were your wings, no one else's. While he turned the plane in the air, he tried to think of other ways to humiliate Esterburg. Maybe he could rig the plane so it would never start again. That would fix him. *Then he would have an antique piece of shit for his collection.*

As Carson turned to head back toward the runway, he received the first warning that something wasn't right. The rudder was no longer operational. Then... silence. The entire power system failed. There was no power to any of the instruments or to the engines. He felt his stomach rise into his throat as the hunk of metal descended.

This is it... this is how I die.

He beat on the dashboard of the jet hoping that it would correct whatever electrical short had occurred, but his thrashing helped nothing. There was the slim possibility that the emergency eject still contained its parachute, but without proper power there would be no guarantee that ejection would even work. He had begun descent before the failure, so there was no way to climb enough to convert the extra forward speed into height. The higher the jet could have climbed the less air resistance with which to contend. Below he could see the air field in clear sight. The crash was inevitable, and the tragedy would unfold in front of all those people. They would have his death captured on film to play for his sister repeatedly.

Why didn't he refuse to fly the hunk of metal in the first place, claim the engine wouldn't turn over?

Why didn't he graduate the Aviation Academy?

Why didn't he go into the Skyforce as his father had wanted?

Why didn't he ever return the call from the cute guy at the auto body shop?

Carson's mind filled with confusing regrets, all swirling at once. In his mind, he wished he could drive the plane into the ground where Esterburg stood, take the old man with him. But at that moment, something peculiar happened. He felt the urgent need to get out of the plane, as if breaking out of the cockpit would save his life even though he was thousands of feet from the ground. The eject mechanism was inoperable, but he saw Dennis' big, red wrench in the console. He grabbed it and unbuckled his safety belt. With a smashing thrust, he beat against the windshield. He slammed the heavy tool against the glass repeatedly until it shattered around him, the force ripping him from the cabin and sucking him into the cold air. The wind burnt his lungs. As he watched the jet plummet to the ground below, his back began to burn like fire. It felt as if someone was driving hot irons deep into his shoulder blades. He cried out and tried to reach behind, ripping his jacket and shirt from his torso.

Without warning, Carson was flying, soaring high into the sky. Specks of blood splattered the great white wings that protruded from his torn back. They carried him higher and higher, into the wind. He had actual wings, wings like an eagle. His vision grew focused, pronounced. He could see for miles ahead of him with utmost clarity, like the eyes of a hawk. He focused on the ground below and zeroed in on Esterburg. His mind was no longer his own; he was something else, an animal, rough and savage. Tucking the great wings behind him, he dove toward the land below in front of Esterburg and his crew. He landed with a mighty pound that shook the earth beneath his feet. The force rippled through the area, throwing Esterburg and his men to the ground, busting media equipment, and shattering all the windows from the nearby buildings.

Lisa stepped out of the shadows to witness the sight of her brother, standing tall. The great, feathered extensions protruding from his back that must have measured over twenty feet when extended to capacity. His eyes shined a luminescent white light— bright, pure. As he stepped forward, the antique jet crashed into flames in the distance. One of the service men jumped to his feet, pulling his gun and firing at Carson twice, hitting him in the shoulder, but it was as if the angel hadn't felt the bullets rip through his flesh. As he continued to step forward, he kept his radiant eyes fixated on the petrified Esterburg. With one arm, he lifted the hefty man from the ground with ease and handed him the keys to his prized antique that now lay in smoldering wreckage before them. Then, he dropped him to the ground.

"Enjoy, you son-of-a-bitch," Carson said in a multi-layered voice that intertwined on itself.

"Carson?" Lisa said stepping closer.

46

He glared at her. At first, his cold and unfeeling expression didn't change at all. However, as he recognized his sister, the light in his eyes subsided. The huge wings shrank back into his torn shoulder blades. He winced with pain as he fell to his knees on the ground. Lisa began to run to him.

"Stop! Don't come closer," Carson warned. The camera crews in the distance scrambled to find any operable back-up equipment to capture the event. He knew that for his sister's safety he couldn't allow that to happen. He had to get away and find a safe place to hide until he could figure out what just happened. As he stood, he cradled his bleeding shoulder. With tears in his eyes, he screamed, "Your brother is dead!" He gave Lisa a final glance before he ran as fast as his weary legs would carry him, the lost angel, disappearing into the thick woods behind the air field.

THE SEED OF HOPE

"**H**ello? Are you there? I said may I take your order?"

Hudson rubbed his fatigued eyes. His mind rumbled with questions about the inexplicable "electric girl." What was her name? What did she look like? Did she favor Victoria Conner?

"Sorry, sorry… yes. Um, I would like a Double Bacon Bliss combo, please." Fast food did for his nerves what vodka did for the alcoholic. Stress led him to drive-thru windows, and it was fortunate anxiety wasn't common for him. Although, if current events kept progressing, he sensed he would pack on substantial poundage at the hands of Shakey Burger.

He picked up his order at the window and headed home. Working late often had benefits, like avoiding the bumper-to-bumper traffic of Region H. *Region H… what crap*, he thought. To him, it would always be Seventh City. He thought back to when Parliament divided the world into geographical regions instead of countries. So many significant changes were hurling at the world that people found it difficult to keep them organized. It became obvious early on that there was little the human race could do to prevent the "positive" changes, veiled threats camouflaged as recommendations, guidance, what was *best for us*. Sure, the remaining Insurgence tried to push against the establishment, but it did little good. The struggle created futile conflict—us against them—and *they* always won. At first, the Insurgence did well in the resistance. But more and more revolutionaries vanished, disposed of in the most politically correct manner possible. Parliament reconditioned those they deemed useful and transformed them into emissaries for the government. The smaller the Insurgence became, the weaker it grew, and weakness brought silence. In the present world, one could no longer hear the voice of protest; its vocal chords had been torn from its throat. Parliament would be less than pleased to recognize that Hudson, the genetic king of the world, deliverer of HRV-EST, had been a key player in the underground resistance.

He tossed his keys into the bowl by the front door and sat down at the kitchen counter to consume his bag of cholesterol. All the old emotions were creeping over him again. His acceptance of Keating's world, his pitiful surrender to the uncontrollable, was now giving way to feelings of insurrection. He would locate the electric girl; he had no doubt. But he had to be careful, search off Parliament's grid. Hidden eyes monitored all online traffic; he knew that. They had been watching for years, listening for the signs of defiance. The only connection off the grid was the Core, the abandoned headquarters of the once mighty Federation. He hadn't been there in years, too many years to remember. He used to visit the place often after his friends had passed. It made him feel connected to them, part of their energy. But the man he was now no longer had time for such reveries.

He threw the half-eaten burger into the bag and tossed it into the garbage. What he wouldn't have given to go back and change the past, but a glass of bourbon and a bath would have to do—bourbon because it reminded him of Steve, and a bath because…well, he smelled like ass. He soaked in warm water and self-pity, drinking his bourbon. His weary mind wandered to the night he first met Wrath and how his life had changed with abrupt speed.

Taking down Evelyn Karns was no easy feat, and the Federation understood that. Not because she couldn't be caught, mind you, but because she couldn't *remain* caught. She was a master at covering her tracks, clouding evidence, and confusing nervous jurors. During her illustrious career, the courts had brought her to trial nine times, and not once did anything stick to her. In the rare instance evidence came to light, it somehow managed to disappear. Witnesses became frightened...or dead. So, everyone believed it would take someone on the inside to make things fall into place and stay there. The problem was that no one on the inside was brave enough to take up the gauntlet.

Hudson was a tough kid. Steve had seen that. Also, Steve was smart enough to discern that Evelyn would do nothing to harm a child. Hudson was one of her favorites. So, he would be unscathed regardless. Hudson was the undeniable diamond in the rough, and Steve had realized he needed to appeal to the boy's potential.

"Don't you want something better?" Steve once said. "Just ask yourself, will picking pockets be enough when you're twenty years old, thirty...forty? Or will you have to graduate to murder to make ends meet by then?"

There were others who had been in Evelyn's company much of their life, those who had grown up, lost their innocence, and stolen more than cars. Rickety Lewis was one of Evelyn's best when he was a boy. Now twenty-four, Lewis stole his first kidney to sell on the Organ Train. Nancy "Bubbles" Edmonds went from pick-pocketing to being one of the most expensive prostitutes in Evelyn's collection.

To Steve, evil was relative and the protection and love the Madame gave her younglings was only intended to cultivate them into the proficient villains they would become. In those days, Hudson knew of no one who left the business with success. Still, he had a hard time believing Evelyn was all bad. Maybe it was because she was the only mother figure he knew.

Evelyn taught him street smarts, determination, and grit. Steve taught him science, cunning, and stealth. Those life lessons made

Hudson worthy of the name *Hacker*. He remembered how it had surprised Evelyn to learn that he was the mole who led to her capture at the hands of the Federation. Steve was against Hudson visiting Evelyn in prison. However, the Federation couldn't help but be impressed that in exchange for her full cooperation Evelyn asked that all of "her kids" avoid prison time in Hold. She requested their enrollment in social services for rehabilitation instead.

Finally, four months after the trial, Steve caved in and took Hudson to see Evelyn at the Block, one of the largest, most complex Hold facilities in the world. Built right outside of Seventh City, the facility housed the world's most dangerous criminals. Evelyn seemed pleased that she was considered ruthless enough to be kept there. Hudson sat there waiting for her to be led into the visitation room. The thick, bulletproof glass stood between him and the visitation cell.

The buzz of the door startled him as they led Evelyn into the area. Hudson didn't understand why he needed to see her. A part of him felt that he owed her an apology; he wasn't sure. After all, he took her down, gathered a plethora of evidence against her, and collected everything the prosecution needed to close one of the swiftest cases Seventh City had ever tried. After being in the Block a year, Hudson had expected that once their eyes met Evelyn would turn on her heels and walk away, but instead she looked into his eyes and smiled. And not a cunning smile, but genuine, as if she was glad to see his face.

Evelyn sat down and took the phone. She looked strange in her subdued getup: the gray uniform, her natural hair, and no make-up at all. Humble. Quiet. Hudson picked up his phone. "Andre," she said. "It's good to see you, boy."

"Uh, thanks," he replied with apprehension. "How... how are you?"

"Ah, well, you would think bad, but actually... pretty good." She looked around the room. "As you could imagine, this is quieter than the life we used to lead, right?"

"Yeah, I bet."

"So, how are you, son? Is the Federation taking care of you?"

"Yes, Ma'am."

"Good. I knew they would." She was quiet for a moment, searching for something else to say through the awkwardness. "Did you know that T.J. has gone back to school?"

T.J. Blackwood had been a good friend to Hudson during their enrollment in the ACE Gang. He was younger than Hudson, rugged, tough, and smart. He could see the finer details of hidden things, which was a beneficial attribute as a car thief.

"Is that so? I thought he was in Juvenile Hold?"

"Oh, he was," she confirmed. "But after that stint, he's emerged a changed boy. Says he's gonna be a cop. Can you believe that? A cop!"

"Well, good for him. I hope he does well."

"Yes, that's definitely great. Old Judge Franklin kept his promise, so you have to respect that. Because of Franklin, all of you kids got opportunities you wouldn't have had... especially not with me." Her positivity was incredible. "Why, boy, you look a little shocked."

"Um, well... I am a little, I guess." Hudson took a deep breath. "I thought you would be really mad at me."

"Do you want to know the truth?"

"Uh huh."

She smiled. "At first I was, I guess. But now? No, Andre. I ain't mad at you." She could tell Hudson didn't know how to respond. "Look, honey, I would've given us another year... maybe two... I would have been killed eventually. Hell, I may even still be put out of my misery. Let's face it—I pissed a lot of folks off. But worse yet, one of you kids would've been killed." She touched the glass. "I've done a lot of bad things to a lot of people, Andre, but I've always drawn the line at you kids. Children need a future, opportunities— opportunities I didn't have a little girl. That's why you kids were just pickpockets and car burglars. Could you have gotten into trouble? Sure. Long term? Not really. But I knew if you were with me you were off the streets, away from the drugs, away from the predators, away from the people who would've taken advantage of you."

Hudson watched her eyes moisten with tears. "You guys were my kids… you *are* my kids. I loved you, and I still do."

A tear ran down Hudson's cheek. Her sentiment touched him so. "Thank you… Evelyn, for everything you did for me. And I am so sorry I hurt you."

"You didn't hurt me, honey. I think you *saved* me. You saved us all." Hudson touched the glass against her hand. "You tell those so-called superheroes that Madame said they better take good care of little Andre, or when I get out of here I'll come take care of them."

Hudson giggled. "I think you may be here a while."

She smiled and stood. "We'll see." And with a knowing wink, she turned to leave.

To her credit, the Madame escaped a mere ten months into her lengthy forty-year sentence. She was the first and last inmate to escape the Block. The good part was that she was smart enough to leave the Seventh City, but not before leaving a box on Andre's front stoop that Sunday. Attached was an Easter card that read: *Always stay young.*

Inside was a chocolate rabbit.

The phone rang. Hudson jerked with a flinch, dropping his half-full sniffer of bourbon into the tub with him. "Dammit!" He scrambled for the phone. "Hello!" he spat with intolerance.

"Andre! It's Blackwood…are you watching the news?" asked Blackwood with a tone of hysteria. Yes, little T.J. had become a cop—a good one—just as he had said he would.

"No, Detective, I'm getting shit-faced, but I am sure you're going to tell me *all* about it."

"Wings!" was all that T.J. said. "The son-of-a-bitch got wings, Andre!"

"Who… who has wings?" Hudson said as he fumbled for the remote control. With his wet hands, he dropped the remote to the bathroom television into the soapy water. "Shi…!"

"What?"

"Hold on." Hudson, wet and soapy, placed the phone on speaker and scampered with caution across the damp marble tile to the television. "What channel?"

"2503. Hurry!"

Hudson turned on the television and got the station set. The newscaster was in mid report.

"Phillip, as you can see, it's totally unbelievable. Arnold Esterburg, retired General of the Parliamental Skyforce, was assaulted today at Quinley Air Field. As most of the public was aware, Esterburg had been staging an event at the local air field to showcase his ability to fly a fighter jet, a fact largely questioned by much of the public."

"Watch this shit!" yelled T.J. from the phone.

Footage played. "The unidentified assailant, seen here…," a circle appeared on the screen highlighting a winged figure, "is believed to have attacked the plane, causing it to fall from the sky, killing an air field employee who had offered to test fly the plane for the General and his crew." Hudson watched the television, his mouth agape. The figure appeared to bust through the windshield of the jet and slope toward the air field. The massive wings spread wide.

"Now, Jane, are those wings? Many people have asked if those are wings."

"Actually, no, Phillip, they aren't. We have received confirmation that what the perpetrator was using was a new model of air glider perhaps stolen from a nearby Parliamental weapons facility."

"Bullshit!" T.J. yelled as the footage cut back to the newsroom. "Those, brother, were wings. Big ass, white wings."

Hudson touched the screen unable to believe what he had seen. "Wings."

"Wings!" T.J. said with a laugh. "Say it again, brother."

"Wings!" they both said with a chuckle.

"I think we need to meet up, Detective."

"I agree. At the usual?"

"Yeah."

"When?"

"First thing in the morning."

"Isn't that place a wreck?" added T.J.

Hudson smiled. "The seed of hope always grows best in the soil of destruction, my man."

THE TWINS

Colonel Arklow walked to the reception desk of the Iron Room, one of the many conference areas at Parliament House. He knew what Keating wanted, and he wasn't pleased. For one, he didn't have time, and for two, there wasn't much to be done. No one knew who or what had attacked Esterburg, or its origin. All ideas were only suspicion, aimless ideas, and it would take more than a hunch to make a sanctioned move. The rapid restructure of the world was leading to unrest with the people, and enough of the Insurgence dwelled in the gutters of the lower Regions to bring about a full uprising if they were to realize their full potential. The rebels were in full recruit mode, and it would take time to get their numbers back down to a manageable level. That meant tapping mobile airwaves, increasing observation, arrests, and, of course, the random accident. Once Parliament subdued enough revolutionaries, they could continue to push control. But that's not how Keating worked. She wanted it completed today, and in the manner she saw fit. Arklow knew if she continued to lack presidential restraint, she would learn the hard way, the *Louis XVI* way.

The receptionist ushered Arklow into the dark conference room.

The large display at the front of the room was black. Sparse lighting gave way to shadows that seemed to follow him, watch him. It wasn't until he reached the head of the long conference table that he noticed a figure sitting in the dimness. "Son-uva!" Arklow muttered as he reacted.

"Walter, you're getting jumpy in your old age," cooed Keating.

"What can I say, Ms. President, you make me nervous." A true statement veiled as an anecdote.

"Do you know what makes *me* nervous, Walter?"

Arklow sighed as he took a seat. "I bet I can guess."

"People with pretty white wings make me nervous, Walter. Little electric girls make me nervous, Walter. Those... *those* are the things that make me nervous." Keating snapped her fingers setting the light above her head aglow, her thin frame draped in a form-fitting black suit. Her short, messy, platinum-blonde hair emphasized hints of make-up that dusted her pale features.

"Nothing is confirmed. As far as that girl, they are saying it was a faulty ground connection to the cooling vat and the water that led to that foreman getting fried."

"And the wings?"

"Well... admittedly, those are a little harder to explain."

Keating leaned forward. "No shit." She spun in her chair and stood, starting her customary pace. "Walter, when I brought you in as Director of Defense, I did so because... well, frankly, you can be an evil bastard. And I like that. But more than that I brought you in because you were innovative, always thinking on the edge. And that's what I need now, Walter, for you to think on the edge."

Walter gawked at her. "I can assure you, I'm on the edge."

Keating laughed. "Well, you can say that again."

"Ophelia, look," Arklow said. "The girl? Nothing to worry about. Trust me. The wings? I am telling you, I've seen the same glider equipment in prototype on the base. Enough people want Esterburg dead. He was trying to fool the public into believing he was in that plane. Someone with a grudge got word and wanted to take him out—plain and simple. You don't really think they've come back from the dead, do you? Because, I am here to tell you—the Federation is very, very dead."

Keating shot him an impatient gaze. "No, Walter, I don't think they've crawled from the ashes and returned. Contrary to popular belief, I'm not a complete moron. But I wonder about the hybrids, the creatures that were in your care."

"They were useless. Corrupt. You know that."

"Were they?"

"Yes, you saw the reports. You were present during final testing. Every splice we tried using Federation and Xeno DNA failed; every specimen died," replied Arklow getting perturbed. "It was impossible to program into the Xenozian genetic code. Nothing we did produced the weapon we wanted. The greatest chance we have now is X25."

Keating stared deeply into Arklow's eyes, as if she were searching for the truth. "And just where do we stand on X25?"

"Completed as of this morning. We should be able to arrange a demonstration soon."

"Outstanding." Keating sat back down. Her mind intertwined on itself with possibilities. She placed her hands on the table. "What do we know about the girl?"

Arklow touched the table activating the bioboard underneath the glass. The display came to life as he logged in. Ellen's picture entered the screen. "Ellen Braxton. Seventeen. A resident of Region H. Mother's name is Dahlia, a former Legal Aide turned homemaker. Father, a lawyer by the name of Charles Braxton, deceased. Dahlia has a boyfriend—some bum named Edward Miller, huge record, troublemaker. Ellen dropped out of school and just started working at Alemede two weeks ago. Beyond that, the girl's record is clean."

"Can we pinpoint her BSC?"

"Regional Authorities are in pursuit. She appears to be traveling to Region G. We're not sure why."

"Keep tracking her. What about our bird man?"

Arklow called up image captures from the air field event. "Not much on this guy, unfortunately. The press captured much more footage, but somehow all media equipment was damaged. We've got all we could get our hands on." He zoomed in on a picture of the wings and highlighted them. Then, he called up a file named *Operation Heaven*. He pulled blueprints and pictures of a glider mechanism prototype. "If you look at the comparison between the gliders the perpetrator has on and the prototype we've been working on under the Heaven project, you'll notice they're almost identical. This guy just managed to perfect it somehow. Probably a mole."

"And what are we doing about these moles?" Keating said with sarcasm.

Arklow rolled his eyes to himself. "If it *is* a mole, we'll find him."

"What about the owner of the air field? The sister."

"Lisa Quinley-Baker. Twenty-four," Arklow said as Lisa's picture came onto the screen. "Married to a Dennis Baker, an advanced engine tech. Her father was Xavier Quinley."

"The fighter pilot," said Keating.

"Yes. He left the air field to her and her younger brother, Carson."

"And where is he?"

Arklow zoomed in on the flaming wreckage captured after the crash and circled it. "In there somewhere. He's the one who was flying the plane for Esterburg."

Keating got up and walked to the expansive picture window of the conference room. She opened her arms, triggering the blinds that opened to show the city once known as Washington, D.C. She paused in silence, observing the world she now ruled, feeling her might, knowing her power. "I'm not convinced."

"Ophelia, dammit," Arklow began.

"Not completely, Walter. Not completely." She turned to him. "It's probably nothing, true. But I didn't get to where I am by being sedate. I want all resources on this. Tell them to do a full scan of any and every suspicious person. I want these freaks caught. Also, I want you to open communication with the Parliamental Media Board. All stories and reports of any more…'strange occurrences' or 'superhuman' happenings will cease effective immediately. All media will route through us, at least for the time being. Nothing gets out to the public that we don't want out. Anyone who disobeys will answer to me. The Parliamental World Summit is right in front of us, Walter. The entire world will be watching us. It is imperative that all goes according to plan." She turned and walked to the large globe in the center of the room. She touched the cool metal, giving it a slow spin. "The population can't get on the rebellion bandwagon. This is just the hope the Insurgence needs to relight old fires. We can't have any more heroes. *We* are their hero, Walter, and we need to remain the hero."

"Understood," Arklow said. "I'll put out the APB and contact the Media directly." He stood up, closed his file, and walked away.

As Arklow left the room, Keating walked back to the window and beheld the city. "Find them—that girl and our mysterious glider man—find them, and *kill* them," said Keating to the empty darkness.

"We thought you would never ask," Snitch said as she arose from the shadows.

Another figure crawled from the ceiling beams and completed a soft backflip to the floor. "Can we *play* with them first?" Scoundrel asked, taking a seat.

Keating turned to the young twins, the only remnants of the planet Xenoe left on Earth, her secret weapons. "Play with them, talk with them—I don't care as long as they're dead when you're done."

Snitch pulled her thick, bushy hair back. "Do you want bodies?"

Keating thought. "No bodies, but samples will be useful. Tissue—skin, blood."

"Oh, we can bring blood, can't we sister?" purred Scoundrel. Snitch laughed, her long tongue flipping in the air.

Keating knew that should it ever become known that Parliament had two Xenozians on its payroll, it would be detrimental for the government's reputation. As far as the world knew, any remaining aliens evacuated the planet over two decades ago, extinct from the moment that *Keating* destroyed Goliaric. The aliens were humanoid in appearance, aside from their obvious reptilian biology.

Distinguishing characteristics of Xenozians included solid black eyes, small grayish scales, and long, fork-like tongues. Their tails, having formidable strength, could be used like an additional limb. They could spit a gooey substance that caused temporary blindness, and long fangs contained a toxin that forced hemorrhaging in victims. Advancements in prosthetic flesh compound hid most of these features from an unwary public, allowing Scoundrel and Snitch to move about unnoticed. By nature, the creatures were agile fighters, stealthy, and cunning. The unscrupulous dealings of Parliament required the complex talents of the twins on many occasions, and Keating knew this matter would prove to be no exception.

Keating took a seat with them. "I trust you can remain undetected?"

Snitch smiled.

H A N A

It took a moment for the elevator to power up, so long that Hudson wondered if it would work at all. So many years had passed he had almost forgotten the location of the Core. Steve built the huge technological bunker well before he met Hudson or other members of the Federation. The team completed the construction together, adding their own personal touches. HANA was Hudson's personal touch.

He hoped she would still recognize him. Twenty years before, Hudson and Voltage designed a technological breakthrough, an artificial intelligence schema they dubbed *Human Adaptive Neurological Automation*. He never shared the technology with others, because the potential for exploitation was too great. HANA understood moods, verbal context, facial queues, and body language. Against Steve's wishes, Hudson also fitted her with a rather extensive language module that contained all the latest slang and references in popular culture. In fact, Hudson had molded her from his vision of the perfect girl.

He walked around the large warehouse trying to remember the sensor's location. "I could have sworn it was over here," he said as he pressed around with his foot.

"Wasn't it by the double doors over there?" T.J. suggested.

"No, that is where Steve used to keep that van."

"Oh, yeah, that van… the Wrathmobile," T.J. laughed.

Hudson giggled. "That *always* pissed him off."

"He couldn't stand it," snickered T.J..

Hudson eventually found the trigger that lowered what appeared to be a standard warehouse crane. He stepped into it and placed his hand on the control panel. As it imaged his palm, a retina scanner completed the second part of the verification. "Verified: Andre Hudson," said the female voice. Once the system accepted his identity, it went silent. Hudson raised his eyebrow with curiosity.

"Do it again," T.J. said.

Hudson repeated the steps, but again there was no response.

"Is it broke?"

Hudson sighed. "It's not broken. HANA… HANA, can you hear me?" There was no response. "HANA, come on."

"I'm not talking to you, Andre," said the woman's voice with a harsh tone.

"I'm sorry. I know it's been a while, but…"

"From my records, it's been eleven years, four months, twenty-two days, seven hours, ten-minutes, and thirty-two… thirty-three seconds. Longer than 'a while,' don't you think?"

T.J. looked concerned. "She sounds pissed, dude."

"Is that T.J.?" HANA asked.

T.J. smiled. "Hi, HANA."

Hudson leaned toward the console. "HANA, listen, I'm sorry for not being here for so long. It's… it's been difficult… for me… I guess. I had to have time." HANA gave no response. "Look…I need you."

There were a few moments of silence before the voice sighed. "Fine…."

The floor in front of them separated, and an elevator lift rose to greet them. After the men boarded, the elevator descended to the lower levels of the Core.

"She likes me," said T.J. with pride.

"Big whoop—she's always liked you better."

Once they reached the main floor for Core control, the lights in the area illuminated section by section. A thin veil of dust covered the place. The main monitors flickered and came to life, filling with updates and patches that were long overdue. A small digital holographer from the center of the ceiling activated and scanned the area. A holographic figure then appeared in the center of the room. She faded in and out before coming into full view. HANA was just how Hudson remembered her. She looked dated, like a frigid, steel android from decades past.

He smiled as he walked toward her. "Hi, HANA."

She smiled. "Hello, Andre. I've missed you."

"I've missed you, too."

The hologram twitched as it moved. "You look old."

"Thank you," Hudson replied. "I think we could both use upgrades."

"Access Mainframe...uploading," said the hologram. HANA's image changed into an enhanced android female, her face a hybrid of cybernetics and flesh. Her long hair was pulled into a thick ponytail atop her head. Her left eye was human in appearance, the right one digital. Sections of brilliant metal clung to her hourglass frame, and a greenish hue shined from underneath the connected body segments. "Is this more with the times?"

"Hot!" said T.J. in awe as he stepped closer.

HANA walked over to the sofa and took a seat. "Right? So, let's catch up while we reboot. I imagine I have about a billion petabytes of information to download, so it may take a while."

T.J. took a seat next to her. He continued to gawk at her figure, amazed by her appearance. Hudson took a seat in the dusty armchair across from them. "Make me one," T.J. said, pointing to HANA.

"Down, T.J.," Hudson said. "HANA, we need your help. It's about Project Phoenix."

HANA's image twitched as she closed her eyes, accessing Mainframe. "*Project Phoenix,*" confirmed the Mainframe's monotone vocal processor. "*File Code A-3791.138. Subjects: Steve A. Sutherland—Codename: Wrath, Victoria L. Conner—Codename: Voltage, Willahelm C.*

Vogel—Codename: Ascendor, Margret A. Casiano—Codename: Fleet, Olivia E. Keynes—Codename: Tempera." As each name was announced, an image of both their alter ego and hero guise projected into the middle of the space. T.J. couldn't help but notice the stunned expression on Hudson's face. It was as if Hudson was literally looking at ghosts from his past, on display, reminding him of a long ago too painful to recall.

"Uh…yes," Hudson said as he recovered from the rush of images. "We're not sure, but I think that somehow the project may have actually worked."

HANA gave him an inquisitive gaze. "Really? But I thought we had concluded that the environmental circumstances had not been suitable enough to cultivate effective growth? In other words… it *sucked.*"

"Well, I thought so. I really did. But something has happened over the past few days that could prove otherwise. Are we live, yet?"

HANA's eyes shuddered as she again accessed Mainframe. "Yes, we are now at one hundred percent."

Hudson leaned forward. "Outstanding. Is the Core secure?"

"Yes," she confirmed. "I am ninety-six point thirty-two percent sure we are secure. If you want full range, it will take longer. There are a lot of firewalls to validate and restructure."

T.J. looked concerned. "We don't need to reach out to the net without full range Hard-Core, Andre. No way. Parliament will be on us in two seconds."

"It will take twenty-three minutes and thirteen seconds to achieve full range," HANA confirmed.

Hudson took a deep breath. "Fine. We have time. I'd say we've got some cleaning up to do around here, and that should give us something to do while we wait."

And so, Hudson and T.J. began to straighten up the large control room known as the Hub, which was in desperate need of polishing. Steve would have been beside himself with shock if he were alive to witness such a mess. The Hub was a literal treasure trove of memories—scrapbooks, trinkets, badges, photos, newspaper clippings—name it, it was there.

Every so often, Hudson would have to stop and pull his mind from the past long enough to stay to the task. It was a peculiar feeling, a nostalgia that was both comfortable and excruciating all at once. Layered into the compunction of middle age, it was sometimes too much to bear. There were so many decisions he could have made, much more he could have said. It could have been possible to mend broken relationships—even between him and Steve, whose bond had become strained in the final days. But death is ultimate and forever. Regardless, present notions of resurrection drove him forward with determination. It was the opportunity to set the world right, to save the weak, the potential for redemption.

Hudson remembered when Steve had first showed him the Core, known at one time as the Den. The first thing Hudson said was…

"That's a stupid ass name, man."

"What's stupid about it? The Den… get it? Like a lion's den?"

"Oh… oh, I get it," Hudson replied. "Why don't you call it… the Hive?"

"No, we can't do that. Drone has already used that for his place, and I'm sure he's trademarked it," Steve said taking a seat at the old multi-network console that used to be where Mainframe now stood.

"The Refuge?"

"Doesn't that sound like you're *retreating* to somewhere?" Steve said.

Hudson thought. "Yeah…yeah, you're right. Oh! Here we go… the Hall of Jus…"

"Core," said a voice from the shadows. "Why don't you call it the Core?"

The boys jerked to full attention at the intruder in their midst.

"Who the hell are you, lady, and how did you get in here?" Steve demanded as he walked toward the figure.

A woman's form appeared through the silver-like electrical sparks that buzzed through the air. "I wouldn't do that if I were you, cowboy," she said in a thick English accent causing Steve to pause. "I'm looking for some guy called Wrath. He told me to meet him here."

"Voltage?" Steve said.

The woman stepped into the light, tall, long, thick red hair, voluptuous, dressed in a tight silver costume tailored with thin, blue electric-like patterns that covered her body. "Voltage...electrical goddess. Nice to meet you." She made her way toward him. "You're a lot cuter than I thought you would be."

"Uh, thank... thank you," Steve said as he swallowed the air in his mouth. "How did you get in here?"

"I followed you here."

"And how did you get past the security?" barked Hudson with aggression. She strolled over and took a seat beside him.

"Let's just say electricity comes in handy." Voltage snapped her fingers causing a flash of sparks to snap and dance around her fingertips.

"Impressive," Steve said. "You're the one who saved that bus of kids in Anchorage, right?"

"That's right. That's me. And you're the big guy who can leap tall buildings, eat bullets, crush things...?"

"Affirmative, that's me."

"You stopped that bomb in Chicago, right? Held it right in your bare hands. Kept it from blowing up all those people?"

"Well... I didn't, like, *hold* it. I sort of drilled into the ground deep enough to..." Out of his peripheral vision, Steve noticed Hudson, who was feverishly shaking his head, signaling him to stop making a fool of himself. "Well, you get it," finished Steve with an air embarrassment.

"I get it. Good for you, tough guy. You know, being serious, you guys do need to beef up security. All this password encryption stuff won't work against someone like me."

Hudson smirked. "Well, in your *professional opinion*, what would you recommend?"

She thought for a moment. "I'm not sure, but if this was my place I would try to develop some kind of artificial intelligence infrastructure, something that would recognize it was me."

"Good idea," Steve said. Hudson looked at him and rolled his eyes. "I'm glad you came. I've heard of you and a few others like us, and we thought it may be good if we meet, get acquainted with each other."

"Can't have enough friends, right?" Voltage said with a smile.

"Sometimes you can," Hudson said.

"So, what's your power, stud?" she said to Hudson.

"Uh…I don't have one," replied Hudson modestly.

She smiled. "Oh, I bet you do. I bet you have all the girls gushing."

Okay… maybe she isn't so bad, Hudson thought.

Steve smirked at Hudson's red face and then turned to Voltage. "I was wondering if you'd be interested in hooking up… I mean, uh, getting together, and uh…" Steve was going down in flames.

"He thinks you're hot," Hudson said.

She smiled.

And that was the day that Steve Sutherland lost his heart and never found it again. It was no longer his. It belonged to the woman with the electric body.

"Oh, hell! Look! It's BIT!" said T.J. with a hearty laugh.

"What?" Hudson said, unsure to what T.J. referred.

"BIT, man, look. Don't you remember?"

It wasn't until Hudson saw the small silver disk he remembered T.J.'s one attempt at building a robot which he named *BIT*. Time had worn on the small machine leaving it busted and unable to generate power. The petite bot was a disk-shaped animatronic that had the ability to transform into many things. It could be a screwdriver, a voice-note recorder, Bluetooth speaker extender, an MP3 player, and a host of other meaningless items. Its programming code was no more advanced than BASIC. In spite of its elementary programming language, it had full Wi-Fi connectivity and communicated over a range of networks. In its true form, it stood about three inches high. It was bright chrome with two miniature arms tipped with intricate mechanical fingers. The head was square with two blue eyes that blinked. It rested on a small caterpillar track that made it very nimble. Overall, the bot had little use, outside of entertaining T.J., and that was good enough.

"Andre, Hard-Core is at full capacity," HANA confirmed. Hudson tapped T.J. on the shoulder and they made their way to where HANA was seated. "So, where do we start?" she asked.

"We need to search the accident at Alemede Component and the assault at Quinley Air Field," Hudson advised. HANA accessed the media reports. Since Mainframe was off the primary grid, it was simple to reach data that was otherwise inaccessible. Reporting and photos from the Alemede and Quinley incidents filled the middle of the room. "Let's start with our winged friend at the airfield." Hudson touched an image of the air field.

Mainframe pulled all applicable images of the air field incident.

"There's our little bird," Hudson said pointing to an image of the figure in the sky. "Capture image… zoom twenty-five percent." The image cropped and zoomed. They saw the blurred figure of a man. The figure was moving at such a rapid speed that resolution adjustment wasn't possible. The headline read: MILITARY GLIDER USED TO ASSAULT GENERAL.

"Pull image three," Hudson instructed, which showed a better angle of the figure's back. "Zoom fifty-five percent and tune image." The blurred image was difficult to detail, but not useless. "Adjust sharpness thirty-five percent… forty." It was then they noticed there were no mechanics strapped to the man's back. He had a large tribal tattoo that covered his left upper arm and stretched around his shoulder blade. It was plain to see the imagery of the white wings that protruded from the man's back.

"Glider—my ass," T.J. said.

"I'm telling you they're real, and apparently he was injured when they tore through his back. I think that's blood," Hudson said pointing to the reddish hue on the image. "HANA, do we have an identity?"

"The system could not make an identification match based on the images," she confirmed.

Hudson rubbed his exhausted face. "How about the girl, Alemede." The images landed on Ellen. "That's her. Who is she?"

"Ellen Braxton, age seventeen. Last known residence—Region H-81," Mainframe said.

"Uh, oh. Not the rough 80s," T.J. said. Regions 80-86 were home to some of the more unfortunate citizens.

"Does she have a record of any kind?" asked Hudson.

Mainframe searched. "There is no criminal history for Ellen Braxton. School records indicate above-average intellect. 3.98 grade point average. Student of Region H High School until thirty-seven days ago."

"What school did she transfer to?" asked Hudson.

"No other school on file. The current educational code for Ellen Braxton is W-Withdrawal."

Hudson turned to T.J. "Now, why would a girl with a 3.98 GPA drop out of school six months before she was to graduate?"

"Beats me," T.J. said. "She was in a bad part of town. Maybe she had to. She'd just been working at Alemede for a few weeks, right?"

"Yeah, two weeks."

"There ya go," T.J. said. "Lots of kids in the 80 Regions have to drop out to support themselves, or their deadbeat parents."

"HANA, can you still access the HRV-EST server?" Hudson asked.

"Yes."

"Can you see what gene batch she was in?"

HANA looked through the multiple file lines in a matter of seconds. "She was in the batch delivered to Region H-73."

"Is that the one?" T.J. asked.

Hudson sat back slowly, a wide smile crossing his face. "I'll be damned."

"Ha!" T.J. said, clapping his hands. "Then that's it, man!"

"Now, let's not get too excited, Detective. That could be a coincidence. And anyway, we don't know if this girl has any *real* power or not. Could have been a freak accident." Hudson pondered for a moment. "HANA, do we know where her last known GPS location was?"

HANA ran the search. "BSC—Ellen Braxton, Serial Number 345294700, shows her location at the Region G Water Treatment Facility."

"What the hell is she doing in the sewers of Region G?" T.J. said.

"Hiding, maybe?" suggested Hudson.

"Or maybe she's not," HANA said. "If you take note of the area of the plant where the chip is presently located, a human body wouldn't be able to fit in these narrow pipes and filters. It could be possible her BSC is not with her any longer."

"Flushed it. She dug it out and flushed it," Hudson said. "Clever girl. We may never find her, then."

"I can find her," T.J. interjected.

Hudson turned to him. "Where would you even begin to look?"

"Look...trust me," replied T.J. with confidence. "I'll start with her house, go from there. Tracking runaways was my bag. I used to be one. I know how they think."

Hudson ran his hands through his hair and opened his eyes wide. "Fine, and I know I don't have to tell you this, but be discreet. I got class in a little over an hour. Text me if you find anything. Either way, let's meet up again here... 'bout 10:00 tonight. We have to get to her before Parliament does."

"You got it."

With that, Detective Blackwood made his way into the rain.

GUNNER

Focus. All he had to do was focus and get through the next hour. Hudson's head was everywhere but in the lecture hall. He thought of every possible excuse to forgo class that evening. The stomach flu would have been a good explanation. It had been a while since he had taken sick time. But essays on Gregor Mendel were due that night—no exceptions—just as he said. *This is ten percent of your grade, so I will not accept any late submissions*, he had said. *Late papers are zero papers. If you are in the hospital, have the nurse fax it. If you die, have your next of kin bring it.* Surely, an impromptu cancellation was impossible after those statements. Yes, it was best to muddle through it, get it over with. Then, back to the warehouse to meet with T.J., who had been searching for the elusive Ellen Braxton since early that morning.

He received at least some information early that afternoon from T.J., who located the girl's mother. To T.J., the woman seemed unconvincing when he asked about the last time she had seen her daughter. However, a good source advised T.J. that the woman had been questioned several times, and her story never faltered. There wasn't much to tell, really. Her daughter left for work the morning of the incident, and that was the last time the two of them had spoken. She maintained her daughter's innocence. The most important thing was that T.J. believed her, especially after locating all the sexual assault claims against "Buster" Lawrence that conveniently went without filing. If the young Ellen had killed old Buster, it was clear the pedophile had asked for nothing less.

"Okay... so, looking at mutations," Hudson continued, running his fingers through his thick hair. "Umm... we can have two separate mutations that are completely unlinked and associated with a clear plate phenotype. So, you could cross one of the two strains to N2 males, and then cross the subsequent heterozygous males to the second mutation to generate the proper trans-heterozygote." A student in the middle of the room raised her hand. "Yes, Ms. Abrams."

"So, distances in the strand matter? Or can you get around that during sequencing?" asked the young woman.

"You can," confirmed Hudson. "The farther apart the mutation is from the marker, the more likely that a recombination event might lead to the mutant allele separating from the proper marker. So, I would always recommend creating several independent lines, like a test, so to speak. Then you can validate the correct genotype. Mr. Williams..."

"But how would you complete the proper validation?" asked the young man at the front of the lecture hall.

"Well, either by the sequencing of the transmuted locus or by getting consistent results from several independent isolates."

The questions kept him engaged, at least on the surface. It was common for his students to watch the clock, count the minutes, wanting to be anywhere but there. But on this night, he was the impatient one. His mind continued to reel with possibilities and hypothesis. Steve had taught him how to juggle several notions at one time, and that skill came in handy on more than one occasion.

"But can it all go wrong?" asked a discreet voice from the center of the room.

"Come again," said Hudson, turning to the students.

Damian Gunner, the ambitious student who had visited him at work the other afternoon, rose to his feet. "Can the sequencing be corrupted?"

Hudson pondered on the odd question. "Anything is possible, Mr. Gunner, but with the complex technology and processes in today's genetics management, I would say you have more probability of getting hit in the head with a meteorite made of diamonds than finding errors in genetic code mapping with today's methods."

"But it could be possible," insisted Damian.

"I don't think so."

"So, HRV-EST... someone can generate their child, get everything they need for the offspring to be perfect, and nothing... absolutely nothing... can cause the offspring to be a freak... of nature?" Damian probed.

Hudson heard something more than a mere question in Damian's voice. It sounded like shame, doubt, even fear. "Damian, look, sure. Something could go wrong. But I assure you, the DNA sequencing validation that occurs during mutagenesis is near perfect. If the sequencer found anomalies in the sample, it would abort and start again. The offspring wouldn't be allowed to go to full term. It would be against the law."

And that seemed to satisfy Damian for the moment, at least for the moment, though Hudson could tell that the boy was not comforted by the idea of perfection. He realized it would be impossible to sidestep speaking with Damian that evening. Dodging him again would seem like intentional avoidance, which on this night would have been true. Hudson continued through the remaining points in the lecture and let the class leave twenty minutes early. He feigned the early dismissal as "giving them a break" since they did so well. In reality, it was to allow more time to meet with Gunner, and then get back to T.J. as soon as possible. As Hudson picked up his satchel and turned to meet the boy, he saw Damian filing out of the room with the other students, a somber expression on his face.

"Mr. Gunner!" Damian turned to him. "Could you come here for a moment?" Damian walked down the steps to Hudson's desk.

"Yes, Professor. I didn't sound disrespectful, did I?"

Hudson smirked in a silly manner. "You actually sounded like an ass, and I don't appreciate it." By the look of horror on the boy's face, he knew he could have knocked Damian to the ground with a feather. Suddenly, Hudson broke into laughter. "Lord, Gunner, you need to lighten up. You didn't sound disrespectful at all. Superb questions."

"Oh, okay… it's just I know that your career has a lot to do with what we have in genetic science today, and I always feel like I am criticizing you. It's feels weird sometimes is all."

"I can see that. But, science doesn't get where it's going without being questioned, Damian. Any scientist who pretends their theories are infallible should not practice science. Understand?"

"Yeah, okay."

"So, you wanted to see me?"

Damian appeared worried. "Well, only if you have time. I know you're…"

"Not busy at all, Damian. Let's go up to the office and we can talk, okay?"

Damian followed Hudson up the back stairwell to his quaint office on the second floor. "Do you follow sports at all?" Hudson said trying to make small talk.

"No."

"Thank, God. I loathe sports. Do you like music?"

"Oh, yeah."

"What kind."

"Steel Pop."

Hudson didn't understand what that meant. "Oh, that's cool. I'm more of a Classic Rock kind of guy myself." They walked into the office, and Hudson placed his satchel on the desk. "Have a seat." Hudson sat down and picked up that trusty pencil, the one with bite marks, his anxiety-relieving chew toy. "Oh, I have your paper done. Thanks for turning that in early."

"You're welcome. I type fast," Damian said.

Hudson got up and walked to a small filing cabinet. He reached into his pocket for his keys, but they weren't there. He sighed. "Well, it seems I left my keys on the podium downstairs. I'll bring it to you next week. Good job, though. Great paper. A+."

"Wonderful. Thanks, Professor." Damian watched Hudson take his seat again and pick up his pencil. "What flavor is it?"

"Come again?" said Hudson.

Damian smiled and pointed at the pencil.

Hudson giggled. "Oh, oh, yeah. It's a bad habit of mine. I have done it all my life, not sure why. I think it's like my worry stone. You know, the rocks with the thumb impression? You rub them and stuff? There's no telling how much lead poisoning I have from chewing on old fashioned number two pencils." He sensed Damian was beginning to relax, which was good. Damian Gunner's method of speaking was as dry as stale toast, a kid that was sometimes too smart for his own good. "So, shoot."

Damian leaned forward, placing his elbows on the desktop. "I'm certain you recall the accident... in the lab... the explosion?"

"Well...sure. It's pretty unforgettable," Hudson said growing a tad apprehensive. He felt Damian was about to confess to something unscrupulous, which would not only be very disheartening since he liked the boy, but would delay getting back to T.J. He bit down harder on his pencil.

"Well, I saw that one girl, Keisha..."

"Keisha Donovan?"

"Yes, her. She was with her lab team at Table A, and we were all getting ready to prep the experiment to examine the different effects of oxidation. Professor Leakey primed potassium chlorate and had a heavy container of it sitting on his table. So, he was called out of class; I don't know what for. While he was out, the students were goofing off. So, Keisha wanted to show some 'trick,' she said, to her table using potassium chlorate and sugar."

"Yeah, I've seen that trick," Hudson said.

"Well, she used a beaker to boil the sugar in water to break it down. She got the chlorate ready, then she asked that other girl at their table to hand her a screen so she could mix the ingredients together in the proper fashion. But that girl grabbed the screen that Professor Leakey uses for sulfur."

Hudson leaned back. It all made sense now. "And boom," he said, chewing on his pencil.

"Indeed... boom. It wouldn't have been so bad if they hadn't left the lid off the container of potassium chlorate. And all of this would transpire right next to the open container of chemicals, so I knew the results would not be positive. So..."

Hudson waited for a moment, but Damian said nothing more. "So?"

Damian took a breath. "I got everyone out."

Hudson looked at him with interest. He couldn't figure out why Damian seemed so apprehensive. "Well, it's good that you were paying attention to what was going on."

"I got everyone out... in 1.274 seconds."

Hudson laughed a little. "Now, what?"

Damian sighed. "Professor, I am expeditious." He paused, waiting for Hudson to reply. "Your expression leads me to believe you don't understand my statement. So, to simplify, I mean I'm *really, really* fast."

Hudson leaned back and allowed his mind to process this information. He wasn't sure where Damian was leading him, but he was very curious to find out. "Just how 'expeditious' is that, son?"

"Fast enough to grab this out of your mouth without you knowing I had." Damian held up the chewed pencil.

Hudson felt a cold sensation hit him in the chest. He chuckled without realizing he did. He hadn't even noticed the pencil leave his lips. There had to be an explanation. "No, shit."

"No, excrement of any kind, Sir," Damian replied.

Hudson sat forward. "So, if I were to pick up this paperclip and spin around in this chair, you could reach around and snatch it out of my hand before I made one full rotation."

Damian smiled. Then he got up and walked to the door. "And I can do that while standing over here."

Hudson shot him a crafty look, snickered, and pointed at him. "Oooh... you're on." He picked up the large clip. "So, ready?"

"Ready."

Hudson readied himself, and then spun once in the chair. Sure enough, when he rotated back to the front of his desk, less than five seconds, the clip was gone. He looked to Damian.

Damian smiled and held out his hand showing Hudson the clip. He walked over and handed it to the amazed Hudson, who smiled and cocked a cynical eyebrow. "Oh!" Damian continued, reaching into his pocket. "And I retrieved these." He tossed the file cabinet keys onto the desk.

That was the point where Hudson lost his cool. Sure, the pencil was a neat trick. The clip was impressive sleight of hand. According to the laws of physics, there was no way a human being possessed the ability to run down a flight of steps, across a hall, into a large lecture hall, grab the keys from the podium center stage, and make it all the way back to their starting position in five seconds. "Ha! Good one, son. But these *aren't* my keys." He got up, smirking confidently, and walked to his cabinet, never once breaking eye contact with Damian. With a click, the cabinet unlocked.

Hudson leapt backward, slamming against the wall. "Woah, woah, woah! Now... wh-wh-wh-what is that, man. What are you saying?"

Damian rushed to his side. "Professor... please, calm down. Come now, calm down. That's why I have wanted to speak to you."

"I mean, that's like *fast*, dude. Really f...f...flippin' fast!"

"Yes, yes, fast. Why don't you sit back down, Professor, okay? Come on." Damian took the bamboozled Hudson by the arm.

"Cause you couldn't have known about the keys, man. I mean, I didn't mention them to you until w-w-w-we were up here, and then that paperclip thing and all. Like woosh!"

"I think I may need to leave," Damian said as he gathered his things.

It then occurred to Hudson that confessing the secret must have caused Damian a great deal of anxiety, and he just had a complete meltdown on the kid. "Wait! Wait, Damian, please... please don't go." Damian stopped, and then turned around, not looking Hudson in the face. Hudson got up and walked over to him. "Look, buddy,

come on. Come over here and sit down. I should've reacted better."
The men took their seats. Hudson didn't know what else to do, so
he offered Damian a piece of candy from his desk.

Damian smiled. "I think you need to chew on your pencil."

"Or maybe my shoe." They both laughed. "So... have you always
been... fast?"

"No, not always. It began, I would say, six months ago. Our
neighbor's son was playing in the front yard. I agreed to watch him
while his father washed the car. I assure you—the kid was in the
street before I knew what had taken place." Damian took a piece of
candy from Hudson's jar. "And that's when it happened. Before I
realized, I was in the street with him in my arms and back to the
front porch. I had moved so quick, that he vomited. A few minutes
later, I did, too, but I cannot tell if it was because of the speed at
which I had progressed, or my reflexive response to vomit in general.
I'll explore that."

"G-force. It was too quick for you. Your body wasn't used to it."

Damian looked down in thought. He remained for a moment
before he said, "Professor... am I broken?"

Hudson shook his head with a smile. "No, son, you aren't
broken."

"Because...I feel very much like a freak," said Damian, becoming
upset. "I've thought something was broken with my DNA, as if my
genome came from a spoiled batch."

Hudson took a lozenge from the candy dish and popped it in his
mouth. "You know... I knew a group of people like you once, one
in particular who was pretty fast."

"Really?"

"Oh, yeah." Hudson leaned back in his chair and crossed his
arms. "Extremely fast. I mean, like..."

"... *expeditious*," they both said in unison.

Hudson chuckled. "Gunner...I know this may sound strange,
but would you be interested in meeting me and a friend of mine
tomorrow night? Say, 9:00? I think I have information that may help
you with all of this."

CORNERED

The sound of the morning traffic roused Ellen from her dreams. Her skin felt sticky and cold from the morning dew. The night before, she found a hiding place under the Southbridge overpass that allowed her to stay away from scavenging eyes while she rested. She shook herself awake to once again face the dawn, leaving her faceless prince in the eternity of her dream world. How she wished he were there to save her.

Ellen walked for what seemed like miles. Her feet felt swollen and blistered. *Maybe I should have grabbed different shoes*, she thought as she stared down at her tattered slip-ons. The BSC she had flushed into the filthy waterways controlled her means to Centicoin. No coin meant no train, no taxi, and most of all, no food. There was the chance she would find someone sympathetic enough to give to a poor homeless girl. If she would have to resort panhandle, best to do it in Regions farther west. There was far too much competition with other less fortunates closer to home.

In the distance, she noticed an inconspicuous café hidden in the marketplace corner of the Old City. She slid past the patrons waiting in line and ducked into the restroom. Her wrist was beginning to feel better, the ache subsiding. She turned on the warm water and dampened a paper towel. Then she pulled her arm from her jacket and unwrapped the bloodstained hand towel to assess her wound, which was certain to be infected by now. As she slowly removed the dressing she was surprised that nothing was there—no wound, no torn flesh, no scar—it was as if the injury had never even occurred.

"What the hell," she said to herself.

"I know, right?" shrilled a nasal voice from the stall behind her. Ellen recoiled and stuffed her arm back into the jacket. The woman flushed the toilet and then walked into the main restroom lobby. "I'm telling ya', that is the roughest toilet paper I have… ever… seen. I might as well wipe my ass with a porcupine on a sandpaper cactus!" The woman stepped to the sink beside Ellen and washed her hands. "It's not like we ladies need a tissue made outta chinchilla fur, but, Christ—softer than that." She turned off the sink and blotted her lipstick. "Not *too* soft. You get some of that cushy stuff, your finger can just *rip* right through." The woman fluffed her hair. "I hate poo-poo finger."

Ellen wasn't sure how take part in a discussion about the consistency of toilet paper, or especially poo-poo finger. But she was positive she wouldn't be shaking the woman's hand. Once the lady left the restroom, Ellen ducked into the adjacent stall to avoid engaging in other unwarranted discussions on bathroom tissue stability. She lowered the toilet lid and sat down, examining her wrist closer. It was bizarre, unbelievable. Apparently, in addition to being electrically charged, her body could heal ten times faster than others. She looked at her left hand with interest and gently rubbed her fingers together. Tiny blue sparks began to dance around her fingertips, like static scattering around cotton sheets. Faster and faster, she rubbed until the small charge flared with a pop, like an overloaded fuse. The scent of electricity hung heavy in the air. She heard the hinges on the bathroom door screech as someone entered.

"Elma, ya' need t'have Willy check the plugs in the lady's crappa! I smell something burning," said a voice entering the restroom.

Ellen recoiled and put her hand under her leg. With care, she stood and pressed her face against the stall door to see the waitress walking to the stall next to her. Once the woman locked the stall door, Ellen flushed the toilet and zipped through the door. Her mind overflowed with equal parts of confusion, fear, and fascination. What was happening to her? From where did this ability arise? Why was it happening to her?

It was time to move. Best not to linger in one area too long. Regardless of her direction or destination, somehow she had to find something to eat, or she would drop dead of hunger. She stepped back into the cafe, pulled her jacket hood over her head, and walked to the edge of the counter.

"Elma!" a husky voice shouted from beside her. Ellen turned, tightening her coat around her. She saw a big man, tall and bald, with a thick beard and a round belly, wearing an apron. "You're not gonna like it!"

"What?" called a voice from the kitchen.

"I have to throw out almost every bit of that Raisin Mint Cinnamon Bread you made. I told you no one wanted something with raisins, mint, and cinnamon."

The voice sighed. "Fine! Okay, fine. Just pitch it out. It was worth a shot."

"I mean, it's just gross," the man continued.

"I get it. Throw it out," the voice called.

He picked up a slice of the bread and tapped it against the countertop. The stiff bread made an audible drumming sound, like a knock at a door. Some customers seated at the counter chortled. "And the junk is as hard as concrete, too,"

"Stow it, Willy! Get that trash taken out and get back here and stir this damn gravy!"

Willy laughed and began to gather the rest of the trash. He wrapped the stale bread into a small white bag and sat it on the counter. Then, he emptied a container of pasta into another container to get it ready for the trash. Discarded food had to be sealed in the white food bags to keep the scent from attracting unwanted pests, especially Rot Rats. While the cook's attention was elsewhere, Ellen noticed her chance. Quickly, she snatched up the two bags and scampered out of the side door toward the alleyway. She ducked next to the large trash receptacles to stay out of sight. The sun was beginning to set, which allowed her to take shelter in the shadows. She held the bags in her hands, looking at them, weighing the risks.

Ellie, you cannot eat this junk. You don't know how old it really is. You could die, you know.

You don't have to do it. You'll find something somewhere.

Yeah… but where? And how am I going to buy it?

Really, it's not like it's gonna be rotten. They were just now throwing it out.

Her internal conversation convinced her it was worth the try. She ripped open the bag of pasta, which actually smelled fantastic. It was warm still. Without further hesitation, she sunk her fingers into the food and began to eat. There wasn't much left, and what was there was obviously going dry, but food was food. The bread, on the other hand, was nearly inedible. She tried to squeeze it, but it was hard as stone. *Hell, Willy, that is brick-bread,* she thought.

Once night had fallen, she realized she was no longer alone. The smell of the food had brought forward a host of other scavengers, eager to pick through the day's winnings. Though she couldn't see what crawled inside the gloom, the sound of churning resonated from inside the overflowing dumpster, as if a host of thousands of worms were feasting on the putrid mess.

The back door to the cafe swung open. Covered in grease, Willy exited the double doors with three bags of trash and two smaller food bags in his hands. Ellen pressed herself hard against the main dumpster and waited for him to leave. With her head against the cold steel of the container, she could make out the clamoring and scurrying of other animals who were awaiting food, the little feet of things best left in the dark. *I'm going to puke… right here; right now. And then I'm going to be arrested.*

The hiss was low, but audible. It sounded like a light puff of air coming from a deflating balloon. From her peripheral vision, she detected something watching her, something alive. She widened her view and saw the fat Rot Rat eyeing her every move. The beasts were as big as house cats and territorial. They were also vicious, their sharp teeth and claws perfect for spreading Scourge. The plump little beast hissed once again and crept toward her. There were stories of the rancorous rats picking bodies clean of flesh in a matter of hours. A smaller rat ran from behind her, scurrying over her ankle. She shivered with disgust. The larger rodent continued to creep closer while Willy hoisted the second bag into the container. Again, it hissed and snipped at her ankle. She kicked at the thing, causing it to back away and hiss once again. Ellen closed her eyes and concentrated. She closed her hand and pumped her first. The pulse of energy built in her forearm as if she was prepping a generator's engine to ignite. If she wanted to stay under the radar, it was imperative she remain selective about when she used her newfound talents. She imagined Willy wouldn't be amused with an electricity-charged vagrant taking shelter at his dumpsters. The rats never traveled alone, so she knew better than to lack caution. The thing reared back and spread it foam-riddled jaws wide. She closed her eyes. It leapt.

Crunch!

Just as it came for her, Willy crunched the fat beast with the heel of his steel-toed boot. Several other rats ran from the shadows, making their escape into the night. "Nasty little bugger!" said Willy. "So, little lady, how did you like the bread?"

Ellen stood. "Um…uh…" She was desperately searching for something to say. "Mister, please don't call the Authority, okay. I… I'm sorry," she said as she started to walk away.

"Wait now, sister!" called the man. "Wait just a minute. Just calm down. We need to make sure you didn't break any teeth on that bread, now."

She stopped, unsure if she should trust his humor or not. Kindness from strangers wasn't a thing to which she was very accustomed. "Uh…okay."

He stepped to the back door. "Hey, Elma! I found our little customer out here. She loves your bread!" He turned to Ellen and winked.

Just then, a small woman stepped to the back door. She was short, round, salt-pepper hair, and had a wonderful button smile. She lifted a questioning eyebrow. "Oh, God, what did you find? Do I need to get the shotgun?" She took one look at Ellen and said, "Oh, honey, honey, honey… look at you, sweetness." She came from the back door and walked to where Ellen stood, taking her by the hand. "What's your name, honey?"

"Uh… Mary," Ellen said. "I was just on my way through town, and I have to catch the train. So, I should go…"

"Are you hungry, baby?"

"Yeah… yeah, very much." With no Centicoin to speak of, Ellen did not understand how she would pay for food. She touched her small pendant. While it broke her heart to think about parting with it, she had to eat. She took off the necklace. "I have no coin, but I can give you this."

Elma stopped her. "Honey, don't you worry about a thing. It'll be on the house, 'kay?" Elma took the containers out of her hand and handed them to Willy. "You can't eat this stuff. It's awful. Come on in. We'll get you taken care of."

Ellen shook her head as she choked back the tears. The kindness hit her so hard and so unexpected that it welled in her throat.

Elma didn't say another word and took Ellen by the hand, leading her inside through the kitchen. "Go on over there and wash your hands, honey. You've been out in the nasty alleyway. You probably have all kinds of critters on your hands."

Ellen smiled and walked to the sink. "Thank you so much," she said to the nice lady.

Elma led Ellen into the main diner where a handful of patrons remained. One couple sat at the far end of the room, another woman sat at counter. Soon, a young man with a beard entered and took a seat across from her. He opened a newspaper as the waitress from the restroom asked him what he would have. *Don't let poo-poo finger lady touch your food, dude.*

"Now, you sit here and peek at this menu. Whatever you want, okay?" Elma said.

"Okay," Ellen replied. Soon, Elma returned and took Ellen's order. In no time at all, the hot meal was ready for her, and it was the most welcomed sight. As she ate, the buzz of the twinkling neon "Open" sign flashed red light onto her plate in a steady rhythm. Soft, smooth, and consistent, the sound became rather lulling. The difference that was made by having something in her stomach was remarkable. The food picked her up, energized her, prepared her to tackle whatever was coming next, and she was certain something was coming. She looked up again at the man with the beard. She didn't know why; he was in her direct line of sight. That he was attractive didn't hurt matters. For a second their eyes met. She wasn't certain, but he seemed familiar. She continued to finish her plate, avoiding the man's occasional gaze.

Her thoughts wondered, her mind rambling with possibilities and outcomes. She wasn't sure what she expected from her adventure. Where would she go? Aunt Janice's house would be impossible. They would look for her, and her family would be monitored with persistence. The only person she could think of was an old school friend who was going to Lenore Community College in Region K, miles away. Without her BSC, her travel options would be limited. It would be impossible to make it on foot, but once she was clear of the inner city, it would be safer to try hitchhiking. She didn't want to risk encountering the wrong people—she had fried one scumbag already, and that was enough.

The bell on the front door jingled as two Authoritans walked into the café. Ellen tightened her hood around her head and continued to pick at her plate, trying to appear as composed as possible. Her insides twisted, sick with angst. She couldn't help but notice that the bearded man also had a prickly reaction to Authoritan presence.

"Elma!" said one of the Authorities. "You know what I am dying for?"

"Well, I hope it's my double-decker apple pie?" Elma returned. "Because if you gentlemen don't eat it, I'll have to pitch to the rats."

"Now, *that*… would be a crime, Elma," said the other officer with a coy grin.

Elma laughed. "Honey, would you like a refill on that tea? Mary. Honey, can you hear me?"

It took a second for the name to register with Ellen. She looked toward the counter. "Uh, no... no, that's okay," she said with a trace of hesitation. The dark-headed officer looked at her as the other placed an order to go. She kept her head down and remained quiet. The soles of his heavy boots clomped against the tile as he walked to her.

"Hey... uh, Mary is it?" said the officer.

Ellen looked up at him, trying to keep her hood and her hair in front of her face. "Yeah."

"What's your last name, Mary?"

Oh, hell... what's my last name? A Roberts Ketchup bottle was on the table. "Roberts."

The officer stepped closer. Ellen focused on the buzzing of the neon light, trying to stay calm. "Oh, like the ketchup," he said in a skeptic tone. He leaned down to take hold of her right wrist. Ellen realized he was about to scan her BSC, the BSC she no longer had. She flinched as he reached for her. "I think you need to let me see your wrist, Mary."

Ellen stretched out her arm allowing him to examine it. He turned it over scrutinizing it for wounds or scars. Her progressive healing had taken care of that, however. The Authoritan reached to take hold of the BSC scanner on his belt, and as he did, Ellen happened to catch sight of the bearded man across from her again. The officer scanned her wrist.

"Scanning," said the electronic voice of the scanner.

The man with the beard stared straight into Ellen's eyes, as if he knew her, as if they were in this together.

Buzz! "Error—Chip Not Detected."

The man with the beard gave her a knowing nod.

With a quick, bright blue pulse, Ellen shocked the officer, sending him off balance and falling into the stools behind him. The bearded man knocked the other officer to the floor as he began to rush her.

"Freeze!" shouted the officer as he picked himself up off the ground.

"Come on! Come with me!" said the bearded man, taking Ellen by the hand.

She trusted him. She didn't know why, but the sense was undeniable. "Okay," she said.

"Freeze or I'll shoot!" warned the Authoritan.

The two of them dashed through the thin screen door, ripping it from the hinges, and as they stepped onto the sidewalk, a high-voltage taser struck Ellen in the back. It popped and buzzed, surging electricity through her. She stopped and looked down at the taser clamps that pulsed volts through her body with a droll expression. The high-pressure voltage gun used by Authoritans could bring the biggest assailant to his/her knees, but Ellen couldn't feel a thing. It was as if the pulse was charging her, energizing her body, giving her more power than any food could have. She turned to the astonished officer. He held the taser gun tight in his hand, his fingers pressing hard on the trigger, his knuckles white from the pressure of his grip. Ellen snatched the cables from her jacket, and with a quick thump, she sent a massive round of voltage back toward the officer. The force knocked him backward seven feet and blew the gun into ashes. She turned to the man with the beard.

"Oh, now, that was cool!" he said with a huge smile, taking her by the hand. Together they ran down the street as the other officer sprinted from the cafe.

"Yeah, I think it's her," said the officer into his relay. "They are heading down 11th Avenue toward Waverly now. Send back-up. And do not use tasers. Repeat—*do not* use tasers."

Ellen and the bearded man almost skidded off the sidewalk as they hunkered into an alleyway. He led her to a large brown town car. "Get in!"

"Where are you taking me?"

"The hell away from here! Get in!"

Ellen jumped into the car. As it rumbled to a rough start, they sped down the empty alleyway. Sirens blared all around them. They whipped past the gaggle of buildings, and Ellen caught the glimpse of possibly a dozen Authority Combat vehicles heading toward their location. One of the SUVs caught sight of them and turned into the alleyway.

"He saw us! They're coming!" she yelled. A multitude of construction cones and asphalt repair equipment blocked the alleyway leaving them with a dead-end. "What are you doing? Stop! You'll kill us! Are you crazy?!"

"Hold on!" yelled the man as the car leapt high over the unsteady ramp at the end of the alleyway, diving into the lower reaches of the abandoned subway system. A hubcap from the passenger's side tire cracked from the wheel, smashing into the heavy concrete of the median. The bearded man continued to speed through the dark passageways, driving deeper and deeper into the dusky underground of what was once Seventh City.

"Oh, my God! Who are you?" she shouted over the commotion.

"Blackwood. T.J. Blackwood. And I'm here to help."

H - 73

egion H-73.

Hudson was familiar with it. His quick student, Damian Gunner, had originated from the genetic batch assigned to Region H-73, just like Ellen Braxton. Though he did not understand how, his experiment had worked; he was beginning to realize that now. And, if so, there was much to be done. Presently, they knew of three—the electric girl, the speedster, and the boy with wings. If they were fortunate, there would at least be one more. They needed muscle, strength, power, the supremacy that Steve Sutherland had retained in the atomic construction of his DNA.

Hudson sat there in the dim Hub of the Core waiting for T.J., who was a half-hour late. It was possible that T.J. was fortunate in his quest for the young Ellen, but for now, Hudson needed to find out more about those magnificent wings. Who was the guy? Where did he come from? Hudson had looked at the images from the air field so many times he could recall them from memory and in perfect detail. The thought of viewing them again was painful. He leaned back, his hands over his eyes, and moaned. "I'd rather have a root canal, dammit!" he shouted to the darkness.

"Now, that is no way to talk," said the hologram appearing in the room.

"HANA, I am going nuts," Hudson said, his eyes red from strain.

"No, you're not *going* nuts. You've been a proud resident of nuts for years," she said taking a seat across from him.

"How are we going to find this guy? I mean, he's his own airline. And these things," he said pointing to the wings. "They *have* to be real. And if they're organic, this dude doesn't depend on gears and clockwork. He could be anywhere by now!"

"You'll figure it out. You always do."

Hudson took a bottomless breath, and then accessed additional news on the air field incident. The bulletins stated that Esterburg was now under observation at an undisclosed mental facility. *That's overdue*, he thought. He attained new footage of the incident, but it wasn't of anything notable, just people in panic, rushing through the field. He came across the clipping about the boy who died in the crash, Carson. In the photo, he stood with his sister and their father, posed before the Quinley Air Field sign. NEW AIR FIELD HAS TALENT, read the headline. Hudson shook his head. This was a stranger…not Bill. Bill was dead.

So what if they never located the man with wings? Was he that important? Even if they found him, he wouldn't be Bill Vogel, the hero Ascendor. Maybe the guy had some of Bill's abilities, maybe more, but he wasn't Bill, that was for certain. It was then that Hudson realized he needed to set realistic expectations of what was at hand. He hadn't waved a magic wand and brought his friends back to life. If it was possible at all, it was only the basic essence of the Federation in other people, different people—people who may even be evil, and what a bad turn of events that would be.

"There's something I'm not seeing," Hudson said, scratching his chin. Again, he poured through the articles, photos, and eyewitness accounts. Nothing made sense. Why had this guy attacked Esterburg? What was the motive?

"Going blind will not help, Andre," HANA stated. "You need to step back and see things from a different angle. Only then will you see more clearly. Turn all of this off and get some rest."

Hudson yawned and tossed his gnawed pencil to the desk. "You're right." He got up and paced around the room, his mind rolling with ferocity, but with no clear direction. He turned and looked at the range of monitors littered with stories of the air field. It was at that moment, gawking at the plethora of pictures from afar, that he realized what was before his eyes. In the promotional photo of the Quinleys, the young Carson wore a white tank top shirt printed with the winged logo of the air field. Up the boy's right arm and shoulder was a dark, tribal tattoo. Hudson leapt to the workstation, accessing the clearer image of the mysterious winged perpetrator.

"I'll be a son-of-a-bitch, HANA."

"Most often you are, Andre," countered the hologram.

"There! Right there!" he said pointing at the comparison between the photos. Just then, the elevator lowered. Hudson stood up hoping it was T.J., and he was not disappointed. "T.J.! We have to go. I think I got a lead on our flying stooge. Did you have any luck in finding…"

It was like seeing a ghost. Though Ellen Braxton wasn't the carbon copy of Victoria Conner, the girl could have certainly been Vickie's daughter.

"I did better than that. Hudson, may I introduce Ellen Braxton," T.J. said with a smirk.

"Uh… uh… hello," Hudson muttered through his surprise. Shaking the haze from his mind, he walked over to the young lady. "Dr. Andre Hudson." He held out his hand.

"Ellen Braxton. Do I… know you?" she said as she shook his hand.

"Perhaps," Hudson said smiling. "It's possible you do. Oh, and this is HANA, our resident hologram."

HANA stood and smiled. "Good to meet you, Ellen."

"Ellen, Dr. Hudson would like to talk to you about…," T.J. began.

"Wait… come here." He led both of them over to Mainframe and pointed at the screen. "What do you see?"

T.J., caught off guard by Hudson's excitement, examined the

screen for a moment. "Um…I…see…the same photos we've looked at a thousand times. Are you going to tell Ellen…"

"It's the same person," Ellen said stepping toward the screen. She touched the screen, focusing on the image of the boy, finding him familiar. They were silent, surprised by Ellen's deduction.

"Okay…how did she connect that's the same person? Cause if she only took two seconds to get it, apparently I'm an idiot," T.J. said. Hudson pointed to the elaborate tattoo. "Ha! So, flyboy isn't dead after all. Tricky, tricky, tricky."

"Listen," Ellen began. "I realize you guys, like, have some *things* going on right now, but when you have a second, I'd like to know what the hell is going on? Who are you people?"

Hudson turned to T.J., and pointed to Ellen. "This is an interesting result. See, I didn't realize that some memory transference could occur at the genetic level. I'll need to study that more and teach it in class."

"And…that doesn't help," Ellen said.

"HANA, can you tell me where Mr. Quinley's genetic bank was located?" Hudson asked.

HANA accessed the HRV-EST databanks. "From the batch assigned to…"

"I bet it's Region H-73," Hudson said with a grin.

"Region H-73," HANA confirmed.

"Do we know where Mr. Quinley's BSC is located right now?" HANA activated the BSC GPS.

"Wait. I didn't think BSCs could be tracked," Ellen stated.

"Now, a part of you realized that was bullshit, or you wouldn't have dug yours out of your arm," Hudson said.

"How did you…"

"Quinley is en route to Region H-42," HANA said.

"And what are the areas of interest in H-42?" T.J. asked.

HANA searched the location map. "The main thing in H-42 is the university hospital, guys."

"The boy's going to the doctor. He's been shot," Hudson confirmed. "He needs us there for moral support."

"Moral what? Do what?" T.J. said as he watched Hudson throw on his coat with excitement. "Andre, we can't go to that boy. We won't be able to get to him. We're not family."

Hudson looked at T.J. with surprise. "T.J., how could you say that in front of his sister?" Hudson pointed to Ellen. They all looked at him as if he was insane. Noticing they didn't get the joke, he stopped. "If I have to explain all my witty puns to you guys, we'll be here all night. Quinley has a sister; they won't know what his sister *looks* like. If we figured out this guy is Carson, it's just a matter of time before Parliament figures it out, too. They'll finish going through that wreckage and find that no human remains are there. And when they do, they'll find him. If we don't get to him now, we'll never get to him."

Ellen looked hesitant. "I don't mean to be a bitch or anything, but I'm not completely comfortable with this. You need to explain some things to me, or I'm not being anyone's sister."

Hudson looked at the photo of Carson's sister on the workstation monitor and then back to Ellen. "Pull your hair back. You look more like her that way."

"I don't think you heard me, man," Ellen continued.

"What the hell, you look better with it down," Hudson replied, ignoring her comment. "T.J., keys!"

THE RESCUE

Carson opened his eyes, feeling groggy and confused, as if he was in a fog. Some things were clear to him. He remembered wandering in the woods for what seemed like forever, getting lost, losing direction. And the bleeding; he couldn't get it to stop. The bullets inside him were alive and digging themselves deeper and deeper into his flesh. He had stumbled through the forest above a campground where a redheaded little girl played at a creek down below. At that moment, things went black. The next thing he knew was that he was rolling down the hill, toppling and tumbling without control. His consciousness returned momentarily when he landed in the creek water, its icy-cold temperature shocking his system. It was so frigid it felt nice on his aching body. The little girl came to him, knelt beside his shoulder, and kept asking him if he was okay. At least he thought it was a child; sometimes it was the little girl, other times it was his sister. His mind was failing, and his thoughts were adrift. He could still feel the protrusions from the wings on his shoulder blades, which were now only numb areas of deadened tissue. The next thing he knew, he was in some type of camper. A man was at the steering wheel, and a rather distraught woman was in the passenger's seat.

"We should go home. We know nothing about this boy!" she said.

"We can't leave him there to die, can we?" said the man.

"Can't we? We don't know what he did to get those gunshot wounds. He could wake up and kill us at any minute."

"Really? The boy can't even stand up, Sophie. He's lost about ten gallons of blood. He's been shot at least twice, and both of his shoulder blades appear to be broken. What do you think he'll be strong enough to do to us?"

The woman went silent. "Fine. Let's get him there and leave him. We sure don't have the Centicoin to pay for his hospital stay."

Hospital. I can't go to the hospital. They'll find out who I am. Lisa… they will go after Lisa. Carson wanted to get away, but he wasn't even strong enough to lift his head, let alone hurl himself from a moving vehicle. He'd have to deal with the repercussions later. Of course, there was always the chance he'd die before they reached the hospital. Whom was he going to fool? It was only a matter of time before they knew he was the one who had attacked Esterburg. Then, Esterburg would have him and Lisa murdered. His only hope was that Lisa and Dennis had fled the Region.

Carson felt the camper stop. He cracked open one weary eye enough to see the hospital entrance. The next thing he knew he was on a stretcher being wheeled into the building. The nurses stabilized him and sent him to X-ray to image his wounds. Once he was back in his room, the nurse gave him medicine to manage his pain and prepare him for surgery.

"He has two of them," a man's voice said. "One lodged under his left clavicle and the other to the left of his sternum, about three inches from his carotid artery. Lucky dude."

"You're telling me. Can't figure out all of these shattered bone fragments in his shoulders, though," a woman said.

"Probably shattered them when he fell down that hill," the man said. "Have you seen that hill? The steep one at Alder Hill Falls? That is one big hill, man. My mom and dad used to take us out there to camp all the time. If he fell down that sucker, I'm surprised he's even alive at all!"

"Did you contact next of kin? I'd like to have someone here before we take him into surgery."

"Didn't have to. His sister got here before we even called her. She's in the lobby with his uncle and cousin."

Uncle and cousin? I don't have any uncles or cousins. Carson heard the squeak of the heavy door as someone else entered his room.

"And who are you?" asked the man. "Hey, get away from him!"

A struggle began, two bodies crumbled to the floor, and then silence. Carson forced himself to pry open his eyes. A nurse and orderly stood by his bed. "Who... who are you?" His mouth was so dry he could hardly move it.

"I am going to give you a shot, and then take you to have your x-rays," said the nurse.

"But I've already had my x-rays," Carson said in a drunken mumble.

"No, these are *different* x-rays." The nurse then motioned for the orderly to raise Carson, allowing her to see his back. "It's him."

"I...I had a dream I was flying," Carson muttered to the nurse.

"Oh, honey, you'll be flying in a minute," the nurse said as she drew a red liquid into the syringe.

"Sure will," giggled the peculiar orderly. "How do we get the body out of here, Snitch?"

"Shut up! He can hear you, *stupid.*"

The orderly smirked. "It don't matter. What's he gonna do? He is drugged out of his mind." The orderly leaned to Carson's face. *"Na, na, na, na, naa, naa... you're gonna die.* See... nothing."

And the orderly was right. Carson couldn't find the strength to move a single muscle. *So, Esterburg found me,* he thought. *That didn't take too long.* In some way, he thought he wanted to die. It was better than spending the remainder of his life running. He relaxed, focusing on the slight numbness the pain medication gave him, taking comfort in it, wrapping into it like a warm blanket. *Well, if this is how I'm going out, then so be it. Maybe with me dead they'll leave Lisa...*

As the needle slid into Carson's vein, he heard a soft click, and then everything went still. It was then that he heard another voice, a man's voice.

"If you know what's good for you, *Nurse Ratched*, you'll pull that needle out of his arm now and back away…slowly," T.J. warned as he cocked the gun. The needle withdrew from Carson's skin. "Move and *you'll* be flying. Got it?"

"I got it! Be cool, man. Be cool. That's just his… vitamins, see. Just his vitamins for the night," said Snitch.

Carson took the syringe of red liquid from her hand and tossed it to Hudson. "Sure… yeah. Now, back up. Where's she at with the wheelchair?

Snitch and Scoundrel backed away with caution.

"Whew! I got one," Ellen said as she hurried into the room pushing a standard blue hospital wheelchair.

Before them was their most elusive prey, the girl Keating sought. Snitch and Scoundrel looked to one another and leapt into attack mode. Snitch bounded high into the air, kicking the gun out of T.J.'s hand. Scoundrel jumped onto Carson's bed in an unnerving panther-like stance and shot forward toward Ellen, knocking her to the ground. He scratched at Ellen's throat, pulling at her necklace. Hudson grabbed the nimble elf and slammed him to the ground with a clunk. Scoundrel booted Hudson deep in the gut, bashing him against the defibrillator machine in the corner of the room.

Snitch maintained focus on T.J., engaging him in a rigorous bout of hand-to-hand. "I can't hit a girl!" T.J. yelled to Hudson. The wicked nurse moved so cat-like it was hard to tell from which direction her punches would fly. He kept blocking and pushing her as much as possible, hoping to prevent her blows from making contact. She looked away from him, turning her focus to Ellen, who was rushing to Carson's bedside to shield him from the battle. Hoping to keep focus on him and away from Ellen and Carson, T.J. punched Snitch hard in the face. The shift of his body weight added extra potency to the hit. Snitch stumbled backward against the wall hard, holding her face as T.J. felt a surge of guilt. However, his regret was gone when the vicious nurse scowled at him with a solid black eye, the greyish scales showing from under the torn human skin used to cover her true self. "Sonuvabitch! They're Xenozians!"

Hudson turned to Snitch, shocked by her alien appearance. He couldn't believe what he was seeing. Xenozians had vanished, driven from the earth after the fall of Goliaric. Scoundrel slammed Hudson against the wall and grabbed him by the neck. The thing leaned in close, flicking its forked tongue in the air. "I can *smell* your fear." The tail of the alien rose into the air, whipping back and forth, preparing to attack.

Hudson heard the defibrillator beep and signal ready. "That's not fear—that's garlic," he choked. "I had pizza for lunch." He snatched the paddle of the defibrillator, placed it against Scoundrel's head, and sent a charge through his brain, burning his rubbery flesh of his face. Scoundrel screeched and fell to the ground.

Carson opened his eyes to see the commotion and the young girl standing valiantly by his side. Ellen looked down to him. Their eyes met, establishing a connection, a link that took the wind from their lungs. They had been two magnets placed at opposite ends of a table. Now that they were this close to one another, their bond was colliding together, locking them in place. Ellen stepped away from Carson and moved toward where Hudson and Scoundrel struggled with one another. With a wave of her hand, she sent bright blue electricity across the room and up Scoundrel's spine. He howled in pain as he fell to the ground. Ellen held him in place with a steady connection of energy, her eyes shining bluish-white.

Carson's wings erupted from his back as he took Snitch by the neck and carried her into air. She struggled against his strong grip, her forked tongue lashing back and forth. His eyes mutated into bright white light. As the two hung in the air, blood dripping from Carson's wounded shoulder, he cocked his head like a curious canine, examining her. Then, he shouted a short, high-pitched cry, like an immense eagle, a sound that caused them all to stop in their tracks. The thick windows of the hospital room cracked under the reverberation. As he tightened his grip on her throat, Snitch spat a gooey green substance into his face. He dropped her to the floor and struggled to wipe the gunk from his eyes. Scoundrel hissed at them and leapt forward, taking Snitch under his arm. He leapt through the damaged hospital window, fleeing into the darkness.

Carson, weary and wounded, dropped to the bed, his wings sinking into his flesh. His shoulder had once again poured with fresh blood. Ellen looked around, stunned, unable to recall the details of what had taken place. Hudson soaked one of the white hand towels with water from the bedside pitcher and wiped the substance from Carson's face. Then, a loud alarm sounded throughout the hospital.

"Quick!" Hudson said. "Grab his legs. We have to get him back to Core."

Together, they got Carson into the wheelchair. Ellen donned the nurse's jacket that Snitch had worn and together they pushed Carson through the chaos of the emergency room and into the parking garage where they set course for safety of the Core.

GATHERING

In the dated infirmary of the Core, HANA used the surgical bots to carefully remove the two shells from Carson's shoulder. It was curious that his body showed signs of healing around the bullets, telling her that advanced genetic restoration, a trait of all superhumans, was already starting to show in him.

"I'm glad you got him here," HANA said. "Looks like his healing has just kicked in. Two more hours and these things would have lived in him permanently."

Ellen and T.J. stood behind the glass in the Hub watching the procedure. The fluidity of the androids was fascinating. One of them dithered for a moment, causing a concerned looked to cross HANA's face.

"Uh, that's not good," T.J. said. They saw Carson move one of his thick wings. "Those are the most magnificent things I have ever seen in my life."

"Andre, if we're going to do this for real, you guys have got to get better equipment in this place," HANA said as she had the animatronics add the final dressing to Carson's site.

"She's not going to sew him up?" Ellen asked.

"She doesn't need to now," Hudson said. "You guys shouldn't stay wounded long. As time goes on you'll find that you heal faster and faster."

"And you owe me... owe *us* an explanation of all this," Ellen said. "Enough with the mystery. We got this guy, now let's talk."

"You are absolutely right," Hudson said, looking at the clock. "And in about an hour and ten minutes we will do just that."

Ellen shook her head. "Why an hour and ten minutes?"

"We have another guest who's supposed to show up," Hudson said as he poured a glass of water for himself and one for Ellen.

"Who?" asked T.J.

"Fleet," Hudson said with a smile.

"Whaaat?" cooed T.J. with a grin.

"God, so who is Fleet?" Ellen's impatience was obvious, which was understandable.

"He wants to speak to her," HANA said over the intercom system, pointing to Ellen. "And he wants someone to contact his sister to let her know he's okay."

"You got it," Hudson said. "Did we find out what they were trying to shoot him up with?"

"Some type of weird iodine-thiobarbital derivative," HANA said. "The doctors would've just thought he had gone into cardiac arrest. It has a ten-minute half-life, so it disappears quickly. Whatever it is, it would've definitely killed him in the state he was in."

Hudson opened the large door and led Ellen into the surgical room. They both walked to Carson's bedside. "Hi, sport," said Hudson. "Those are impressive appendages you got there."

"Oh, sorry, hold on," Carson said as he closed his eyes, allowing the wings to pull back into his flesh. He winced.

"Does it hurt when you do that?" Hudson asked.

"Not as bad as it used to. I have a few questions," Carson said, exhausted.

"Join the crowd," Ellen spat.

"Yeah, do we know each other?" Carson asked her.

"Literally? No. Figuratively? I would say that's a yes," Ellen advised.

"My name is Doctor Andre Hudson. I teach at the Harland University. I have a story to tell you guys, but I am waiting on another part of our team to get here."

"Team?" Carson said in confusion.

"Yes. So, look, I'll send T.J. to talk to your sister, but we need to know where we can find her, okay? We shouldn't be using phones to discuss any of this."

"Okay," Carson said as he sat up, throwing his legs over the side of the bed. "She's at her other job tonight. A little bar called the Hip-Hop, downtown on Ailor Avenue."

"Got that, Blackwood?" Hudson called.

"Got it. I know where that is. I'll go now," T.J. said over the speaker.

Hudson turned back to them. "I'll get you guys something to eat. Rest. Talk. I'll be back soon." With that, he left the room.

"Please tell me you understand what's going on," Carson said.

"Not a clue." Ellen held out her hand. "Ellen."

"Carson," he replied, shaking her hand.

Ellen pointed to the Mainframe monitors that could be seen through the glass of the infirmary. Scenes from Carson's accident were still displayed on the monitors. "You look good for a dead guy," she said as she hopped onto the bed across from him.

"Thanks."

"So, uh… you got wings."

"Apparently so. Let me guess—you're a freak, too?" Ellen looked a bit insulted by the statement. "Sorry, I didn't mean it like that. That sounded like an ass."

"No, you're right," she smiled.

"So, what can you do?" he asked. He watched her snap her fingers, sending out sparks of electricity. "Nice!" he said with a grin.

"Yeah, I'm still getting used to the idea," Ellen said as she examined the infirmary.

"Me, too. So, you married?"

"Lord, no. You?"

"No. Boyfriend?"

"Nope. Girlfriend?"

"Gay."

Ellen smiled. "Shut the front door! Really?"

Carson smiled. "Really."

"See, you were too cute to be straight. I knew I liked you for a reason."

"You like gay guys?"

"I *love* gay guys," Ellen said, tossing her pendant into her mouth. Carson laughed. "What the hell are we doing here?"

Ellen spit out the pendant and sighed. "Well, Carson, I'm not sure, but I think it'll be interesting."

Hudson soon returned with sandwiches for them. "Here you go, guys. I wasn't sure what you liked, so I made you bologna."

"Andre," HANA said appearing in the room. "Your visitor has arrived."

"Wonderful! Show him to Tech Briefing Room A. We'll be in there in about ten."

After they had finished the sandwiches, Hudson led Carson and Ellen down a hallway to a large conference room. He opened the door and ushered them into the space. A silver table with a black glass top sat in the middle of a military-like meeting room. Large screens surrounded all four walls. On each screen was a grayish-white circle, and in the middle of the circle was a brilliant, blue, four-pointed star under a red letter "F." Light blue wings surrounded the emblem like a crest. The animated emblem turned counter-clockwise in a steady motion. There was another boy sitting at the table waiting for them. He stood when they walked into the room.

"I would like for you two to meet Mr. Damian Gunner. He's one of my students at the university." Damian nodded to them. "Mr. Gunner, this is Ellen Braxton and Carson Quinley." They exchanged odd hellos while they examined each other. Hudson noticed the exchange. "Do you know each other?"

"No," Damian said. "But you both appear really familiar to me.

Do you attend the university?"

"No, but we're doing the *déjà vu* thing a lot these days. Don't sweat it," Carson said.

"Please have a seat." Hudson motioned toward the front of the room as HANA appeared. "And this is what I call 'Human Adaptive Neurological Automation,' but since that would piss her off, we call her HANA. She is my right hand lady and controller of security here at what we call the Core."

"Intriguing," Damian said.

Hudson took a seat. "Before we get started, guys, I want you to keep an open mind about what I am going to say. I'm about to send a boatload of info your way. See…before this city was part of Region H, it was a common U.S. metropolis known as Seventh City. It was typical in every way, except one: it was headquarters to a group of guardians known as the *Federation*, and this building was their base."

"The special forces group…with the military, right?" Carson said. "My Dad told me about them."

"Certainly," Damian said. "The group of top secret soldiers."

Hudson smiled. "Well, that is what *most* people today think." He walked to the front of the room and took a deep breath. "This will be hard to believe."

"Ha!" Ellen said. "Try us."

Hudson moved his hand over the black table causing the surface to illuminate. The surrounding screens displayed the same images. "The Federation protected planet Earth for many, many years. And they weren't part of the military. They were *superheroes*." An image of Steve Sutherland entered the screen. "*Wrath*, leader of the Federation, possessed superhuman strength and invulnerability." Each time Hudson waved his hand over the table, a different member of the Federation appeared on the screens. "Next, we have *Voltage*, controller of electricity. She could generate heavy electrical current. *Ascendor* had formidable strength, telepathic ability, and a very high intellect. He designed those great mechanized wings you see there. *Fleet*, the fastest woman on the planet, could move in super-sonic speeds of up to MACH 4. And last, but not least, we had

Tempera, who could control both fire and ice. These heroes lived among us, protecting the human race from everything…including ourselves."

Ellen laughed. "Okay…you're being, like, serious, right?"

"I'm serious, Ms. Braxton. A little over three decades ago, man learned he was not alone in the universe. We got a visitor. This guy." Goliaric appeared on the screen. "His name was *Goliaric*, ruler of the planet Xenoe in the Zanbar dimension. Using gateways called *Odysseys*, his plan was to come to earth's dimension, enslave the human race, steal all of our natural resources, all that fun jazz—a nasty little habit he had gotten into with several other worlds. But we had the Federation, our own secret weapon. And that pissed him off. For years, Goliaric tried to take over Earth, but the Federation always stopped him in his tracks. He tried everything—death rays, mind control, time travel, nuclear attacks—but the Federation was always able to stop him, until they were betrayed. While most of the human race valued the Federation, there were those who found them a threat. Namely, this woman." An image of President Keating appeared on the screen.

"Pardon me, Professor, but is that…the President?" Damian asked.

"Yes," Hudson confirmed. "Well, she wasn't the President then. She was just the good old Secretary of Health and Human Services under this man, President Edward Collins. Ophelia was against the Federation from the start, said they were a threat to humanity. She tried to claim that Goliaric attacked our planet because these guys existed, a statement that was an outright lie, one of the many lies this woman has told. President Collins gave her permission to attempt negotiations with Xenoe, and for a while, we saw progress. In reality, though, she was setting things up for herself. But, no matter how bad things got, the Federation was always there to save us."

Damian shook his head. "Now, to reiterate what you have communicated. You're telling us that the President of Parliament, of the world, worked with a giant from an alien planet to take over the Earth, and this alien was slain by a band of superheroes in tights?"

Hudson paused for a moment and cocked his eyebrow. "Well, they didn't wear tights, but you've about summed it up."

The kids exchanged gapes of disbelief.

"Okay, let's say you're not a psycho. How have we *never* heard of this?" Ellen asked. "My mom has told me stuff, some wild stuff. My dad had tons of conspiracy theories—those theories killed him. The superhero bit is one thing, but wouldn't we know if aliens invaded Earth once upon a time?"

"We've not been able to work out the technology, yet, but we suspect it has to do with implementing the Biotic Scan Chip," HANA confirmed.

"Mind control?" Damian hypothesized.

"Not *control*, so much as suppression," Hudson said.

Ellen leaned forward. "How do you remember all of this, then?"

Hudson tapped his wrist. "Fakes. When BSCs came to be, T.J. and I fitted ourselves with altered facsimiles."

"So, then what happened? If these guys were superheroes where did they go?" Carson asked.

Hudson leaned back; a somber expression overtook his eyes. "*I happened.* Wrath, or Steve, as I knew him, was a great friend of mine. Steve called me *Hacker Hudson* because of all the tinkering I did with computers."

"So, you were his sidekick?" Damian smiled. He turned to see Carson giving him an odd stare. "So what… I read comic books."

"Well…I guess so," acknowledged Hudson. "Steve and I had many disagreements, just like any friendship. I was around, say, nineteen going on forty, thought I knew it all. I met this genetics intern at a company called Evolutions Service Technologies, a girl named Nancy Woodrow. You know it today as the genetics conglomerate that oversees the HRV-EST program, but at the time, it was a start-up company the government was beginning to take some interest in. Steve never trusted Nancy, which pissed me off. I couldn't figure out why he didn't have confidence in someone as kind and sweet as Nancy seemed to be. After about a year together, I asked Nancy to marry me, and she said yes. Steve was furious…

said I was throwing away my life, that she was no good. Well, I had had it. That was the last straw for me. About two weeks before we were to be married, the two of us were lying around, having pillow talk, and we got on the subject of Steve, superheroes, immortality, all that stuff. Since this was the woman I was going to spend with the rest of my life with, I had no hesitation in sharing."

A curious look crossed Damian's face. "What could you have confided in her that was that unscrupulous?"

"Do you always talk like that? Is it an Asian thing?" Carson asked.

"Like what, bigot?" inquired Damian.

"I told her their weakness...every last one," Hudson said. "Tempera, like most superhumans, had accelerated healing, but it didn't help her once she became exposed to *hydrargyrum*. You know it as mercury, the same element once used in many temperature-gauging devices. The liquid metal would render her powerless should she be covered in it. And if injected with it, her cellular structure would disintegrate; she would literally melt. And it wasn't long before that flaw was used against her. Fleet was lightning fast. It was both her power and her weakness. She could sustain controlled momentum up to speeds of MACH 5, but if she pushed past that, she'd lose the ability to control it. Speeds past hypersonic would rip her to pieces. Goliaric poisoned her with Pyrophetamine, an illegal amphetamine. Once he turned her loose, she ran until she turned into dust.

"Ascendor could be incapacitated with a high-pitched frequency that prevented him from using his telekinetic abilities. With the heightened sensitivity of his sonar, excessive supersonic pitches could rupture his blood vessels causing aneurisms. Voltage could be handicapped by water, and if it entered her lungs for an extended period, her internal organs would short-circuit. Think of it like throwing a radio into a bathtub. And last was Wrath, whose only known weakness turned out to be an alien toxin called *Xenathium* from the waters of Xenoe. Though harmless to common humans, it weakened the cellular structure of Steve's flesh. Once crafted into a weapon, such as a bullet, it was the only thing that could pierce his indestructible skin." Hudson rubbed his tired face. "I can't tell you why I felt possessed to share information so vital."

Ellen leaned forward. "You thought you could trust her."

"No one should be trusted with something so important...not even me."

"Who did Nancy tell?" Damian asked.

"I have no idea. All I know is that I woke up the next morning and she was gone, never to be heard from again. Soon after, Tempera was murdered. I knew it was the information I had volunteered that led to her death, and I was beside myself with guilt."

"Did you tell Wrath?" asked Carson.

"I told him...eventually."

"And what did he do?" Carson added.

"What Steve always did—he consoled me. Me! Of all people. Told me not to feel guilty, that it wasn't my fault. But we both understood whose fault it was." The room fell quiet for a moment. The emotion in the room was so profuse it could almost be seen with the naked eye.

Ellen was the first to speak. "You didn't realize."

"Anyway," Hudson interrupted, hoping to avoid pity. "Wrath was the only hero left, and he intended to kill Goliaric and drive the aliens back to where they came from. It was a huge battle, massive. I had never seen Steve so insane, so vicious. The Federation had a no-kill policy. They captured villains, imprisoned them, but *never* killed them. It was their creed. But something snapped within Wrath. He tore through the aliens, literally ripping them apart, ruthless and crazy. He knew Goliaric would use Xenathium against him, so he had to make every bit count. Finally, he killed Goliaric, but Steve was hurt too bad to pull through. Once the forces of Xenoe fled, Ophelia pulled the wool over the eyes of the world. She held this big press conference telling the people that her and Steve had been working together for months preparing their attack on Goliaric and his troops."

"And everyone believed her," Carson stated.

"Political tactics," Damian said.

"All politics," Hudson confirmed. "And that's when the changes started. One world government, Parliament, dissolution of individual countries, BSC, Centicoin, controlled reproduction—all points of control that Ophelia has been using for years now to blind us all. It was strange how everyone forgot about the Federation, the *real* Federation. They forgot about Xenoe, Goliaric, everything. And things are about to get worse…for all of us."

Ellen leaned back in the conference chair. "So, how do we fit into all this?"

"Project Phoenix," HANA said.

"You're referring to the bird?" Damian asked.

"A project to locate the next generation who'd fill the shoes of the Federation," Hudson said, feeling the tinge of guilt pierce his heart. "The same genetic triggers had to occur sooner or later, and I hoped they would happen again in my lifetime."

The group sat there taking it all in, processing it, allowing the data to congeal.

Carson stood. "So, we're friggin' superheroes! Awesome! We got a flying dude, electric lady, and… and… what do you do, dude?" he said pointing to Damian.

Damian held his hand forward and tilted his palm left and right. Faster and faster he went until you couldn't see his hand at all, only traces of lightning-like energy.

"I can't believe it," Ellen said.

"Awesome!" Carson said with a smile. "Okay, wings, electric, a fast dude…who else? Do you think we will find others with abilities like we have?"

"If we're lucky," Hudson said.

"So, how do we find them? They could be anywhere in the world," Ellen said.

HANA appeared beside Ellen, causing her to jump with a twitch. "We continue to watch media and social networking. We are looking for anything, news stories, tall tales, anything at all that could lead us to others, should they exist."

Hudson stood. "Parliament has already locked down the media.

They know something strange is happening. But this entire complex is off the Parliamental grid. We can monitor anything, including their transmissions. If they share any information about someone out of the ordinary or superhuman, we'll catch it."

Carson picked up a soda from the small refreshment counter. "So, who were the terror twins at the hospital? Do we know?"

"Twins?" asked Damian.

"We'll fill you in later," Ellen replied.

Hudson looked to HANA, who shook her head. "Not yet," HANA said. "But we're running the information through the database. No known Xenozians fit their description, so we don't know how they got here. We'll continue to look into it."

"So, what is our directive?" Damian asked.

Hudson looked to Ellen and Carson. "Young lady, you removed your BSC, so you are off the grid. And Carson 'died' in the plane crash. So, I imagine that you two have little options. I intended for you guys to stay here if you choose. Mr. Gunner, what about you? What would you think about rooming here?"

"Living on campus drains much of my disposable income. If you insinuate that I could stay here for free, it would be illogical not to take advantage of that opportunity," Damian said.

Carson again scowled at Damian with an abnormal expression. "Dude…seriously…are you, like, from *Vulcan* or something?"

"You got it," Hudson continued. "There are several rooms in the second level. I will go make sure they're in order. It's been a while since anyone has stayed here. After we get you settled in, we'll need to remove the rest of your BSCs. The structure of the Core is protected against all GPS and bug tracking, but I have a feeling we may never recognize the full potential of what those chips can do."

Damian looked concerned. "Wait. How am I supposed to go to school without my BSC?"

"We'll implant in each of you BSC clones that carry all capabilities except Parliamental GPS, the same kind T.J. and I have. Painless. You won't feel a thing. We'll be the only ones who can track us. We'll load them with identities, historical information, and a small amount of Centicoin—your first week's paycheck."

Carson didn't seem convinced. "All of this seems good, too good to be true, actually. But...I don't understand how to be a hero. And I don't think you guys know either."

Hudson walked over to them and sat on the conference table. "I get that, guys. I do. And I don't want you kids to do anything you don't want to do. I couldn't take being responsible for the deaths of any more heroes. All I am asking is for you to try. HANA is certified to train each of you, and she is ready to do so starting tomorrow. Give it a shot; try to hone the skills you have. See how comfortable you are in that skin." Hudson's phone vibrated. He reached into his pocket and looked at Carson. "It's T.J. Your sister is fine. He talked with her and advised her to lie low. He told her we would be in touch."

Carson nodded.

Damian gave a modest smile. "I expect it would be astounding to be a superhero."

"I would most agree with your assessment," mocked Carson playfully.

As the kids made their way out of the briefing room, HANA turned to Hudson. "So, you're not going to tell them about Phoenix?"

Hudson felt it best to not respond.

SUSPICION

Keating sat in the examination chair inside her majestic office. The straps around her right arm kept her hand palm-up to prevent movement. It was essential she remain still while her prosthetic was adjusted. The technician opened the box from Alemede Component and retrieved a small chip printed into a plastic board. The tech broke the piece out of its frame and tested it. Once the chip passed, he fitted it into the prosthetic. The semi-organic flesh that covered her forearm and hand helped hide any sign of the cybernetic substitution. Once the chip was in place, the tech touched each of the hydraulic tendons causing her fingers to flex one by one.

He leaned back and undid his sanitary mask. "Ms. President, I think you're done." He resealed the flesh around the mechanics. "This piece has always been some of my finest work."

"Yes," Keating said, holding the robotic hand before her face in wonder. "You would never realize."

"I still say what you did to save the world was brave."

"Thank you. My arm is the least of what I'd give to save the human race," Keating said in a tone that dripped with fabricated sincerity.

"We are all so excited to hear what you have to share during the World Summit. It's been a long time since the world has heard from you." The tech gathered the last of the tools and devices and turned to her. "Okay, if you feel any hesitation in the joints, call me. The new AI chip should give you much more control and enhance the fluidity of your movement."

"Thank you, dear" Keating said, smiling as the tech turned to leave. As the tech exited through the door, Keating could see two figures hovering at the doorway. "Come." Snitch and Scoundrel entered the room. "I trust you have good news for me?"

The twins stood in front of her desk. Snitch spoke first. "We confirmed that it was the boy, Carson. He was the one with wings."

Keating stared into her eyes. "And the sentence that ends that statement should be, 'And he's dead.'" The twins didn't respond. "So, you didn't kill the boy?"

"We weren't able to administer the drug in…"

Keating held her forefinger and thumb against the bridge of her nose in pain. "*How* did a young man, drugged out of his mind, make an escape?"

"It's them," Scoundrel said.

"Them… who?"

"The heroes," he clarified.

"Wait… there was someone there *besides* the boy?" Keating asked concerned.

"The girl was there, too…Ellen." A tense look crossed Snitch's face as she awaited Keating's response.

Keating smiled and leaned back in her favorite chair, which looked more like a throne. They were lucky to locate Quinley's BSC signal once they discovered no chip or human remains in the wreckage. It was simple to trace him to the hospital where he was to be disposed of with a shot of Iodinisium, leaving foul play undetectable. Braxton had not been so easy to pinpoint. They recovered her chip from a debris filter at the Region G Water

Processing Plant, so it was a blessing they stumbled upon the girl. Keating laughed. "So… so, let me get this straight, children. You had not one, but *both* of them there…and left them *both* alive and well. Would this be correct? Did you buy them chocolates? A get-well teddy bear?"

Scoundrel looked at her. "They had help."

"Who?"

"We don't know for sure," stated Snitch. "Two other men, older."

Keating spun around in her chair. "Have a seat. Tell me everything that happened. Everything, Snitch."

The twins took seats in front of Keating's large writing desk. Snitch did most of the talking; it was best that way. Snitch cleared her throat. "After we took care of the nurse and doctor, we checked to make sure it was him. We saw the markings on his back, so we knew he was the one with wings. I got the shot ready, just like you said. I was just about to do it when the two men came in and caught us. The girl showed up with a wheelchair and…"

"So, they were coming to take the boy," Keating said.

"It would seem so," confirmed Snitch. "We tried to fight them off, but it was four against two."

"Four against two *Xenozians*, which shouldn't have been an issue," Keating clarified.

"But the boy and girl had their power. We saw it!" exclaimed Scoundrel.

Snitch rolled her eyes, wishing he hadn't spoken.

Keating gave him a defiant gaze. "I didn't ask you to speak."

"He's right, though," Snitch said, diverting her attention. "It was just like the Federation. But how did they know about each other? Nothing connects Quinley and Braxton. We checked. They grew up in separate locations, different schools, different everything. We don't understand how they found one another."

Keating got up and walked to the window. She cupped her hands behind her back. "Is that all? Have you told me everything?"

"Yes," confirmed Snitch.

Keating turned to them. "Are you sure?"

"Very sure," Snitch said. "It's safe to assume we have new superhumans to deal with."

Keating walked back to her chair and took a seat, contemplating, pondering the implications of what she was hearing. It couldn't be that simple. "I assume nothing, Snitch. I think you are both right...and wrong." Her mind continued to churn. "It has to be more meticulous, more...strategic, more than coincidence that another group of heroes exists." Keating rubbed her chin. "Too organized. No, this has been planned."

"But how would you..." Snitch began.

Keating put a hand up to silence her. Then she turned to her workstation. She pulled personnel files for Braxton and Quinley and ran a side-by-side comparison on every piece of data in their historical files.

"We gave you the complete report," Scoundrel said. "We compared everything from the time of their birth until now and nothing."

"Yes, but did you search *before* that?" said Keating.

"Why would we care the time before their birth?" asked Scoundrel in a confused tone.

Keating dug deeper into their history, diving into their creation. That's when the common link unfolded. Visiting the HRV-EST genetic birthing files, she saw that both Ellen and Carson's genetic map originated from same Regional farm, Region H-73.

"Odd that both of them come from the same genome assignment region, don't you think?" posed Keating.

"Not really," Snitch replied. "Those batches contain hundreds and hundreds of potential subjects. It wouldn't be uncommon for them to have come from the same batch, right?"

Keating didn't reply. She only stared at the screen, thinking, running the scenarios. "It could be nothing, but I don't imagine these heroes exist by happenstance, children. I think they may have been intentionally *grown*." Keating continued to search other files in the HRV-EST database, and then she stopped, a wicked smile crossing her pale face. Pleased with herself, she got up and walked back to the window. "Now you have a new task ahead of you. I want you to comb the HRV-EST files, *all* of them. Look for all genomes seeded the day we cremated the remains of the Federation. Then, section out those assigned specifically to *Region H-73*."

"But that could take forever," Scoundrel said.

"I do *not* give a damn how long it takes!" Keating growled.

"What are we looking for?" Snitch asked.

Keating turned to them. "Just get the data. That's all." Snitch and Scoundrel gathered themselves to leave. "Oh, and, children—let's keep a close eye on this boy." She turned her screen around showing the final Region H-73 personnel file she had accessed, a young man by the name of *David W. Porter*. "I've always suspected he would be...*important*."

LEARNING

The weeks went by in an instant. Ellen had never seen so much information, and she didn't know how she was to retain it. There was so much to learn that there wasn't time for much of anything else. Ellen's mysterious prince continued to visit her in her dream world, which always elevated her mood. Together on the sands of a beach that overlooked infinity, they talked about the world, their hopes, and how together their aspirations would come true. It always put a smile on her face, which she needed now that training had spent her. She finished her final lesson, shut down the Federation database, and sat at her station rubbing her pendant on her lips. HANA was to arrive soon to close out their final lessons, and then they could continue with physical training. She looked over to Damian, who examined his screen with studious effort, while Carson stared at his screen with confusion.

Weeks before, the morning the group had begun their training, Ellen didn't understand just how much she was about to change, how all of them would change. Each of them awoke that first day to find a white exercise outfit with red stripes in their room. When Ellen had tried on her suit, she thought it was large for her, especially around her butt area. *My ass looks massive*, she thought. But when she saw how small Damian's suit was on him, they realized they needed to switch. They traded outfits and met in the Hub for breakfast, and afterward the group proceeded to a glass elevator past Tech Briefing Room A.

As they rounded the corner, they happened upon a row of large display cases. Each case had its own engraved nameplate and contained a specific uniform. Once they were close enough to read the wording, they could see that the cases held the uniform for each hero of the Federation.

"Were these their costumes?" Ellen asked with a smile.

"Yes," HANA replied. "Each designed and created in the Armory here in the Core."

"Oh, I would so love to have an exceptional costume," Damian said.

"Calm down, Mr. Gunner," HANA said. "Let's jog before we run MACH 5."

After entering the elevator, they traveled downward to the training area.

"God, how big is this place?" Carson asked.

HANA looked up at him. "Mainframe—basic history on the Core."

"Certainly," said the polite synthesized voice. "Construction on Core Complex finished on July 17th, 2073.56-2. An underground, multi-layered compound, it serves as headquarters for the members of the Federation. Overall, the unit has 227,000 square feet divided over eight levels, including a functioning infirmary, containment facility, and hangar unit."

"Damn," Carson said.

"Negative," the voice corrected. "The Core does not use hydropower. So, no dams are required. Energy is supplied through a network of Solar Fusion panels and the Core's Primary Nuclear Fusion Reactor. This amalgamation allows for an infinite power supply."

Carson smiled and looked to Damian. "Are you two related?"

The elevator door opened. "Level 9—Core Training Complex."

Two sanitation automatons completed final touches on the dormant gymnasium.

"As you can tell, this place hasn't been used in a long time," HANA warned as she led them into the small arena. Section by section, the overhead lights came on as they went on their way. "This is the primary training area of the complex."

Cushioned mats sat in many areas around the hardwood floors at the lower end of the court. Several sparring automatons stood motionless to their right. An upgraded computer bay was to their left. A multitude of exercise equipment sat throughout the perimeter.

"This appears to be a gym on steroids," Damian said with a smile.

"It has a functional computer lab, sparring androids, and training machines tailored to each of the Federation's... *your* talents," HANA said as she showed them the facility. "A hydrotank for soaking all the muscles we're going to overwork sits back there. And Damian, since your metabolism is so extensive, Hudson had the snack room stocked for you."

Ellen took it all in. "I don't mean sound rude...or ungrateful, or anything. But, how does Dr. Hudson pay for all of this?"

HANA smiled. "Let's just say the Federation took care of him."

"How does Parliament not find this place curious? Do they not question why the professor is buying all this equipment, the food, supplies? It must take a great deal of effort to operate an establishment this substantial," Damian said.

"We get all we need from suppliers in the Underground," HANA replied. "So, much of it goes undetected."

"So, it's all stolen," Carson alleged.

HANA stopped them and turned to him. "The Underground is not all thugs and thieves, Mr. Quinley." They continued to walk. "Over sixty percent of the dealings are legitimate. It keeps buying fair and prevents Parliament from claiming most of the merchant profit, profit that would be used for far more illicit dealings. Does that make sense?"

"Uh, yeah," said Carson, regretting his statement.

"What are we to train first? Will I get to spar with one of those animatrons?" Damian asked with excitement.

They made their way to the computer bay. "First thing's first," HANA instructed. "Please take a seat. I have called up the personnel file for each of your counterparts. It has their alter-ego data, power and strength detail, and an expanded history. The powers they came into back then are much like the powers you have come into now."

Damian looked at the hologram as he took a seat. "I must admit, the thought of supplementary homework doesn't sound agreeable. I thought we would train?"

"Knowledge is half the battle, Mr. Gunner."

Carson shook his head. "But what will reading all this do?"

HANA turned to Carson. "We have noted the abilities you carry are much like the abilities of the earlier members of the Federation. Hudson's hypothesis is the more you learn about them, the more it should help you realize your own capabilities."

Ellen looked at the data load for Vickie Conner, a.k.a. Voltage. It was a mass of information, her life story. "So, which parts do we need to read?"

"All of it."

"*All* of it?!" Ellen said. "There must tons of reading here!"

HANA winked. "The headphones to your left will walk you through the data. And pay attention to the screen. It will show you various press clippings and video files."

Carson scratched his head. "So, is this all we're going to do?"

"Monday, Wednesday, and Friday, your schedule will be: 8 AM to 9 AM Breakfast, 9 AM to noon, Learning and Development…"

"What?" Damian said. "I am already responsible for a massive amount of studies with the university."

"That's right, Mr. Gunner… but just on Tuesday and Thursday nights, correct? You'll still have those two days for your studies at the university."

"Distressing!" Damian said as he threw his head back.

"Noon to 1 PM—lunch, 1 PM to 2 PM— cardio training, and 2 PM to 3PM, strength training."

Ellen couldn't believe her ears. It was as if she had joined the Parliamental Militia and was going through Basic Training.

"Break from 3 PM until 3:30. Then, finally, Self-Defense from 3:30 until 5." HANA looked at the pained faces of her new students. "What did you think, guys, you would just get powers and bam— you're rock stars?" She walked to the door. "You can summon me anytime for questions. Have fun!" And with that, HANA disappeared.

"Horseshit," Carson said. "I don't read."

"You don't read, or you can't read," Ellen said with a smile.

Carson smirked. "Oh, ha-ha. Your ass still looks huge in those white pants."

Ellen stuck out her tongue. She turned around and looked at the screen. "This is like military school."

"I must agree!" said Damian.

Ellen accessed the file and dove into the history. Vickie, or Voltage, was quite the athlete. She played everything from lacrosse to basketball. An outgoing student from London, she seemed to keep better-than-average grades all throughout school. Her interest was in physics, and she became accepted into Carter Technological Institute, a prestigious university based in Chicago, Illinois, at the age of sixteen. While working late one night on a new fusion laser with her lab team, another student became trapped in the fusion room as the laser was about to spike. As the generator fed energy to the laser core, Vickie attempted to unplug the optic reactor cable, sending an atomic charge of 13,000 milliamps through her body. Except for the short-term memory loss, she had no physical injuries, which surprised everyone. Her powers arose about a month after the incident. Vickie found she could alter various types of energy and control electrical output on a molecular level. Her bio-conductivity could reach over 500 megawatts, more than a small nuclear power plant. She could not generate voltage in liquid, especially standard water, her primary weakness. If water entered her airways, it could lead to a biological short circuit, internalizing her energy and resulting in excessive electric current to her internal organs.

Even though he was against the study, Carson became engrossed in Bill Vogel's life. He had never been much of a reader, but Bill's story mesmerized him. Each training day he couldn't wait to get down to the training room and read more of the file. Willahelm Vogel was a young, up-and-coming psychiatrist from Berlin, Germany determined to cure dementia and strengthen the human mind. After losing the grandmother who had raised him to Alzheimers, Bill investigated the mind, searching for various methods to strengthen the human synapses. Working with his partner, Dr. Kelly Jäger, they developed an investigational serum by combining the cerebrospinal fluid of several animal species, namely oscine passerine birds such as crows, ravens, and even birds of prey, like the eagle. Birds, who possessed keen intellect and problem-solving skills, were ideal in the experiment. In attempts to murder Bill and claim notoriety for herself, Dr. Jäger attacked him and injected him with the unstable drug. The treatment was far from a complete compound, and once in his bloodstream it shut down his nervous system, leading to paralysis and death. A full two hours after his heart had stopped, Bill awakened with newfound abilities, including telekinesis. With his newfound understanding of the mechanics of flight, he created a breathtaking set of mechanized wings that could carry him through their air with great speed. His weakness was his own advanced mental skills, which could be distressed by certain high-pitched sonic vibrations.

In pouring through Maggie Casiano's files, Damian learned she had grown into her ability naturally. She lived in a rural town in Puerto Rico, quiet, a loner. Shy and introverted, she made decent grades in school, but was non-existent to the other students. Her father worked as an engineer in San Juan at Dillion Skyforce Base, an experimental military complex. He took her to the base on weekends while he worked on designs and blueprints. The details of the mishap were sketchy, but her abilities first showed themselves when she was fourteen years old. One weekend at the compound,

Maggie used her advanced speed to stop a massive jet engine from crushing her father. She and her father would keep the secret for a long time. Eventually, she decided to use her abilities for her own notoriety, becoming a track star, even qualifying to compete in the Olympics. Her conscience soon got the best of her, and knowing the unconventional abilities she possessed, she dropped out of competition citing injury. She retired from the sport, and a year later, she joined the Federation. Her weakness was loss of control at near-hypersonic speeds, which could lead to total physical atomic instability.

Day after day, week after week, the group learned more and more about the past and themselves. They grew closer to one another, sharing experiences, understanding who they truly were. After over a month of mental and physical preparation, the group felt stronger, faster, and healthier. Their minds were quicker, more agile, as were their bodies. Their powers were a different matter. It was difficult to continue to hone something that appeared to be aggressively growing and expanding. Regardless, they had come a long way from where they had been. With most of the historical studies behind them, they spent more time honing their strength and abilities.

"Done!" shouted Carson, a massive smile on his face.

Ellen leaned back and rubbed her tired eyes. "Me, too. Thank God." She turned to Damian and was caught off guard by the odd expression on his face. "Are you done?"

"I've been done," Damian replied.

"Then why do you look so pissy?" asked Ellen as she tossed a small wad of paper in his direction.

Damian looked at her, rubbing his chin. "Something's not right."

Carson turned to him, eyebrow cocked. "What are you talking about?"

"All of these heroes came from all over the globe. Most of them came into their powers by accident."

"So?" Carson said.

"Isn't it a strange coincidence that we each developed our power naturally?" Damian watched inquisitiveness drape across their faces.

"I know I didn't endure some scientific experiment gone awry to wake up with my abilities. Did you? And we've all lived within a couple of hundred miles of one another. Isn't that peculiar?"

"I don't find it peculiar at all, Mr. Gunner," HANA said as she appeared in the room.

Damian leaned back. "So, how would you explain it?"

HANA took a seat on his desk. "I don't think it's always possible to explain things like this. Even in the histories of your predecessors, we can only guess how they all became who they became at that precise moment, right when the world needed them." HANA smiled and leaned toward him. "There are moments, Damian, where I believe fate is more powerful than science. And I believe fate has placed each of you right here…right now."

"To save the world?" asked Carson with a sly grin.

"Yes," HANA replied as she rose to her feet. Though Damian's smile told her he conceded to her theory, she knew it didn't fully appease his analytical mind. "So…moving forward. I wanted to tell each of you how well you've done. Over these weeks what have you learned about the lives of your former colleagues?"

Carson stretched. "I learned that this bird guy needed to pick better friends."

HANA shot him a droll look.

Damian raised his hand. "What was the point of reviewing this information?"

"Evolution," HANA replied. "When you understand how the Federation handled their powers, it will arm you with knowledge they never had. Speaking of which, come with me and let's test you out." She led them into the main training area. In the far end of the room, a thick steel plate rose from the floor. Attached to it were wires that led to a voltage meter. "Ellen, you've read all about Vickie. The trick with your power is summoning it on command and then controlling the output. What I want you to do is connect with the sensory plate right there and raise the voltage meter indicator to the middle. Then, hold it steady for five minutes."

Ellen tried once. She tried twice. She tried over and over again.

Over a solid half-hour, she only summoned electricity twice. She couldn't understand why it was so difficult.

"Concentrate, Ellen," HANA said, stepping around the metal plate.

"I am concentrating!" Ellen shot a quick bolt through the hologram. HANA grimaced. Ellen was over it. The energy was coming and going, difficult to trust. She was tired, and she was irritable.

"Okay, maybe we should take another break," suggested HANA.

"No, no...I *will* get this," Ellen said with determination. She would do it if it killed her. During each of the instances where her power had materialized, she had been distraught, frightened, or angry. She had to control the energy if she wanted to master it. She rolled her eyes and focused on the sheet once again, blocking out the surrounding sounds. Then, a humming rattled in her ears. The energy rose in her forearms, and without warning sparks escaped from her fingertips, colliding with the steel sheet. The voltage meter attached to the sheet rose fast.

"Oh, my!" yelled Damian, who had not witnessed Ellen's gift before that moment.

"That's it! Now stay calm," HANA said. The voltage meter danced back and forth. "Try to keep the meter balanced."

Ellen could sense the energy fluctuating in her fingertips. It was difficult to keep control, but she got the meter to stay steady at the midpoint. After a minute and fifty seconds, she was still holding the meter level. "I'm doing it!" she said, growing excited. However, her sudden delight affected her output, which began to power past the designated midpoint.

"Wait! Hold it... hold it," HANA said.

"I'm trying!" Ellen asserted. But the voltage continued to get stronger. The energy from her hands grew bright white. Small sparks sputtered into different directions.

HANA grew alarmed. "Okay, back off, Ellen. Take it down."

"I can't!"

HANA turned to the boys. "Run!"

Damian grabbed Carson's arm and zipped behind the bleachers of the training room just in time for a bright flash to light up the room.

"Dude! You about broke my arm!" Carson fussed from behind the bleachers. He poked out his head. "Hey… is everything okay?"

"I'm never going to get this!" Ellen said disheartened. To everyone's amusement, her hair rose in the air as if she was touching a static ball. She stomped over to the bleachers, miffed, and plopped down onto the bench. The sanitation automatons arrived and put out the flaming metal which glowed like red molten rock, dripping onto the floor.

HANA turned to the sad girl. "You did great. At the end, things got a bit…" one robot sprayed a final spritz of flame retardant on the metal. "… heated. But, still you did well."

"I was impressed," Carson said as he jumped onto the bench beside her. "Your hair looks fabulous, by the way." Ellen looked at him and smiled.

"Gunner?" said HANA.

"Here," Damian said from behind the bleachers.

"You can come out now," confirmed HANA.

"Uh… no, I'm… I'm good, thank you. I'll just hang out here."

HANA turned to Ellen. "You take a break, and we will try it again. Okay?"

Damian crept out from behind the bleachers and sat on the other side of Ellen. He patted her on the shoulder in an attempt to comfort her. "It'll be all right. You'll get the…" Just then, a small blue spark shot from Ellen's shoulder and popped Damian in the arm. "Ow! Gosh-darn…look, I sympathize with your predicament; but I'm going…to go…like, sit over there." Ellen couldn't help but snicker.

"Carson, let's see how you do," HANA said.

Carson walked to the center of the gym with the hologram. "Okay, so what do I need to do?"

HANA pointed at his back. "I've been dying to ask. Let's see them."

Carson smiled and took a breath as the back of his tee shirt stretched. "Ow, ow!" he said, realizing he had forgotten to take off his shirt. He pulled the shirt over his head. Then he stood back, stretching his wings open wide and proud. "Sorry, they got caught in my shirt." He took ready stance. "You want me to fly?"

"No."

Surprised, Carson said, "Why not?"

HANA looked at him with a smile. "Because you can. Actually, I'd like for you to get that." She pointed to a thick metal ball sitting on a table thirty feet away. Carson smirked and walked toward the table. "No, I want you to stay right where you are and make it come to you...with your mind. You've studied Bill enough to know that he could move things using his mind."

Carson smiled. "You're joking, right?"

"No," HANA said. "Let's see if you can do it."

"Look, just because Bill had these mind powers don't mean I have them. I didn't get injected with bird fluid. I was just...well, born with this stuff."

"Yes, I understand that. But since you share so many common characteristics, we need to determine your full abilities. Try it. Just believe it can happen. Concentrate on that ball. See it lift off the table and come to you. Ninety percent of telekinesis is visualization." The hologram walked over and sat with Ellen and Damian. Carson began to walk toward the ball. "No, I want you use..."

"Wait," he said. "I want to get a sense of it. It's my first time." He walked to the table and lifted the ball which must have weighed at least five pounds. With a deep breath, he sat it back down on the table and returned to his starting point. "You gotta be kidding me." He stretched out his hand and concentrated.

"Just breathe," HANA said.

No matter what he did, the ball would not move. Carson closed his eyes and again envisioned it. He could see it moving from the table, rising high into the air, and then floating to him at his command. Then, he felt a strange sensation, like a tingling in the middle of his forehead, something he hadn't experienced before. The ball wiggled on the tabletop.

"It moved!" whispered Damian.

"Shh," Ellen warned.

Carson's eyes slowly cracked open, shining brightly. His mind connected with the ball. Without hesitation, the ball flew from the table with considerable speed, slamming into his chest and knocking him backward into the bleachers.

"Oh, God!" HANA said as she ran to him. "Breathe easy…easy now. You knocked the wind out of yourself."

"Ugh… that was not fun," Carson grunted.

So, there was poor Carson, sitting on the bench alongside the charred Miss Braxton, holding an ice pack on his left wing. It was difficult not to laugh at Ellen, who was still trying to keep her hair from standing on end. Now, it was Damian's turn. HANA called forward a huge bulk of protective padding, which must have been twenty feet thick, from the far wall behind a state-of-the-art treadmill.

"What is all that for?" Damian asked.

"To keep you from flying through the wall," HANA said.

"I am quite proficient in speed. I see no need for such safety measures. All I need to do is run," he said with assurance as he stepped onto the large treadmill.

HANA smiled. "And that's true, but Fleet used to run a standard MACH 4, close to MACH 5 when she put her mind to it. Let's see if you can do…MACH 3, maybe?"

"That should be no obstacle." Damian smiled. HANA activated the treadmill starting it at a running speed of 6 MPH. "Oh, come on!" Damian sneered. "Give me something better than this." HANA took the speed to 25 MPH, and Damian kept the pace with ease. 40MPH, 60 MPH, 80 MPH, 100 MPH.

Ellen and Carson watched in amazement as the speedster took to the pace with ease, his legs and arms transforming into undistinguishable haze. At 375 MPH, Damian appeared strained. Once at 600 MPH, he looked concerned. The treadmill rumbled and hummed with force as it increased in speed.

"We're almost there," HANA said as she grew excited. "MACH

1!"

Damian was now pushing his physical boundaries. The electricity burnt his muscles, which began feeling like gel.

"Woo! Go, Gunner! Wear it out!!" Carson cheered.

At last, the stress exceeded his capacity. Damian lost his footing and flew backwards like a bullet, smashing through the tables and burrowing through nearly fifteen feet of the protective matting behind him. They hurried to the insulation that encased him as Hudson and T.J. entered the training area.

"Gunner! Tell us you're not dead," Carson yelled into the ripped padding.

"Uh… I am alive," his muffled voice called through the cushions. "I don't believe I will be able to pry myself out of here, however."

HANA smirked. "Aren't you glad I left these out?"

"Yes, Ma'am," Damian moaned from inside the cushions.

Hudson was in awe at the melted steel, ice packs, and the mounds of detonated foam around the room. "Looks like we've missed the excitement. Decided to make the most of the last day of school, huh?"

"Well…as you can see, it's not gone so well," Ellen said as she walked past Hudson and T.J., trying to keep the last strands of hair from standing high.

Hudson smiled. "I think we need to spray down Ms. Braxton's do, throw a splint on Carson's wing, and dig Mr. Gunner out of the pillows so we can get something to eat. HANA, you've been patient, even for a computer. Let's have a break."

"All right, guys," HANA said. "Enough training for today. We can finish the final points tomorrow." HANA stepped onto the elevator with Hudson. "They're getting curious about their real origins, Andre," she advised. "How long are you going to keep them in the dark?"

Hudson sighed.

FLESH 84

Alex and Derek strutted into David and William's room with colossal smiles on their faces, which meant they were both up to no good. David sat there alone with his laptop, trying to work on his term paper and ignore them. But, as usual, that would be of no use.

"I can see you're going to stand there until I acknowledge you," David said, not looking at them. "You're acknowledged. Now go away. I've got a paper due."

"We have awesome news," Alex said.

"And what is your *awesome* news?" David said with sarcasm.

"Orchestra seats to *Flesh 84*, and that is, indeed, awesome, my man!" Alex said as he held up a bundle of tickets.

"Agreed!" Derek giggled.

Flesh 84 was the premier adult nightclub in the area, so exclusive it was impossible to get tickets, which were mostly reserved for patrons who were more well-to-do. It was known to be high dollar and high class. Nobody they knew had ever set foot inside.

"Dude," David said, sliding back from his desk. "First, how the hell did you get tickets?"

"Derek's old man," Alex said.

"Your dad?" David said as he looked to Derek, who shook his head. "And what does your Dad do?"

"He's a senior partner at Wilks & Harlen Law," Alex said on Derek's behalf. It was common that Alex spoke for Derek in most conversations that didn't call for the word *agreed*.

"And he's a perv?" David asked.

"Agreed!" Derek said with elated excitement.

Alex bounced onto David's bed. "Catch this…his dad got the tickets to take a bunch of his lawyer buddies to the club tonight, but his *mom* found 'em. And, boy was she pissed! So, his dad lied and said they were Derek's instead."

David laughed. "Really? You're kidding me."

"No shit!" Alex said. "Here she comes strutting into that kitchen, mad as all hell with that bundle of tickets in her hand, demanding to know whose they were. Well, his dad just sits there with his mouth hanging open like a freak. When she asks him again, he denies they're his. Then, she turns to my man Derek, here, and asks if the tickets belong to the frat, and, of course, he says…"

"Agreed!" Derek giggled.

"You ought to have seen how pissed his dad was when she reached across the table and tossed them to us." He handed the silver tickets to David.

David counted through them. "Dang, man, there has to be twenty tickets here! That's about 1,900 CC!" David looked at the shiny silver tickets emblazoned with the Flesh 84 logo. The laser printing kept them from being forged. The only problem was that David wasn't up for going to a club. "But I have to study for this mid-term."

"And me, Charles, Pete, and Lenny are skipping out on drumline field drill—what's your point?" Alex added.

David thought for a moment. "Man…you know we could sell

these and get that big screen for downstairs?"

"Titties," Alex said.

"Or, that pool table you guys wanted?"

"Titties," Alex repeated.

"Get a Nexus 1900 game system for every room in the house?"

"Uh…let me think. Yeah, I will take Titties for five hundred, David."

"Or level the back yard, finish the pool… *and* get a deck," David said, pulling out the big guns. The frat had tried to install an above-ground pool, but the cost to level the ground had been excessively high.

And on that note, Alex and Derek looked at each other for a second, pondering having an awesome above-ground pool with a sick-looking deck—the parties, the envy…and the parties. They turned to David, and with a smile, they both screamed, "Tittiiiieees!!"

David smiled and tossed the tickets at them. "Fine, fine. You guys win."

The two sprinted from David's room and recruited other brothers to go on the adventure of a lifetime while he continued his paper. Maybe it would be good to get out of the house, go somewhere, do something, get Abernathy off his mind. Boy, would Oscar have loved going to Flesh 84. His expression would have been priceless. He pictured them all at the club, Oscar in tow, his face aglow with a smile and visions of…

"Titties," David muttered to himself with a laugh, shaking his head at the ridiculousness.

It would have been something to see. He finished the paper, saved it, and printed out the final version on clean, white paper. He placed it in his folder, kicked off his shoes, and flopped onto his bed. Now that he had finished the work, he could relax for a while. If legend stood correct, the club didn't open until 10:00 that night. It was two hours away, so they would have to leave around seven if they wanted to get there, get parked, and get inside before the show began. He took a deep breath, closed his eyes, and drifted away.

In his mind's eye, he began to picture what the club might look like, how it may smell, the sound of thumping music. The girls there all had *special* talents, gimmicks used in their show. Not anything one would consider trashy, mind you. For example, one girl was said to be a contortionist who balanced on a high wire above the stage. There was another girl who apparently juggled knives (which could end up being especially painful without clothes). The star attraction, however, was supposed to be a girl who was a fire-eater. She was a legend. It would be something to see.

His legs relaxed, his large frame sinking into the soft bed. With his roommate, William, still at work, he had time to be alone and rest. His mind wandered to other things, other more peaceful things. And then he began to dream. His angel came to him as she always did. Taking him by the hand, she led him forward into a new, unknown place. He found himself inside a large dusty theater full of empty seats. She led him down the aisle of red chairs toward the grand stage before them. When she turned to him he saw his angel's beautiful eyes for the first time. As she pulled the thick velvet stage curtain open, she said two words: *Help us.*

The world was on fire. Destruction was all around David as his angel vanished into a white fog. Strange alien aircrafts buzzed overhead emitting a rumbling pitch that hurt his ears. In the distance, he saw dozens of them, their gray, scale-covered skin dripping with a thin coat of slime, their eyes black as night. They attacked the people around, placing them in shackles and leading them aboard the strange aircrafts. It was then that he saw Oscar, bound and on his knees, before one creature. Oscar's eyes met his, and he yelled something to David, something he couldn't quite hear. He yelled it repeatedly. At last, David could perceive the word. It sounded like *wrath.* The alien in front of Oscar smashed his face with the butt of his gun, breaking his glasses. Blood poured from his nose and mouth. The sight of Oscar broken and battered caused a fury to take over David, an anger he had never known. All he wanted to do was kill these creatures, slaughter them any way possible.

David broke into a full run forward. One by one, he jerked the creatures up into the air, ripping them to pieces. It was horrendous, brutal, ferocious. He shredded the heads clean from their shoulders, murky blood spilling to the ground. Others he tore in half. He punched through the chest cavity of one, ripping out its two hearts and squashing them to mush. And he continued to pulverize the beasts, one by one, stomping through the corpses on his way to rescue Oscar.

Then, a large figure broke through the smoke and fire, a tall, hulking mass. A metal helmet with curled, demon-like horns hid its face. Bright, red eyes glowed from within the helmet, and from the creature's back flowed a thick, tattered cape. David continued to march forward, confident and furious. The two titans stood toe-to-toe and examined one another. Then the battle began. They swung at one another with violent force, brutalizing each other in the middle of the battlefield. The beast pivoted upward with force, connecting to David's chin, knocking him up into the air. David landed hard onto the ground, losing much of his wind. He sprang to his feet and charged the monster, tackling it full-force like a linebacker and running it into the side of one of the massive ships.

David stumbled backward and noticed he was no longer on the battlefield, but in a massive engine room inside the alien craft. He and the creature continued to spar with one another. A thick layer of blood and dirt covered David's face, his left eye swollen shut from the trauma. The beast again charged him, but instead of running forward, David placed all of his weight behind him, like an anchor. He used his strength against the force of the charge to punch the creature in the face with all his might. It was as if it had smashed into a brick wall. The thing's legs flew from underneath it as it landed hard on its back, cracking the floor. Its helmet flew high into the air, and as it looked up at David, he noticed its thick, scaled flesh, ripped and bleeding, its red eyes glaring at him. David lifted his leg high into the air and stomped the thing in its chest, feeling the bones crack underneath his foot. It grabbed David's foot, throwing him backward.

As David rose, he noticed the thing now brandished a large spear-like weapon made of an iridescent metal. He then saw poor

Oscar on his knees, holding one of the alien's guns to his own head. As David screamed to Oscar, telling him not to pull the trigger, Oscar shot himself through the skull, his lifeless body falling to the side into a puddle of blood on the floor. With David's attention focused on Oscar, the thing charged him and impaled him with the spear, shoving it through his chest. The hot metal seared through David's flesh and bone. The monster looked at him with a seditious glower and dropped him to his knees. It turned to walk away, leaving his life to run from his body.

With both hands, David took hold of the spear and pulled the metal through his chest. He used his last bit of strength to stand tall. Before the creature knew he was near, David rammed both of his fists into the alien's back and through its chest, ripping it into two halves. He dropped the slimy carcass to the floor, and then he stumbled forward, falling to the ground in front of Oscar's body. As the light left his eyes, he looked at Oscar and whispered, "I'm sorry."

Oscar raised his head and smiled at him. "It's okay, Dave," he said. "Now, wake up."

David bolted straight up in his bed, dripping with sweat, panicked, unsure of where he was. Above him was the wall of the alien ship. With a mighty roar, he punched clean through the four-inch metal.

"Daaang!" said a voice. David turned in the dark to see a figure standing at his bedroom door.

Lenny flipped on the light and stood there holding a smoking bong with a guise of skepticism on his face. "If I wasn't high as shit right now, which...I *am*, by the way...I would think you punched through William's bed."

David looked above him. He had punched a hole clean through the thick bunk bed above him, ripping through the thick metal frame and the seven-inch thick pillow-top mattress. He looked back to Lenny with shock.

"If this is real, dude..." Lenny said as he took a final toke from his bong. He blew out the long bellow of smoke. "Will gon' be pissed," he finished, choking back the hit.

David stood in the shower allowing the hot water to run over his body. He found himself overwhelmed by the vivid dream, a dream he felt was somehow real. He had experienced nothing at all like it. It made him anxious, jumpy, and on edge. He was now easily startled, which was strange. David Porter just wasn't a timid guy, and that's why he always went first at haunted houses. As they were getting into the car to head to the club, he almost swung at Alan, and Derek's driving nearly made him climb the walls. Once they were out of the car at Flesh 84 and in the fresh air, David grew calmer.

They experienced some trouble getting in at first. The usher thought that this group of frat freaks had stolen the tickets. But once the tickets were proven legitimate, the boys were given the full VIP treatment, for which Flesh 84 was so infamous. After a couple of beers, David felt much better, almost like his old self. The layout was everything David thought it would be. He noticed the whole room decorated in a deep wine red, gold, and white color palette, very sophisticated. Thick, white tablecloths covered the tables, and in the center of them sat small iron lamps that added to the ambiance. Attached to the chairs at each was a CC scanner where you tipped your favorite dancer. Once you did so, a light would come on above your seat. The more the tip, the redder the light would shine, and tips equated to direct attention from the ladies. The balcony was divided into several individual sections, each with its own grouping of tables. Elegant hand-carved embellishments detailed each wall, which lent to the antiquated appearance of the establishment. A high wire stretched about the vast stage, and thick, red curtains with golden tassels hung from end to end. Each waiter was dressed in a neatly pressed tuxedo. David smiled as the lights dimmed.

"Oh, my God! We can almost touch that stage," Alex yelled. "That's awesome!"

Derek laughed. "Agreed!"

"Gentlemen!" shouted the MC entering the stage. The animated man wore a tuxedo with tails and donned a black top hat. The crowd cheered. "For those of you who don't know us, I bid you welcome. For those of you who do know us...don't you have a home?" The crowd laughed. "Tonight we have for your viewing pleasure nine of the most gloriously beautiful females on the planet… and *one ugly one.* And we are bringing them out just for you. But first… the *rules.*" The crowd booed. "Unless invited, do not get on the stage. If you get on the stage, you will be carried off…and *out.*" A snare drum and cymbal crash accented his remark. "Next, if you want to touch yourself, please do so under the tablecloths, but we ask that you do not touch these classy women. If you do, you will be carried off… and *out.*" Again, the snare drum and cymbal sounded. "Last, but not least, please conduct yourself in a proper manner. You are in a gentlemen's club, after all. Do not toss food, phone numbers, or boxer shorts onto the stage. Doing so will get you carried off…" The MC placed a hand to his ear.

"And out!" shouted the crowed.

"Superb! Now, let's get things started! Please welcome, the lady of flexibility, *Benderella!*"

The crowd went wild, and for good reason. David had never seen anything like it. The woman could bend into just about any shape. Following her act was a sword-swallowing gypsy girl they called *Karmi the Great.* However, David couldn't help but grow nauseous at the high wire matron they called *Swan.* It didn't help that at the end of her act they faked a fall, sending the unsuspecting crowd into panic.

The MC took the stage again as a siren sounded. David perked up, his nerves taking hold. Others in the crowd appeared to grow anxious.

"Uh, oh!" said the MC. "I think someone just called the fire department! Please welcome to the stage, the star of our show, *Laila—the Fire Eater!*"

The house lights darkened as the boom of the music rattled through the foundation. The curtains parted and the lights shimmered with brilliant sparkles from ceiling to floor. Fog bellowed from the two prop buildings on the stage as a beautiful young woman dressed in a tight-fitting firefighter's uniform strutted down the middle of the stage, dragging a chair behind her. A pole lowered from the top of the stage toward the front. The crowd exploded into applause, and chairs lit up with tips left and right. The young woman had obvious talent, a tremendous and coordinated dancer in her own right. She performed complex choreography that would make a gymnast hide his/her face in shame. She stopped at the chair in the center of the stage and dusted it in a teasing manner. Then, she paced back and forth to the beat of the music, looking for the lucky man she would bring up on stage with her to have a seat. She chose one older man from the side of the room, and he walked up to the stage. She sat him in the seat and began to dance for the lucky fellow.

Once the man's turn in Laila's special chair was through, the ushers escorted him off the stage and back to his seat. Then, a young man toward the front of the stage got his turn. It was at that moment that the fire seemed to engulf the stage. It appeared that the woman could shoot great bellows of flames from her palms into the air. The crowd was overrunning with energy, and Laila appeared to be having a wonderful time. And David was glad he came. The club helped him put his strange dream to the back of his mind. All was going well until his eyes locked with the young dancer's. Laila stopped cold on the stage, staring into David's eyes, and he into hers.

Without a tip being offered by a member of the frat, the young woman walked off the stage and onto the tables, all the while keeping her eyes on David. He froze, unable to move. Something within him knew her and knew her well. She jumped onto the tabletop where David sat and whipped her hair in a circular motion.

"Come on," she yelled, taking him by the hand.

Alex appeared taken by surprise. "Wait, sugar, why doesn't he have to tip?"

Without thinking, David stood up and walked with her over the tables to the stage. The crowd went wild. "Do... do I know you?" he yelled over the music.

"Funny, I would ask you the same thing!" she yelled as she sat him in the seat. With a swift kick, she threw a long leg over his head and straddled him.

"Woah! Uh...I don't know... I *think* so!" he called to her.

"Do I owe you money?" she said as she slithered down his leg, setting David into a state of shock.

"N, n, no... no, I don't think so," he said.

"Do you owe *me* money?" she asked as she slithered in front of him, parting his legs forcefully.

David gulped. "Dear, God! *Not yet!*"

She slinked back up by his ear. "What's your name?"

"David! David Porter!" he called. "I go to URU." David startled when she fell into a complete split in front of him.

"Hold onto something," she said as she grabbed the back of the chair. As she leaned backwards, she spewed bolts of bright flames into the audience from her mouth. She snapped upright.

"Oh, sweet GOD... what's your name?"

"Laila," she yelled.

"That's your real name?"

Boom! Bang! Pow!

The sound shut down the music, and the audience fell quiet. As David got his bearings, he saw approximately seven men armed with large shotguns, all except one. The unarmed man wore a suit, a very expensive suit from the looks of it. His bald head glistened under the lights. The lower house lights came on as the man stepped onto the stage. Taking the microphone from stage left, the man said, "Good evening, Gentlemen. You may know me. My name is Bernardo Canstanza. But some of you may know me as the *Bishop*. I'm... uh... sorry to bust up your little party here, guys, but, you see, Niki there owes me some money." He pointed up the balcony to Nicholas Zee, the owner of Flesh 84. "So, Niki, uh, since you weren't able to pay up, I think I'll take a loan from these nice gentlemen in the audience. Now, Nik...if you sit there and shut up, your customer's good Centicoin will buy you some time. But, if you move, Niki...everyone dies. Got it?"

The men with Bernardo pulled CC scanners from their coats. As they did, Laila moved around in front of David in a deliberate manner. "Stay quiet," she whispered.

"So, my guys are going to come around to your tables and collect coin from you's nice guys. Okie doke?" He looked at Laila. "And I will, uh, walk over here, and, uh, get *entertained.*" He strutted to Laila with a perverted grin and attempted to run his large hand up her cheek. "Hey, sweetheart. If you like doing shows, why don't you, like, drop down here and bob on my junk for these nice men. Show them your *real* talent."

Laila yanked her head backward. "I'd advise you to get the hell away from me."

He grabbed her by the back of her head, pulling her thick hair into a knot. "Or what, bitch?"

David stood and took hold of the thick steel firefighter's pole. Then he heard a multitude of shotguns cock, preparing to fire. "What, fly boy. You a tough guy?" Bernardo said. "Ha! Look at this big sonuvabitch, Louie! Think I can take him?"

"You can take him boss," called a voice.

David felt a rage well up within him. "Why don't we find out?" he growled.

Bernardo smiled. "Nah, that would take too much time." He reached into his pocket and whipped out a silver handgun. "How's about I blow ya ugly head off instead?"

"Stop!" shouted Laila.

Bernardo looked at her. "*One of us*, is getting blown, sweetheart. Me...," he cocked the gun with a click. "...or him."

"Wait!" Laila shouted, causing Bernardo to pause. "Okay, okay. Fine. But I need music."

Bernardo laughed. "Listen, if you're gonna do me, I will whistle Dixie for ya, sweetheart." His gang laughed.

She looked at David with confidence. She reached up and took his hand, making him let go of the pole. That's when she noticed that David had crushed the four-inch thick metal with his bare hand. "Don't move," she said. "DJ! Play something...get me in the mood." A fast-paced beat with a thumping rhythm pulsed through the speakers. Bernardo's men howled.

She took Bernardo by the hand, led him to the chair, and eased him into it.

"Yeah, baby doll," he said.

She put her fingers on his lips to silence him and danced around him for a while. As she did, his gang lowered their guns and applauded and cheered. Her provocative motions captivated Bernardo's men.

"You wanna kiss, sweetheart," she asked the gangster.

"Hell yeah!" he yelled.

She shot David a rebellious glower as she bent down, placed her lips against Bernardo's, and breathed frigid, sub-arctic air deep into his lungs. David watched Bernardo's eyes widen in bewilderment and then turn into two frigid orbs of ice. Once she stepped to the right of the spotlight, the audience noticed Bernardo frozen completely through, a horrific expression plastered on his icy face. The white frost covered his entire body, which was now thick, dense ice.

"What they fu...?! What did you do?!" yelled one of the men.

"You bitch!" yelled another before firing his gun. The shots hit the corpse of Bernardo, shattering him to pieces. The crowd burst into panic.

"Run!" she yelled to David. But he knew there was no way she would make it across the stage in time without being riddled with bullets.

"No!" he yelled as he grabbed her, turning his back to the audience. A horde of shots fired, riddling David's back. The bullets shredded his jersey as he held Laila tight. She leaned back and looked up into his eyes expecting to see his dead body topple to the ground, this boy who had just saved her life. Instead, he said, "You need to go, now!" She stared into his eyes unable to understand how he was even alive. *How is he...they missed,* her mind quickly explained. *They had to have missed him somehow.* "Go!" he yelled again.

She backed up a step. "Heather," she said.

"What?"

"My name is Heather."

David felt her cold lips kiss his cheek before she disappeared through the thick red curtains, the girl of fire and ice.

THE NEWS

During "graduation" dinner, the group told Hudson and T.J. all about what they had learned during their weeks of adventures. HANA was nice enough to print them makeshift diplomas. That didn't mean they had learned all there was to know, just enough skill and knowledge to understand the basic principles of what they were facing. More training was in store. It felt nice to relax. Carson kicked back in his chair, rocking back and forth. Due to his unconventional metabolism, Damian continued to eat ten times what the rest of them would have been able to consume. Ellen sat with her head down on the table, playing with a little silver disk she had found on the workstation, spinning it around like a top.

"It must be nice," Ellen said, looking at Damian.

"Hmm?" he muttered, his mouth full of food.

"To eat like that and be as skinny as you are."

Damian swallowed the glob of food. "My metabolism has increased to match my physical speed."

"I'd love to eat like that," Ellen said as she spun the disk around and around on the table like a coin. "I'd tackle that chocolate cake. It wouldn't live to tell the tale. Guys have it easy."

"We do not!" Carson said.

"Oh, please, yes you do," Ellen said as she sat forward. "Men don't age...*really*. All you have to do is stop drinking soda and you drop a thousand pounds. We girls think about food and our asses blow up. And we wrinkle in all the wrong places."

Hudson giggled, looking at T.J. "Well, that is one thing you guys don't have to worry about. At least not like me and T.J. do."

"What, gaining weight?" Carson said.

"No, aging," Hudson clarified.

Damian smiled. "So, would we be akin to immortal?"

Hudson shook his head. "Well, no... not exactly. The advanced make-up of your DNA structure allows for aging modification. I can't recall what the ratio was. T.J.?"

"I think it was two to one." T.J. leaned back. "I think that's it. We'll have to ask HANA."

"What does that mean, two to one?" Ellen asked.

Hudson stood up and walked to the large point tablet on the wall behind them. He picked up the stylus and scribbled a timeline on the transparent board. He drew another one under it, longer, with intersecting lines spaced further apart. "Superhumans, though the same on the outside, are very different from regular people, even down to the atomic structure of your cells. The nucleotides of your developed DNA structure are more tightly woven than the standard human. So, the cells in your bodies behave differently. In the normal animal, cells go through a life cycle. They are programmed to commit suicide, and that death plays the very important role of population control by balancing cell growth and multiplication. Your cells don't behave that way. They still die off and replace themselves, but at half the speed that mine would. The only time your cellular activity increases is when the foundation is broken. A black eye, a cut, a bullet wound—these types of cellular disruptions cause a hyper-reactive response from the atoms in your body. They rush to repair themselves to support the integrity of the organism."

"So, you age twice as slow, and heal four times as fast," T.J. said.

"Exactly," agreed Hudson.

Damian looked confused. "Then, why do I still have an injury from my shaving mishap yesterday?"

"Well, that's the thing. Just like your powers came on gradually, the genetic anomalies that will make you *super* come on with time. I am sure none of you woke up when you were three years old able to do what you can do today?" They all shook their heads. "That's because most of these things develop after puberty."

"Ha! Maybe that's why you're a late bloomer, Damian," Carson chuckled.

"*Maybe that's why you're a late bloomer, Damian,*" Damian mocked.

"Puberty is when the human body jump-starts physical changes," Hudson clarified. "That's why most of these things trigger during that phase. So, when did you first notice your powers? Did it come about during something traumatic, like a scary moment for you?"

The room was quiet. Carson was the first to speak. "Yeah... a few days ago I jumped out of a plane with no parachute. That was traumatic. I guess it triggered a fear of splattering all over the ground."

"Well, mine wasn't so horrific," Damian said. "It was two years ago. I woke up late for my final and..."

"Your final? That's traumatic?" Carson said.

"If you knew Professor Ingle, you'd realize that is quite traumatic."

Hudson shook his head. "Ingle is on the crazy side."

"And that's an understatement," Damian added. "If we were even a minute late, she said we would get a zero for the final. My dad would have murdered me if I had failed that class. I was running like a cheetah, trying to get to class. The next thing I knew was that everyone seemed to freeze in time. But it was me who was moving at an excessive rate."

"What about you, Ellen?" Carson asked as he leaned back looking her way.

Ellen didn't respond at first. She found it impossible to mention.

What was she to say? That she was about to be raped by this old pervert and she fried him like chicken? "I don't want to talk about it. Let's just say it was traumatic."

"Was it recent?" Damian said.

"Recent enough."

"Did it all happen at once or…"

It was then Hudson realized the door he had opened. "Regardless, there could be things that haven't really manifested in you yet," he interrupted, buying Ellen time to breathe.

"What do you mean?" Damian asked.

"Well, like your shaving incident, for example. There could be aspects of the cellular foundation that haven't come forward, yet. You could still be in for surprises."

"So, Ellen," Carson said. "Were you, like, in front of people when it happened for the first time?"

"I said I don't want to talk about it!" Ellen said with a firm tone causing sparks to fly from her fingertips and snap against the small metal disk. She jumped back with surprise. The disk shuddered on the table as a tiny power indicator illuminated red for a moment and faded away. Ellen smiled. "Okay, what the hell is that thing?"

She reached over and picked it up, holding it in her hand. It felt alive, organic, and she could sense it was frightened. Lifting it to her face, she began to link with the machine on a subconscious level. Sparks and electrical current danced around her hand. The disk hopped out of her hand and onto the table.

All at once, bright streams of blue current from Ellen's fingers connected to the small disk. It shivered and shook around the table as it fed on her energy. Its once dull chrome shell shone like new as if it was mending itself; its circuits and indicators danced and sparkled. Then, the little disk transformed into a tiny, three-inch animatron. It looked up at them in wonder, its small rectangular head moving from side to side as if he was trying to decide what they were. It looked to Ellen and beeped and squeaked.

"Oh, well, nice to meet you, BIT. My name is Ellen," she said to it. Again, it resounded with meaningless twitters and beeps. "Uh, no,

I don't know how long it's been. We'll have to ask him," she added, looking in T.J.'s direction.

"Uh…do what?" asked T.J.

"How long has it been since you created him?"

T.J. was astonished. He had almost thrown out the old bot, which now stood before him as if it were brand new. "Uh… I don't know. About twenty years. Wait, you can talk to him?"

Ellen smiled. "Yeah, can't you hear him? He speaks fine."

BIT repeated in Ellen's voice, playing back what she had just said. "Yeah, can't you understand him? He speaks fine."

"Ha! That's funny," Carson giggled.

"Seriously, you guys can't hear him?" Ellen asked.

"It sounds like a bunch of beeps and blinks to us," Damian said.

BIT rolled toward her on his small caterpillar tracks and spoke to her once again. Ellen smiled. "He says…he can communicate perfectly fine with someone who is smart enough to understand him. Ha! Really? You guys can't understand this?"

T.J. leaned into Hudson. "Was Vickie able to talk to robots?" he whispered

"Never," Hudson confirmed as he watched in amazement.

T.J. reached over, picked up BIT, and examined him. BIT struggled against his hand, fighting to get away. As soon as T.J. sat him back down on the table, he rolled back to Ellen, placing his small shiny hand on hers. At that moment, BIT had all but fallen in love with Ellen Braxton. For the rest of the afternoon, he demanded to be carried in her pocket at all times. The two of them huddled on the couch and carried on conversations only they could understand. BIT showed off his various capabilities, transforming into a host of practical items ranging from a flashlight to a whistle.

HANA appeared in the room. "Hudson, I think we have a hit."

"A what?" Damian asked.

Hudson hurried to the display to see that social media was on fire with a story that was just unfolding from the early morning hours at Flesh 84, the gentlemen's club. "Guys, I think we have something!" They all gathered around Hudson. BIT perched on Ellen's shoulder like a small bird. "Early this morning, the Bishop had an incident at a club called Flesh 84."

"The strip club?" Carson asked.

"That's the one," confirmed Hudson.

Damian looked confused. "Who's the Bishop?"

T.J. stepped forward. "Bernardo Canstanza. He's the head of the Canstanza crime family. Responsible for the deaths of a lot of important people."

"Or *was*," Hudson clarified. "Seems Bernie is dead, along with twelve other people."

"You're shitting me!" T.J. said.

"No, Sir. According to this, he and his gang busted into the club last night to collect a debt from the owner, but since he couldn't pay up, they tried to rob the customers. Old Bernardo threatened one dancer there, the 'fire eater.'" He gave T.J. a knowing look. "Apparently the fire eater didn't like that too well, so she, get this— 'froze him solid' in front of hundreds of people. Wait…I think we have pictures." Hudson clicked on one of the JPEGs, but then one by one, every post related to the incident began to disappear.

"What's happening?" asked Ellen.

"I don't know. I don't know." Hudson said as he tried to recall the posts. It was no use; they vanished before his eyes. "Turn on the television. Channel 2503. Quick!"

T.J. turned on the television and switched to the local news channel. There was a live report of a man arrested that night for making the illegal drug called "Tie-Dye" in his apartment. Also, there were reports of delays of the new bridge construction downtown. There were even stories on the new chocolate factory opening on Waverly Avenue. But there was nothing on the murder of one of the largest crime bosses in the Region.

"Why are they not reporting anything?" Carson asked.

Hudson sighed. "They've been *told* not to." He gave T.J. a knowing look. "Keating knows. Without a doubt, she knows. She's locked the media down."

T.J. rubbed his exhausted face and flopped into the adjacent desk chair. "Dammit! So… what do we do now?"

Hudson stood up and reached for his coat. "I think we need to pay a visit to Flesh 84 and meet our mysterious fire eater."

THE MILKMAID

"So, you got no idea why Canstanza thought you owed him money?" asked the Detective. "You didn't, like, take a loan from him to run this fine establishment of yours or anything?"

Nick Zee leaned over the sink in his office, running water on his face. The room was in shambles. All the windows shattered, bullet casings littering the floor. The safe in the corner was cracked open and void of contents.

"I told ya'. I didn't know who Bernardo Canstanza was. I don't know why he was here, and I don't know why he would have thought I owed him a damn thing."

The Detective walked over to the desk and tossed a piece of paper onto it. "Well, then take a peek at this invoice then." Zee walked over to the desk and picked up the paper. "Seems that someone in your building is doing business with Canstanza

Cosmetics and with Canstanza Corp Wine & Liquor. Somehow, your ladies are staying pretty and your patrons are staying drunk with the help Canstanza's companies—and at a discount to boot."

Zee shot the Detective a rebellious stare, wadded up the invoice, and tossed it in the trash. "I don't know where that came from, I told ya."

The Detective smiled. "Oh, yeah, yeah. That's what you say." He lit a cigarette and began to make his way out of the room along with the other two cops. "But, if I were you, Niki, I wouldn't get too far away from Region H, got me? I think we'll have a few others invoices to share with ya'. Have a good night."

Zee watched them walk down the hall and disappear through the side exit door. "Son of a bitch," he muttered. He smashed the intercom button. "Diane! Get your ass in here. I need someone to get this cleaned up. Pronto!"

He spun around in the chair and unlocked the lower desk drawer. Inside were all the contents from the burgled safe. To be sure to get the max return from the insurance, he was clever enough to submit the safe valuables as stolen. "Damn you, Bernie," he muttered to himself. "I told you I'd get your money. I told you! You didn't have to come in here, busting up my place." He sat back and slammed the drawer. "I'm glad you're dead. Good riddance!" Someone entered the room. "Diane! Get all this friggin' glass cleaned up…"

Then, Zee went blind.

By the time Hudson and the team reached Flesh 84, the crowd had dispersed. The place appeared to be abandoned, except for an expensive luxury sedan parked in the lot. The license plate read *ZEE-1*, apparently one from Nicholas Zee's fleet

"Is anyone even here?" Ellen asked.

"Zee wouldn't have left that car here, trust me," T.J. said.

As they approached the door, T.J. raised his hand to knock, and that is when he noticed that the door was slightly ajar. He reached behind his back and pulled his gun.

"What is it?" asked Hudson.

"Something's wrong," confirmed T.J.

With prudence, they entered the lobby of the dark club. The emergency lights cast a red hue over the area, which was in absolute shambles. Standard crime scene lasers sectioned areas of bloody evidence. Bullet casings and Ripper cartridges covered the floors.

"What are those?" Damian asked.

"Ripper cartridges, Authoritan issue. Fitted with a smartchip. Once the bullets enter the target they'll locate the closest organ or artery," informed T.J. "Hello? Anyone here?"

There was no answer as they continued to make their way through the space with caution. They walked up the steps to the office floor where they could see lights. T.J. called out again, but received no response. As they entered the main office, they could see Zee seated in his office chair, his back to them.

"Hey, Zee, it's Blackwood." T.J. held up his hand instructing the others to stay at the door. "Hey, you guys remodeling?" He made his way around to the back of the desk. His face went sour as he motioned for Hudson to come examine the body.

Zee's jaw had been ripped from his skull. His hands, bound behind his back, were blue and pooling with settled blood. Thick, green goo covered his eyes. "There," he said, pointing to the ooze. "Seems like our little E.T. buddies came to pay him a visit. Which means they're looking for the fire eater, too, I bet." T.J. poked through the debris, searching for evidence.

Ellen examined the file cabinet at the far end of the room. "Looks like her name is Heather Isles, but the file is empty."

Hudson walked to her. "How do you know?"

"It's got her stage name on it," she said as she handed him the folder.

"*Laila, the Fire Eater...* cute," Hudson said. "That's got to be our girl."

"We should go check out the lockers. Maybe we can find something," T.J. said.

T.J. led the troop to the abandoned backstage area. As they rounded the corner, it surprised Hudson to hear T.J. yell, "Freeze! Authority. Hold it right there."

A very tall woman stood there shivering, a small Centicoin bank in her hand. A look of horror was plastered on her face. She had long blonde hair and wore short-shorts with a halter top and light blue jacket. "Hey, I'm just getting what's owed to me, okay? Zee didn't pay me this week."

T.J. walked over to the girl and began frisking her. "Who are you?"

"Wendy McDaniels... I'm the one they call *Mary the Milkmaid.*"

"Never heard of you," T.J. said.

"Oh, come on. Yes, you have."

"Can't say I have," T.J. confirmed.

Wendy sighed and then sang. *"Mary, Mary quite contrary. Milks those cows all day. Those things ain't stilts; her stems is built. She was born that way."*

Carson cracked up, causing Hudson to glare in his direction.

"Okay...Wendy," T.J. confirmed as he pulled her identification from her purse. "I believe ya'. You know a girl named Heather?"

"Heather? No, I don't think so."

"Laila?" Ellen asked.

"The fire girl! Oh, yeah! Really nice. Super-talented. Designs all our costumes. Not sure why she was in a dump like this. She had smarts."

T.J. handed her CC bank back to her. "Do you know where we can find her?"

"She's not in any trouble is she?"

"Not if we find her first," Hudson confirmed.

Wendy pondered a second. "Not really. She rooms with one of the other girls here, Rhonda. Rhonda Fitzburger. A lot of us girls stay at a little apartment building out on 17th and White Avenue. Rhonda is in apartment 137."

"Then, I say we go there," Hudson said to T.J.

"But...if you *really* want to catch sight of her," Wendy added. "Every night she goes and sees her sister. She's a waitress at the Tippy Top out on Broadway. The little diner that serves all the ice cream. Laila...uh...Heather goes there every night."

"Thank you, Wendy," T.J. said. "Now, you best get out of here and go home. It's not safe."

The troop hurried through the back door.

"Eh… you're telling me, brother," Wendy said as she continued to shove CC banks into her purse.

THE FIRST BATTLE

Night crept across the city like a phantom. Heather knew it would only be a matter of time before the Canstanza family came for her. She didn't take them to be the understanding type. They would come for her, they would find her, and they would kill her, most likely in the most painful manner possible. Worse yet, they would hurt Elizabeth, and she couldn't allow that to happen. Liz had gone through enough tragedy in her life, much of it because of Heather. Sometimes, the hardest apology to accept is your own.

The goons had ransacked the apartment before Heather got there. Rhonda would be pissed. She wouldn't believe that Heather had nothing to do with it, though. Saturn House, the small, rundown apartment complex where most of the Flesh 84 talent lived, was in a shadier part of Region H. It wouldn't be a stretch to assume that they were victims of common burglary. Salvaging what she could of her belongings, she marched into the night—to where, she had no idea. She was no stranger to the streets or surviving the night. She would wander the city like she had before, allowing the storm to calm. Then, she would emerge again in another life, another line of work, another path. That was the beauty of being alone.

A traffic accident a block from the Tippy Top would hold the attention of the crowd, who would be waiting for blood, gore, and drama. With the distraction, it would be easy to duck into the diner and make it to her favorite corner booth that sat away from the main lights and windows. She could practically live in that booth, and no one would realize she was there. There were times she had remained at the diner for hours on end. The longer she was there, the more the owner—old, forgetful Stanley—mistook her for different customers. Half the time Stanley couldn't remember Liz's name, and she had worked there for three years.

In the distance, the blinking neon of the Tippy Top flashed and danced. Her sister's beautiful red hair could be seen a mile away. She appeared to be waiting on her favorite customer, the one named Andrew. Heather couldn't recall the man's last name, even though Liz had told her a hundred times. He did something in real estate. He was nice, and better yet, he was nice to Liz. That was all that mattered to Heather.

The tiny silver bell on the door jingled as she walked inside. Liz turned around and smiled at Heather with that big, bright smile as Heather made her way toward her favorite booth. Regretfully, a rather surly looking man occupied the seat, and that was unacceptable.

Heather walked up to the man. "Dude, you drive the red pickup right?"

He looked at her with an odd expression. "No, a white sedan."

"Yeah, that one. Someone is breaking into it."

"Dammit! Are you serious?" he yelled as he picked up his coat.

"Yeah, some woman."

"Blonde?"

"That's the one."

"Bitch! She got enough in the divorce. That car is mine!" With that, he grabbed his coat and ran out of the diner to save his car.

Heather giggled, took her place, and waited on her sister. Liz finished speaking to Andrew and walked over to her. "What did you just say to that man?"

"Nothing," Heather said. Liz was skeptic. "I didn't do a thing!" Heather said with a smile.

The silver bell jingled again. The man walked back to where Heather and Liz were talking. "Hey… no one is stealing my car."

"Oh, sorry about that," Heather said as she picked up the menu and glanced over it.

"You're in my seat."

"Sir," Liz whispered. "I am so sorry about this. This woman is in here all the time, and she's crazy as hell. Her mind is just not right. She has to sit in this seat because it's the only place where she can't hear 'the voices.'"

He looked at them, skeptical of what he was hearing. With a sigh, he rolled his eyes, shook his head, and walked to a booth down the aisle.

"Woman, you're getting as bad as me," Heather said.

"I get it from you."

"Whatever! You're older."

"Yeah, yeah, yeah. You better order something or Stanley's gonna crap a cracker."

"Fine," Heather said. "Bring me some…tomato basil soup. *No crackers!*"

"Ha, ha… be right back."

Outside, the last of the wreckage from the accident appeared to be cleared. A light mist of rain peppered against the cars. Heather watched the droplets of water as they ran down the windowpanes. Liz brought her a glass of water and she took a sip of it finding it was too warm for her taste. She took hold of the glass and sent frost through it, chilling the water to perfection.

"Heather, you need to quit doing that out where everybody can see you," Liz said as she took a seat.

"Oh, they'll be fine."

"Not everyone is as understanding as I am, Heather." Liz noticed

Heather spy the deep scars around her neck, causing Liz to pull her collar up to hide them.

"Speaking of which, how are Mom and Dad?"

"Mom wants you to come home."

"Dad doesn't."

"He'll come around, Heather. He loves you."

"No…he doesn't Lizzie. He thinks he is supposed to because I'm his kid."

Liz looked at her with pleading eyes. "*I* want you to come home. I hate you not being there, Heather. Stop all this dancer nonsense. Come back and let's get you back in school, have a normal life."

Heather laughed. As she leaned forward, she lifted her right hand and rubbed her fingers together, causing a small flame to generate. Liz took the cloth napkin and wrapped Heather's hand in it, dousing the fire.

"I'll never have a normal life, Lizzie."

The door opened and a man entered with a young girl around Heather's age.

"You could have a normal life, Heather. You can control all this now. It's not like when we were kids. You can handle it perfectly. There's no reason you can't come back home."

"Sorry," said the young woman approaching the table. "I hate to bother you, but is your name Heather Isles?"

"We're kind of talking here," sighed Heather.

"Sorry," Ellen said. "I thought you may be her."

"What if I am?" Heather said as she sat back with assurance. She examined Ellen curiously. "Hey…have we met? You work at 84? Isn't your stage name Princess-something-or-other?" It was that strange feeling, like déjà vu, the same feeling she had experienced when she met the frat guy in the audience.

"No. Uh, my name is Ellen. And this…this is Andre. Would you have a second to talk?" Ellen could also feel the connection to Heather, so they had the right person. It was a peculiar bond, like being tied together with thin silk thread.

Heather glared at both of them. "Like I said, I'm talking to my sister here. You'll need to…"

"I think you can help us," Ellen added.

Liz patted Heather's hand and stood, allowing them to take a seat. "What can I get you guys?"

"Oh, nothing, thank you very much," Hudson said.

"You, honey?" Liz said to Ellen.

"Water, maybe? Thank you."

Ellen and Hudson took a seat. "Thanks for talking to us," Ellen said.

"I've not talked to you, yet," spat Heather with suspicion in her voice.

Ellen looked at Hudson, who then took the lead. "Ms. Isles, my name is Dr. Andre Hudson. We wanted to speak to you because we think you're…special."

Heather laughed. "You got that shit right, mister. You don't realize how special I am."

Ellen looked at Hudson, who nodded to her in approval. Ellen leaned her hand forward. "I think I do." Ellen held her fingers wide allowing sparks to dance up her fingertips.

Heather flinched with surprise. "What the hell is this?" She started to rise to her feet.

"Wait, wait," Hudson pleaded. "Please, don't leave. Give us a second."

Heather calmed herself and took her seat. "Who are you?"

"Well, that will take a while to explain, and I wouldn't feel comfortable going over all of it here," Hudson said. "If you are willing to trust us, we have a place where we can talk."

Heather laughed. "You have to be kidding me, man. So, did Canstanza's guys send you?"

"No, no," Ellen said. "I never even heard of that guy until today. I promise."

Heather looked through the diner window to the car out front and noted three other guys sitting there. "So, who are the jackasses in the car? The one you came in?"

"Uh…let's see," Hudson said turning to the window. "The

gentleman in the front is my friend T.J. The two guys in the back are Carson and Damian."

"They're special, too," Ellen added. "Well, T.J. is special in a *different* way."

Heather looked at them. "So…what do you want?"

"We have need for someone with talents such as yours, Heather," Hudson said. "All we want to do is give you more information. I think we can explain why you are the way you are. Then, after you have all the information, you can decide if you would like to hang out with us for a while."

Heather leaned forward as Liz returned to the table with two glasses of water and a basket of breadsticks. She sat them on the table. "I brought you something anyway, guys."

Heather saw Hudson's eyes wander to the scars that ran along her sister's neck. "Uh, thank you."

Liz patted his shoulder and walked away.

"Hey, I understand how weird this is," Ellen said. "Trust me. It's new to me, too. This just started up with me a few days ago. It was scary. I've been staying with Hudson and the guys for a few weeks now. I know how you feel about having such a weird ability, not having a place to go."

Heather smiled and leaned forward. "Did you notice her neck, princess? That is what my 'unique' ability does. I'm used to it, because mine started *years* ago." Heather leaned back and stirred her water with a straw. "The two of us were fighting like sisters do— over a doll or some crap. Well, things got a little *heated*. Before I realized what had happened, I set my big sister on fire in our living room, right there in front of our dad." She stared at the glass of water with empty eyes. "I was nine years old…and petrified. At first, our parents tried to act like it didn't happen, like it was an accident. But the more afraid I got, the more dangerous I got. So, my dad sent me to a special hospital in Region L, a real *shithole*. And they just shut me in a room and left me there. No one cared about a crazy little black girl, least of all rich white doctors. I stayed trapped there until I was about thirteen and then I broke out. And I have been on my own ever since, doing whatever I needed to do to survive." Heather turned back to Ellen. "So, don't walk in here and get all compassionate with me like you know what I've been through, okay?"

Ellen was so shocked by the hostility she almost couldn't respond. "Oh, I didn't...I mean..."

"Come with us," Hudson said. "Don't you think you've run long enough? Wouldn't you like to have some answers?"

"I have to get back to work. My boss owes me..."

"Your boss is dead," Hudson said.

Heather looked at him with a blank expression. "What?"

"Zee was killed this morning. The club is gone," he confirmed.

Heather sat still for a moment, thinking of options, directions, possibilities. "Well, that's just another career change I get to make," she said as she stood. "So, if you'll excuse me, I'm going to go get my stellar résumé updated and..."

"Oooh," they heard someone moan. "Oooh, yeah, baby. Watch me work it!" Snitch stood on top of the far table, holding onto the pole in the middle of the booth. She twirled and swayed her hips as if she was dancing a striptease. Hudson and Ellen shot upright. "Oh, wait now! Wait. I ain't through." Snitch continued to grind the pole and bent all the way backward with incredible dexterity that would break the spine of most *real* people. They heard her bones crack under the pressure. She smiled at them. "What did I tell you—pole dancing ain't too hard, is it, girl?"

Heather had no idea what the weird girl meant. "Who the hell are you?"

"Fans!" called another voice. "We have come all the way here to meet the legend!" said Scoundrel as he stepped from the back along with two Parliament soldiers in full gear. "The heat-seeking rump shaker!" One soldier dragged Liz from the back, laser rifle held to her temple. "The girl who can lit'rally... *drop it like it's hot!* Can I get an amen?"

The handful of remaining customers ran from the diner and into the street.

167

"Hallelujah!" called Snitch as she sprang from the table. "We found you out, Hudson…Dr. *Andre*. Yeah, we know who you are now, *Hacker* Hudson. We've been doing our homework." Snitch walked over to him, circling him, ruffling his hair. "Just give up, man. There's nothing you can do. You didn't think you'd be able to pull off this little reunion, now did you? We *always* find out."

Ellen took Heather by the hand and stepped backward. A slither of blue spark caught the attention of Heather, who saw Ellen's other hand sizzle with bluish current.

"And so, you can either send them with us, or we can just kill all y'all now," Scoundrel said. "What'cha think? Just to show ya' that I mean what I say, I'll have my man here blow this bitch's head all over that nice mound of ice cream. It'll be like when you stick a plug of dynamite in a…"

A swoosh of wind scattered about the diner. Before anyone could understand what had occurred, Liz was gone and with her the soldier's weapons. The two guards looked at each other in complete disbelief.

"Where'd she go?" Scoundrel yelled.

With massive force, Scoundrel suddenly stumbled backwards as a blurred image swung and punched at him faster than he could comprehend what was happening. The front window of the diner shattered as the winged figure burst through and hovered in the air, knocking Snitch to the ground.

"Kill their asses!" Snitch screamed, scrambling to her feet.

Nine additional soldiers rushed the diner, Taser Batons in hand. Carson made quick work of two of them, snatching then by the collar and soaring through the shattered window. Higher into the air he soared as the men screamed in terror. He carried them over the dark, leech-infested Western River.

"Put us down, you freak! Now!" yelled one of them.

"Oh, I do what I'm told, boys," said Carson before dropping them sixty feet to the frigid water below.

Inside the diner, Snitch targeted Heather. She bounded high in Heather's direction, knocking her to the ground. Snitch snared her wrists and held them tightly as Heather fiercely struggled against her. The more Heather struggled, the higher her body temperature climbed. Finally, Heather's hands burst into brilliant white-hot flames, forcing Snitch to wail loudly. The organic flesh melted like hot wax from Snitch's hands, exposing her scale-covered skin. As her head rolled backward in agony, her jaws unhinged in a snake-like fashion, long razor-like fangs lined her gaping mouth, dripping with toxin. Snitch snapped forward, preparing to sink her teeth into Heather's face when Heather exploded into a mass of flames. Ellen appeared from behind and grabbed Snitch around the neck, sending hundreds of volts through her body. Snitch toppled to the floor, jerking and shuddering, giving Heather the room she needed to stand again.

A soldier rounded Ellen and with great force, jabbed her hard in the back with his Taser Baton, which did little to stop her. Another approached fast behind him, Light Rifle in hand. Working together, Heather pulled Ellen to the right while she leaned to the left. Heather threw a mass of frost at the one soldier, busting his visor and freezing his face to the bone. Ellen grabbed the Taser Baton of the other soldier, reversing the voltage, causing it to pulsate through his body, knocking him to the ground unconscious.

Heather looked at Ellen, impressed with her actions. "Thanks."

"No sweat," Ellen said.

As Hudson and T.J. continued to fend off the remaining soldiers at the other end of the diner, Scoundrel had his hands full with the mysterious blur. Greenish-black blood dripped from his busted nose while he swiped and struck at the mysterious figure. As the thing broke away, Scoundrel snatched the live Taser Baton from the unconscious soldier on the ground. Throwing a pitcher of cold water to the ground, he tossed the charged baton into the liquid in time for the blur to come in contact. With a loud snap of electricity, Damian flew hard against the adjacent wall, knocked off balance by the shock.

"Ha! How ya' like that, smartass?" Scoundrel shouted as he slithered up behind the dazed speedster. His thick tail whipped from behind him, wrapping around Damian's throat. As it tightened, Damian found it difficult to remain conscious. The beast held Damian tight while it licked him with its sticky forked tongue on the side of his face. "Ooh...tastes like Kung Pao chicken."

Damian took a deep breath, closed his eyes, and began to shudder all over, every inch of his body pulsating. Scoundrel bellowed as he tried to maintain his hold. The quivering became more focused and brutal. Scoundrel soon found it impossible to stay attached to the vibrating hero. Damian evaporated from his grasp so forcefully the vigor caused Scoundrel to retch. Suddenly, Damian reappeared, landing another round of blows to Scoundrel and knocking the alien backward into the booths.

"So gross!" Damian shouted as he wiped the slimy saliva from his face.

After the last soldier fell, the two lizard-like creatures scuttled from the building to lick their wounds in defeat. The victorious team gathered themselves together for the first time. Carson landed in the middle of the diner that was now in complete shambles. Ellen pulled her ripped jacket around her shoulders, and Heather wiped the soot from her eyes. The weary Damian walked toward them, joining the huddle. Hudson and T.J. held onto each other's shoulders and smiled. As they examined one another's disheveled appearance, they broke into congratulatory laughter.

"Who the hell are you people?" Heather said through her laughter.

"We don't know!" chuckled Damian.

"And, you have wings!" Heather shouted to Carson.

"The hell you say!" he said as he turned and looked at them.

"Hey," Heather said with sudden panic. "Where is Elizabeth?"

Damian was still trying to catch his breath. "Her...and the old guy...under the East bridge...ten blocks...thataway."

The loud rumbling of the Terratank could be heard for blocks. The team froze quietly listening to the sound, attempting to gauge its distance. The large military vehicle contained enough firepower to level a city block with ease. As it pulled square in front of the diner, Hudson backed away. "Guys…I think we need to go." Just then, the vehicle separated into war-mode, large guns spinning from its sides. "We need to go now!"

Damian snatched Hudson and T.J. and bolted from the rubble. Carson took Ellen and Heather into his stout arms and soared into the air just in time for the remains of the small diner to explode into flames. And as the diner burnt to the ground, they realized that together they had won their first battle.

TRIAL PERIOD

Heather was more open to being blindfolded than Hudson thought she would be. Not that she wasn't somewhat hesitant, but Hudson could tell that she was beginning to trust the group, at least on some level. This was probably due to the innate teamwork the group had displayed during the altercation at the diner. Once at the Core's location, the group exited the car, and Hudson and T.J. led her through the warehouse toward the elevator.

"I'm going to feel *so* stupid if you guys kill me," Heather said, holding her blindfold.

"You're fine, Ms. Isles," Hudson replied with a smile.

"But we are taking a bunch of goofy pictures of you to post to the net," Carson giggled.

Heather could sense the large freight elevator descending. The air became colder, refreshingly cleaner. The echoes that bounced from the surrounding walls told her that the area was large and spacious. Finally, Hudson undid her blindfold, and as the massive lights illuminated the Hub of the Core, Heather rubbed her eyes, unsure of what she was seeing. She stepped past them, taking all of it in, allowing it to process. It was amazing.

Ellen stepped around her, beaming. "Yeah…that's how I looked when I first saw all of this."

Heather walked down the steps to the main floor. "What is this place?"

"It's called the Core," Carson said, as the flopped down on the small couch.

"The what?" she asked.

HANA appeared next to her. "You must be Heather."

"Ahh!" Heather jumped back in defense.

"I apologize, Heather. I have gotten so used to these guys being around that I pop up here and there." HANA walked toward the center of the room.

"And who the hell are you? Okay, someone needs to explain some things," Heather said.

HANA and Hudson debriefed Heather, giving her much of the same information as the remainder of the team, though not quite all. They walked through the basics—how the Federation was formed, the rise of Keating, the alteration of the free world—all the technical points. There would be far more than that for her to absorb.

"Now, now… let's stop right there for a moment. I'm sure you have questions," Hudson said.

Heather's blank expression was obvious. "Ya' think? You're telling me that no one remembers this big ass alien dude because of tracker chips?" Heather asked, holding up her arm.

"That's right," Hudson said.

"If we can be tracked by these things, and we are on the world's Most Wanted list, why aren't there soldiers swooping in here right now?"

HANA looked to her. "The inner walls of the Core are sealed from the BSC tracking frequency."

"Uh huh," Heather said. "So, how are they not tracking you guys outside this place?"

"The ones we have are modified. It includes all required scan data, but none of the GPS ability or neuron suppression," Hudson said. "And if you stay with us, we'll give you one."

Heather sat there looking at all of them as if they each had three heads. She turned to Damian. "Do you buy all this bull?"

"Well, uh…" Damian began.

"Do you believe us?" T.J. asked.

"I believe *you* believe it. And that just means you're crazy. Trust me, no one can make this crap up," said Heather with a smirk. "So, okay…let's say all of this is gospel. There were all these super guys running around saving people and stuff, and this big alien guy came and tried to take over the world, and now the President is working to enslave the human race, and yadda, yadda…how does that fit in with us…with me?"

"I've been convinced that given enough time, I may be lucky enough to encounter superhumans again, those with the talents necessary to challenge the tyranny of Parliament," replied Hudson.

Heather giggled. "So…you want *me* to join a band of alleged superheroes in tights?"

"There aren't any tights…we asked," Damian corrected.

Carson shook his head. "Yeah, I ain't doing tights."

Heather rolled her eyes. "Okay, maybe it's a noble thing you're doing, brave, and so-forth, and I may be a little stupid, but not stupid enough to join a cult trying to overthrow the government. Thanks…but no thanks."

"It's not like that," Carson said. "We're not, like, trying to take over the world."

"Well, that's what it sounds like," Heather said. "So, you guys have fun. Good luck. And goodbye. Show me how to get out of this place. I'm not into this."

Hudson couldn't help but feel like someone so reluctant would only jeopardize their current situation. There was no way to hold Heather. The only choice was to let her go and hope that she would eventually come around. "And that's your choice, Ms. Isles, though

I regret it." Hudson turned to T.J. "Walk her out."

With disappointment, T.J. began to lead Heather away when Ellen yelled across the room. "Heather," Ellen said as she went to her side. "Before you go, can you come with me for a minute? Just a minute. Promise. Then you can go."

Heather looked at her. She cared little for whatever Ellen had to show her. She needed to get out of this place, get her life back on track, and figure out what she was going to do. But there was something about Ellen's face, something sincere. Heather huffed and then rolled her eyes. "What... *fine*. Hurry."

Ellen led her to the elevators and took Heather to the room in which she was staying. Ellen scanned her updated BSC to unlock the door. Heather sighed and followed her inside. The room was nice, cozy. It was like a studio apartment, complete with kitchenette and bathroom. "Have a seat."

"Look, princess, what do you want? Hurry up." Heather sat down in the chair.

Ellen walked to the small refrigerator and got them both a can of soda. She handed the cold can to Heather and took a seat on the couch across from her. Then Ellen took a deep breath. "Before you go, I want to tell you something...for two reasons: first, because I haven't told the guys; second, you're the first girl I've seen in ages." Ellen began twiddling her pendant as she sat back and took a breath. Heather sat there, a dismissive expression on her face, unmoved by Ellen's plight. "A while back...did you hear about the guy who died at that big computer company in Region H-70? Alemede?"

"No. I'm not one to follow the news," Heather said with a raised eyebrow. "I'm sure that shocks you."

"Well, I used to work there. I hadn't been there long...about two weeks or so. Things with me had been a weird for a few months. I guess my electricity thing was kicking off in some way. I was experiencing odd crap...like shorting out my hairdryer, my lamp, my cell phone. It sucked."

"Did you suspect it was you that was burning things out?" asked Heather.

176

Ellen deliberated for a moment. "No…not really. I mean, there were a few times I was like—*damn, I need to quit walking so fast across the carpet.*"

Heather giggled. "Right?"

"It wasn't obvious then. More subtle. My mom is dating this pervert of a drunk who used to be a big shot electrician, so I thought it was because of his, quote-end-quote, *repairs.* Anyway…I go to work and I am checking all these computer parts, these expensive Gene VDUs for HRV-EST. And… *pop*! I fry the whole batch. The foreman, gross old guy…he flips out, takes me to this press room to tell me I have to pay for the damage. He can take care of it if I do him *favors.*"

"Oh yeah, it's always the *favors*, right?" Heather growled. "Men are friggin' pigs. So, what did you do?"

Ellen took a drink of her soda. "I did him…right there on the floor."

Heather almost slid out of her seat. "Girl?!"

Ellen laughed. "What do you think I did? I told him hell no." Ellen's laugh subsided as her face went somber. "That's when he attacks me. He drags me over to the cooling bin, this big vat of nasty water, and starts dunking me in it."

"That son-of-a-bitch."

Ellen looked into Heather's eyes. "And that's when I killed him."

The air in the room froze. Heather looked at Ellen with a serious expression. "Like—for real—killed him?"

Ellen took a deep breath. "When he held me under the water, I don't know, I felt my body react. Then, it was too late. I ran huge volts through the man. I literally cooked him." Heather could see Ellen grow upset by the horrific memory. "I'll never forget the smell; it was God awful. It was like bleach. Have you ever got around a bunch of bleach and then you smell it for hours? That's what it was like." Ellen looked up at Heather, who actually seemed moved by the story. "And I never told a soul. Dr. Hudson knows, but we've never talked about it. This is the first time I've told anyone at all."

Heather's mind drew a blank. "That's heavy. I mean, in my time

I've seen a lot of stuff, but nothing like that."

"And that's what I'm doing here, Heather. I want to learn about what's happening. Master it. Then, I want to get my mom out of that hellhole and away from that alcoholic deadbeat forever. I'm done with my old life. Screw that. I need a new one. And this is it."

Heather sat back and smiled.

"Why are you smiling?"

"Girl…that is messed up," Heather said. "So, maybe you're not such a princess after all."

"No, I'm far from a princess," Ellen said as she took a sip of her drink.

Heather could see that Ellen was still very distressed by the ordeal. "Hey, girl, the guy asked for it. If it hadn't been you, it would have been someone else, and there ain't no telling how many other girls he would have gotten to beforehand. Trust me…I've dealt with perverts a lot!"

Ellen smiled and looked down, turning the cold can in her hand. "How did you make it so long on your own?"

"Well, like I said, I was trapped in hospitals for a while. When I broke out, I stayed at a halfway house for a few years. It was nasty, but it kept me safe."

"Did you have to…like…you know, with guys to get coin?"

"Hook?"

Ellen was a little embarrassed. "Yeah."

"One time I almost had to, but it never came to that." Heather leaned forward. "So, now I want tell *you* something…something that you won't believe." She paused for a moment before quietly saying, "I've never *been* with a guy." Heather couldn't understand why she was so open with Ellen, this girl she had known for mere hours. Even as the words were leaving her mouth her mind was saying, *Are you completely insane? Don't tell her that.* It was that connection that made her feel comfortable, the bizarre link the two girls shared, as if they had known each other forever.

"You're a *virgin?*" Ellen said in a tone of disbelief.

"Shut up! Listen…I've messed around. But *all* the way? Nope.

And I swear my hand to God if you tell the guys I'm not a *big old ho*, I'll be pissed off."

Ellen laughed. "Why do you want them to think you're a big old ho?"

"Keeps me looking tough...streetwise." Heather cocked her head. "Sister, I used to dream about doing something with my life, making this *grand statement*...one for the whole world to see. But you'll learn that half of life is *fake it till you make it*, honey." Heather snapped her fingers and sat back with a smile.

They laughed, and it was good to laugh, to have much needed girl-time. Ellen hadn't been able to relax like that since she had left school, and Heather had been cautious of other girls for so long it was refreshing to just sit with someone and talk. No competition, no ulterior motives.

"Why am I telling you all this?" Ellen said.

"I was sitting here thinking the same thing," Heather replied. "I don't know...it's like we've known each other somehow. Those guys, too. I'm not sure how, but I do."

Ellen sat back, looking at Heather. "Stay, Heather."

Heather sat back in the chair. "Ellen, girl, I don't know how to be no superhero."

"You looked like you were doing pretty good at the diner tonight."

Heather shook her head. "No, I mean I can use my power and all. But, I've had to watch out for just me for so long, I couldn't watch out for the world."

Ellen smiled. "Think of your sister."

"Do what?"

"Think of your sister. That's what I do with my mom. I picture my mom, and when I do it makes me want to...save her, I guess, save the world."

Heather pondered on that for a moment. It made sense. In reality, Lizzie was her motivation for most things. "That's not a bad idea."

"Works for me." The two of them sat in silence for a moment, not sure how to direct the conversation further. "Stay," Ellen said again.

"This is crazy."

"Stay…just for two weeks. After that, if you don't want to be here you can do whatever you want." Ellen could see that Heather was contemplating it. "Consider it lying low from the Canstanzas. It'll be like taking two weeks to hide out and figure out what you're going to do next."

Heather looked to her. "Why do you want me here so bad? Most girls think I'm a bitch. Don't you?"

"Without a doubt, I think you're a bitch," Ellen said with a hint of mockery. "But, it would be nice to have another girl here for a while. I like HANA, but though she can tell you what PMS is, she's never had it."

They laughed. Heather considered for a moment more. Sure, Ellen was right. It would give her somewhere to go for a while. She wasn't a prisoner. She could leave whenever she wanted. And she would get a place to stay, somewhere safe to shower, things to eat, and a brand new BSC, one that would prevent her from being monitored. Really, it was a win-win.

"Okay, princess, you got it. *Two weeks*, though. That's it."

MELTING

Keating met Colonel Arklow in Center Hall and together they walked to the set of Sub-Level elevators at the end of the corridor. Arklow held his thumb against the bioprint scanner to activate the lower-level subfloor access. Soon, they arrived at Bioscience Level 2. As the elevator doors opened, Keating saw the bustle of the technicians inside the laboratory. Arklow allowed Keating to step from the elevator first. A young tech saw the President and shifted into a short-lived panic mode. He alerted the doctor who ran to greet them.

Doctor Thomas bolted to the laboratory lobby. "Ms. President, Colonel, I am so sorry. I didn't think you were coming for another hour."

Keating stepped up to him. "Oh, calm down, Thomas. I've got things to do. Better to get this over with now." Thomas nodded in agreement and led them into the lab. "And according to your reports, the serum has been ready for a while now."

"Oh, it has!" Thomas confirmed. "And I think you'll be very

pleased with the results." Thomas led them to the lab station at the right side of the room. He motioned to one technician who handed him a small, silvery, computer-like device, about the size of a business card. "First, I would like to introduce you to the Xtron Z-33." He handed the Keating the module. "We've worked out the final kinks with the Xenathium secretion. We've also intensified the alpha waves, which should rectify any of the earlier defects we experienced with control." He led them to a cage sitting atop an observation table, which held a large white rat with a similar module attached to its head. Once the doctor activated the module, shiny metal webbing made from the alien toxin began growing from it, wrapping around the rodent's flesh. One technician fed data into the computer at the table, giving the rodent instructions to follow. "As you can see, unlike our earlier demonstrations, the subject is now under full control."

"Outstanding!" purred Keating.

"And now, if you will follow me," said Thomas.

They proceeded through the main lab to the surgical prep rooms at the rear of the corridor. Several small sterile operating rooms lined the left and right of the bright white hallway. Keating could hear a woman scream in the distance. Another man yelled in agony. In a room to her right, a half man/half dog creature ran about on all fours. As they entered the last room, Keating could see a young man sitting on a surgical table in the center of the lab.

Thomas turned to them, handing them special gloves and bio-protection masks. "Here, put these on. We're not going where the patient will be treated, but I don't like taking any chances." The three of them donned the protective gear and entered the observation area of the room. "Have a seat."

Keating and Arklow sat down as the lights inside the surgical room before them lit. Two nurses dressed in protective garb prepped the area. With the room sterilized, another nurse and doctor walked to the healthy young man. The doctor instructed the man to lie down and remain calm, and the nurse administered an injection that appeared to relax him.

"What are they giving him?" Arklow inquired.

"Sedative," Thomas answered.

Tension in the man's body began to subside, his muscles becoming weak and loose. Once the patient was sedated, they prepared the leather harnesses. They proceeded to strap the patient onto the table tightly.

"If he's sedated, why does he need to be secured?" Keating asked.

Thomas leaned to her. "You'll see."

The doctor walked to the patient's right arm and injected him with a syringe filled with a green liquid. They watched as dark green lines began to make their way through the man's veins. As the substance coursed through the man's body, his head fell to the right, his eyes opening. Keating saw that the patient's right eye had turned milk-white with a thin line of blood pooling at its base. What appeared to be thin slices and abrasions appeared over his face and traveled their way across his body. The nurses and the doctor stepped back to get to a safe distance. When the patient began to convulse, they left the room, sealing the door behind them. The flesh over ninety percent of the patient's face appeared to be rotting away, leaving putrid muscle and gelatinous skin exposed. Deep, festered lacerations now covered his entire body. Though what she witnessed was of her own design, for a second in time Keating felt as if she would be sick at the sight. The convulsions slowed as the man flat-lined.

"Dear God," Arklow exclaimed. "Is he dead?"

"Almost," Thomas said.

With a gurgling clamor, the patient liquefied into a puddle of ooze, dripping onto the floor of the surgical room. Arklow turned his head to avoid the gory sight.

Proud, Thomas turned to Keating. "The victim first experiences a loss of muscle function, which leads to paralysis. Their tissue structure becomes unstable leading to complete degeneration."

"This is insane!" Arklow spat. "We can't have people leaving Medical Resources and turning into puddles of puss in the streets! That man died in less than five minutes. We need something far more subtle."

Thomas shook his head. "Calm down, Colonel. The serum we use to suspend the virus can be adjusted to just about any timing release we want. All you have to do is let us know how long the virus is to remain dormant, and we will make it happen."

Keating smiled. "Thank you, Doctor." She stood and gathered her things. "We will get back with you on timing. I would like to have the final serum production-ready by this fall."

"That will be no issue," Thomas advised.

Keating and Arklow left the floor and proceeded to the elevator. "You don't look so good, Walter."

"That is the most disturbing thing I've ever seen."

"Oh, buck up, solider," Keating joked. "This is precisely what we need to rid ourselves of the Insurgence once and for all."

Arklow rubbed the sweat from his face. It was all too horrific. "Isn't there another way?"

"No, Walter, there is no *other way*. I don't want another way. I want this way."

The elevator doors opened, and they stepped back into Center Hall.

"There must be something else we can do. I don't know if I can go through with this, Ophelia."

"Sure you can, Walter. It isn't like you'll have to witness it."

"But all of those people..."

At that juncture, Keating's patience had reached its end. She spun to Arklow and pushed him against the far wall. She raised her hand to his throat, the tissue separating from around her mechanical fingers. The long, steel blade stretched from within her droid-like appendage and touched Arklow's neck.

"Listen...*Walter*...this is the plan, it's what we need to do. I've brought you this far because I pegged you for a man of integrity, guts! I can't afford loose ends. You know far too much to get off this rollercoaster, and I can only have those with a strong constitution along for the ride. The Summit *must* go without interruption. You don't have to visit these Regions; you don't have to witness the roaches die. These people have to be dealt with—once and for all. What did you think? We were just going to line them up and stuff them into Hold camps? It has to be this way. It has to be quick, and it has to be now. If you can handle that, wonderful." She leaned closer to him. "But trust me when I say, Walter, if you have any intention of becoming an obstacle for me or my goals, I will dispense of you in the most appallingly creative manner possible. Do I make myself clear?"

Arklow shook with fear. "Yes...yes, Ms. President."

Keating loosened her grip and stood back, straightening herself. Her hand transformed back into its normal state. She then leaned forward and straightened Arklow's jacket and tie. "There you are, now, Walter. Good as new." She winked at him and walked away leaving him to revel in the repulsion he had witnessed. Making her way up the main stairs and into her office, she touched the phone pad and dialed a number. As the speakerphone rang, she undid her jacket and draped it across the back of her chair.

"Hello?" said a woman's voice.

"Yes, may I speak to Cecelia Porter, please?" said Keating in her most professional tone.

There was hesitation. "And could I ask who is speaking?"

"Yes, this is President Ophelia Keating, calling to speak to her about her son. Is she available?"

"Yes! This is Cecelia! I thought that was your voice, Ms. President, but..." While the ecstatic voice droned on and on, Keating rolled her eyes.

"Yes, yes...Cecelia. I would like to talk with you about David. I have a particular interest in him. He would make a fine addition to a new...*task force* I'm putting together."

FINDING MR. PORTER

Heather not only found interest in her new world, she excelled at it. What took the the rest of the group weeks to learn, Heather mastered in around fourteen days. She had used her powers for so long that she was quite skilled at them. The history lessons weren't too fun, however, and she had all but refused to take any examinations. Still, she studied enough about this Tempera character to get by, and that was about all. Heather was comfortable in her skin and found no benefit from learning how someone else used a power she had to master the hard way. Ellen looked up to Heather Isles. She was rough, rugged, street-smart, and kept all that together in a sexy package that Ellen yearned to emulate. Heather taught her some tricks to mastering her powers, and Ellen showed Heather the ropes of the Core. In no time at all, the two girls were getting along quite well.

Ellen knocked on Heather's door. "Hey, open up...it's the Authority."

Heather opened the door with a smile. "Hey, girl. Hold on, let me hide all this weed."

"So, what'cha doing?" Ellen asked as she plopped into the chair. On the table in front of her were sheets and sheets of used sketch paper.

"Remodeling."

"Remodeling what?"

"Us," Heather said.

Ellen laughed. "What are you talking about?"

"Did you catch all those freaky costumes that the Feds used to wear?" Heather asked smiling.

"They weren't that bad, really," Ellen said.

"Whatever! And those names? If you think someone is gonna call me 'Tempera' you're crazy as hell. Sounds like Chinese food." Heather looked up and placed a hand over her heart. "Not to speak ill of the dead, Miss Tempera...love you, girl."

Ellen leaned back. "Well, then what did you think up?"

Heather handed her the sketchpad. "Back at the club I used to design all the outfits for the girls. It was my thing, I guess."

Ellen looked at Heather's updated design for the Tempera uniform. It was a very creative ensemble, elegant yet powerful. The sketched figure hovered in the air in a powerful pose, fire surrounding one hand, ice surrounding the other. The suit itself was brilliant white and crimson. Sleeveless, the suit wrapped up the neck, complete with red thigh-high boots. For homage, she had positioned the Federation emblem on the right lapel of the uniform. In the corner, Heather had tried out several names, but had circled one. "Celsius? Ask Ellen."

"I liked it. Not too girly, but not too in-your-face, either. Sexy."

Ellen smiled. "I love it. Make me one!"

'Turn the page," smiled Heather

Ellen flipped the page of the sketchpad to see what appeared to be her—her hair whipping about, hovering in mid-air, electrical beams covering her body. The suit was black and blue; a diagonal electrical bolt separated the two colors. Her outfit also had the Federation emblem, but covering the stomach of the uniform. Underneath the figure was the name *Kilowatt*. Ellen couldn't help but laugh. "That. Is. Hot! I love the name. Oh, my God, I couldn't pull that off. I'm not built for that."

"Girl, please. You're built fine. You could dance at the Flesh for sure…have those guys flipping out and tossing Centicoin all over the place." Heather snapped her fingers.

"What about the boys?" Ellen asked.

"I'm working on them. I'm not done yet. I haven't designed a lot of things for guys. They keep looking like drag queens."

Ellen flipped to other pages and saw outlines for a hero named *Velocity*, which would be Damian, and a beginning sketch for one named *Axillar*, which Ellen assumed would be Carson. "Velocity and Axillar? Those sound cool. Where did you get the name Axillar?"

"Axillary feathers are part of a bird's wing. I Googled it."

Ellen giggled. "That is awesome. The boys will flip out!"

"So, tell me…will you tell me?" Heather asked, leaning forward.

"Tell you what?" Ellen said with a smile.

"Which one of the guys do you think is the cutest?"

"Hmm," Ellen thought. "Carson is cute, but he's gay."

Heather snapped upright. "Shut the front door and eat the key! You're kidding me."

"No, Ma'am."

"That figures. Those wings were just too hot. My gaydar is usually dead on, though. How have I missed that over the past two weeks? Well…what about the fast guy?"

"Damian?"

"Yeah. He's too smart for me, though. He's the kind that would examine sex too much to do it right. Still, he's kind of cute."

"He is."

What then followed were several puns about "speed" and how that could "work against" Damian, followed by wild laughter. They continued to talk for well over an hour, comparing life stories, preferences, taste in clothes and guys, dancing dangerously close to veiled secrets.

"So, I wonder if the last guy is cute."

"What guy?" Heather asked.

"Well, so far we have everybody from the Federation but the strong guy…uh, the one they called Wrath." Ellen pictured his features. How tall would he be? Would he be able to wrestle a bear? "He may not even exist, though. Or maybe not yet."

"Or *he* could be a *she*," added Heather.

"True," conceded Ellen. "But what if he's a he and what if he's hot? I wonder if he'll, like, be able lift diesel trucks, jump over skyscrapers, catch bullets with his teeth…"

Catch bullets. Heather almost injured herself as she leapt straight to the floor. "Oh. My. God! How did I not remember that?"

"What?! Remember what?" called Ellen, growing concerned. "What's the matter?"

"That guy…oh…dammit! What was his name? This guy at the club!"

"Who?"

"How could I have forgotten about that? There was this…some guy there the night Flesh 84 was raided by the Canstanzas…he with a bunch of frat dudes. I saw him and, and, and it was just like when you guys walked into the diner the first night we met. He looked so freaking familiar! I didn't know what that feeling was like then, but…"

"What?" Ellen asked.

Heather took her hands. "I'm telling you…he's the strong guy… the last one of us. He has to be!"

Together, the girls bolted back to the Hub to tell the rest of the group. They busted through the main door, making T.J. leap out of his skin.

"Meats and cheeses!" T.J. shouted.

"It's him!" Heather said.

Damian and Carson looked up from their video game.

"What? Who?" Hudson asked.

"I know the guy, the strong guy. He was at the club that night. It was him. I…I…I brought him up on the stage with me right before Canstanza busted in. He, like, crushed this metal pole on stage, like, with his bare hands. That thing was solid!"

Hudson stepped to her. "Heather, you're not making any sense. What guy?"

"I remembered looking at that pole and thinking, wow this guy is on steroids or something. Then, after I killed Canstanza, they shot at me. And he, like, jumped right in front me to keep me from getting hurt. He should have been Swiss cheese, but he was fine! The dude wasn't even bleeding!"

"And why did you not think to bring this up before now?" smirked T.J.

"I don't know," Heather replied. "A lot happened that night, and...I don't know! I think maybe I thought they missed him or something. Then I ran out, and I met you guys, then the fight at the diner, then all this damn training..."

Hudson took her shoulders attempting to calm her down. "It's okay, Heather, just breathe."

"Can you remember what he looked like?" Carson asked.

"Uh...yeah...he was really, really tall, a big guy. Sandy-blonde hair," Heather added.

"Did you get his name?"

"Yes!" she said, taking Hudson by the hand with excitement. "David...David...uh...uh." A pained looked crossed her face. "Oh, I can't remember! But he said he goes to school at URU. And he's with some fraternity."

"Do you remember the name of it?" T.J. asked.

Heather rubbed her head. "No, he didn't say the name. But one of them was wearing a shirt with Greek-looking letters on it."

Hudson marched to Mainframe. "HANA, can you call up the Greek alphabet for us? Heather, come...look." HANA projected the Greek alphabet to the middle of the room. "Now, take a look at these letters and see if any of them stand out to you."

Heather searched her memory. It was so difficult to recall. "Um...it had the letter 'P' in it," she said, pointing to letter *Rho*. "And...I think this one." She pointed to the letter *Psi*. She continued to drill through the letters trying to remember the last one. The last letter seemed much like all the others.

"What did it look like?" Damian asked.

"I can't remember, dude!" she said. "Like the letter 'O', but that could be this one, this one, or this one," she finished, pointing to the letters *Theta*, *Omicron*, and *Phi*.

Hudson took her by the hand. "You are *dripping* in awesome, Ms. Isles."

Heather look confused. "But I didn't…"

"HANA, search for a fraternity on the United Regional University campus using the Greek letters Rho, Psi, Theta, Omicron, or Phi."

HANA scanned the Mainframe web. "I have three fraternities that match that description. Rho Theta Omicron, Theta Psi Phi, or Psi Rho Phi. All three have houses on campus."

"Can you find all the boys named *David* in those houses?"

"There are seven boys with the name of David in those fraternities." HANA read off the names as small thumbnails of their student IDs appeared on the monitor. "David R. Stellan, David W. Pierce, David W. Porter, David C. Rodriguez…"

Heather looked. "Yes! That's it! Porter! That's him, right there." She pointed to David's picture.

"Thank you, Ms. Isles!" Hudson said as he walked toward her, arms wide. "You've been a very," he kissed her cheek, "very," he kissed her other cheek, "wonderful asset. HANA, can we locate Mr. Porter?"

"I show he registered for fall semester today and…he accessed his student account to buy textbooks," HANA confirmed.

Hudson rubbed his chin. "We will need to track Mr. David Porter of URU's Psi Rho Phi house. Where is here right now?"

HANA searched. "Something's wrong. I can't lock on his BSC."

Hudson looked at her with interest. "What do you mean?" He walked to where she was standing.

"What wasn't clear about that statement?" HANA said mockingly. "I mean something is going on with the boy's BSC. It's blocked."

"By whom?"

"I'm not sure, but someone doesn't want us to find him."

Hudson thought for a moment. "She knows. Keating found out

who he was after the incident at Flesh 84."

"No, I don't think that's it." HANA added.

Hudson shook his head. "It has to be."

HANA looked at him. "Parliament has had the block on his BSC since he was *six years* old."

T.J. cocked his eyebrow. "Why would they block the BSC of a six year old?"

"And that, sir, is the question of the day," Hudson replied.

T.J. got up and grabbed his jacket. "Well, let's get to it then."

Hudson grabbed his arm. "Wait. Maybe it's not such a good idea to do anything tonight."

"Why wait?" Damian asked. "Let's recruit him and complete the set."

"Hey, I haven't signed anything, yet," Heather said.

"The twins found us at that diner, and they recognized Heather. If they knew Heather don't you think they may know who David is?"

"Then why haven't they taken him?" Carson asked.

"My guess? Bait," Hudson added. "They could be waiting for us. No, we need to be cautious about this one, guys." Hudson took a seat. "Trust me. No one wants to get to this guy as much as me. But we almost didn't make it out of that diner. They could be waiting for us as we speak." Hudson began chewing his pencil, his mind filtering through their options. "I'll go in the morning alone."

"Why alone?" asked T.J. sternly.

"If it is a trap, then it's best I be the one in danger."

"But, what if you're caught?" Ellen asked.

"Then, I guess I'll need heroes to come save me." Hudson winked.

T.J. took a seat. "Listen…if anyone is going, *I'm* going." He noticed the look Hudson was giving him. "And don't start on me, Andre. If something happened to you, who's going to lead these kids? Huh? So, end of discussion. No more on it. I'll wait until tomorrow. Then I'll bring the guy back here. We can give him the rundown, size him up, see if he's worth it, and then see if he's interested."

"Are you interested? Your two week trial is up." Hudson said, turning to Heather.

Heather looked up at them.

"She's staying." Ellen walked over to her. "You ain't going anywhere."

Heather shook her head and smiled. Where was she to go besides the Core? Her world had once again turned on a dime, but that was common. Nothing was ever simple in her life, and in many aspects, she liked it that way. Change was something to which she had grown accustomed. Who were these people? Would she be willing to give up the complete independence she had known? Or, rather, was that in fact loneliness? Within those doubts sprouted the curiosity of what it would be like to belong to something more, something bigger than herself. It would be interesting to try; she would never get the chance again.

"I must be out of my damn mind," Heather replied in concession. She saw the boys laugh and give each other high-fives. "And don't think I ain't getting one of those fine ass rooms, either. I want room service, and fresh towels, and some new clothes, and some..."

T.J. sat down beside Hudson and leaned close. "Man, how are we going to make it? We're too old for this," he said with a smile.

Hudson watched the kids gathering with one another, standing at the cusp of adventure. He hoped he was doing the right thing, the noble thing. If he was, if it was fate, destiny, so to speak, together they could save the world.

"I don't know about you," Hudson said with an endearing smile. "But I've missed this."

AN OPPORTUNITY

Blackwood didn't want to seem like a cop; better to look like a student. He may look like an older student, but his young guises could certainly pass for "twenty-something," and his thick beard hid the years on his face. He went for a more *hipster* appearance, the party guy. He pulled the tan knit beanie over his head and threw on thick-framed glasses. As T.J. stepped back from the mirror and gave himself a final glance, he nodded with a smile. "Yeah…I'm still hot." When he walked into the Hub, he heard whistles and a *woo-hoo* or two.

"Wow, T.J., you're pretty cute," Ellen said.

"Thank you, thank you," he replied.

Heather held her nose. "But what are you wearing? Is that cologne?"

"Patchouli," T.J. replied. "I thought it would make me…authentic."

Hudson entered the Hub, nose in a newspaper. "You smell like Willie Nelson's beard," he said without looking in T.J.'s direction.

Ellen smiled and patted his shoulder. "You smell fine, T.J."

Hudson sat back in the desk chair and folded the paper. "Okay… so, what's the plan?"

"I'm going to Psi Rho Phi house, like I'm looking to join. Then, once I find Porter I'll get him alone, give him the basics, and bring him here."

"And you'll do that by…knocking him out and tossing him in the trunk, I presume?" Hudson said.

"Don't be a smartass, Andre," T.J. said. "I'll improvise. I'll get him here. Don't worry." T.J. threw on his flannel jacket for added effect and picked up his keys. "According to his register schedule, his last class lets out around 3:00 PM. The campus is in Region I about three and a half hours away. I hope he'll come straight in from the lecture hall. If not, I may have to wait around."

Heather sat back on the couch. "So, if you get this guy, let me make a suggestion, okay? Maybe instead of running him over with superheroes and aliens, you can show him the news files HANA walked me through this morning. That was easier to process."

Hudson smiled. "Noted."

T.J. was unaware that David had skipped out of Biology. David's mind couldn't take sitting there for an hour listening to Professor Rollins monotone vocal resonance, which was as dry as toast buried in the Sahara. His head hurt, and he still didn't understand how to process the incident at Flesh 84. Apparently, the guys didn't quite know either. They hadn't said much to David in the past couple of weeks. Some of them seemed terrified of him. It was as if there was this huge elephant in the room, this strong, impenetrable pachyderm, and no one was going to acknowledge it was even there, least of all David. On the plus side, everyone seemed to go out of their way not to annoy him. William purchased a new bed without batting an eyelash, not even stopping to mention that David had punched through his other one. It was difficult not to notice that William had stayed with his girlfriend a lot more than usual. He could only assume that it was because William feared for his life. David had turned into a human wrecking ball—literally. Now that he was a menace, chaos sprang up in his path no matter which direction he took. He felt strange, studied, examined, as if he was being watched by a million people light years away.

As he drudged up the porch steps, he put the key in the door and turned it, but snapped the key in half with no effort at all. He looked up to the sky with a wounded expression. "Aw, come on!" He couldn't gauge the power sometimes, and it was getting worse. It seemed that the simplest touch could cause mass destruction. He didn't know who he was, or from where he had come. Maybe he was a real-life Superman, an alien sent to the quaint blue sphere called Earth by his birth parents to save him from his dying home world. *Yeah, who would believe a story like that*, he thought. It would still be the most plausible of explanations.

The front door popped open. Alex stuck his head out like a timid fawn. "Uh…hey, man," he said. "Had a little *boo boo* with the key, huh?"

"Yeah," David sighed.

"Oh, don't worry man, those keys are cheap." Alex opened the door.

David drug himself into the foyer to see an unusual sight. All the brothers gathered in the lounge of the house. "Am I missing a meeting?"

"Dave…my man…come on over here and sit down for spell, okie doke?" Charlie said as he took David by the arm and led him to a chair at the far end of the circle.

With an apprehensive expression coating his face, David took the seat. He studied the guys, watching their movements, trying to decide what was taking shape. It appeared to be an intervention. He raised up to better position his chair and noticed that four of the brothers jumped with a jolt. That's when it hit him. "You guys are about to pitch me out, aren't you?"

They looked at one another. Alex spoke up without hesitation. "Absolutely not, man," he said with confidence. "You're our bro."

Lenny leaned forward. "Psi Rho Phi sticks together, man. Right?"

"But…," began Alex. "We do need to talk to you."

"Okay," David said with an air of relief.

Alex took a deep breath and sat down across from David. "And we don't want to piss you off, dude." Various "nos" and "absolutely nots" sounded around the room.

"You won't piss me off, Alex. And if you do, it's cool. We get mad at each other. That's just the way it is. I won't flip out, attack you guys, or punch through William's…" David looked around the room. "Where's William?"

Alex looked at Lenny, then back to David. "Uh, Will withdrew from Psi Rho Phi this morning."

"Because of me, right?"

Alex looked at him. "Dave, what's going on?"

"Nothing, guys," said David, even though he realized what they meant. "Everything's fine."

"William's bed, bro…you shredded his bed," Lenny said. "And my electric razor you borrowed—the thing looks like you've been grinding concrete with it."

"And the refrigerator door," Phillip said. "My dad got us that, man, and you slammed the thing and bent the door down the middle."

"Now, I didn't slam it. I just shut it," clarified David.

"The railing on the stairs," someone else called.

"Agreed," Derek said.

"And the door to the dryer. Don't forget that," another said.

"And the stuff at Flesh 84," Alex said. The room went silent. That was the silver bullet, the incident that no one knew how to explain.

Alan leaned forward. "Man, they shot you. I mean…*blam*…shot you—a lot—and nothing—not a scratch."

"I told you they missed, guys. The shots went…"

"They shot you, David," Alex said firmly. "I was sitting right there. Those bullets shredded your shirt, but didn't leave a mark on you. They bounced off you like you were rubber."

David groaned. What was the use? There was no point in acting like something wasn't happening to him. "Guys…toI don't know what's wrong with me. I think I'm sick, a disease or something. I don't know my own strength. I don't..." Everyone grew quiet. David couldn't say anything more. Was there anything else left to say?

"Can you pick up the sofa?" Alan said with a smile. "I mean, like with the guys on it?"

David looked at him with amusement. "What? Are you serious?"

"No!" said Lenny who sat on the end of the sofa with four others.

"Yes! I am serious," Alan said. "Do it. I want to see you do it."

David chuckled and rose to his feet. "You're not serious."

"Man this is bullshit," laughed Alan.

David walked around to the back of the sofa, bent down, and took hold of the bottom. He scooted to the left to center himself. Then, as if he was lifting a bag of groceries, he boosted a reclining sofa with four grown men seated on it, which must have weighed a thousand pounds.

"Woah, woah!!" yelled Alan as David hoisted them into the air. "Dude! Dude, put us down."

"That is *stupid* brilliant," Alex said as he stood up, his face overshadowed with amazement.

David wasn't even breaking a sweat in lifting the group. He sat the guys down gently. Alan sprang from the couch, rubbing himself, like he was covered in bugs. "That is just creepy, man!"

Alex cheered. "I think it's excellent!"

"Agreed!" yelled Derek.

And so, for the next several hours the brothers made him lift almost every weighty object in the house. David held the oven up long enough for Derek to get his signature hacky sack from underneath, which Alex had "accidentally" lost. With the community car jack being out of commission, he could hold Lenny's Volkswagen up long enough for the tire to be changed. But most beneficial of all was the unleveled ground in the backyard. Using his bare fists, David broke up the uneven ground enough to level it for the long-awaited pool. And the brothers loved it. They were in absolute awe of David's power. What were small, yet amazing, chores to David made him feel more normal than he had in weeks. After all the attention, he began to feel that having these uncommon abilities might not be so bad after all.

Outside, T.J. pulled to a stop in front of the house. He studied it for a moment, looking for anything that would be suspicious, but there was nothing out of place. It appeared to be a normal fraternity house. He reached behind him, making sure he had his gun in case of anything unexpected. Placing his sunglasses on and fluffing his hipster beanie, he stepped from the car and made his way to the door.

The guys walked back into the house reeling from everything they had just seen. It had been miraculous. Lenny was determined that they would be rich. He had plans to enter David into every single Strong Man contest in the Region. He convinced himself that David would be the next wrestling champion of the world.

"Listen, guys," David said as he made his way to the sink. "I don't think we should tell a bunch of people about this, okay?"

"Man, why not?!" Lenny exclaimed. "You don't think the world is ready?"

"No, I don't think *I'm* ready, guys," he explained. "I can't handle this, yet. I need time to…figure this out."

Lenny sighed. "Fine…but you at least have to enter just one Strong Man contest. Just one!"

David laughed and turned on the sink to wash the thick mud from his hands.

"I swear," Alex said. "It's like you're some superhero."

"Agreed!" Derek said with a smile.

T.J. walked up the porch steps to the front door and knocked.

"Hey," called Alan as he looked out of the window. "Someone is here, guys." Alan went to answer the door, and a moment later yelled, "Yo, David! It's for you."

Frankly, David wasn't sure who would be asking for him. He dried his hands and walked into the lounge to see Alan standing there with none other than Dean Kidmon along with two young agents, male and female, dressed in pressed black suits and sunglasses. Two

Parliamental soldiers accompanied them.

"Uh, I'm David," he said. "Oh, hi, Dean Kidmon."

"David, we have very exciting news for you. This is Agent Harris and Agent Pike. They've come to speak with you personally!"

Snitch stepped forward and smiled. "Sorry we're late. We're running behind. How are you?"

David shook her hand. "Uh…Fine. Late for what?"

Snitch looked at Scoundrel concerned. "Did you not get a notification? A phone call or something?"

David chuckled. "No, what's this all about?"

Snitch smiled. "Well, Mr. Porter, the President is reaching out to gather young people to be part of an advisory task force who will plan the future of our world. Someone should have contacted you to let you know to expect us."

"No…no one called." David didn't believe a word of it. The girl seemed sincere enough, but something about her didn't seem right to him. "And I'm guessing that Parliament told my mom all about this, right?"

"Oh, yes. You can call her if you like?"

David continued to dry his hands, looking at Agent Harris with an untrusting gaze. "I think I will. Hold on just a second." He reached into his pocket and took out his cell phone. Then he noticed that he had several missed calls and three voicemails. They were all from his mother. He clicked the call button to redial her. "Mom? Hey…fine, and…yeah, sorry about that. I had my phone on vibrate and didn't even see it until now. I was just about to call you…"

"Guess who called this house?" his mother interrupted with nervous excitement.

"Uh, who, Mom?" David asked, though he already knew by the excitement in her voice.

"The President herself! Is that not crazy?"

"Yeah, that's what I wanted to talk to you about. There's people here who say they're supposed to take me to meet with the President."

His mother was overjoyed. "Yes! Is that not wonderful! I told you they were watching you, honey. Keating said she is driving you out today. She apologized for not calling sooner to get you ready. She wants you to be part of the new Youth Advisory Board of Parliament. Is that not wonderful?"

Not really, he thought. He had no idea what a Youth Advisory Board was. As far back as he could remember, government officials had been part of his family's life, so he was familiar with the drill. But there was something about these agents that was out of sorts, different, abnormal. He stepped into the hallway attempting to get out of earshot. "Mom, are you *sure* that was the President who called you?"

"Without a doubt! I'd recognize her voice anywhere."

Though he would never admit it to his mother, David had never cared to meet with the President; frankly, he wasn't a fan. He recalled going to Parliament when he was younger, and it was the most boring thing he had ever done in his life. Political fame was his mother's dream, not his. Yet, knowing how important notoriety was to her, how was he going to refuse the invitation? He hung up with his mother and turned to them.

"David, isn't this an exciting opportunity?" asked the Dean.

"Oh...yeah, yeah. And this...this is great. Can you guys come back in a couple of hours though? I have to get cleaned up and..."

"My apologies, Mr. Porter. I must insist that we leave now," Snitch said. "We are far behind schedule, and it will upset the President if we're not on time. There are facilities at Parliament House where you can freshen up when we get there—promise. After the meeting, we'll bring you straight back home."

David looked to the guys warily, then back to the agents. After a moment more of deliberation, he picked up his jacket. "I *will* be back tonight," he said to Alex.

The agents turned to leave taking David with them. "Oh, and one thing," Snitch said turning to the boys. "One of our Detectives may come by to pick up David. We've not been able to reach him to tell him we were picking him up instead." She gave a small, flat package to Alex. "Tell Detective Hudson we said we'll be in touch soon."

As they walked out of the door, Alex looked down at the package and saw one word written on the front: *Hacker.*

CRUMBLING

Three blocks away, T.J. continued to knock on the door until a young girl answered.

"Hey, there, can I help you?"

T.J. could see other girls in the house behind her. "Uh…yeah, I'm looking for Psi Rho Phi house?"

The girl laughed. "Oh, we are Psi Omega Phi." T.J. looked at her with confusion. "Don't worry; people do this all the time. Psi Rho Phi is at 2814 University Circle, and we are at 2814 *West* University *Avenue*. People get us confused a lot. They're just about three blocks that way, though. You don't have far to go."

As T.J. walked back to his car, he paused for a moment to allow a long, black limousine to cross the street. Little did he realize that David Porter had driven right under his nose. The guys at Phi Rho Psi weren't aware of much outside of what they had heard from the Agents and the Dean during the peculiar visit. However, it was obvious that they were fully aware of how special David had become.

"Any idea why these Agents would've been interested in David for this group they're creating?" T.J. asked.

"Yeah… David is, like, a super…" Lenny began before being ribbed by Alex.

"Dave is a special guy, Detective," Alex corrected. "His mom works for the government, so we think that's why." Alex looked at the package on the table. "They were weird, though. We could tell Dave thought so, too. Something wasn't right with the situation. Oh, and they gave us this for you. You're Detective Hudson, right?"

The mention of Hudson's name rattled T.J. to his core. Alex handed the small package over. "No, but he's my partner. I can deliver this." T.J. thanked the brothers for the information and left the house to begin his long drive back the Core.

"Hey, Detective," Alex called. T.J. turned around to him. "Listen…if there's anything we can do to make sure Dave doesn't get hurt, call us. He's our bro."

Derek nodded his head. "Agreed." It was a heartfelt statement that confirmed the brothers didn't trust the agents, the reasoning, or the situation.

T.J. said goodbye and got into the car. Before starting on his way, he pulled out his signal chaser, a small device used to find tracking and locator bugs, and scanned the package. Once it checked clean, he stuffed it under his coat and started on his way. His stomach was in knots the whole way back to Region H. He could hear Hudson's angry voice in his mind. He pulled into the lot and turned off the car. Sure enough, he was correct—Hudson was upset.

"What do you mean, someone picked him up? Who?" Hudson spat.

"See…I knew you'd be pissed. I don't know who *they* were, Andre. The guys just said that the Dean had shown up with these agents who wanted David for a special advisory panel with Parliament," T.J. said, growing impatient. "I have a feeling the guys suspected they were shady, though, that something wasn't right about them. Also, it's pretty obvious that they know about David's abilities."

"What? How?" Hudson asked.

"He's living in the house with the guys, I'm sure it's come out somehow, especially if David was scared of what was happening to him."

Hudson got up and began pacing steadily, back and forth. "Parliament got him."

BIT beeped and booped at Ellen. "Good point," she said to him.

"Why did they wait until now to pick him up?" Ellen said as BIT wiggled around her fingers.

"Maybe…they just figured out who he was," Carson said.

Damian shook his head. "That's plausible. We didn't realize who he was until now, correct?"

Hudson turned. "No, they've known. I feel it. They've been watching him for a while. It's something else—something we haven't figured out."

"And there's this," T.J. said. He reached into his satchel and pulled out the small package wrapped in brown paper. "The guys said the agents wanted them to give this package to a Detective *Hudson* if he showed up." Hudson slowly reached out. "I scanned it in the car; it's clean."

Hudson took the package and looked at the front. "Hacker?" He unwrapped the bundle to find a thin tablet, about four-by-four inches. The screen was glowing with the Parliamentary shield. "Shit…"

"What is it?" Heather asked as she stepped closer. The others followed her. As they gathered around Hudson, he turned on the tablet which began to play a prerecorded message.

"Hello, Dr. Hudson," said a voice.

"Is that the President?" Ellen asked with a flabbergasted tone.

"I guess I need not tell you who this is, do I?" the voice cooed with a sinister chuckle. "Oh…I would *love* to see your face at this very moment. You sitting there with the meta-children you've collected from your experiment, realizing the most important piece to your puzzle has slipped through your fingers. And, bravo, by the by…I admit I was impressed when I figured out what you accomplished, how the number one patsy of the Federation hid his identity all…these…years." A photo of the young sidekick, Hacker, shined on the tablet. "To be frank, I thought you were dead. I was surprised to learn that Hacker was none other than the prize-winning Dr. Andre Hudson, the man who had made many of my dreams a reality," she chortled. "That must really piss you off.

"At first I didn't understand how you did it. I pulled at my brain trying to figure out how these powerful human beings were rising once again to be a thorn in my ass. That's when I remembered our friend Mr. Porter. I've had my eye on David for quite a while." Photos of David when he was a young child appeared on the screen. "He came to my attention as a five-year-old. His mother, that vile, materialistic creature, was hell-bent on getting him enrolled in Granger House, one of the most prestigious preparatory school in this part of the world. That meant David had to go through a rigorous round of testing, which included DNA charting to make sure he was free of communicable diseases. It was during those routine examinations that we noticed how similar his genetic code was to Steve Sutherland; we saw the…*potential*…the boy possessed. But your little secret was still safe. I presumed that if the boy was growing with certain powers, he was doing so naturally. I didn't realize he was *invented* with intention."

Hudson felt the thick ball of shame swell in his stomach.

"Parliament has spent the past sixteen years monitoring Mr. Porter, waiting to see if he would become a threat. I took his revolting mother into the fold, made her think she was important to the structure of government, all so I could keep a close watch on him." The screen illuminated with Ellen's photo and the story of Alemede. "I didn't suspect something was amiss until Ms. Braxton murdered the lead foreman of Alemede." Next, Carson appeared. "Quinley confirmed my suspicions when his wings sprouted. And, by the way, tell him I enjoyed the jolt to Esterburg. That old fool is a jackass of the lowest stature." The social postings from the events at Flesh 84 appear ed. "When the whore from that skin club surfaced, I had to get to the bottom of things." Heather was not pleased about Keating's description of her. "Those old pains in my ass returned. It was too perfect, methodical. But it wasn't long before I found the common thread that connected all of these young people...*Region H-73*."

The shame steadily rose into Hudson's throat, choking him. It was the one piece of information he had withheld, Project Phoenix, and he was sure the revelation would cause the fragile binds of his young team to unravel. He could feel the eyes of the team locking onto him, targeting him.

"That's when it all made sense. You arranged to somehow be in contact with the bodies of the Federation. I'm not completely sure how, but it was you who corrupted all of our samples. And you kept the uncontaminated DNA strands for yourself. Since you knew the ins and outs of the HRV-EST program model, you fed those genes into the farm hoping that one day your gallant team would rise from the ashes. Bravo, Hudson—brilliant work. Though, putting them all into the same Regional batch established a detectable connection. It was the only flaw in your otherwise excellent plan, and it has led to your undoing.

"I had Mr. Porter picked up today so he could fulfill a lifelong dream of mine. As you may have suspected, my main goal for taking genetic code from the Federation was to create the perfect warrior, the supreme biological weapon, and now I have the means to reach that goal. I have developed a unique manner of ensuring that Mr. Porter will join my ranks, and once I have him recruited...I am sending him after *you*. I will have your own invention, the strongest being on the planet, rip you and your team apart, limb by limb." Keating gave one final laugh. "Well, I've rambled on enough, Hudson. Thank you for being such a...*good sport*."

With that, the tablet dissolved into dozens of tiny microbots which scattered and scampered around the floor.

"Get them, quick!" Hudson yelled.

The group stomped and crushed the little bots until they were nothing but bits of smoking circuitry on the floor. The silence grew thicker and thicker. Finally, Hudson turned to them and took a deep, labored breath. "I know what you're going to say, and..."

"Tell us about Project Phoenix...the truth," Ellen said as she placed BIT in her pocket, her voice stern.

Hudson got up and paced. He ran his hands through his hair and closed his eyes to give him courage. "Before the cremation of the Federation's bodies, Parliament ordered EST to take samples from each of the heroes for 'medicinal' purposes, to cure diseases, heal the world—all that nonsense. But I realized it was for something more malevolent than that. Aside from my work with The Federation, I moonlit as a young genetics tech at EST. I'd been living the double life of genetics guru and young sidekick for a while, so I arranged it to where I would be the one designated to take the samples from the team. I knew what the government would do with them, so I added chromosome-chain breakdown code to each sample leaving it healthy on the surface, but rendering the samples useless. Those are the ones I submitted to Parliament. The good batch, I kept. I wouldn't have made it out of the lab with what I had stolen. The only choice was to plant the real samples into the HRV-EST network hoping that one day the dominant genetic code of the superheroes would revive somehow during the genome selection process for reproduction. I grouped all the samples in the same region—H-73. At the time, it seemed like a good idea. I thought that way, should the plan work, I would have a way to track the genomes used and confirm the batch. Also, it would keep you closer to one another and not scattered around the planet."

"See...I knew it!" Damian said. "I told you guys! So, that's why our powers parallel the Federation's with such similarity." Damian turned to HANA. "It wasn't *freak* genetic chance that caused our powers at birth, or *fate*...you *intended* it. The genes you planted made us like them."

"Yes," Hudson said. "But you're not a perfect match. I mean, I've already seen abilities in you that differ from the Federation."

Carson leaned forward. "But we're not original. We're copies, right?" he said with a tone of frustration.

"No...not copies. You are each unique. Different. For example, your wings. Somehow, the bird compound in Bill Vogel's DNA mutated in you, leading to your advanced abilities. I never imagined something like that would occur. Also, Ms. Braxton's ability to communicate with technology. That's never been possible before. Your powers are different, more pure, and I suspect they will become stronger as time goes on. I wasn't trying to make perfect clones," answered Hudson. "I didn't *create* the sex of the child or the personality. The fact that you seem to genetically remember one another somehow is another odd side effect I hadn't expected, either. Instead of being born with functioning abilities, it's taken strong emotions, or traumatic events, to bring them to the forefront. I didn't know if you guys would look like the original Federation, or act like them." Hudson smirked at his egotism. "Hell, looking back, what would've happened if you had turned out to be criminals?" He looked at them with pleading eyes. "The world was going to need the Federation again, and you would be our only hope against a world that has indeed become a prison to the human race, ruled by Ophelia Keating. I believed…" He stopped and looked down in shame. "I thought what I was doing what was best…for the greater good."

Heather had been silent. Hudson realized early on that Project Phoenix would be more difficult for her to accept, especially knowing what she had gone through as a child, her loss, her sister. After her story in the diner, he dreaded telling her the truth more than anyone else in the group. And he was right to be apprehensive.

Heather stood up and walked around the room. Her anger hovered in the air, and everyone could sense it. "And you asked nobody," she said flatly. She turned to Hudson, who had a hard time looking at her. "You didn't ask a soul. And now, on top of all that, there could be this freaky-strong, invincible maniac roaming the streets?" She stepped forward angrily. "See…that's what wrong here. You took power like this and threw it out there like an idiot, threw it up in the air just to see where it would land. You didn't even think about how it may screw up a kid's life, did you?" She walked toward Hudson. "That's the problem with all you science types. You think because you *can*, you should. Well, what if I don't want to be a freaking superhero? Huh? Can you take it back?" She stopped in front of him. "If I asked you tonight to take it away, could you?"

Hudson groaned. "No, Ms. Isles, I could not."

"Of course, not. No, because that could fix your mistake, correct what you've done. You doctors never think about that, do you? You do whatever you please, whenever, and you don't think of anyone. To you, we're all idiots, stupid animals who don't understand what's best for us."

"Heather, I realize how this must be for you," T.J. said, trying to add logic. "Try to understand what Hudson was trying to do here, what we are trying to save."

"You guys had your chance to save everything, and you failed!" she yelled. "And…what, you think you get a do-over? And you sure as hell don't get to say you 'understand' how I feel about anything. My family threw me away. Away! I almost killed my sister. My dad, who still doesn't acknowledge I exist, took me to a priest thinking I was possessed. How dare you act like you understand how any of us feel!" The tears rolled down Heather's face, which only added to her fury. For a split second, she raised her hand to Hudson, her fingers shining with heat.

"Heather, don't!" Ellen said.

Heather stood there, staring into Hudson's eyes. She considered setting him ablaze, but she couldn't bring herself to do such a thing. She was angry, but she wasn't immoral. The most disheartening part was that he didn't flinch or move to protect himself in any way. His eyes looked into her heart, begging to be set free, weary, tired, almost as if he wanted to be put out of his misery. She lowered her hand. "Screw this. I don't want to be in your freak club anymore. None of us should. I'm getting the hell outta here."

Heather turned on her heel and walked out of the Hub. Hudson couldn't bring himself to look at the others, who soon followed Heather out of the room, shaking their heads with disappointment and shame. No one said a word for what seemed like an eternity, not even HANA.

T.J. walked to him and laid an understanding hand on his

shoulder. "They were out of line, Andre."

"No," Hudson corrected. "They were not out of line. They were right. Absolutely right. The shitty part is, man, I wouldn't do something like that today. I couldn't. If I knew then what I know now…the person I am this very second…I would have seen how this would be the disaster it's turned out to be. Heather was right, too. I did it because I could, because I was guilty, not because it needed to be done, and I ruined the lives of those kids, all of their lives." Hudson got up and picked up his jacket.

"Where are you going?" asked T.J.

"I don't know. I don't care."

HANA stepped forward. "If they leave, they leave knowing where the Core is."

Hudson walked to the elevator. "Without them we don't need this place, anyway."

FRANKENSTEIN

As promised, they gave David the opportunity to tend to himself once they had reached Parliament House. Once they left the frat house, the girl known as Agent Harris called Keating let her know David was in the car, and they were on their way to Parliament. As they traveled to the Capital, no one had said a word. It was the most boring drive David had ever taken, and he had driven from coast to coast with his parents. Nevertheless, he was happy to be out of that limo and alone to gather his thoughts.

Something about the whole ordeal didn't seem right to him. It seemed arranged, rehearsed, anomalous. And those two agents— there was something about those freaks that made little sense. They were strange, and they smelled funny, an odd scent he had never before noticed. He wanted to text message the guys to say he was there, but his phone hadn't been able to connect since he entered the limousine. Regardless, it would be over soon. He would go in, listen to the craziness that was about to be shoveled down his throat, and then smile and wave goodbye. His mother would be happy, and he could get back to school to figure out what he should do to understand the abilities he now possessed. Maybe he would take Lenny up on the offer to enter a few contests. It would be a new adventure for free.

There was a knock at the door. "Mr. Porter, the President will see you now," said the voice of Agent Pike.

David rolled his eyes, wiped his face, and then walked through the restroom door. He followed the Agent to the lower end of a large, white hall, which was impeccable. *How could someone have so much white and none of it be dusty or stained? What am I going to eat when I got home? What time will I get home? Will I be able to skip a class or two in the morning?* As they led him to the large office, random questions filled his mind. When Parliament was the White House, they called the room the Oval Office. Seeing it in person, he could understand why it would have had such a name.

He took a seat and sat there patting his leg, waiting on Keating to grace him with her presence. He wondered if she looked the same in person. She had always looked so stern to him on television, so rigid. As Keating entered the huge double doors, David noticed she looked even harsher in person. Mustering all the sincerity he could find, he stood, smiled, and held out his hand. "Hello there."

"David Porter!" Keating cooed as she rushed forward, taking him by his huge shoulders. "It is so nice to meet you in person at last. I am so pleased. Did you have a good drive?"

"Affirmative," David replied.

Keating turned to him with an odd expression. The word reminded her of someone from her past, someone who had died long ago. "How *martial* you sound, Mr. Porter. I like that. Please pour yourself a drink and have a seat. I would like to have a little chat with you, a conversation I think you will find most interesting."

David got up and prepared a small drink and took his seat. "My Mom is super-excited about me being here."

"And she should be!" Keating said with a smile. "She should be proud. I would be if you were my son." She leaned forward and picked up a pen from the desk. Then she opened a file and shuffled through papers. "David, dear, I wanted to talk with you, because I think you can help me."

"Affir...I mean, yeah. The agents said that you are putting together a new advisory board, right? For youth?"

Keating smiled. "Well, somewhat, but not quite. I'm afraid it's a little more focused than that." Keating got up, walked around to the front of the desk, and took a seat across from David. "We have a growing concern here at Parliament, David. We have cause to suspect that a man is trying to organize an uprising, a mutiny, if you will."

"A mutiny? For what?"

"To take over our world," she answered. David gave her an odd look. "Let me show you something." Keating waved her hand at the adjacent screen on the wall. Pictures and information filled the display. "I want to show you some pictures, and I would like to know if you have ever met any of these people, if they have ever approached you. Okay?"

"Sure."

She called up a picture of Hudson. "This man is known as Dr. Andre Hudson, the ring leader of a terrorist organization. He has a band of specialized soldiers he is organizing in an attempt to overthrow the Parliamental board. He is intelligent and extremely dangerous."

Though the man looked somewhat familiar, David shook his head. "No...I don't think I've ever met the guy."

"Good," she said smiling. "Next, we have Ellen Braxton specializing in technology and electronics, a keen programming expert. We expect that she has attempted to hack into our secured systems on numerous occasions."

"Hmm... no... don't know her, either."

"What about this young man? His name is Damian Gunner. Weapons expert?"

"No, Ma'am."

"Carson Quinley, aviation specialist and engineer. He is their lead technician. Ring any bells?"

"He doesn't ring any bells, Ms. President. He seems a little familiar. Probably because he looks a lot like my cousin, though."

Keating took no amusement from the comment. "Heather Isles, trained assassin."

When David saw Heather's picture, he froze in place. It was then he realized that his suspicions were true. If Keating expected him to believe the young dancer he had met at Flesh 84, the one whose life he had saved, was an assassin trying to take over the world, she had another thing coming. He had seen this girl, looked into her eyes, and he had known her, somehow, once upon a time.

Keating continued. "Ms. Isles has killed multiple Parliamental officials and is one of the main threats to our way of life." She turned and looked to David waiting on him to say he didn't recognize Heather.

David hesitated for a brief second. "No…I've not seen her before."

Keating gave him an intrigued squint. "So, you've never met this woman face to face?"

David swallowed. "No."

Keating stood up and walked to the back of the large desk in the middle of the room. David could sense that she didn't believe a word of what he had just told her. He had completely lost his ability to lie some time ago. He felt threatened, in danger.

"David…are you certain you have never seen that girl? Something about your response…I don't know…it leads me to think you may not be telling me the truth."

"Well," David began, as his mind raced. "Well, you're right," he said with a sigh. "A few months ago, me and some of my frat brothers went out for my birthday. We went to this club…"

"What type of club, David?"

"It…it was an *adult* club. I think the girl in that picture worked there," he said feigning shame. "I'd appreciate it if you wouldn't mention it to my mother. She doesn't really understand things like that. I didn't wake up this morning thinking I'd be telling the President that I've been to strip bars."

The lie seemed to fool Keating. It was reasonable. It was even true in a sense. Keating smiled and took the seat at her desk. "Well, we're only young once, right, Mr. Porter?"

"Right!" he said with a wide smile. "So…what would you like for me to do? Since I've never met these guys, I'm not going to be much help, right?"

"I would like for you to find these people for us, David. You are young, trustworthy, they will believe in you. Then, you can relay that intelligence back. We have to stop them, David. Our lives depend on it."

No, his mind exclaimed. *No, I don't trust this at all.* "President Keating… listen, I'm so, so honored that you thought of me for this; really I am. But, I've not done *spy* work before." Agents Harris and Pike enter the room dressed more casually than the suits they had worn earlier. "I haven't had training for anything like that, you know? I'm sure you guys have someone who is better suited for something so important."

Keating said nothing at first, though she obviously wasn't pleased with his resistance. She circled around the desk and leaned against the front of it as the two agents took their places in each corner behind her. She pointed to one of the display cases scattered about the room. "Do you see that artifact, Mr. Porter?"

It looked like a long, pewter object. It was triangular, about twenty inches long, and came to a point at the far end. Along each of its three sides were odd symbols etched in the metal. There was something familiar about it, the markings in particular, like he had seen it somewhere, perhaps in a photo. He had a sudden flash to his strange dream, the surrounding fire, and the hole he had punched in William's bedframe. "Yeah," he said. "Nice. What is it?"

"It's a relic, a weapon from a great war."

"You mean like World War III?"

"Something like that," she said with a smile. "It's coated with a very special and rare toxin. It's called Xenathium. Have you ever heard of it?"

"Uh, no," David replied, his nerves rising. He didn't understand why he was growing so frightened, why he wanted to be home, anywhere, as long as he was far away from Parliament.

Keating walked over and touched the case. The agents made their way to the other end of the room. "It belonged to a great warrior I knew once. It's the only one of its kind, the only weapon like it on our planet." She turned to him. "And, coincidentally, the only thing that can *kill you*."

David looked up in surprise. "What?"

"Yes, Mr. Porter. I know all about your little gifts, your talents. I've always known about them."

David gave her an insolent stare and stood, but there was a sudden, intense pain in his right temple. Agent Harris held the object against David's head allowing it to take hold. Complex arms extended from the small device and latched onto David's face, allowing the Xenathium toxin to break down his skin just enough to enter his body. It felt as if it was boring into David's skull. He fell back into the chair, unable to move. His body was rigid all over, petrified. "*What... are... you... doing to me?*"

"The contraption we fitted you with is a little invention we perfected just this week, Mr. Porter. It's called the Xtron Z-33, a synapse modification device." Keating went and knelt down beside him. David writhed and squirmed against the control of the device. "You see, most mind control can be achieved by drilling through the skull into the neuropathway. Although, that trick wouldn't work with someone as special as you. I know who you *really* are—invincible David Porter, strongest man on the planet. We wouldn't be able to break the surface of your skin, let alone drill into that pretty little head of yours. So, I had to achieve the same level of control without direct neuron connectivity." She leaned closer to him. "Oh, I've watched you for years, boy, waiting on your powers to come to light." She rubbed the sweat from his cheek. "And now I have you, my perfect weapon."

"Should we start the homing bots now?" Snitch asked, making her way to Keating's side.

"Yes," replied Keating as she rose. She patted David on his head like a good dog and walked away.

Snitch accessed the monitor and touched the screen. "Initiate homing sequence Q21-816." The words *sequence initiated* appeared on the lower left-hand part of the monitor. A map of the larger Region appeared on the screen. Various red dots searched for a target location.

Keating heard David groan as he continued to fight against the device. She looked at him and rolled her eyes as she took a seat at the desk. "Oh, stop being so dramatic, Mr. Porter. It will all be over soon." She sat back, pleased with the progress, and watched as David's blue eyes faded into white orbs of nothingness, empty, lifeless. Silvery veins appeared across his flesh as the apparatus took final effect. Sluggishly, her new creation stood. "What is your name?"

"Xtron 5460887," replied her creation in a multi-layered robotic tone.

"Upload his targets," Keating instructed.

Scoundrel walked to David's side and plugged a USB connector to the device on his skull, uploading the data to his imprisoned mind. "Done."

"Now," Keating said. "Let's see how well Dr. Hudson and his children fair against my unconventional *Frankenstein*."

CYBORG

The east bridge was Hudson's safe place, his sanctuary. During his time with the ACE Gang, the bridge was a very effective hiding place he used to avert the Authoritans and agents. In his special hiding place under the old abandoned bridge, he simply couldn't be found. It had been abandoned for eons, however. Its structure was so unsound that even stray dogs shied away from it, but that mattered little to Hudson in his present state. He located his "office," as he used to call it. Dry mud from the torrential rains caked the floor. Beyond that, most of the area remained intact. He sat down at the decrepit desk and took a deep breath before he sank deeper into his ocean of self-pity.

That terrible day, the beginning of the end, Steve was sitting on the desk waiting for him.

"I knew you would be here, Hacker," Steve said. Hudson said nothing. He couldn't even look in Steve's direction. He turned to leave. "Andre...wait...wait, okay?"

"What, Steve?"

"I believe we need to talk."

Hudson turned to him. "And what is there to talk about?" he
choked. "I know what you'll say, Steve."

"It's not your fault."

"But it is, it *is* my fault," Hudson said as he kicked the chair. "I
shouldn't have told her a damn thing…it was none of her business."

Steve leaned forward. "She was going to be your wife, Andre. It
wasn't like you had only known this woman a week…you had been
in a relationship for over a year."

"But *you* didn't trust her. You saw through her."

"Because I wasn't in love with her. You were."

"And that makes it okay?"

Steve scratched his newly grown beard as he stood upright. He
looked weary. With Vickie gone, Hudson realized Steve had nothing
left. Besides Steve, she was the last of Federation, and, to him, the
most important member. The grief coated his face like war paint, a
symbol of his pain, agony that Hudson believed he himself had
caused.

Steve walked toward the broken wall, peering into the night. "I
would've told Vickie."

"What?"

"I would've told her…everything. I did tell her everything," Steve
said. "If you loved Nancy like I loved Vickie, how could I be angry
with you? It means…you were blinded by what you felt. And who
hasn't been?"

A tear welled in Hudson's eye. "I killed her, Steve." It was too
much to hold back. The dam broke. The grief rushed over Hudson
as he sobbed. "I killed them all. Every one of them." Hudson felt
Steve's arm wrap around his shoulder.

"You killed no one, Andre. You loved those guys."

"It was me," Hudson sobbed. "I killed them. I could have run
the knives in their backs myself." Hudson put his arm around Steve,
his head falling into Steve's chest.

"You didn't kill them, Andre. And…whatever you think you've
done…I forgive you." Steve patted his young apprentice's back.
"I've got a plan."

Hudson leaned back, wiping his eyes. "What? What plan?"

"It's time we go underground, Andre, make Goliaric think he's bested me, like I've run away. Then, when he's confident he's won, I'll have him."

"But, he'll kill you," Hudson said.

"Maybe...maybe not." Steve walked away and stood at the wall again. "The Federation took an oath a long time ago that we would never kill for the sake of killing. Arrest, detain, sure...never kill. Killing made us no better than the scum we fought. But...we've moved beyond that now. I've got one chance, and I won't accomplish anything by just handcuffing Xenozians. They have to be exterminated once and for all."

"You can't do it, Steve. You'll die," Hudson said. "They know you can be affected by the toxin."

"If so, that's okay, Andre. Someone has to give everything. And it's all I have left." He walked back over to Hudson. "And listen; you have to find a way to stop Ophelia. She has plans for the world, big plans. With no Goliaric, and no Federation, she'll have nothing to stop her. She'll try to take over. That's why she had President Collins assassinated. And if she can arrange for the President of the United States to be murdered with no one batting an eye, she has far more influence than we thought."

Hudson looked up at him. "And how do you stop someone who can kill a President?"

Steve turned to him and patted his shoulder. "You'll think of something, Hacker. You always do." With that, Steve walked over to the desk and picked up his baseball cap. After he placed it on his head, he walked back to Hudson and hugged him. "I love you, little brother," he said. And then the hero made his way into the rainy night.

It was the last time Hudson ever saw him alive.

Hudson wiped the stinging tear from his left eye and tried his best to pull himself out of the painful memories. He wondered what was happening at the Core. Whatever it was, he was certain it involved heated conversation. He had given the kids plenty to discuss; that was for sure.

"What are you doing?" asked Damian.

Heather marched about her room gathering her belongings, throwing them onto the bed. "Getting my crap together."

"For?"

"What's it look like? I'm getting the hell out of here. I'm done. Through!"

"So, that's it, then?"

Heather turned to Damian, a look of anger across her face. "Look, dude, I like you guys. I do. But sometimes you can be a little naïve."

"I'm not naïve," Damian said.

Heather looked at him. "What does your dad do?"

"He's a dentist."

"Your mom?"

"She manages a bank."

"Do you have any brothers or sisters?"

Damian looked at her with a strange expression. "No, but I don't…"

Heather sat down beside him and patted his knee. "Sweetness, your parents are both big-shot professionals, which means you've never been broke. You've never had to share anything with brothers or sisters. And you're going to one of the best universities in the Region." She touched his shirt. "I bet that shirt cost more than my whole wardrobe. Trust me, you're naïve. Look around you, honey. This is all a lie."

It was true; Damian didn't have much in common with the others. He didn't live in the lower Region like Ellen, he didn't lose his father like Carson, nor did he live on the streets like Heather. But he understood what it was like to be afraid.

"Okay, you're right, Heather. I've not been through the things you and the others have endured. But you inaccurately assume that I have this…this *perfect* life, and that's where you're wrong. I've never had a choice…in *anything*. My parents have always decided what I wear, what sports I play, what school I go to, who I hang out with, what career I'll have. I've not had a say in my life at all, not one time." Damian looked to the floor with humiliation. "I was fortunate enough to have a few good friends in my childhood years. My mom didn't find them agreeable, though. They weren't…*proper* enough, significant enough. She said she had to settle for 'trashy friends' when she was a girl in Japan, but I didn't. But my friends weren't trash. I liked them." He turned to Heather. "When I was turning ten, I wanted a birthday party. Normal, right? My mom agreed, and I couldn't wait to tell my friends about it. So, when my birthday rolled around, I was so enthusiastic about it. I ran home after school, and when I walked down to our den to join the party, I noticed I wasn't familiar with any of the kids sitting at the table around my cake. That's when my mom told me she had invited *new* friends for me, 'better' ones. One of them told me she had even paid them to be there."

Heather wasn't certain how to respond to his story. Noticing his eyes glistening with tears, she patted his shoulder. "Did they at least bring good presents?"

Damian giggled before he could help himself. "I fail to find the humor in such a crass statement…bitch." The two of them laughed as he wiped the moisture from his eyes.

"Ha! Oh, my God, you're awful!" Heather giggled.

Damian looked at her. "Look…you're right about this place, but does it have to be?"

"Be what?" Heather asked impatiently.

"A lie. Why can't we make it what we want?"

"Right," said Carson as he stepped into the room.

Heather rolled her eyes. "Oh, now, don't you start." She stood up and threw a wad of her clothes into her duffle bag. "This has all been nuts. I don't even know what I was thinking."

"The same thing we were all thinking," Damian said. "How great it would be to be a superhero. I know I was." He picked up her sketchbook and thumbed through it.

Heather scoffed. "What a crock of… It's just not fair."

"So, what do we all do now?" Ellen asked as she stepped around the corner of Heather's door.

"I guess I'll start over, like I always do," Heather said. "I'm good at that."

"I'm not," Carson said. "I'm not sure what Lisa and I will do now. Maybe we can sell the air field and move to another region somewhere. Who knows?"

"I get to go back to the humdrum life of a Chemistry major," Damian said. "On the bright side, I can shake test tubes so fast that I'm my own centrifuge."

Ellen smiled as she fell back onto the other end of the sofa. "You're such a jackass, Gunner." She pulled her long hair into a ponytail. "I guess I'll stay here."

"What?" Heather said. "Why?"

"I have nowhere else to go."

"Well…come with me, then, gal," Heather said. "We'll figure something out."

Ellen smiled. "I wouldn't make a good dancer."

"We don't have to dance, we can do whatever we…"

Taking the sketchbook from Damian, Carson said, "So, what has you more pissed, Heather. That we were lied to…" He held up the sketch she had made of herself as Celsius. "Or that you don't get to be her?"

Heather looked at the sketch, realizing Carson was correct. She had gotten used to the fact that they would be superheroes, saviors. For the first time, she had the opportunity to be something more than who she was, to belong to something bigger, and the chance now ran through her fingers like sand. She sighed, fell face-first onto the bed, and screamed into her mattress. "Yes! It pisses me off! It sounded so cool."

Ellen took the sketchbook, turning to the page where Heather had sketched a revised version of the old Federation emblem. "We still belong to something, guys." She stood up and walked to the front of the room. "So what? So, Hudson didn't tell us about

Phoenix. Does it matter? Does it matter how we came into the powers?"

"Not to me," Damian said.

Ellen looked to Heather. "Ask yourself...does it matter where you got your power from? We've all dreamed of this, everyone has at one point or another in their life. We can now take that dream and make it ours—for real. Wouldn't you like to use these powers to help the world regardless of how we got them?"

Heather beamed. "You go on with your dream, Martha Luther King."

"Revolution!" Carson cheered.

Heather noticed the serious expression on Ellen's face and rolled her eyes. "Okay. Yeah, yeah, I'd like to help the world."

"What about you?" Ellen asked Carson.

"You don't have to ask me," Carson said. "I'm ready to roll."

Damian smiled. "So, what's next, *Kilowatt?*"

Ellen grinned. "Well, first we need to get HANA and T.J. up to speed. We'll tell them that the Federation is staying." Ellen picked up the sketchbook and looked to Heather with a smile. "And there's an Armory around here somewhere. We could try to build these designs?"

Heather smiled.

At that moment, they felt the strange rumble under their feet.

"What was that?" Damian asked.

The roar then rattled up the walls, shifting the pictures that hung along them.

"Something's wrong," Ellen said. "We need to..."

A thunderous boom sounded throughout the area. Red emergency lights switched on as they all ran from Heather's room. As they rushed to the Hub, their eyes couldn't process what they were seeing. T.J. hid behind a large steel table exchanging heavy gunfire with at least a dozen Parliament soldiers. A thick fog of smoke poured from the camouflage canisters the soldiers used to hide their location.

"What the hell?!" yelled Carson.

"How did they get in here?" Ellen screamed, as they took shelter against the entryway.

"Better yet…how did they even find this place?" Heather added.

Like a shot, Damian ran through the area, assessing what they faced. He returned in an instant. "We have thirteen…" T.J. took down another soldier. "*Twelve* soldiers—heavily armed. They've used something heavy to break through the foundation at the elevator so they could get inside."

Carson pulled off his shirt, allowing his wide wings to expand. "Can we take them?"

"Twelve?" Heather said. "Oh, we can try it."

"You look for any excuse to pull that shirt off, don't you," Ellen added.

The new Federation flooded the war zone. Damian took two soldiers out before they even realized what was upon them. He zipped through the area so fast he was nearly invisible. As everyone in the room froze in time, Damian stepped between the two soldiers and armed them with their own Taser Batons. He touched the end of each baton to the steel-lined helmets the soldiers wore. After he had pressed their fingers down on the triggers, he zoomed away. As he slowed to normal velocity, he saw the high charge from the tasers knock the two soldiers backwards, tossing them to the ground, unconscious.

T.J. looked up from behind the table to see the young team coming to the rescue. With a huge smile, he yelled, "About time!"

Carson soared high into the air. He spread his wings wide and flapped them with force, pushing the smoke from the room, allowing them to get a better view of the soldiers who remained. One soldier pulled his rifle, took aim at Carson's chest, and fired multiple rounds. Carson's eyes illuminated a vivid white light as he lifted his hand forward, stopping the bullets mere inches from his body. "Not today," Carson commanded in a multi-toned vocal. He lifted the soldier into the air, throwing him to the side with ease.

Heather ran forward with all the might she could muster while her hands bursted into thick flames. The force propelled her forward, throwing her into two of the soldiers. Both the soldiers and Heather fought to get to their feet as another adversary fired an Annex Net at her. She tumbled to the ground as the wire net swung around her body, binding her in place. The more she fought against the net, the tighter and tighter it became, cutting into her flesh. With both pain and fury, she screamed, pulling against the wire. As she did so, her hands turned a shade of brilliant red, sweat pouring from her body. With a fierce blast, her palms mutated into a solid red flame, melting the netting from around her. She then reached forward and took the soldiers by their helmets, melting the gear to their skulls. The men fell to the floor, writhing in agony.

Ellen was holding four of the soldiers at bay at the far end of the room. As she marched forward, sparks crackled from her feet. She opened her arms and turned her hands palm-up, blue static dancing around her fingertips. Fear overtook the troops as Ellen's eyes began to shine with a bright, electric blue radiance. In chorus, they unloaded their rifles at her, shooting dozens of rounds toward her. She easily deflected the bullets by holding her hands forward, the metal bullets bouncing away from the magnetic pulse of the energy. She stretched her hands forward and lifted the men high into the air as they yelled in fear. As Ellen tossed the men upward and out of the complex, the true threat dropped from the ceiling, landing with a rumble onto the ground.

T.J. stepped from his hiding place to get a full view of the sight. Carson floated behind T.J.'s shoulder as Damian joined them. "What. The hell. Is that?" T.J. said, his mouth hanging open.

The thing appeared to be mostly human. It stood a towering six-foot five inches tall with wide shoulders. The thick arms flexed as it clinched its bulky hands. Its eyes pulsed with a silvery light. The glow moved back and forth between its eye sockets, as if it was processing the surrounding data. Attached to the right side of its head was a peculiar gadget. Circuitry webbed down its face, growing thicker as it extended down the neck. Chrome-like steel covered its right arm, and small veins of shimmering lights moved around the metallic flesh of the cyborg.

"Oh, my God. That's him!" Heather yelled. "David."

The thing stomped through the Hub, tossing rubble back and forth, in search of something or someone. It grabbed T.J., peered into his face, and then threw him hard against the wall. Ellen charged it head-on, but it snatched her from the ground by the neck. She struggled against him, trying to break free, but it was useless. As it continued to pace the room, Heather used the blaze of her hands to propel toward them. Ellen screamed in pain, the thing choking the breath from her lungs. Heather sent a blaze of flame at the droid, being careful not to strike her friend. The fire singed the fabric of the cyborg's shirt, exposing its shoulder and chest, but left its flesh unscathed. The hybrid punched Heather with a violent uppercut, sending her airborne, dousing her flames as she landed in a heap of rubble.

Carson dove toward the robot that still held Ellen in its steel hand. Focusing his telekinetic force, he managed to lift it from the ground. He called forward wires and metal scraps from the rubble beneath it, which wrapped around the droid, encasing it in metal. But the wreckage was no match for its strength; it shook off the bindings with ease. As it broke free, it fired a beam of energy toward Carson. The winged hero threw his hands forward, holding the pulse at bay. Stronger and stronger the robot pushed, the beam growing intense and more harsh, until Carson couldn't suppress it any longer. The pulse finally tossed him against the wall, knocking him out cold.

Suddenly, Damian began to whip around the thing. Faster and faster he went, stirring up a small vortex of wind. He moved so swiftly it was difficult for him to see his surroundings. Burning tears ran from Damian's eyes as the robot lost its balance. It fell to the left, keeping a tight grip on Ellen, who had nearly passed out from the pressure. Damian's speed amplified as he pummeled the bot with punches and jabs. Ultimately, he managed to strike it directly in the neck, damaging a small unit of the mechanical webbing. At that moment, the droid had had enough of Damian's antics. It produced a single forceful pulse that pushed the rubble and wreckage across the room and knocked Damian off balance. The speedster flew into the adjacent wall headfirst.

Damian's distraction had allowed Ellen to reclaim her wind, and she sent of a charge of electricity at the cyborg, belting the device attached to it skull. The shot momentarily stunned the android. It shook off the attack and looked at her with irritation. It drew back its large fist preparing to pummel into her face. But as she looked into the cyborg's glowing eyes, Ellen felt it, that link, that instant of connectivity all of them had experienced with one another. And in that moment she recognized that this mechanical creature that held her in its grasp was none other than her faceless prince of whom she had dreamt all these years. The revelation was so staggering that she could no longer fight against the android. She closed her eyes as the thing continued to rear back, but then something caused it to stop. Slowly, she opened her eyes and peered into the blank, lifeless face of the robot to see that the intensity of its eyes had dimmed. Did it recognize her, too?

She reached up, placing a soft hand against its cheek. "Please," Ellen said as a tear dropped from her eye. The controls on the side of its head sparked once again setting the robot into a rage. It looked at T.J. one final time, its eyes bright, and then bent down and leapt through the broken elevator shaft, disappearing into the rubble with Ellen as its hostage.

RUBBLE

"They invaded the Core."

After those words, Hudson heard nothing else T.J. uttered. The ringing in his ears was far too loud.

"What did you say?" Hudson said.

"They found us, Andre. I don't know how. But they did." T.J. was frantic.

Hudson drove so desperately he thought he would kill himself on the way back. There were moments he barely kept the car on the road. Arriving at the warehouse, the first thing he noticed was that there was no longer an elevator. Something had completely demolished the elevator shaft. He saw the ruins of the Hub scattered below. The sight nearly made him vomit. Carson stood below him, a shocked expression splashed on his face. He, too, was just as shaken by the sight of the surrounding destruction. Noticing Hudson standing at the crater above, Carson spread his wings and joined him.

"You're not going to like this, Doctor," he said, as he took Hudson under his arms and flew him down to the Hub.

HANA's scattered image stood at the far end of the room. "... lcome to the Core... or... ore," the hologram muttered repeatedly like a scratched vinyl record.

Damian threw his ruined shoes into the pile of trash, the soles smoking and melted from the force of his pace. Heather strode back and forth, her mind turning, furious and intent. Carson made his way around Hudson and pulled his shirt on as his wings disappeared into his back.

"What…what…" It was all Hudson could get out of his mouth.

"Soldiers," Damian said. "Lots of them."

"And David," Heather added.

"Who? Porter?" Hudson asked in amazement.

"Or, at least what used to be David," Carson said as he sat down on the torn sofa.

T.J. looked at Hudson. "They were controlling him somehow. Cybernetics, or something. He had something on his head."

"If that was David, he is exceptionally resilient. I would hate to upset him," Damian added.

Hudson looked around the ruins. "Where's Ellen?"

"He took her," Heather replied.

"To where?"

"No idea," Carson finished.

Hudson didn't know what else to say. It was all so unbelievable, so surreal. He staggered over to the sofa and found a suitable place beside Carson to sit. "I don't get it!" Hudson said. "How the hell did they find us? This place is off the grid. Tracking devices are unable to get an outside signal."

"With this," T.J. said, tossing a small object to Hudson. It looked like a small bot, a residual spy left over from Keating's present earlier that day. Its legs pointed upward forming a small, dish-like parabolic antenna. "From the tablet. I found it under the coffee table after they left. I don't know what frequency it uses. We'll have to open it up and match the code to block it."

As it pulsed with a red glow, Hudson felt fury overtaking him. He smashed the bot into a crumble of sparks. "Dammit!"

"Where would they take her?" Heather asked.

Hudson thought. "It could be anywhere…anywhere in the

Region."

Hudson thought to himself. "It's been forever since Keating has held a formal address. The entire planet has eyes on Parliament, and knowing Keating, she is planning quite a show for everyone. But it's the only place we can start."

"Where?" Carson asked with surprise. "You mean, like, Parliament House? The Capitol?"

"That's the one," Hudson confirmed.

"We'll find her," said Heather with determination.

Hudson grew quiet for a moment. "I'm sorry I didn't tell you about Project Phoenix." The group looked at each other. "I didn't tell you...because deep down inside I knew what I had done was wrong." He thumbed at his watch. "I didn't think so then."

"You were trying to give people hope, Professor," Damian said.

"No, you don't understand. At the time, I understood what I was doing, the risks involved, and the result I hoped to achieve. But it wasn't until I met you guys...I realized what I had *really* done." Hudson sat back. "You kids are all so smart, special...when I heard what you had been through in your lives...well, that's when I saw how selfish I had been." Hudson stood up and walked to the broken Mainframe. He retrieved a watch-like device out of the top drawer and used it to call HANA. The broken image at the far end of the room faded as she appeared on his wrist.

"Hi, Andre," she said somberly.

"HANA, T.J. and I will need access to Parliament added to our BSCs and full blueprints of the structure."

"It'll take a moment. We are still getting the main CPUs back online," she confirmed.

"Understood. T.J., let's get all the sanitation automatons to this level. This place has to be put back together. We'll reinforce it later. The lab on Level 8 will be a good place to..."

"Wait," Heather said. "What do you mean, Parliament?"

"It's the only place to start," Hudson replied. "We'll tackle Keating head-on."

"Look, I'm not excited about jumping into the belly of the beast myself. But will we not be going with you?" Carson added.

Hudson turned to him. "Ellen is captured. No telling what they've done to David. I can't ask you guys to break into the Capitol."

"So…you're giving up on us?" asked Carson with concern.

"No, I'm setting you free."

Heather gave him a peculiar look. "Free? I don't need to be *set free*! I'm already free. You're just going to pitch us out?" She saw Hudson's surprise. "I want a normal life, and we've already determined that ain't going to happen. I'll never be… *normal*. So, this is all I have. It's all *we* have."

"I don't want to go back to way things were," Damian said.

"We can do this," Carson said. "We did good tonight, Dr. Hudson." He saw Hudson look around the room. "Well, okay," Carson continued, "it *looks* like we got our asses handed to us, but we did better than you think we did."

"Carson, it's dangerous," Hudson said. "You guys are far too green. If they took Ellen to Parliament, I can't have you going up against them. You could be charged with treason and spend your lives in Hold, if you keep your lives at all. T.J. and I will get Ellen and David—I assure you. We have the experience to…"

"We can do this, Hudson." Carson walked over to him and placed his hand on his shoulder. "You guys can't get through it with just the two of you. It's an impossible mission."

"We can stop Keating… save Ellen and David. We can save them all," Damian smiled.

Heather got up and walked to where they were standing. She looked at Hudson with a stern gaze. "I don't know how to feel about what you did," she said. "But I understand why you did it."

Hudson looked at them, these new heroes, and he smiled. It occurred to him that they had taken on a slew of Parliamental soldiers and a hyper-powered cyborg and lived to tell the tale.

Hudson shook his head. "The seed of hope always grows best in the soil of destruction." He smiled. "God, I'm so going to regret this…okay, let's do it."

The team cheered.

HANA soon appeared behind them. "Andre, Mainframe is back online. We've diverted power from the environmental systems while we repair the Hub."

Hudson patted Carson on the back. "All right, guys, it's now or never." He rose to his feet. "HANA, we need a trace on Ellen's custom BSC. There has to be a way to find her. She can't be too far." He turned to them, and with a wide smile he said, "Welcome to the Federation."

ƎIT

As she regained consciousness, Ellen felt the aching pain in her throat and wrist. She rubbed her dry eyes while the room came into focus and then she examined at her arm. Bandages covered her right wrist, the same wrist that contained her modified BSC from the Core's infirmary. Bright LED lights above her shone down upon her holding cell, which was made of a thick poly-glass material. There were holes in the ceiling and around the bottom to allow air to enter. An exchange slot around fourteen inches long was located in the wall in front of her. There was a single cot, a sink, and a small toilet that was hidden from view, all made from the thick plastic material. *At least I can pee in private*, she thought. The cell was in the center of a dark, spacious room. The marble floors and walls made the chamber cold and reverberant.

In the distance, there was an elevator. To her right was a large round metal door beside a type of mechanical station area. Electrical conduits and cables connected to a primary coupling that fed into her robotic captor, who rested as he regenerated. The plugs appeared to connect into the unit attached to his head. The steel-like material appended to his skin was alive, growing, and getting worse, like a cancerous tumor. His condition seemed more severe than at the Core. Now, the disease covered his right arm and extended down his left bicep. The thin layer of silver almost hid half of his face. The webbing continued to expand, eating away at the last of his humanity.

Feeling in her pockets, she realized that she had lost her phone. Also lost in the scuffle was her necklace, the only part of her father she had was now gone, never to be seen again. "Shit," she muttered. She squinted her eyes and held her hand over them, attempting to decipher more of her surroundings. "Hello?" The sound of her voice seemed to affect the charging station where the cyborg rested, causing it to pulse with the echo. "Can you hear me?"

The gears of the elevator turned. The floor indicators lit one by one until it reached the final floor where Ellen sat. As the glossy black doors slid open, a tall, thin woman dressed in a pressed suit stepped out, her platinum blonde hair styled into a spiky fauxhawk. Without a doubt, it was the President. The woman lifted her head, smiled, and walked toward the holding cell. A chair rose from the floor in front of the cell.

"Good evening, Ms. Braxton." she said. Ellen didn't respond. "Do you mind if I sit?"

"I don't give a *damn* if you *fall*," Ellen spat.

Keating laughed. "Touché, Ms. Braxton." She sat down and crossed her legs. "So, I suppose you realize who I am."

"Yes, I know who you are."

"Good. And I know who *you* are, my dear." Keating leaned forward and rubbed her chin. "I am so pleased to meet you. I trust you've met my friend here." She looked to where the cyborg rested.

Ellen looked to the charging station and then back to Keating. "That's him, isn't it? David."

"Brava! Yes, Mr. Porter is a very special, someone I've been eyeing for a quite some time. He was out there, waiting, gestating like a brilliant butterfly, waiting to break through his cocoon." She looked at Ellen. "But *you*...you surprised me, Ms. Braxton. In fact, all your little friends left me staggered. I had hoped I'd have Hudson in my clutches, but I suppose you will have to do." She cocked her eyebrow at Ellen. "I loathe surprises. And so…now comes the part where the evil villain begins her monologue, telling you all the little points of her plan. Typically, I wouldn't dare." Keating smiled. "But it's so damned clever I have to tell someone."

At that point, Ellen jumped up and threw forward a fierce charge of electricity, intending to shatter the glass that held her, but the energy bounced around in the cell like rubber balls. Ellen yelled and covered her head until the charge dissipated. Keating smiled. "That was fun for me." She grabbed the base of her chair and pulled it closer to the cell. "You're being kept in a bicarbonate holding chamber. Everything inside is safe from your energy. You can fire your little charges all you want, and the only person you'll be hurting is yourself."

Ellen glared at her with insolence. "What do you want?"

"I want you to die, Ms. Braxton." Keating said. "And you will. My only regret is that I can't have a bigger audience." Keating leaned back. "You've heard all about the mighty Goliaric and how he wiped out the Federation, including your predecessor, Voltage, n'est-ce pas? He actually used the same box that you find yourself in right now." Keating looked around the empty room. "And on live television… in front of *millions* of people. It was outstanding. I don't have enough of the world under my boot… *yet*. If I were to kill you in such a public manner, my popularity would plummet."

Ellen looked up at her. "Why would you care? It's not like public opinion matters."

"Oh, but it *does* matter," Keating said, placing a hand on Ellen's cell. "It matters a great deal—at least for the moment. But that will change, my dear. That's what the World Summit is for. Tomorrow evening, in front of the entire world, I plan to pass my most significant decree yet." Keating reached inside her coat pocket and pulled out a vial of radiant green liquid. "Vaccine X25."

Ellen waited for Keating to continue. After a moment of needless dramatic silence, Ellen sighed and rolled her eyes. "Blah, blah,

blah—what is Vaccine X25?"

"I thought you would never ask," Keating cooed with a leer. "What I hold in my hand is a breakthrough immunization for the disease Scourge—the ailment that plagues the lower Regions of the world. Years ago, when we created the Scourge virus, I had hoped it would wipe out the filthy Regions of the deprived."

"Wait," said Ellen. "*You* created Scourge?"

Keating smiled. "Oh, yes. But over the years it's proven to be a bit of disappointment, I'm afraid. While it has shown results since its introduction, it hasn't had the…lasting impact I had hoped. So, I will announce this vaccine at the Summit tomorrow, which we will give for free to all indigent citizens, and the world will once again think I am a god." Keating stood, her face twisting into a sneer.

"So you created a vaccine for a virus you manufactured just to get the world to like you?" asked Ellen. "That's one stupid campaign strategy."

"It's not quite that simple. It's what inside the vaccine that really counts. In reality, it's an augmented version of the Scourge virus, one that lays dormant. This particular formulation remains inactive for approximately ninety days. Once awakened, the virus replicates at an exponential rate, killing the host in a matter of hours, leaving nothing of them but a puddle of goo."

"Won't the deaths of thousands of people who received the vaccine hurt you in the polls?"

Keating stepped to Ellen's cell. "At that point my popularity will no longer matter. There will be no more Unfortunates left to stand against me. The Insurgence will be no more. I will then steamroll through the remaining population, recruiting those who stand with me, and crushing those who stand against me. Then, and only then, the world will be *mine*."

"Yeah, you're one sick bitch," Ellen hissed.

"True… true," Keating said as she took her seat and crossed her legs. "So now, all that's in my way is you and your little friends. I've no doubt they'll come running to your defense, Ms. Braxton, and I'll be so ever disappointed if they don't. I've already ensured their visit.

I think you've noticed your wrist is now absent the customized BSC Hudson gave you."

Ellen looked down at her injured wrist. "What did you do?"

"They'll track that BSC signal, which will lead them miles from here to a facility tailored to every weakness the fools have. First to go will be your friend, Mr. Gunner. We have special ammunition just for him, laced with hybrid derivative of cathinone known on the street as *MPH*. What is just a good time to many humans will be a metabolic reaction inside Mr. Gunner of... *nuclear* proportions. Next will be your good friend, Ms. Isles. She'll be slathered with enough boiling mercury to shut down her entire nervous system in seconds. Then, we will welcome to the stage, Mr. Quinley, who'll be pummeled with a special Sonarium of my design, which produces frequencies so high it will burst his head like a melon." She laughed and clapped her hands. "Last, but certainly not least, we will bid adieu to the infamous Andre Hudson, the cause of all our pain. I've not thought about a flashy way to undo Andre." She touched her chin in contemplation. "After I make him watch them all die, I think I'll slice his throat myself." She stood and walked to face Ellen. "And then, there's you. Once I have disposed of your friends, you'll be of no further use for me. Underneath your feet is enough water to fill this box all the way to the top. It will enter your lungs and cause your body to cook itself, like a deep fryer. Just like poor Victoria Conner."

Ellen looked to David. "And what about him?"

Keating laughed. "Oh, he'll be my weapon, my guarantee that all will bow before me." With that, Keating walked away.

Ellen looked at Keating with such fury it hurt. "You won't get away with it. They know your weaknesses, too."

"Silly girl," Keating laughed as she boarded the elevator. "*You* are my only weakness."

The elevator doors closed.

Ellen sat down, solemn, broken. She got up, walked to the small door of the cell, and examined the structure. The one entry point appeared to have no lock or hinges, only a square control panel with the shape of a hand. There appeared to be no way to break through the confinement. She laid her hands against the glass and pulsed power through the structure, hoping to crack the glass. If she could find a way to crack it, it could be shattered. She closed her eyes and pulsed faster with increased intensity. The hum of the electricity grew louder and louder. Sweat began to bead on her forehead.

When she opened her eyes, she saw the cyborg standing mere inches away from the glass. The green laser scope of the blaster on his forearm aimed at the center of her chest, a warning for her to back away. Alarmed, she jumped backwards. The hybrid's eyes shined brightly as it lowered its weapon. It stood there, staring at her, guarding her escape.

Ellen studied the cyborg, the machine that was once her faceless prince. With caution, she approached the glass once again. The closer she got, the brighter the droid's eyes grew, cautioning her to stay at a safe distance. But, her curiosity drove her forward. She placed her hands against the glass.

"Hello?" she said. "Can you hear me?" The thing didn't move, nor did it acknowledge her voice. "Look…if you can understand me, your name is David. Is that right?" Again, she received no response. "Well, I'm going to call you David. So, David…somewhere in all of that machinery you are… *you*. I know you can understand me." The cyborg acknowledged nothing. Ellen placed her forehead against the glass in defeat. It was hopeless. Even if she broke loose from her prison, she would have to deal with Super-bot. Then, an idea fluttered into her mind like a tiny butterfly. She placed her forefinger into one of the ventilation holes of the glass. With a quick zap, she touched the hybrid with her energy. If she could communicate with machines, maybe she could communicate with the mechanic humanoid.

"Hello?" she said to it. The thing didn't move. She pulled back her finger and pounded on the glass in anger. "Say something!" Her eyes stung with tears.

"… Who… are… you?" said a voice inside Ellen's mind. The voice moved like wind, carrying through both of her ears in a rebounding manner. Startled by the sound, she stiffened, inspecting the surrounding space.

"Who's there?" she called.

"… Where… am I? I can't see," the voice continued.

Ellen looked to the motionless cyborg standing guard at her cell. "David? David is that you?"

"… Affirmative… who… who are you?"

"My name is Ellen, David. Ellen Braxton." With the mechanical virus attached to his body, Ellen could communicate with him as if he were any other electronic device.

"Who? Why can't I see you? Everything is dark…"

"David, listen. We're trapped, being held prisoner," Ellen tried to explain.

The voice groaned. "I can't hear you," it called.

Ellen closed her eyes and allowed her mind to awaken. Her body radiated with a faint hue of energy. She felt serene as she diverted her focus. "Is that better?" said her subconscious.

"Yes…much…much better," he said, his voice now clearer. "What did you say your name was?"

"Ellen Braxton."

"Ellen, what's happening? Where are we?"

"We're being held prisoner."

"By Keating?"

"Yes."

"I remember," he said. "I was with Keating. She…she had that agent, that boy, put something into my brain."

"Yes, David, your mind—she's tried to take you over, make you do things you don't want to do."

"How do we get out?"

"I don't know, David. But if we don't she'll kill us and thousands of other people.

"Are you with the Authority?"

"No, I'm with a group called the Federation," confirmed Ellen.

"The what?"

"Federation. We're special…unique, I guess you could say, not like normal people. We have gifts, powers. I don't think you're like other people, either. You have abilities, don't you, David?"

The voice paused. "Yes…"

"That's what Keating is using you for. She's controlling you right now. Stop her, David. Break free…"

The voice groaned. "I can't. I don't know how."

Ellen held her focus steady. "What do you see, David? What's around you?"

"I'm in a room…there's like…lights everywhere, circuits… cables."

The technological prison was a large white room draped in circuitry, processors, and electrical conductors, all exchanging information. The room seemed to be growing smaller, confined. It was as if the mechanisms were trying to overpower his will, possess him. In the center of the room was a nucleus, a bright, glowing orb that powered his cell. From it, stretched rope-like power lines that confined him, wrapping around his arms and legs, holding him tight against the wall.

"David," Ellen thought to him. "Is there any way out…a window…a door?"

"No… nothing. I can't move. It's got me tied up. I can't get free."

"David…listen to me. Yes, you can. It can't hold you. You're stronger."

The voice grew afraid and distraught. "It'll kill me! I can't get away!"

Ellen had to calm his mind and make him concentrate. She pushed her mental capacity as far as it would allow. At that moment, a vision of Ellen appeared inside David's prison. The glowing image of her stepped out of the energy of the nucleus. She raised her head and looked at David, seeing the astonishment on his face. He closed his eyes and turned his head as she approached him. "David, don't be afraid. It's me. Look at me."

David opened his eyes to the being made of light. "How did you get here?"

"I can sort of talk to computers. Long story," she said with a smile.

"It's good to see you," he said, as he looked at the glowing figure with wonder.

"It's good to see you, too, David," she said. His words caressed her heart, warming her. In actuality, she didn't know this boy, nor did he know her. But they were not strangers to one another, nor passing acquaintances. Their awareness of one another was on a profound level, a seed planted in the soil of the mind and bloomed within a beautiful dream. Though the faceless prince and the angel had not touched in life, the interwoven thread of their hearts created an intricate tapestry of promise and dedication. It was a love that had survived death, organic and flourishing within the smallest atoms of their very DNA.

"Where did you come from?" he asked. "Are you real, or is this just another dream?"

"I'm real, David. I'm in a holding cell inches from where your physical body is standing," Ellen said as she touched his arm. "Keating had you kidnap me."

David thought, the memories becoming clearer. "A warehouse. I remember a warehouse. Soldiers were with me. I broke though the floor to let them in. I was supposed to get the doctor, some man... I can't remember..."

"Hudson."

"Hudson!" David confirmed. "He wasn't there. There was the man with wings. The fast one moved too rapid to spot. And a girl made of fire." David raised his head and looked at the vision. "The girl...Heather...from the club. I saved her."

"Yes, yes, David. The man with the wings, his name is Carson. The fast guy is Damian. We're like you—unique. We are trying to use our abilities to defeat Keating before she kills us all."

"What has Keating done to me?"

"I'm not sure, David," Ellen said. "She has you trapped with some device that is manipulating your mind and trying to overtake youto. She's going to use you to kill the people who resist her."

David looked at his restraints and tried to pull against them, but they grew tighter. "I can't get out of it!"

"Try, David!"

Again, he pulled against the machine, and using all his might, he almost pried himself from the wall. Sensing his resistance, the nucleus boomed with fury, growing bright. It attacked Ellen, ripping her energy apart.

"No!" he roared. "Leave her alone!" The nucleus shot forward, slamming him against the wall. The binds tightened, securing him in place.

Ellen fell backwards in the cell, sweat covering her body. She felt drained. The connection she had made to David spent her energy. With her last bit of strength, she pulled herself onto the cot and tried to catch her breath. She had to save him, save them all, but how? She looked to the cyborg that stood at her cell. Though it seemed nothing had changed, it flustered with a slight twitch, its eyes fading in and out.

David's internal struggle had begun.

At that moment, it felt as if Keating would win. Ellen couldn't help but feel the despair in her soul. Keating would lead the team into the trap and kill them one by one. Then, she would take care of Ellen. And now, David, her faceless prince—he wouldn't know what he was doing as he crushed the life out of the Insurgence, and would be unable to stop himself.

It was hopeless…or was it?

She felt an odd stirring in her back pocket, as if there was a mouse in it. She reached in and pulled out the small silver disk, the multi-bot, BIT. He snapped from her hand and onto her belly. After he transformed, he rolled forward on his tracks with great concern in his digital eyes.

"BIT," Ellen said, a tear rolling down her cheek. It was a relief to realize she was no longer alone.

BIT beeped and whistled, but to Ellen he said. "Why do you leak, Miss Ellen?"

"I'm just happy to see you," she said.

"BIT is happy to see you, too. Why for are you in prison? Did you do bad?"

Ellen laughed. "No, not bad, BIT. We need to get out of here. We have to reach Dr. Hudson and the team. If we don't tell them where we are, they'll walk into a trap. They'll be killed."

BIT jumped back and covered his eyes in fear. The silver bot shook. "Oh, no. We cannot let them be dead, Miss Ellen. What to do? What to do?" He turned, hopped onto the floor, and rode around on his caterpillar tracks scanning the structure of the holding cell. He rolled back to her. "May you pick BIT up, please?" Ellen picked him up from the floor and placed him back on her stomach. "BIT have bad news, Miss Ellen. There is no way for to open prison."

Ellen dropped her head back and sighed. "Then, it's over, BIT. There's no way to tell them where we are."

BIT blinked his blue eyes. "But I can tell them. BIT can tell them. Watch. BIT will show you." BIT converted into a small communication module. His tracks rounded into a small dish with an antenna that shined with a red beacon. "BIT call T.J. He will hear. You just wait. He will hear. BIT will fix."

At that moment, if there was anyone who adored a machine, it was "Miss Ellen."

THE MESSAGE

"We have a bounce on Ellen's BSC," HANA confirmed. "It will take a few minutes to pinpoint, but the signal is live and strong."

Hudson rolled his chair over to Mainframe where the hologram sat. Sanitation automatons had at least cleared enough of the debris for them to use the network, and repairs around the main entrance progressed. He looked at the signal on the screen. "Perfect! This should pinpoint her location, and once it does, we'll organize."

"What's the plan?" Carson asked, as he took a seat on the desk.

"It'll depend on where she is being held. We'll need to strategize and map out our movements," Hudson said.

Heather walked over to Hudson and HANA. "I hate to admit it…because it'll make it sound like I was wrong…but I'll miss this place."

"Where are you planning to go, Miss Isles?" asked Hudson with curiosity.

"Well…now that they know where we are, don't we have to find somewhere else to bunk?" asked Heather.

Hudson smiled. "You don't build a multi-million dollar

253

infrastructure like this and not provisions to be prepared for infiltration. The Federation always knew something like this could happen. That's why there are around seven entrances and pathways built into the Core that span the whole city. All GPS satellite data for this location has been erased. We will block off and reinforce that elevator entrance as if it never existed. If soldiers return, all they'll find is an old, empty warehouse. It will be like we were never here at all."

Mainframe beeped with an alert.

"I think we have a lock, Andre." HANA touched the screen to zoom into view on Ellen's location.

"Where is she?" Carson asked, as he stepped up behind them.

Hudson followed the trace until it locked on the destination. "She is…at 4213 Avenue C80, Region H-65 Lock 44578, the old Wickerbrook Lumber Room."

T.J. joined them. "I know that building. It's where gangs used to deal drugs before Parliament sanctioned it and turned it into a forensics center. Why would they take her there?"

Carson huffed with relief. "Thank God she's not at Parliament."

"Let's hit it, then" T.J. said, grabbing his coat.

Suddenly, Hudson wasn't so sure. "Wait. Wait…doesn't this seem too easy?"

T.J. rolled his eyes. "Andre, we don't have time for you to analyze this to death like you always do."

"Look at how strong the BSC signal is," Hudson said as he pointed to screen. "That place is about seventy miles from here and that output is ranging at 6.32."

"So…" said T.J.

Hudson pointed at a graph below the main grid. "Compared to this output signal." The range was 6.92.

"Well, whose is that?"

Hudson looked at T.J. "That's yours."

"Look…I don't understand why you're seeing what you are seeing, but we have to go, Andre. Keating won't hold her forever. She knows everyone's weaknesses and she won't hesitate to use them all against us," explained T.J.

Hudson sat there a moment, thinking, turning it around in his mind. It was their only shot to save Ellen, and the only way they would ever locate her. "Fine," he said dissatisfied. "But, we have to be extra careful."

Hudson, T.J., Carson, Heather, and Damian prepared themselves for their greatest challenge yet. They made their way to the main elevator, but something still wasn't right with Hudson, and everyone could sense it. He didn't seem nervous, excited, mad—he seemed skeptical, as if he knew there was something else hiding in the shadows on the other side. They took the elevator to Subfloor 9. They exited to see two sleek, white transport cars attached to a railing.

"This is one of the additional pathways I mentioned, Ms. Isles," Hudson confirmed. "This particular tunnel leads to the north-most end of the city." They stood there waiting for Hudson to enter one of the transport cars, but he just stood there, waiting, thinking about what they were about to do.

"Dammit, Andre," T.J. whispered.

Hudson sighed and swiped his wrist against the door. As they entered the car, his stomach grew tighter and tighter. Just as Hudson reached to start the rail, HANA's voice came over the inside system. "Wait a minute guys. Hold it. I think Hudson may be onto something. Come back up here."

Hudson smiled at T.J. as he opened the door and held his arm out to usher them back into the corridor. T.J. rolled his eyes. "Why do you always do that, Andre? God."

Once they were back inside the Hub, Hudson sat down at Mainframe. "What do you have?"

"I have no idea, but it's coming into us right now," HANA advised.

Unsettled, Hudson leaned forward taking the monitor into his hands. "That's not possible."

It was true—something had managed to establish a direct link to the Core network. Hudson squinted. "What the hell is that, T.J.?"

T.J. looked at the screen to see a series of numbers:

010101000110100001101001011100110010000001101001011 10
011001000000100001001001001010101000010111000100000 01
000100011011110010000001101110011011110111010000100000
011001100110111101101100011011000110111101110111001000
000011000110110100001101001011100000010000001110011011
010010110011101101110011000010110110000101110001000000
101010001110010011000010111000000101110001000000010101
000111001001100001011011100111001101101101011010010111
001101110011011010010110111101101110001000000110111101
100110001000000110001101101111011011110111001001100100
011010010110111001100001011101000110010101110011001000
000011100100110010101100001011001000111100100101110001 0
000001010000011100100110010101110011011100110010000 00
100010101101110011101000110010101110010000100000001 11010
001101111001000000111001001110101011011100010000001010
010010001010100001101001100010011110100001100111010

The sequence repeated over and over again. Damian leaned forward. "I haven't practiced BASIC in a long time, but if I am not mistaken, and I am never mistaken, I would declare that's binary code... simple textbook binary."

"Well, I *declare* you're an idiot," Heather said. "Let's say this in *stupid-Heather* terms, guys."

Damian turned to her. "Computer language uses two binary digits: 0 and 1. So, on a keyboard, every letter and number have a binary representation. The binary code assigns a bit string to each symbol or instruction. In computer processes, the codes are used for different methods of encoding data, like character strings, into bit strings. Computer talk."

Carson leaned forward. "So, what do all those numbers mean?"

Hudson looked over to HANA. "HANA, can you translate?"

HANA waved her hand over the control panel. The numbers fed

into Mainframe. Then, all of a sudden, words appeared on the main monitor in the front of the room:

```
This is BIT. Do not follow chip signal. Trap.
Transmission of coordinates ready. Press
Enter to run RECLOC:
```

"Shut up!" T.J. smiled. "She has BIT with her!"

Carson laughed. "How did the bot end up with her?"

Hudson beamed with excitement. "Are you kidding? That thing hasn't been out of her pocket since it fell in love with her. He has direct network access here, so she's using him to communicate with us."

"Press Enter," Heather urged.

When Hudson did, another set of information ran onto the screen:

```
38.897676
-77.036528
```

"Is that more code?" Heather asked.

"A password?" T.J. interjected.

Hudson examined the numbers. "No. If I'm not mistaken, that's longitude and latitude numbers, locations on a map." Hudson activated the mapping system. "Northwest Region I, Parliament Centerline."

"What? So, Keating actually had enough balls to take Ellen to Parliament?" Carson asked with surprise.

"I won't speculate to the size of Keating's testicles, but looks like it's the belly of the beast after all, Mr. Quinley," Hudson confirmed.

"Oh, joy," replied Carson with sarcasm.

T.J. shook his head. "I can't believe she would take Ellen there. The Summit is tomorrow night. Is she nuts?"

Hudson sat back. "She must be pretty damn confident we'll end up at Wickerbrook Lumber. She duplicated Ellen's BSC and ramped up the tracking so we would lock onto it."

"Impossible," T.J. said. "These can't be duplicated. Each chipset is one of a kind. If Keating has it, she physically removed it from Ellen. That would've been the only way."

"She would have never taken Ellen to Parliament if she thought we would find her there," Hudson said.

"What could Keating be planning?" Damian asked.

"Whatever it is, we're supposed to die at the end," Carson confirmed.

"More code is coming," HANA said. She ran the numbers through Mainframe.

Must save David. Stop Keating.

"Tell BIT we're coming. Hold tight," Hudson said. He turned to the group.

"How the hell are we getting into Parliament?" Carson asked.

Hudson turned to him. "That's a very good question, Carson. We'll have to improvise."

T.J. shook his head. "We'll be lucky to get within fifty square miles of Parliament without being shot by Authority. I am sure they're on the lookout for us."

"Then how will we get into the city? They'll be waiting for us with roadblocks everywhere," Heather asked. "We sure can't walk."

"I could run each of us there? Going my fastest, they'll never see us," Damian said.

Hudson shook his head. "The extra weight would push you. After getting the second person there, you'd be spent, and we would be disoriented from the force."

Carson smiled. He stood up and walked to the front of the room. "What if I could fly us there?"

"Carson, those wings are impressive, but I would calculate they would need to have approximately another ten feet added to each wing to..." Damian said.

"No, no," Carson said. "I mean, I can *fly* us there...in a plane, my dad's plane. He built one from the ground up. The thing is decked out, loaded. With its airspeed, we could get to Ellen in about fifteen minutes." Carson placed his hands on the desk and leaned into Hudson.

"They'll detect an unknown aircraft entering the Capitol, Carson," Hudson added.

Carson smiled. "Not if it's fitted with a Camouflage R18."

Hudson rubbed his chin. "That's not possible. Those radar mufflers were banned ten years ago?"

"Sure they were," Carson confirmed. "But you'd be surprised what you can find in the Underground. I'm telling you, no one is gonna see us coming. I could land that sucker *on top* of Parliament, and they wouldn't even know we were there."

CONNECTIVITY

"**A**re you still there?" David asked.

Hearing the voice echo in her mind, Ellen raised her head and looked to the cyborg. It examined her, waiting. She closed her eyes. "Yes…yes, David, I'm here."

"Can I see you again?" he asked.

Ellen couldn't divert the energy needed to enter the cyborg's CPU and supply BIT with enough power to maintain contact with the Core's network simultaneously. "I'm not able to right now; I'm trying to get us help."

David hung his head, powerless against his restraints. He looked around his digital prison, searching for holes, weaknesses, anything that would allow him to break free. The room was growing smaller, caving in on him, waiting to take him over. "I have to get out of here. I don't want to hurt anyone."

Ellen heard the pain in his voice. "We'll get you out. I promise. I won't leave you."

David tried to picture her face in his mind. The image looked so much like the elusive figure who had visited his dreams, the angel who was always so kind. "Can you talk with me?"

"Yeah, I can do that." Ellen slid BIT under the cot to hide him from view.

"Good…I'm going nuts in here from all the buzzing," he replied. He stared into the nucleus of the prison as if she still stood there. The walls grew closer, his restraints tighter. He closed his eyes, trying to focus on the sound of Ellen's voice. "I think I dream of you," he told her.

Ellen looked up with surprise. She got up and walked to the edge of her cell where the cyborg stood guard. She stared into its lifeless eyes hoping to catch a glimpse of the real David, something human.

David smiled; sweat beading on his forehead. "I don't know how, though. We've never met before…in reality, that is."

"Maybe it was a past life," she said.

"Have you dreamt of me?" he asked.

"I don't know. But I feel like we've met, like I've known you before."

"Me, too," David said. He closed his eyes, trying to picture her again. "I wish I could see your face. It's a really nice face."

Ellen smiled. "Why, Mr. Porter, are you hitting on me?"

"Yes," he said with a smirk. He closed his eyes again as the walls grew closer. "So…how did you become…electric, I guess."

"It's a long story," Ellen said.

"Well, we seem to have time." Actually, he wasn't so certain how much time he had. Soon the surrounding walls would close in, crushing him into nothing.

"True," she replied. "Well, you and me…we were created, in a way."

"In HRV-EST?"

"Yes, and no. Someone gave our abilities to us through the HRV-EST program."

"Who?"

Ellen paused. "Someone who wants us to save the world."

David chuckled. "God, I can't save the world. I'm not doing so good for myself right now."

"David, you don't sound well. Are you okay?"

David swallowed back his groan as the restraints tightened again. "Yeah…yeah…I'm okay," he lied. There was no point in upsetting her by telling her the details of his predicament. "Uh…have you always had your powers?"

"No…not always."

"How did you find out about them?" David asked.

"Well, it's complicated," Ellen replied, hoping to avoid the story of Alemede. "I can say it freaked me out, though. I didn't understand what was happening to me. What about you?"

"I broke our driveway."

Ellen laughed. "What? How do you break a driveway?"

"I was working on this piece of crap bike I bought to mess with, rebuild and stuff. One of the bolts dropped down into the engine block, and I got pissed. I slapped the driveway, and I cracked it—I mean, like twenty-five feet of concrete—cracked that sucker right down the center. My mom thought we had had a tremor or something."

Ellen snickered. "Really?"

"Oh, yeah…I was only fifteen years old. I freaked out. It seemed to come and go back then, though. It wasn't constant until now." He smiled at the memory, recalling how long ago it all seemed to be. He shook the sweat from his eyes. "So, these other guys with powers—what all can they do?"

"Well…you met Heather," Ellen said.

"The girl that does the fire and ice stuff."

"Yeah. She's awesome. Then, there's Damian. He is super-fast. Last, there's Carson. He has these big wings that come out of his back, so he can fly and move things with his mind."

"Like, real wings?"

"Yep…big ones."

"And you guys are called the Federation, right?" David asked.

Ellen stood and walked to the edge of her cell. She stood in front of the lifeless robot. "Yes…and we want you to be a part of it."

"I'm not sure I'd fit in," he chortled. "But it'd be fun to try." He felt as if he would soon lose consciousness. The walls closed in further. "Look…Ellen…I'm not sure I'll make it out of this."

"Sure you will, David. I'm going to…"

"If I don't," he interrupted. "…I won't be me anymore. Don't let me hurt you guys."

Ellen put her hands on the glass of her cell. "What are you talking about? What's happening?"

"I think the android is trying to stomp out the last of me, my human side. And if it does, I won't be me anymore." He looked into the nucleus. "Don't let me hurt you, Ellen, or anyone else. Keating can't be allowed to use me. I know how you can kill me."

Ellen didn't know how to respond to that statement. She wanted to say nothing at all.

"Ellen, are you still there?"

"I couldn't kill you, David."

David looked up at the nucleus, which was glowing brighter. "In Keating's office, she's got a weapon she says can kill me, like a big spearhead. You'll see it in a glass case at the far end of the room. Get it and take me out."

Ellen's eyes stung with tears. "Look, I won't let you hurt anyone. But I can't…"

David sighed. "But I won't be able to be trusted. I won't…I…"

Then, the voice was silent.

"David?" Ellen said with her mind's voice. "David, can you hear me?" She grew disconcerted. "David…are you are alright? Answer me!"

He was unable to react. Within in his mind's prison, the synthetic binds from the cyborg wrapped around his jaw, gagging his mouth. The more he struggled against them, the tighter they became. The prison grew bright.

All of a sudden, the illumination of the cyborg's eyes grew intense. It turned its head and then stepped away from the glass. As it did, a figure approached her cell. It was the girl, the twin from the diner, carrying a tray of food. She stepped to the glass and smiled in a contemptuous manner.

"Hi." Snitch said. Ellen didn't respond. "So, Keating ordered me to bring you food. I'd let your ass starve."

"You're so kind," smirked Ellen. Snitch sat the tray into the exchange compartment. Ellen picked it up and placed it on the cot. "I wonder what it'll be like to watch you die," Snitch jeered. Ellen looked at her and walked back to the wall of the cell where Snitch stood. She stared her in the eyes. "You first."

Snitch laughed. "Ha! It's cute you still think you guys will make it through this. Just like a human. All that hope…and faith…and other bullshit. We studied the human emotional cortex years ago. I think it's your coping mechanism, a way to deny the inevitable."

"The only thing inevitable is my kicking your ass," growled Ellen.

Snitch broke into laughter. "That sense of humor, too. It's priceless." She stepped to the glass and glared at Ellen. "You and you friends will die, sister. When this aquarium fills up with water, and you're swimming around in it like a fish, I'll be standing here when you short-circuit." Snitch grabbed her own throat and jerked as if electricity was shocking her to death. She made glugging sounds before breaking into laughter again.

As Snitch continued to mock Ellen's demise, Ellen slid her finger through one of the ventilation holes of the cell wall. With a quick buzz, Ellen sent a massive shock to Snitch's hip. The twin yelped with pain as she jumped in the air like a feline. Her slacks were singed, and her human skin was blistered and bleeding. She glared at Ellen and stomped toward the cell. Furious, she placed her hand against the door panel to open it, intending to return the blow. Just as she was about to do so, she stopped, smiled, and looked deep into Ellen's eyes.

"Ooh…good one. Clever girl. All I needed to do was open this door, right? Let you wiggle out of there. No, you'll drown, bitch." And as Snitch walked through the darkness toward the elevator, Ellen's opportunity for freedom slithered into the shadows.

ESCAPE

They crouched in the darkness at the perimeter fence of Quinley Air Field. They had to hurry if they wanted to reach Ellen in time. Parliament Authority patrolled the grounds, and it was no surprise they had altered all the entry codes to the base. Sleek black government vans sat around the perimeter of the main office. With his highly developed vision, Carson focused on the office building to assess their situation. He could see Lisa sitting at the desk, working. It felt like he hadn't seen her in decades. He wanted to get to her, hear her voice, but the night had something else in store for them.

The three of them would have to work together to get into the office, get the keys for the Cloak, and get the plane onto the runway. Everyone had a job—T.J. was the locksmith, Damian was their stealth, and Carson was the guide. Getting the keys was the easy part. The difficult feat would be reaching the Cloak, starting the engine, and taxiing to the runway without being blown to bits by the Authority.

Damian crouched beside Carson. "So, how do you suppose we tackle this equation?"

"The keys are in a safe that sits at the side of the big desk in the middle of the office," Carson said. "The trick is to get in there without being spotted."

"Is it a combination lock? If you can tell me how to open it, maybe I can just whoosh in there and get them."

"That's the thing…Lisa has the keys to the safe. We have to get to her."

T.J. crouched beside them. "If you had a disguise, maybe you could get in there to talk to her."

Carson gave him a dense look. "Awesome. You got a trench coat and a spare beard handy?"

T.J. pointed toward the agents walking the perimeter. "Those guys…we can cold-cock one and strip him down. Bam…instant disguise."

"What size do you wear?" Damian asked.

"Extra-large," Carson replied.

"Get me in," said Damian to T.J.

T.J. looked at the entry pad for the back perimeter fence. He pulled a radio device that had two small directional from his pocket. He turned on the tool, held it close to the entry pad, and it blinked. Gently, he turned the directionals in various ways, waiting for the wave lines on its screen to match in pattern.

"What is that?" Damian asked.

"A KeyGen. Instead of breaking code to bust a lock, it uses concentrated waves to target the lock's algorithm." T.J. continued to move the sticks around until the lines were almost parallel. "And once it does…" the entry pad lit green and beeped. "You're in."

Damian slipped into the fence. "Wish me luck."

"Here," T.J. said. "Take these with you." He handed Damian two small silver vials with glass centers. "These are Authority-issued Ether Casks. Once you are close enough to one the agents, bust it in the center with your thumb. It will release a powder that will knock him on his ass. And keep it at least twelve inches away from your face, or it'll knock *you* on your ass. I only have these two, so make them count."

With that, Damian zipped away. They watched as he rocketed by the four guards on the far side of the office. In a flash, Damian was back at the fence. "I found none of those suitable. Two of those gentlemen appeared to be about seven feet tall, one seven feet wide, and the one in the back seemed to take great pleasure digging into his nostrils and wiping the contents onto his lapel."

"Shoo, damn, Damian! You don't have to be so gross. Did you see anyone else...who *wasn't* digging in their nose? There have to be more guys than that." Carson said.

"I'm looking!" Damian sped away again, this time going to the back of the office building. He stopped at a large oak tree in the middle of the path and pressed his body against it. He peered around the tree into the darkness. Hidden in the shadows, he could see one agent buried inside a stack of boxes, sleeping the night away.

Damian smiled. "Slothful. You're an beefy dude." Damian was about to step around the tree when he dropped both of the Ether Casks behind him. As he stepped back to find them, his foot crushed the small vials, sending a thick, swirling cloud of dust around his ankles. The chemical covered his new shoes. "Dammit, dammit, dammit! I loved these shoes," he whispered.

Facing the guy head-on was now the best option he had. Maybe yanking the man out of a dead sleep would leave him disoriented. He pulled his dark gray hoodie over his head and drew the strings to tighten it. The more of him covered in dark color, the more camouflage he would have. He grabbed a thick chunk of tree from the field and began to stalk the sleeping agent. He could render the man unconscious, steal his clothes, and be out of sight before anyone suspected a thing. He crept to where the unsuspecting agent lay snoring and snorting like a hog. Closer and closer, he moved until he was right on top of the man. He reared back, holding the heavy branch high above his head. Right before he could pummel the agent, he heard a click beside him.

"Don't even think about it, punk," said a voice to his right. Another agent stood behind him, laser rifle in hand. He pressed it against Damian's temple. "Don't move! I'm gonna blow your damn head off." He pushed the rifle harder into Damian's skull, the steel barrel cutting into his skin. "Charlie! Charlie, ya dumb son-of-a-bitch...wake up!" he shouted.

"What the hell, Paul?" Charlie said, as he roused. Once he saw Damian standing before him with the gun to his head, the agent jerked to his feet. "Who are you? How did you get in here?" he asked, pulling his rifle.

Damian's mind began to calculate how quickly he would have to move to dodge two rifles and render two men unconscious at the same time. While it wasn't impossible for him to do, it had a very low margin of error. One slip and his head would be gone. At that moment, he remembered his shoes were covered in the thick, white powder from the Ether Casks. He closed his eyes, took a deep breath, and placed his heel on the sole of his left shoe, and began to work his feet loose.

"I said don't move, dumbass! Charlie...go get Mike and the guys. We need to take care of this shithead," said Paul before leaning into Damian's ear. "It's been a long time since I saw brains...I've been missing the..."

The events were so swift it was difficult to tell what happened. Damian loosened his chemical covered shoes, hopped into the air, removed them with his hands, and spun, slapping the agents in the face with them. Charlie soon hit the ground, but Paul staggered a moment.

Paul wiped the powder from his face. "What the...what the hell is th..." And then he was out, too.

Damian took a second to gather his thoughts and calm himself. He waited to see if the commotion had brought other curious agents to the scene. After no others approached, Damian removed the heavy ropes from one of the boxes where Charlie had been snoozing and tied the unconscious men to the oak tree. After ridding the men of their suits, he searched for something to gag them with, but couldn't find anything appropriate. He removed his moist socks and stuffed them into their mouths. "You, guys may chomp on my offensive feet." Then, like a flash, he threw his shoes back on and headed to where Carson and T.J. sat waiting.

"What took you so long?" Carson spat. "And where are your socks?"

"Ran into some friends...there, try these," Damian said as he plopped down to catch his breath.

While Charlie's badge looked more like Carson from a distance, his suit was excessively small for Carson's bulky arms. Paul's suit, however, fit perfectly. "How do I look?"

"Like a prick," T.J. said. "Now let's go. We need to get this done asap."

Carson slithered through the hedges toward the office. Damian and T.J. followed. The group separated with Carson heading toward the office building and the others taking post at the hangar where the Cloak rested. Carson carried Agent Charlie's rifle in his hand for added effect. He must have looked convincing, because an agent standing in the sidelines didn't give him a second glance. He began to reach for the door when a voice stopped him.

"She's not going to like it if you go in there. No Authoritans in the office. She's a bitch," called the agent.

Carson thought for a minute. "Tell me about it," he spat.

"Okay, buddy," the agent laughed. "It's your funeral."

As Carson opened the door, Lisa spun to him with a furious scowl on her face. "I told you guys not to..." Noticing it was Carson, Lisa began to rush to him.

"Stop," he warned. "Don't. They'll see. Turn back to the computer like you're working."

Lisa turned back to the PC. "Oh, my God, Carson, are you okay? We've been worried sick!" she said without looking his way.

"I'm good, sister," Carson replied as he entered the room. "All is well." He strolled through the office. "Lisa, I need the keys to the Cloak."

"What? What the hell for?"

"Just trust me. I'm going to walk to the restroom. Lay them on the desk beside you, and I will grab them on my way out."

"Okay...okay," she agreed.

Carson saw her reach for the safe as he entered the bathroom. After he shut and locked the door, he put his hands on the sink to brace himself. His nerves were infested with anxiety. He turned on the sink, filled his hands with cold water, and splashed it on his hot face. He reached over and flushed the toilet, though he didn't quite know why. He opened the door and stepped back into the office. As he had instructed, Lisa had placed the keys to the Cloak on the edge of the desk. With restraint, he made his way past the desk. As he reached for the keys, she grabbed his hand. He looked at her to see tears streaming down her face.

"Carson, I'm so scared. They took Dennis. They said they would kill him if I didn't cooperate."

The words tore through him. His sister didn't cry…ever. The last time he had seen her shed a tear was at their father's funeral. And now they had his brother-in-law. Enough was enough. He squeezed her hand. "Don't worry, sister." He smiled and slipped the keys into his pocket. "We're gonna save the world."

He heard the roaring in the distance. "Sound the alarm! Untie me! I'm gonna get that little shit!" Carson looked through the windows and saw agents scurrying around the building. One of them ran to the large van in the center of the parking lot and activated a siren, alerting the others that something was wrong.

"You got to go, Carson!" Lisa said.

Carson touched her face and then started for the door just as a half-naked agent stepped through the door with a laser rifle. Four other agents filed in from behind with others on the way.

"Freeze, dumbass!" Agent Paul shouted. "Where is your boyfriend?"

Carson cocked his eyebrow. "Actually, I'm single. But you fill those boxers out real nice."

"Shut up!" the agent said as the group entered the office.

"I don't think you want to do that," Carson warned as he lowered his arms.

"I'm telling ya, I'll blow you away. Don't move!"

"I'm just going to give you back your jacket, bro." Carson held a hand up in submission while he slid out of the jacket. He nodded for Lisa to move away to safety. Quickly, he began lunging back and forth, fighting against the fabric of the crisp pressed dress shirt. With a thrust, the large wings ripped through fabric, opening wide in majestic wonder.

"Holy shit!" screamed one of the agents, as they stumbled over one another, backing away as Carson pushed his broad chest forward. He flapped his wings once sending a whirl of air through the room.

"It's the one with the wings! Hurry!" another yelled.

Carson's eyes turned bright as he stomped toward the men. As Paul lifted his rifle and fired, Carson raised his hand stopping the charge in mid-air. Panic ensued as the men rushed around trying to get out of Carson's way. He looked to Lisa. "Come on! Stay behind me." Lisa ran to his back, staying in step with her brother.

With a fierce shove, Carson threw Agent Paul through the door and against the car parked in front of the office. The agent hit the vehicle with such force, an imprint of his body dented the thick metal. Carson ducked through the doorway and continued outside, throwing agents in various directions before taking Lisa into his arms and soaring into the air toward the Cloak's hangar. The men continued to fire at them as they flew to the structure.

Carson put Lisa on the ground and slung open the hangar door, aiming the keys at the Cloak to unlock it. The cockpit of the sleek jet opened. "Get in!" he shouted as his wings sank into his flesh. "Hurry!"

T.J. and Damian helped Lisa into the cockpit. Carson turned to the handful of agents who had made their way to the hangar door. His eyes burned with a bright hue as he took a deep breath. At that moment, he let out a fierce scream that reverberated through the open hangar. The men tumbled backwards, the cry pulling them into the air. He sprinted to the plane and entered the cockpit. As it slid shut, he started the engines.

"What the hell, man? What is going on?" T.J. shouted.

"We're getting out of here. That's what's going on!"

"And...um...who are you?" Damian asked, looking to Carson's sister.

"Oh, sorry, my name is Lisa. Carson's sister."

"Oh!" Damian said with a smile. "Oh, my God! It's so good to meet you! How are you?"

"Introductions later, guys!" Carson growled.

The jet rolled through the open hangar doors. The agents continued to fire on them as Carson taxied to the runway.

"How much room do we have?" Damian asked.

"Not enough," Carson said as he revved the engines hard.

The jet rushed forward, leaving the multitude of agents trailing behind them. Carson groaned as he struggled to wrench back the yoke, propelling them forward into the air. Damian felt his stomach heave as they lifted higher and higher. And as they continued to climb into the black night sky, leaving the stunned crowd below, Carson extended his middle finger to bid them all good night.

A PLAN

The docking bay for the Core was hidden on the opposite side of the ridge at the lower part of the cliffs. Carson radioed Hudson, Heather, and HANA to let them know that they were successful in getting the Cloak, and that Carson's sister was with them. Lisa told them that the Authoritans had taken Dennis about a week after Carson left. The Authority wanted to set up camp at Quinley Air Field to use the long-range scanning and air control ability of its tower. Not to mention they wanted to wait for Carson to resurface. When she refused, they took Dennis into custody. Though she was uncertain where they were holding him, Carson was sure that the advanced network of the Core would be able to locate Dennis' BSC and they could rescue him from the clutches of Parliament.

Hudson met them in the receiving dock of the Core. The sleek plane hovered into the space and landed. Carson had been correct in his description of the customized jet—Hudson had seen nothing like it. They exited the cockpit.

"You must be Lisa," Hudson said as he held out his hand.

Lisa took it. "Yes, and you're Dr. Hudson?"

"Nice to meet you." He looked up at Carson, who leapt onto the floor from the cockpit. He saw the back of Carson's shredded shirt. "I take it by the look of that shirt that things didn't go smoothly."

A snarky look crossed Carson's face as he walked past Hudson. "Don't ask."

"Agents?"

"Unquestionably," said Damian. "A plethora."

"Then Keating knows we have the jet."

Carson smiled. "It's not going to matter. They have no idea what this thing can do." He turned around to the Cloak and pressed a button on the key fob. A static-like charge ran across the hull of the jet making it virtually invisible.

"A superhero with an invisible jet?" Heather said. "Doesn't that sound a little cliché?"

"It's not invisible," Carson explained. "Take a look, Hudson."

Hudson walked toward where the jet used to be, and as he got closer, he noticed the jet wasn't invisible at all. Its surface had become mirror-like, camouflaging its structure using the reflective patterns of its environment. Hudson touched it and small sparks began to dance around his hand. He smiled. "Your father did this?"

"My father was the smartest Skyforce Engineer in the world."

Hudson beamed. "No doubt about that. What did he call it again?"

"The Cloak S-900…and I would like it if we kept the name."

"It's a wonderful name," Hudson said.

"We have to find my brother-in-law. Authority took him and Lisa doesn't know where they're holding him," Carson said, stepping closer to Hudson.

Hudson looked at Lisa, who was distraught. "We'll find him," he said to her with confidence. "We need to hurry."

They joined HANA in the Hub, which was almost operational thanks to the hard work of the army of automatons. What Lisa beheld nearly overwhelmed her. The group had tried to bring her up to speed, but nothing had equipped her for what she was witnessing. All she could do was smile and say, "I can't believe it." Dennis still possessed a Parliament-issued BSC, which would make him very easy to pinpoint. Running the scan, they discovered that he was in general Hold in Northeast Region I, just a few miles away from Parliament, and coincidentally, Ellen Braxton.

"He's there," Hudson said pointing to the screen. "About ten miles from Parliament."

"Where they have Ellen detained," Damian said.

T.J. pointed at the monitor, calling out the area. "That's Precinct Hold 783. I know some guys there."

"So, what do we do?" Lisa asked, looking to the group.

"I can get him released," T.J. said.

"So, you can just waltz in and get him?" Carson asked.

T.J. scoffed. "Pssh... I don't *waltz*, kid. But it'll be a piece of cake. All I need to do is give them a transfer order, like I am supposed to bring him back to this Hold region. They won't suspect a thing."

"And with Carson's jet, we'll be able to get into the city undetected," Hudson said. "And once we're in, I have a safe place for us to set up."

Carson smiled. "Let's get there and break him out!"

"Not tonight," Hudson said.

"What?" exclaimed Lisa. "But we have to get him out now!"

"Let's just get into the city safely while it's dark and get a plan together," Hudson added. "Both Ellen and Dennis are located inside Region I, the center of Parliament. We could go charging in tonight, but think about it. Tonight we have too much security to break through, and I don't think we'll outsmart them all. Tomorrow night, though, every Authoritan, every soldier, every piece of security will be on guard for the World Summit. It will be the prime opportunity to slither in through the cracks."

The group looked at one another.

T.J. nodded his head. "Yeah...okay, I get you. That makes sense. Everyone will be preoccupied tomorrow night for sure. I can go get Dennis and bring him back here to Lisa while you guys go after Ellen."

Lisa stood. "I want to come with you."

"We can't let you do that, Lisa," T.J. said. "It'll be too dangerous. If we're figured out…"

"I'm not going to sit around here," she said. "Not that this place isn't…great…but my nerves won't be able to take wondering what's happening. You could get caught, or killed, or…"

"You won't win this," Carson said, nodding at T.J. with a smile.

"All right, all right. I get you," T.J. said. He looked to Hudson. "I can take care of her. The question is what the plan from your side will be?"

Hudson moaned. "Unfortunately, our job won't be as easy as walking in with a transfer order." Hudson called up the blueprint of Parliament House. "The structure of Parliament is built onto what used to be known as the White House when the United States existed." Hudson walked to the image and moved through it with his hands. "Parliament's upper structure comprises six levels with over one hundred and thirty rooms. It's unlikely that they'd hold Ellen on one of the main floors in the building. I bet she's somewhere here." Hudson touched on the lower part of the image. "There are three subfloors underneath Parliament. The elevator to them is at the end of the Center Hall here."

"What's on those floors?" Heather asked.

"No one knows," Hudson said. "Back when I was working in gene technology I could visit Sub-Level A, which was a Bioscience area. That was years ago. At any rate, I would suspect that Ellen would be somewhere underneath Parliament, being kept well out of view."

"So, Keating grabs Ellen, takes out her BSC, and plants it in this lumberyard," Heather said. "And while we're on a wild goose chase getting ripped to bits, she gets on television to get the world on her side."

"Sounds accurate," agreed Damian.

"As long as BIT keeps his signal connected to the Core network, we'll be able to stay in contact with them. Ellen said she can keep him charged, so we should be good there," Hudson added. "She didn't know what floor she was on, but thought it was the bottom level."

Carson walked over to where Hudson stood. He stuck his hand into the hologram of Parliament. "I think you're missing a big piece of this. How the hell do we get in?"

Hudson sighed. Carson was right. All ideas were moot if entry to Parliament proved impossible. He waved his hand and called up a map of the front grounds of Parliament. "Tomorrow night, every main media conglomerate in the world will be on the front grounds waiting for Keating to take the podium *here*. The east wing will be wide open. The timing will be tight, but from the looks of it, if we can somehow get inside the secondary guest lounge on the third level here, we can make our way down the corridor to Center Hall. As soon as we're inside the building, we'll be able to track where Ellen is by locking on BIT's signal wavelength. If we can be quick, we can get her and slip out of Parliament using this hidden lower-level service exit. With the Summit in progress, no one will even care."

"That's a long way to go," Carson said. "Why can't we go in that service route to start with?"

"We wouldn't be able to get inside in time. It would take too long to break the system, and it may trigger unwanted visitors. We don't have that kind of time." Hudson confirmed.

Heather leaned forward. "And what about David?"

Hudson cocked his eyebrow. "Well, if he doesn't kill us, we'll try to take him along. Maybe we can shoot that thing off his head."

HANA looked to them. "No...you don't want to remove it," she warned. "It would kill him in an instant. We don't know how far that thing has gone into his brain at this point. But I have a temporary solution to that," she said, as she opened the infirmary shades. On the medical table was a small device that looked much like a USB Flash port. "Take this. If you can get close enough to insert this into the input module on his temple, it will circumvent Keating's programming, shutting him down. Once we get him back here, I can examine how to remove the node from him in the safest manner."

"Okay...good enough," Hudson agreed. He leaned back at the desk, chewing his pencil, his mind running. He stood up and walked to the three-dimensional map of the Parliament building again. "I wish there was some way to get in *here*," he said, pointing to the guest entrance to the visitor lobby in the back of the grounds. "If there was some way to get into the ground floor, we could go straight in, take a right, and there we are."

"They will have guards at that entrance to keep out the public," added T.J. "Even if you blend in with the crowd, if you try to enter the building you'll attract attention."

"What if we had a diversion," Heather said.

"Yes," Damian said. "We can have Heather perform some extraordinary pyrotechnics."

"And *that* won't get us shot in the head," Carson spat, flipping the back of Damian's head.

T.J. took a seat in the chair across from him and smiled. "A diversion's a good idea." Just then, T.J. got a brilliant thought. "What about frat guys…crazy frat guys from URU? The university is in Region I about a half-hour away from Parliament. Those dudes have made the news headlines for their bullshit more times than I can count. They said to let them know if we needed help. I say, we take them up on the offer. Get rowdy frat brothers at that entrance to give 'em hell."

Hudson opened his mouth to counter the suggestion, but as he did, it occurred to him it may a workable option. He smiled. "You know…that just might work." He got up and focused on the Parliament map. "If they can think of something creative to pull off at that entrance, it should allow us time to slip inside unnoticed." Hudson waved his hands and moved the map to the data link on his wrist. "We should leave now for Region I. We can stay overnight at the safe house there and finish detailing the plan. Then, we can pay Psi Rho Phi a visit in the morning to see just how creative they can be."

DISTRACTIONS

Hudson found it impossible to sleep. Fear, excitement, anxiety, and hope filled the entire flight to Region I. Hudson could tell the team was enthusiastic and eager. The one thing they lacked was caution. Caution came with time, a part of wisdom from experience. It was the obvious element missing with the team. Yet, how would they gain experience if there were no battles to fight? The clash before them was wrought with risk and danger. There was too much at stake not to go forward, and Hudson couldn't go forward alone. He needed them, and they needed him—it was a mutual dependence.

It was lucky that Hudson had maintained the apartment Steve kept for times the Federation visited the Region previously known as Washington D.C. Once inside the city, T.J. managed to secure a cruiser from one of the nearby Hold offices. They made sure to park far from the apartment complex so as not to draw unnecessary suspicion. As the team slept, Hudson looked at them in wonder. These kids, so young, yet much more cunning than he could ever be; what would he do should one of them be killed? Could he live with the guilt?

Earlier that night, while reviewing possibilities and scenarios, they had each acknowledged that risk, the possibility of no return, and each had accepted it with sincere duty. But was the commitment only the musings of children who didn't understand the full weight of their decision? He got up from the sofa and walked onto the balcony to stare into the night sky. Region I was heavy with traffic and noise, even that late into the night. Planes flew in overhead carrying important world officials taking part in the Summit the following day. Below, limousines and passenger vans making their way to the event jammed the highways. He knew Keating would be beside herself if she knew that Hudson was so close to her.

"You need to sleep, Andre," T.J. said.

Hudson turned around to see him sitting in the shadows. "And you don't?"

T.J. smiled and stretched. "I slept an hour. Hell, I'm good for the week. Authoritans don't get to sleep, buddy, especially us big shot Detectives."

"Yeah, that's what I hear," Hudson said, looking into the sky at the stars. He sighed. "Dammit, Tommy…am I doing the right thing?"

"You're doing the only thing that can be done—right or wrong."

"What if they die?"

"But what if they live?"

Hudson looked at him. "I don't understand."

"What if they live? What then? If we allow Keating to keep on… take over. Won't they be dead anyway? Won't we all be dead?" T.J. saw Hudson shake away the comment. He got up and walked to Hudson, placing a hand on his shoulder. "You're gonna have to let it go, man. You didn't kill them."

Hudson looked into the stars, keeping his eyes away from T.J. "Yeah, I know, I know. It's just difficult to put it aside."

"If you don't, you're not gonna be any good to these kids. We have this shot, this one shot, to take it all back. There's no army of aliens to invade us now, man, no one but Keating. And we can take her—if we do it *now*, before she's made that final move. Once she's wiped out the Insurgence for good, there's no one left. We can fight, but we can't fight the entire world."

Hudson smiled and looked to him. "Sometimes, you're not a dumb shit."

"And sometimes, you're not an ass." T.J. took him by the shoulder and gave him a brief hug. "Now, get in there and get a couple hours sleep."

And Hudson did. He could finally rest, for at least a while. Those few hours of sleep proved to be just the thing he needed to clear his mind. And when he woke, he did so to the sound of clattering in the kitchen. He looked over to see Heather cooking. He stretched and sat up, placing his feet on the floor. The scent of the food was pleasing. Bacon…Heather had demanded it when they had stopped at the convenience store before reaching the apartment. Rising to his feet, he meandered into the kitchen.

"Good morning, boss!" Heather said. She scooped the bacon out of the pan and onto a plate lined with napkins to drain the grease.

"Oh, that smells good. I didn't realize you could cook," Hudson said.

"Yep…Lizzie taught me a long time ago," she said.

"How is your sister?"

"She's doing good. I talked to her yesterday using the phone we gave her. Said she had got on at this nice restaurant downtown, much better coin. So, it's good we blew up her place of employment," Heather said with a grin.

Hudson chuckled. "I'm going to wake the boys."

"Cool…and tell Damian there's enough for *eve-ry-bo-dy*, not just him. I don't care if he has the metabolism of a hummingbird. He can snort a bag of sugar or something."

The group gathered and ate breakfast, and for a while, it was as if they were on a meaningless field trip. They forgot the danger that lay before them, and that was good. The mind needs occasional repose from the horrors of reality.

Soon, it was time to travel to United Regional University, which sat about a half-hour from the apartment, to visit the Psi Rho Phis. The SUV cruiser pulled to a stop in front of the frat house.

"So, what do we do?" Carson said. "Do we say…hey, David's been turned into a killer cyborg and we need to rescue him before he kills everyone in sight?"

Hudson turned and looked at Carson as if he would slap him. "Maybe you should just let me talk, okay?"

They all left the car and walked to the front door. Hudson knocked twice before Alan answered.

Alan, who seemed to have had a coarse evening the night before, smelled of stale vodka and regret. He squinted his eyes to the bright sunlight. "Damn…do you guys know what time it is?" Seeing Heather, he perked up and tried to straighten his appearance. "Sorry, uh…hey! How you guys doing? What can I do for ya?"

"Hey, Alan," T.J. said.

"Hey! Mr. Detective dude! What's going on?"

T.J. stepped forward. "Alan, this is my friend Andre. We're here to ask you guys for help…for David."

Alan's face grew serious. "Is Porter okay? What's wrong, man?"

"We think he's fine," Hudson began. "David is in a situation, and we want to get him out of it. But we will need the frat's help."

"Sure, sure, man…you guys come on in," Alan said. As the group filed in, Alan yelled, "Visitors—*female* alert, guys!"

After a few moments, the gentlemen made their way down to the lounge. The notion of female presence had inspired them. In spite of their apparently hectic evening, each of the brothers appeared in tip-top shape, groomed to perfection. They all took seats in the lounge of the house. As they settled, Alex could not resist staring at Heather with a curious expression.

"Do I know you?" Alex said. "You look familiar."

As was common for Heather, she pulled no punches. "We've not met, but I was the slutty stripper at Flesh 84 the night you guys were having your little fraternity field trip."

The boys smiled at one another.

Alan grinned. "Oh yeah! The one with the fire and ice tricks!"

"You. Were. Awesome!" Pete cooed as the other brothers nodded.

"Agreed," Derek said with a snort.

"Yeah, yeah, guys," T.J. interrupted. "The reason we're here. You guys were right to feel weird about those Agents who took David." He looked to Alex. "They weren't Agents...not really. They were working for the President, who ordered them to kidnap David."

"For what?" Charlie asked from the back of the room.

"You guys have seen David's abilities, correct?" Hudson asked them, causing the boys to look at one another, concerned.

Alex leaned forward. "Yeah...we did—his uber-powerful strength and stuff."

"That's why she wants him," Hudson continued. "She wants to control him."

"Why?" asked Lenny.

"To take over the world," Heather said. The brothers looked at one another with heavy concern.

"That's why we need your help," Hudson said. "See these guys standing behind me? Well, they are all special...just like David."

"You're all strong and stuff?" Pete asked.

"Well, not exactly," Carson replied. "We are all a little different, I guess."

Alex leaned toward Carson. "How?"

The team looked at one another.

"They've seen me...much more of me, so I'm off the hook," Heather said with a smile, allowing her hand to turn into flame.

"Woah!" shouted Lenny. "You mean you can really do that shit?"

"Yep," Heather replied.

Damian cracked his neck and sighed. "My turn." He took a moment to focus and then zipped around the room, stopping at various points to highlight his immense speed.

"Shut! Up!" Alan said in amazement.

"I don't believe that," Pete said, smiling.

Charlie looked to Carson. "And what do you do, big guy?"

Carson smiled and walked to the front of the lounge to give

himself space. He pulled off his shirt and balled his hands into fists. He closed his eyes, took a deep breath, and then the wings unfolded from his back, almost stretching the length of the room. Everyone gasped in surprise. A few of them dashed to the kitchen in fear. Lenny fell off the back of the couch and landed with a thud to the floor.

Alex grabbed the edge of the couch, his eyes flying open wide. "Baby Jesus on a unicorn!" he cried.

"That is messed up!" Pete said.

"Agreed," said Derek, who was in shock.

Carson tucked his wings behind him. "Yeah, they take a little getting used to," Carson said.

"That is so great," Alex said, as he stood. He walked over to Carson. "Dude, can I...like...touch it?"

Carson looked to Heather, who was about to burst into hysterics. "Yeah, man, you can touch it if you want to," he replied with an air of flirtation.

Alex reached out to touch the massive wing, and as his fingertips sank into the soft feathers, the wing flinched. Carson had had no one really touch his wings. He moved the appendage, allowing Alex to feel the inside of it.

Pete leaned forward. "Okay, I'll let you guys use my room in a minute, kewl?" He watched Alex's face turn red as he made his way back to the couch. Pete turned to Hudson. "So, just tell us what you guys need us to do. We'd do anything to help Porter."

Hudson turned to them. "You guys remember the Summit that's going on tonight, right?"

"Yeah, sure," Pete said.

"Well...we need a diversion—at least twenty minutes, so we can get in and get our folks out. We hear that you people are the masters of diversion, right? Do you think you could work us up one?" Hudson asked.

The brothers smiled and nodded at one another.

Alex laughed. "Oh, man...Psi Rho Phis are the *kings* of distraction!"

Derek smiled. "Agreed."

Pete took Hudson's hand. "We got your back. You heroes just get our boy out, cool?"

Hudson smiled. "That's the plan."

ƎREAKOUT

The night crept up on them with a vengeance, as if their fervor had sped up time. The event schedule stated that Colonel Emanuel Arklow would take the front stage at 7:00 PM. He had thirty minutes to speak to global defense and budgeting, with an additional fifteen minutes to accept questions from the media. Next up, was Dr. Amanda Monday, who was to speak on human health and the Scourge epidemic. She, too, got a half-hour with a fifteen minute window for Q&A. Monday would introduce President Keating, who would take the stage at 8:30 PM. She was to speak for an hour with an additional thirty minutes planned for Q&A from the press.

With their diversion secured, they could now take full advantage of the Summit timeline. They had arranged to meet Psi Rho Phi two blocks away from Parliament at the corner of 10th Avenue and Industrial Parkway at 6:00 PM sharp. They would prep, and from there T.J. and Lisa would travel to the Hold in Northeast Region I where T.J. would present the transfer order for Dennis.

During this time, the team would make their way to the south entrance of Parliament where people would gather at the massive digital screens to watch the broadcast. By 6:30, Psi Rho Phi would launch into whatever spectacle they were planning, and the team would slip into the entrance and activate the tracking locator to lock on BIT's signal. They would travel down the hall to the Sub-Level elevators, tracking Ellen's location during the process. Once they had located her, they would first try to subdue David using the device that HANA had provided.

Damian's speed would allow them to attach the unit quickly. Once they had David secured, they would free Ellen. They could exit Parliament undetected through the lower level service route. Both teams would make their way back to the secure location at Steve's apartment. Finally, they would mingle into the crowd that would be leaving the Summit by that time. With the tons of schmoozing that Keating would desire post-event, they would be back in the Cloak and well on their way to the Core before Keating would even know what had happened.

Then, the hard part would begin—planning how to take down Keating, once and for all.

The team pulled into the small parking lot near the 10th Avenue intersection to wait on the frat as planned. As was typical of Hudson, he demanded to arrive fifteen minutes early. They all sat together, quiet, minds twisting and turning. The SUV was thick with tension.

T.J. turned to them and handed them small pins that looked like shiny, black buttons. "Here."

"What is this?" Heather asked.

"Ghost Tags—*highly* illegal," T.J. replied. "They're A/V disrupters that shield you from audio-visual equipment. You won't display on cameras, thermal registers, and so on. Pin it anywhere on your body, somewhere secure."

Carson pinned the tag to his pants pocket and sat in the back, nervously thumbing his pant leg. He had to break the awkward silence. "I don't give a damn what you say," he started, causing everyone to shake with fright. "That Alex dude was into me."

Lisa shot him a gaze of skepticism. "Into you... or her?" she said, pointing to Heather.

"Right?" Heather said with a grin.

"Woman, please…did you see the way he was all about my wings? He wanted to roll around in 'em. They're dead ass sexy, right?"

Heather laughed. "They are pretty, now. You may have me there."

Damian leaned back. "What time is it?"

"5:47," Hudson replied.

Just then, a timeworn, shabby van with tinted windows staggered into the parking lot. The group perked up, hoping that it was Psi Rho Phi. The van parked two spaces from them and turned off its engine. And they waited. After five long minutes, Hudson grew impatient. "What the hell are they doing?"

"They'll get out, Andre," T.J. said.

Another two minutes passed before an old couple exited the van, eyeing the SUV, wondering why in the world Hudson and the group found them so titillating. Hudson looked at the clock: 6:10 PM. "They're late. Why in God's name would they be late for something like this?"

T.J. didn't know how to respond. It was true; time was of the essence, and they couldn't afford to lose precious minutes. "Maybe they got turned around."

At 6:15, Hudson had had enough. "We got to get going. T.J., you and Lisa start on your way for Dennis. We'll walk up and mingle into the crowd at the Parliament building. We'll have to go with the original plan—we'll circulate with the people outside of the visitor lounge entrance. Then, we will break from there and go up the steps to the guest lounge on third level."

"But, if there's abundant coverage of security in that area, how shall we get past them?" Damian asked.

Hudson sighed. "We'll have to play it by ear guys," he huffed with obvious frustration.

Lisa opened the rear door and stepped into the parking lot. T.J. opened the passenger door and looked to Hudson. "You guys please be careful. We'll wait at Steve's until midnight. If you're not there by that time, we'll know something's wrong."

Hudson looked at him and patted his shoulder. "You got it. But nothing will go wrong." He saw the scowl on T.J.'s face. "Well, nothing outside of what has already gone wrong," he said, referencing the absent frat.

T.J. patted his shoulder one last time while Lisa kissed her little brother goodbye. The two got into the patrol car and began on their way. T.J. looked into the rear-view mirror and saw the team separate into two groups, preparing to make their way to the Parliament building.

"He's setting them into two groups." The comment made T.J. feel as if he was still with them.

"What?" Lisa said.

"He divides them up. That way they look less conspicuous," T.J. confirmed.

"Oh, okay," Lisa said. She looked out of the window as they continued to drive on, not saying anything at all.

T.J. turned onto the main parkway and started toward the interstate ramp that would lead them to the local Hold, which sat about fifteen minutes from where they were. He reached over and turned down the radio. "They're gonna be alright, you know."

Lisa started to speak but stopped, turning her statement over in her mind, making sure it was proper. "I don't think you believe that's true—not completely."

"Sure, I do," T.J. said with a smile. They entered the ramp for the eastbound interstate.

"I hope you're right," she added. She was quiet for a moment or two. Making conversation, she said, "So, tell me…what does T.J. stand for?"

T.J. smiled. "Thomas James. Thomas James Blackwood."

"That's a cool name."

"It is," he smiled. "So, have you always worked on planes?"

"Yeah, it was part of our dad's world for as long as I can remember. I was never as good at it as Carson was, though. That boy took to aviation like it was nothing, like he was a bird."

"The boy's got wings, you know," T.J. said.

Lisa laughed. "Well, that's true."

T.J. stuffed a piece of gum into his mouth and offered a stick to Lisa, who refused. "What did you do when you first saw them? The wings, that is."

"I flipped completely out. It was so unreal. There we were, watching Carson go down in that piece o' shit plane as it began to nosedive. I thought I would puke, I swear. I also thought I would put my hammer through that old jackass General's skull. All I could think of was—*God, how am I going to bury my brother? How will I make it after he's gone? Why do I have to lose him, too?* Then, I saw him bust through the shield of that cockpit and jump out, and I kept waiting on a parachute to open. And at first, I thought those wings were the parachute. Dennis was like, *Son of a bitch, Lee, those are wings!* I didn't believe it. We stood there, watching those things flap, watching him soar around the sky like a huge eagle. And I know this sounds dramatic, but when he landed, I swear to God, it was like an angel. I realized how special my little brother was," Lisa said, wiping a tear from her eye. "Soon after, those Agents came. We've got these high-tech, long-range scanning drive. My dad bought them from a buddy with the Skyforce. They wanted to set up camp at the field and use them. Well, at first I told them no, and that's when they took Dennis. They were waiting for Carson to come back."

T.J. could tell she was frightened. He reached over and patted her hand. "Well, I bet you they wish he hadn't now."

She laughed. "Oh, I wish you could've seen this one guy…when Carson threw out those big ass wings. He saw Carson, crossed himself like he was in confession, yelled 'Santa Maria,' and passed out cold."

T.J. laughed. "I don't blame him. I about did the same thing when I first saw 'em." They turned off the main road into the Hold. He circled around, parking the vehicle facing toward the building so that Lisa could see what was taking place. He killed the engine and looked at her. "Okay…I'll present the transfer order to the front desk. All Holds are set up the same. They'll walk me straight back through those blue doors to where Dennis is. I'll bring him out, and we will be on our way back to the apartment in no time, got it?"

Lisa nodded her head. "Got it."

"Okay…gonna leave the keys in case you need them. Give me about ten minutes."

"Okay."

T.J. got out of the cruiser and walked toward the building. As he entered, he could see the main desk to his left. There were two thugs in the detaining area waiting to be processed. Two women waited in the back of the small lounge. The Hold was almost vacant, which was good. He walked to the counter and knocked on the window. The clerk sat there, pushing piles of paperwork.

She turned around and looked up at him, unamused by his presence. She slid open the window. "Can I help you, honey?"

"Yeah…Detective Blackwood here from Region H. Need to pick up a scuzzbucket named Dennis W. Baker. You got him here?"

"Let me check," she said as she entered the information into the database. T.J. stood there, examining the area. One thug stared at him, the same gaze of hatred the public always gave the Authority. "Yeah, honey, we got him. You got a transfer?"

"Yeah, doll, here ya go," he said, as he pushed the form to her. As she looked it over, T.J. leaned back to make sure Lisa was okay. She was still sitting in the cruiser waiting.

The clerk lifted her wrist to her face to speak into her transmitter. "Roger…got a transfer her for Dennis Baker. I'm sending a Detective Blackwood back there to you." She turned to T.J. "Go on back, honey. I'll get his stuff out of inventory," she added, pointing him toward the blue doors.

"Thanks," T.J. said as he made his way to the Tank where they held criminals in small glass cells reminiscent of fish tanks. The doors buzzed him in and Authoritan Roger led him to where Dennis sat with his head in his hands, rocking back and forth in a small tank.

Roger pressed the call switch on the tank. "Hey, Baker, got someone here to pick you up for transfer back to H. Get cuffed."

Dennis looked up at T.J. and stood. Placing his arms behind him, he pushed his hands into the shackle preps to his right, which fitted him with wrist cuffs. Roger opened the tank door and passed him off to T.J. before leading them out. Once back in the lobby, T.J. walked back to the processing counter where the woman waited with a clear plastic box containing Dennis' personal effects.

"Here you go, honey. Have a safe trip," she said.

"Will do," T.J. replied with a wink.

It was easy, easier than T.J. ever thought it would be. *Hell, I wished they moved this smooth in H,* he thought. As they neared the double doors, T.J. could see Lisa smiling. He felt Dennis' arm tense as he noticed her, too. "Stay calm," he whispered in Dennis' ear.

As they were about to exit, T.J. heard, "Honey, wait…where is your Captain's digital signature?"

T.J. closed his eyes. *Dammit—hell!* "Uh, what?" he said in a confused tone as he approached the glass. "Did that ass not sign it?"

"No, honey, I don't see it. And I can't let you take the prisoner without a digital. The system won't finish the process." She looked to T.J. for a moment, waiting for further explanation. "I'll have to call your Hold."

That was it—the last straw. There was no way his Hold knew about this transfer, nor did they authorize it. Not only was this about to expose the ruse, but it was also going to lead to the exposure of T.J.'s allegiance to the Insurgence. "Well," he began. "I don't think Captain August is in today, sweetie. He's out on Annual. Sorry about all this. Is there any way I can…"

"Sorry, honey, no can do. Got to have it. Now, if I can get a verbal from him or his back-up, I can override with vocal command. I'll call, though. I bet they can track one of them down. Hate for you to have to drive all that way for nothing."

"Okay, sweetie," was all he could manage. What else was he going to say? The ruse was about to be over. They would probably shoot both him and Dennis right there in the lobby, in front of Lisa. Oh, God, how awful that would be. At least he had left the keys with her. She could get away. He watched her through the door with worry on his face. He could hear the woman on the phone with his Hold.

"Yeah, Sheila? Barbara from Hold I-16. How ya doin', sweetheart? Good. Listen…we have a Detective Blackwood here. Yeah…yeah…Thomas Blackwood, that's the one. Well, he's here to pick up a transfer by the name of Baker, and your Captain forgot the digital signature. Can we get a verbal? Okay…Okay, I'll hold." She turned to T.J. with a smile. "Be just a second, hon."

The sweat beaded on T.J.'s head. He looked at Dennis, who was as confused and frightened as he was. "It'll be okay," he lied, looking at Dennis.

"Yeah…yeah…I'm here, Sheila." An expression of concern covered Barbara's face causing T.J.'s stomach to knot. "Thanks, hon. I appreciate it. I'll handle it here." She hung up and looked to T.J., torn by what she heard. She looked up at him with sympathetic eyes and sighed. "Honey… I hate to do this to ya'. I swear. You're sweet." She reached for her lapel and pressed the button on the desk. T.J. heard the doors lock. "Roger…we have a break out in the lobby." The sirens inside sounded.

As poor Roger hit the Tank Room door, there was an explosion of glass, iron, and plaster. Everyone in the area fell to the ground in disbelief as they tried to shield themselves. T.J. and Dennis dove onto the floor in time to realize that Lisa had driven the SUV cruiser through the front of the building. The thick steel ram attached to the front of the cruiser shattered the entryway to bits.

"Don't just lay there!" Lisa yelled over the cruiser loudspeaker. "Get in the damn car!"

T.J. smiled. "You have one helluva wife!" he shouted, as he pulled Dennis to his feet.

"You have no idea," Dennis replied.

The two men jumped into the cruiser as Lisa peeled out of the debris. They squealed out of the parking lot, slamming onto the street with full force. She floored the gas as she fled toward the interstate.

"What just happened?" T.J. yelled.

"I'm not certain, Thomas, but I think I drove this car through a Hold station!" Lisa replied. Dennis reached up and put his hands on her shoulder. She grabbed his hand. "Hi, baby!"

"Thanks for springing me, hot ass!" said Dennis.

"Anytime, babe. Hold on!" Lisa sped onto the interstate and merged into the cover of traffic.

As they made their way down the interstate headed to the apartment safe house, T.J. knew his life—their lives—would never be the same. He could never return to his world as an Authoritan. His detective days were now behind him. The odd part was that he didn't even seem to care; for he knew deep inside that what they had done that night would change the course of history forever. Deep within him he couldn't help but feel that after all was said and done that evening, the Authority wouldn't even exist. And that feeling made him happier than he had been in a while. As he took a deep breath, T.J. closed his eyes and said a prayer for the safety of Hudson and his band of heroes.

THE KISS

Hudson and Damian made certain to stay several paces ahead of Heather and Carson, hoping to remain discreet. It was essential that no attention be called to them. Keating had expected to see their dead bodies by now, so to see a heightened level of security inside Parliament wouldn't be a surprise. They would have to be prepared for anything.

"Are you nervous?" Damian asked.

Hudson kept his sweaty palms deep in his pockets. "I'm always nervous, Mr. Gunner. It keeps me breathing."

As the sun sank in the distance, they waited at the intersection for the crossing light to change. Hudson could see the crowd gathering in front of the wide screens where the Parliamental insignia shined. Lines of imperial automobiles, limousines, and media vans leisurely taxied around the back of the building on their way to where President Keating would soon make her most notable appearance to date.

"Can we do this?" Hudson heard Heather ask from behind him.

"We'll be fine. We'll be able to do it as long we're together," Hudson replied without turning.

The light changed, and the group walked forward. After crossing the final median, they filed behind others who were making their way up the great stone walkway to the rear visitor entrance. Hudson looked at his watch: 6:37 PM. He looked to the left of where they stood and could see the narrow staircase they would take to the third level to gain entry to the building. All they had to do was get inside, and then they could trace Ellen's location. If all went well, they would be in and out in a less than an hour.

"Oh, my God!" shouted a well-dressed woman beside Hudson. Her enthusiasm stunned him. "Aren't you excited to be here?"

"Ecstatic," Hudson muttered in a lukewarm tone.

"I am here with my husband. We're here to be part of a historical moment," the woman continued.

"Well, goody for you," Hudson said. He looked to Damian, rolling his eyes.

"What do we do," Carson said from behind them.

Hudson leaned back. "As soon as they start the broadcast, everyone will be glued to the screens. At that point, we'll break from the crowd and start up the stairs. Once we get…"

Heather tapped him on the back. "I think you better look at the steps."

Hudson looked over the crowd to see not one, not two, but *five* Agents lining the steps to the upper floors. There was no way they could take that path, not with so many Agents guarding it. Hudson's mind spiraled. Two guards stood at the visitor entrance, so the team couldn't pass there either. It was a standstill. There were no other options before them. Hudson looked down in defeat as the chance for hope slid down his spine and puddled beneath his tired feet. It was over before it had begun.

"Hey—Hey! URU! Show me what you g'on do!"

A voice boomed over the bullhorn. Followed by a small crowd repeating the chant: *Hey, Hey! URU! Show me what you g'on do!*

"Brilliant!" Damian said, a grin spreading across his face.

Hudson spun around to see the entire Psi Rho Phi frat in the distance behind them. Alex stood on the hood of a van with a bullhorn, leading the group in the rhythmic chant. Alex then jumped to the roof of the van, throwing his fist in the air.

"I said…Hey, Hey! URU! Show me what you g'on do!"

The brothers repeated the chant again. Hudson was surprised to see the crowd beginning to woot and cheer in response.

"Everybody say…Hey, Hey! URU! Show me what you g'on do!"

The crowd repeated the chant as Alex held his hand to his ear.

"Last time! Say—Hey, Hey! URU! Show me what you g'on do!"

It seemed as if the entire audience was singing the chant with the brothers.

Alex pointed at Hudson, and with a wide smirk he shouted, "Brothers!"

"What?!" the frat shouted.

"Line 'em up!"

Out of nowhere, snare drum rolls blasted through the crowd as several others joined the brothers, forming a systematized drumline. The ten of them lined up in front of the van in an angled formation, all armed with brightly colored snares. The group broke into what had to be the most elaborate drumline routine the world had ever seen. Working together in complete unison, the group moved with mirror-image choreography. The crowd, the guards, and the media found themselves enraptured by the sight as the rattle of the snares echoed through the space, bouncing off the concrete and plaster of Parliament. The people exploded into thunderous applause when the lights lining the drums tore through the darkness of nightfall. Not only did the drums ignite with multi-colored twinkling lights, but also each set of drumsticks shined with various colors of the rainbow.

Hudson couldn't wipe the sneer from his face. The brothers had come through, and they had come through in such grand fashion he found it hard to tear the team away from the show. Hudson took Carson by the arm. "Yes, yes—all the pretty lights, but we have to go, guys…now!"

Carson tapped Damian and Heather. Together, the band of four spies slithered through the enraptured crowd toward the now unmanned steps. They slipped into the threshold and turned right, and then they made their way down the abandoned Center Hall toward the Sub-Level elevators. Hudson activated the tracker which locked onto BIT's signal. Then, he ducked behind the large pillar at the edge of the corner to examine the elevator lobby that appeared to be void of people. He turned to them, motioning for them to continue. The group stepped to the pair of silver elevator doors, but as Hudson began to press the down button, the floor indicator chimed and illuminated. Someone had arrived to the ground level.

"Oh, monkey-fart!" Carson said.

"Hurry," Hudson instructed.

They ran back to the edge of the elevator lobby and ducked into the small alcove against the far wall.

"Monkey-fart?" Damian said to Carson.

They were lucky to have gotten out of the way, for when Hudson peeked around the corner, he saw none other than President Keating herself exiting the elevator. She was accompanied by Colonel Arklow, a small band of Agents, and the precarious twins from the diner.

"And we need to keep an eye out," Keating said to the group. "I should've had a dumpster of dead bodies by now."

"Maybe they haven't thought to track the girl's BSC, yet," Arklow said.

"Walter," Keating replied. "Hudson is many things… *stupid* is not one of them. He searched that BSC as soon as the girl was taken. Trust me. They have had plenty of time to get to the lumber yard."

Hudson heard another set of feet running toward the group. "President Keating!" said the exasperated Agent as she neared them. "We have received word about an incident at Hold 435. Someone ran a cruiser through the front of the building."

"Okay…so, the Agent wasn't a great driver," said Snitch.

"No…you don't understand. They took a prisoner—someone named Dennis Baker?"

There was a moment of disbelief before Keating erupted. "Bastard!" she shrieked.

"Ms. President!" warned Arklow.

"Oh, I don't care if the media hears me!" Keating shouted. "It was Hudson. They're here. Tell all Agents to increase security at every entry point to this building. Scour the grounds looking for anything out of the ordinary, and...what the hell is that noise?" Keating asked, hearing the drumline.

"A frat from the university. Some flash mob or something, trying to get their fifteen minutes," answered one agent.

"Shut them down, now!" Keating demanded, forcing the Agent to scurry away. She turned to the remaining detail. "Hudson and those brats cannot be allowed anywhere near this building, do you understand?" The group nodded their heads in agreement. "And you two...you stay near me at all times," she said, pointing to Snitch and Scoundrel.

The communications director stepped to them. "President Keating?"

"What?!" Keating shouted.

"Ma'am...we are almost ready for Colonel Arklow to take the stage."

Keating took a second to calm herself. "Please accept my apologies. Walter, you may go. Break a leg."

Snitch stepped to Keating. "You need to get ahold of yourself."

"I know," Keating said.

"You're about to be on television."

"I know."

"So, get a grip..."

"I know!" Keating growled. "I need to sit. Have some tea brought to me in my room." Snitch nodded and walked away. "And let me know of *anything* at all that is suspect."

Keating's entourage led her to the makeshift green room in the lobby. She took a seat and picked up a copy of her speech from the adjacent table. As her mind wandered, she thought of possibilities, scenarios, and fantasies. She could barely contain her excitement at the thought of seeing the dead, decomposing bodies before her— the so-called heroes, the *new* Federation. What a joke. No...it was her time, her moment to shine once again, to be the champion of the world, a world she would own, a world she would eventually decimate. Little did she know that mere yards from where she sat were the very people she hoped to destroy.

The team remained quiet, motionless, trying to keep from being detected. The Agents following Keating's demands had silenced the drumline. As the space grew quiet, they all took a deep breath and attempted to calm themselves.

"Okay," whispered Hudson. "Damian…zip over there, punch the elevator, and come back."

"Got it." In a flash, Damian was back with them. The elevator ventured back to the ground floor.

Hudson checked the tracker once again to find it still locked onto BIT's signal. Carefully, the group raced to the open elevator and ducked inside the doors.

"Where do we start?" Carson asked.

"The signal is weak, so I would wager she is farther below the grounds. We will start at Level 3 and work our way up," Hudson said. He held the tracker against the bioprint scanner and locked on the frequency, activating the sensor. He pressed Sub-Level 3 on the touchpad, and the elevator doors closed.

Carson noticed the two small security cameras in the upper part of the elevator. "Are you guys sure these ghost thing-a-ma-jiggies work?"

"Well, if we get shot when the doors open, we'll know they don't," Hudson said.

Heather turned to Hudson with a scorned look. "That's not funny." She took a deep breath and tried to relax.

The elevator passed Sub-Level 1. However, as they passed Level 2 the elevator slowed.

"Oh, no…are we stopping?" Damian asked.

"Someone's getting on," Hudson said, as he prepared himself.

They pressed themselves against the walls of the elavtor, hoping to avoid detection. They froze as the doors opened. An unsuspecting lab technician was standing before them with his back turned, engaged in heated conversation. Music blared from the ear buds he was wearing. The glass doors read: *Bioscience Level 2: Phase III Clearance Only*. The clueless tech yelled remarks across to the other three scientists, who were busy in the main laboratory. Hudson could hear the Summit playing through the speakers inside the space.

As they introduced Colonel Arklow to the podium, the tech pointed at the others inside the lab. "Yeah, and I bet she'll want the serum completed and tested in the next hour, right?" he shouted as he stuck his other hand in the elevator to hold the door.

"You know it," called one tech. "But I bet you wouldn't be so brave right now if you knew she wasn't out there waiting to go on stage, would you?" The other techs laughed.

"Forget that bitch!" the tech hissed.

They remained immobile, waiting for the tech to turn to them, pondering what would happen once he noticed the intruders. Heather looked to Carson with dread. As he calculated the environment, Hudson counted five techs, including their friend at the elevator.

"Yeah, she can sit and spin for all I care. I'm done with all that," the tech said. He began to turn, but leaned out again. "I mean, even God had seven days to create the universe. Sheesh!"

"Shut up," one of them shouted back. "Get coffee already!"

With that, the tech waved them off and placed the loose ear bud into his left ear. Then, he backed into the elevator and pressed the button for the upper level fourth floor. The elevator doors closed. Since Hudson had pressed Sub-Level 3, the elevator descended downward.

"Dammit," the tech murmured, as he hammered the fourth floor button on the touchpad, as if that would change his course. He hummed along with the music playing in his ears, oblivious to the elusive passengers behind him.

When the elevator doors opened on Sub-Level 3, the group peered into the large, dark chamber. The broadcast of the Summit echoed through the speakers of the vacant storage area. At the left side, stood the ominous cyborg, plugged into at a hefty energy station. Toward the back of the room, Ellen was laying on a cot in a glass cell, her eyes closed. Her bent knee waved back and forth in a lulling manner as she awaited the saviors who were right before her. The tech hammered on the *Close Door* button until the doors slid shut. However, Hudson had no plans on riding to the fourth floor.

"Hey, buddy," Hudson whispered as he tapped the tech on the back. As the flabbergasted tech spun toward them, Hudson delivered a fierce uppercut. He then took the wobbly tech by the shoulders and used the man's head to block the elevator doors from closing. When the doors slid open, Hudson dropped the man's limp body into doorway to keep the elevator from returning to the upper floors. "There…that should hold off other visitors for a while." Hudson turned to the team and noted the stunned looks on their faces.

"Some students use the idiom *badassary* occasionally, and I have always wondered what that term meant. I believe I now have my answer," Damian said with a smile, as he stepped over the unconscious tech.

They could hear the crowd cheering through the speakers when Colonel Arklow took the stage to feed the world his calculated lies. They stepped into the shadows of the room and made their way toward Ellen's holding cell with guarded approach. Hudson noted the four security cameras positioned at each corner of the room. "We'll need to take care of those."

"Why? They can't see us," Heather said.

"They can't see us, but they can see everything else. We can't deal with interruptions. Damian, handle those, please…*quietly*. We don't want to wake up our colossal friend."

"Got it," Damian said as zipped through the room. The gravity of his speed allowed him to run high against the walls. He darted to each camera, removing the power supply from each unit. He then returned to the ground where the others were standing.

Together, they approached Ellen's cell. Hudson leaned against the glass and knocked on it. Ellen didn't seem to notice the tapping at first, so Hudson knocked once again with more effort. She opened her mouth, preparing to hurl well-rehearsed insults at whoever was disturbing her, but froze once she noticed her friends were standing there. She placed her hand over her mouth, checked that the cyborg was still in sleep mode, and hurried to the glass.

"Oh, my God!" she whispered, placing her hand against the glass. "I am so glad to see you guys! Get me out of here." Ellen looked into the distance and noticed the elevator doors bouncing against the unconscious body of the tech, unable to close. "Is that guy dead?"

"No...just knocked the hell out," Heather added with a smile.

Hudson stepped to the small control panel of the door and examined it. "Dammit! It's shielded," he said, wiping the sweat from his brow.

"What does that mean?" Carson asked.

He pointed at the outline of the hand on the panel. "It's protected from signal hacks." He stood there, thinking, trying to arrive at possible options. He retrieved the signal tracker from his pocket, its status bar now solid green. Then, he pulled the tracker apart to expose a QWERTY keypad. "I think I can find a frequency, but it will be tricky." He held out the device and searched for the lock code. The group gathered behind him, awaiting the key that would lead to Ellen's freedom. At that moment, the device flickered green. "Got it!" Hudson said with a smile.

Just as they began to revel in the bliss of their success, the hand indicator on the panel buzzed a bright red. The snapping sound echoed around them as the ventilation holes on the glass cell capped. All seams around the structure sealed tight. Hudson looked at Ellen's expression of disbelief.

"What's happening?" Ellen asked with alarm.

"It triggered a defense response," Hudson replied.

Water began to fill the cell, rising from below Ellen's feet. BIT scurried up Ellen's leg and buried himself in the pocket of her hoodie. "It'll fill to the top," Ellen called to them.

Heather stepped back and held her hands toward the cell. "Hold on!" she shouted as she pummeled the enclosure with fire. However, the intense heat didn't alter the foundation. She then attempted to freeze a section of the glass.

Carson leaned forward and punched the icy circle with all he had, but the prison was unaffected. The water had nearly risen to Ellen's knees. "Step back," Carson commanded. He pulled his shirt off allowing his wings to open wide.

"Again with the shirt!" Ellen called out.

As he stood upright, his eyes shined. He focused his energy, attempting to shatter the glass with the power of his thoughts. With his power combined with Heather's temperature assaults, he managed to force the structure to bow, but it would not weaken.

"Hurry!" Ellen said as the frigid water reached below her waist. Her mind whirled with images of what would happen to her body when the liquid entered her lungs. In her mind's eye, she could envision her body burning from the inside out, shorting out as if she were radio dropping into a bathtub.

"We're not breaking this," warned Hudson. "It's reinforced Authoritan poly-glass."

"Damn!" Damian said. He placed his hands against the glass and vibrated, hoping to shatter the structure. Still, it wouldn't budge. At that moment, Damian took several steps back, and then ran high into the air. With great force, he came down hard, smashing into the front of the glass. His flaccid body slid down the glass to the floor, dazed by the smash.

The team remained so focused on saving Elle n thatthey didn't notice the cyborg upon them. They looked at the creature that had once been David Porter. His face was no longer human; no flesh was visible. The virus had completed taken over his body.

David Porter was dead.

"Oh, hell!" Heather said as she stumbled backward.

As Hudson attempted to step away from the robot, it struck him in the chest, sending him soaring across the room. He smacked against the far wall and toppled into a mass of storage boxes that lined the space.

Heather looked to Ellen, who was now treading the water beneath her as she continued to rise to the top. "David, stop it!" Heather shouted. The cyborg turned to her and stomped in her direction. It took her by the neck and hoisted her into the air. As it squeezed the life from her body, Heather focused her energy into her arms. She screamed with fury as she raised her hands to the android's face. The fire grew brighter and brighter until the bright blue flames ran over both of her arms. She shot an intense beam of fire into the thing's face, forcing it to let her go. It stumbled backwards, momentarily stunned by the blast. Realizing what had happened, it stepped forward once again, intending to stomp her into the ground.

Its leg shifted downward onto Heather's body with all of its might as Carson soared high overhead, his eyes shining intensely. He spread his wings and circled above, entering a dive-bombing position and piling into the android's spine before it could crush Heather. Carson bashed the thing into the wall in front of it, splintering the sheetrock to rubble. He stumbled back, stupefied by the attack.

Ellen held her hands against the prison ceiling, her air wearing thin. She felt faint from lack of oxygen. Her body was cold, frigid, the water taking her temperature down to dangerous levels. There was no way out of her predicament. Weakness began to overtake her.

Damian regained consciousness while the android was digging itself out of the debris. As it rushed Carson, Damian shot like a rocket toward the robot, driving into it with everything he had. He whacked the droid with such force that the shock wave threw the group backward. The android smashed into a set of large forklifts, crumbling them to bits. Damian stumbled back and wiped his hands on his pants. Then, he took one look at Heather, who was just getting to her feet. "Woman! You're on fire!"

"I *know* I'm on fire!" Heather said as she shook the flames from her arms. The android arose from the wreckage and trudged toward them. At that point, Heather changed, altering her form from fire to ice. Thick frost and ice covered her body as she charged up an intense blast. Slamming her fists together, she sent a whirl of frigid ice toward the android, freezing it in place from the neck down to its feet. She kept the ice beam steady to hold the droid in place and turned to Carson and Damian. "His head!" she struggled. "Get the thing on his head!"

Hudson was shaken from his dazed state by the voice over the broadcast that was calling for Dr. Monday to take the podium. He groggily stumbled out of the debris, seeing Ellen nearly submerged in the cell, barely able to stay alive. He ran to the cell hoping he could find a way to shatter it. "Hurry! She's going to die!" he shouted to the team. Though in Hudson's heart he knew it was useless, he picked up a broken steel beam and beat on the thick panes of the prison with all his might.

Carson and Damian looked to Hudson, and then to each other. Realizing it was David or them, they sprinted toward the android encased in ice. Damian retrieved the USB device HANA had given him from his pocket and climbed the ice. The droid fiercely tossed its head back and forth, trying to shake the heroes from it. Carson's eyes burned bright as he used his strength to hold the android's head still. Then, Damian shot forward to install the device. As his hand connected with the apparatus, the droid pitched its head backward with force, causing Damian to crush the USB device against its metal armor.

"Damn it!" Damian shouted.

Suddenly, the droid broke one arm free and took hold of Damian's leg. As it pulled him forward, Damian's hand snagged against the robot's mental controller, cracking it. The thing shrieked while the bright sparks popped and crackled. It broke from the ice, lifting Damian into the air.

Heather stepped back. "No! Don't rip it off his head! It'll kill him!"

Carson looked back. "Okay, well, we'll be more careful with the monster trying to kill us."

The android tossed Damian into the rubble as Carson tumbled to the ground. Carson rose to his feet quickly, and then he looked back at Ellen's impenetrable prison. It was apparent that Ellen was going to die. They had tried to shatter her cell with every object they had at their disposal...except one. He heard the robot shatter through the ice that remained. Carson grinned and turned to face the machine.

"Come on!" he shouted at the thing. "Come at me, you son-of-a-bitch!"

With a mighty bellow, the cyborg broke into a full run and took Carson by the throat. Hudson ducked as it slammed Carson against the cell where Ellen barely held on to her life. It stared into Carson's eyes, small sparks sputtering from the broken control on its head.

"Come on!" Carson choked. "Put me out of my misery, you bastard! Punch me! Do it!" The cyborg reared back and threw its heavy fist forward to shatter Carson's skull. Carson fought free in just enough time to dodge its powerful fist, allowing it to burrow through the glass of Ellen's cell. The front of the prison shattered. Ellen's weak body poured onto the floor with the mass of water.

Oblivious to the scrimmage below, Keating stood curtain side, eagerly awaiting her turn at the podium. Victory was so close she could taste it on her tongue, like sweet wine. After her announcement, it would be a matter of months before the Insurgence would be dead, rotting in the forgotten streets of the filthy Regions of the Unfortunates. Once the indigent were puddles of gunge, she would have them swept away, washed into the gutters of nothingness. Then, she would reveal her *true* self unto the world. With the unconquerable David Porter at her side, she would slaughter all those who opposed her. He wouldn't be defeated as the only key to his destruction was in her possession. It was perfect, absolutely perfect. Her attention was diverted for a split-second when the floor under her feet quivered against the war buried beneath her.

As Doctor Monday finished her rhetoric, she cleared her throat. "Now, if you please," Monday began. "Make welcome to the stage, our Commander in Chief, President Ophelia Keating." A thunder of applause erupted throughout the crowd. Keating prepared the smile she had rehearsed to perfection and broke through the curtains to receive their devotion.

As the witch above them reached the podium to shake Dr.

311

Monday's hand, Ellen raised her head and took a deep gasp of air. She broke into heaving coughs while the furious droid stomped toward her.

"Leave her alone!" Hudson called.

With both hands, it took Ellen by the waist and raised her into the air. Ellen's head hung wearily in front of her. The cyborg began to squeeze her, intending to squish her in two.

"Stop it!" Heather cried as she stumbled forward, tossing flames at it.

The monster was undeterred. It pulled Ellen close to its face as it squeezed tighter.

"Ellen!" Carson shouted. "Ellen, fight it! Fight back!"

Ellen opened her somnolent eyes and looked at the robot.

"David," she whispered. From the corner of her eye, she noticed that Damian was preparing to dash at it, but she held up her hand to signal for him to remain still. "David," she managed again as she placed her hands on its cheeks. "David, I know you can hear me. You can hear my voice. There is something left of you in there. I know it."

In the prison of David's mind, the room had closed in and grown constricted. The nucleus was absorbing his physical body, devouring him. The binds had choked the life from his weary veins. He was nearly spent, but he heard the voice of his angel as she spoke. And the voice made him open his blood-filled eyes.

"David, please. I know you don't want to do this. You couldn't." She placed her forehead against his, closed her eyes, and whispered. "When I told you I didn't know if I had dreamt of you—I lied. I dream of a man whose face I can't see. And in those dreams I'm alone…and afraid…in the dark where monsters hide in the shadows, waiting for me." As the tears rolled down her cheeks, she felt the grip of the cyborg loosening around her. "And then my faceless prince comes and takes me into his arms. And the monsters run away. He takes me away, far away from all the darkness, far away from all the fear. And he holds me close to him."

The words of his angel filled his heart with a strength he had never known. He fought against the nucleus, pulling himself free of the light, ripping the coils from around his torso. He could feel its weakness, its inability to contain him. The angel had to be found. The android pulled her closer to it, but not to harm her, to sense her, feel her. She rubbed its face gently, feeling the sensation of the cold metal underneath her hands. She connected to it, sparks of energy feeding back and forth between them, a life force of power.

"I've dreamt of my prince all my life, but I've never looked into his eyes. I've never touched his lips. I've never seen his face...until I saw *you*." And with that, Ellen kissed David on his mouth, feeling the warmth spread through his steely exterior. He pulled her close.

Heather held her hands over her mouth in amazement, stepping forward with the others, who watched in awe as the pair ignited with electricity. They seemed to glow, intertwining with one another, becoming one. Suddenly, the cyborg howled as it dropped Ellen to the floor. Damian snapped with a flash and gathered Ellen up, bringing her into the safety of the team. They watched the cold humanoid fall to its knees, writhing in pain. It pulled at the apparatus against its head, ripping it from its skull, and as it did, the metal covering peeled from David's face. He roared with might as he threw the device to the ground and smashed it to cinders with fist.

And the cyborg was no more.

IMPOSTER

K eating placed her hands on the podium and allowed the crowd to continue their praise. She smiled with arrogant pride, staring into the sea of people before her. She raised a hand to quiet the audience.

"Colonel Arklow, Dr. Monday, and good citizens of the Global Parliament—I bid you welcome. You know, it's been a long time since we've spoken, but I trust you haven't forgotten about me." Again, the crowd erupted in ovation. Keating looked into the lenses of the multitude of cameras that lined the front row. "And for all you wonderful citizens at home, I would like for you to be a part of this. Can we turn and show the folks at home who is here with them?" The cameras turned to the cheering crowd. Keating raised her hand once again. As the people silenced, she said, "Citizens…I have come to you tonight to talk about a true problem we are facing as a society today, a plague that is destroying the fabric of our planet—a disease that is draining our families, our economy, and our future. Yes, I am referring to *Caudovirales putrescat*, or as you know it, Scourge." The crowd booed at the word.

Far below Keating's feet, Ellen rushed to David, who rested on his knees before them. "David?" she said dropping to him, taking him by the hands. "David can you hear me?"

With the removal of the control device, much of the metallic exoskeleton had melted from his skin. The right side of his body remained covered in the bio-metal, which extended from his pectoral to his fingertips, but the steel was warm in Ellen's hands. David felt shaken and disoriented. As he realized who Ellen was, he touched her face causing her to smile through her tears.

"Oh, my God...you're real," he said.

Their lips found each other like strangers in the dark. Ellen fell into his arms as he embraced her. "I thought we would lose you," she said.

"I did, too," he replied.

"Are you okay? Are you able to stand?" she asked.

He shook the fuzz from his brain. "Yeah...yeah, I think so."

"You know," Carson said. "This is all sweet and stuff, but we'd like to meet the guy who's tried to kill us... *twice*, I might add."

Ellen hurried to her feet and helped David to his. "Oh, God... sorry, guys. I forgot you were there for a second. David, let me introduce you to the people I've told you about. This is Damian."

"The quickest dude alive," David said weakly, taking Damian by the hand. "You're one quick bastard."

"Appreciations, Mr. Porter," Damian said.

"And this is..."

"Heather," he said. "Yeah, we've sort of met."

"You remember," Heather said with a smile.

David winced. "You don't forget a lady who can spit fire and ice, I don't think."

Ellen pointed to Carson, who appeared to be taken by the tall, stout, handsome man before him. "And this is Carson."

"Wings," David said with a smile. He shook Carson's hand.

"Yeah," Carson said as he moved his wings. "You can't miss 'em."

"Wicked right hook, by the way, man," David added.

"Uh, thanks!" Carson said. As Ellen led David past him, Carson looked at her in wonder, mouthing—*Oh, my God.* Ellen smiled.

She led David to Hudson. "And last, but not least, this is Dr. Hudson, the man of the hour."

"I don't know about that," Hudson said as he took David's hand, scowling in pain. "You must be the infamous Mr. Porter." Hudson ached from the battle.

David smiled. "Affirmative," he said.

The word made Hudson freeze for a moment. It was like seeing a ghost. *Affirmative.* Not only was it the word itself that caused the memory to return, but the manner in which had David said it. He could see Sutherland so clearly in his mind, standing right before him.

"Dr. Hudson, you all right?" Ellen asked.

"Uh, yeah!" Hudson said, as he broke himself from his trance. "Sorry. I'm just realizing that I don't rejuvenate like you guys, nor am I as young."

David held onto Hudson's hand. "Ellen told me what you want us to do, Doctor. And I think it's the greatest thing. I don't know how much of a hero I may be, but knowing what Keating has in store, I sure would like to try for you guys."

"I appreciate that, David," Hudson said. "Tell me…do you remember everything that just happened?"

A look of shame crossed his face. "I'd like to say no, but I do. And guys, I am so, so sorry. I couldn't control it."

"Don't worry, David. We understand," Hudson added.

Ellen's pocket began beeping and chirping. She smiled and retrieved the small bot from inside it. BIT unfolded and looked up at her. "And there's my hero." She turned to David. "And this is BIT, the little superhero who saved both of us."

BIT flexed his petite metal arms.

"Guys, we don't have much time to rest. We have to get out of here," Hudson said. "The Summit is coming to an end soon, and a slew of guards and soldiers will scour this room. I don't want to be here when they do." Hudson said.

"I must concur!" Damian added.

The group gathered themselves and approached the service exit. However, Ellen suddenly found it impossible to leave, not with Keating's plans so close to fruition. What were they to do—just walk away? Once they returned to continue the fight, would it be too late? How many would be dead? She stopped. "Wait...wait. Guys, we can't go."

"Girl, Mr. Muscle here must have knocked the hell out of me, cause I thought you said we can't go," Heather muttered as she continued toward the exit.

"Seriously," Ellen said. The group turned to her. "Look... Keating is up there lying to the world. She's telling them about this new vaccine for Scourge, a miracle cure that's supposed to rid the world of the disease once and for all."

"It's a fake," David added. "It's a stronger version of the Scourge that comes alive in a few months after injection."

"And once it does, it kills someone in a matter of hours instead of weeks," Ellen added. "Worst of all, she's going to offer it to *everyone* in the lower Regions...for free. The entire world will run to the health centers as fast as they can."

A look of horror crossed Hudson's face. "But...that would wipe out all the lower classes, all the Insurgence."

"Everyone—our families, everyone we love," David said. "And once they're dead that's when she'll make her move to take over—for good."

Hudson shook his head. "It's not safe. We're too tired and there are too many of them. Let's go back the Core, get our thoughts in order. Then, we'll come back and..."

Ellen stepped forward. "It will be too late by then! What do you think Keating will do when she comes down and sees this mess, me gone, David gone? She won't accept defeat. She'll get stronger, increase security, and come after us. We'll never have a chance like this again."

And Ellen was right; Hudson knew it. Right now, at that moment, Keating's need for adoration, the worship the Summit provided her, made her weak. She was off guard and unprepared. If there was a time to strike at the heart of immorality, it was now.

"You're right," Hudson admitted with a sigh. "She's weak right now."

Carson groaned. "Dammit! So, what are we going to do?"

"We can catch her when the Summit is over. Hide out," Heather said. "Then, when she's least expecting us, we sneak up and beat the shit out of her."

"Whatever—where would we have to hide, Heather?" Damian asked.

Ellen walked to Heather and took her hands. "We have to make a *grand statement*, Heather…*one for the whole world to see*."

Heather smiled as she remembered her own words. She nodded her head. "Hell, yeah," she replied.

Above them, Keating rounded the podium, microphone in hand. She stretched out her hand to the sea of people before her. "For way too long, we have struggled to treat our loved ones, our parents, our children, our sisters, our brothers." The crowd cheered in agreement. "Scourge has wiped out entire families in a matter of months, families who were too poor to pay the high price of the current treatments, which cost way too much to produce. We… *cower* in the dark, hiding from a monster that is smaller than the tiniest cell in the body. But it finds us. It *always* finds us. It finds us, and it kills us." At that moment, pictures of the infected flashed on the large prompters behind Keating.

"Save us!" yelled a woman in the audience.

"Save *you*?" Keating said as the crowd rumbled. "*Save you*?" The crowd grew louder. "I say, I will *save you all!*" The crowd exploded in applause. "With this!" She presented the vial of serum. "Vaccine X25. For years now, I have kept my head down, working with the brilliant scientists and chemists of Parliament to develop this… this miracle…for the citizens of the world. Vaccine X25 is the first approved inoculation for Scourge, which completely prevents transmission of the virus in *any… living… creature!*" The audience rose to their feet, screaming and cheering at the outstanding news. Keating smiled and wiped an insincere tear from her eye. She held her hand up to silence the crowd. "And to add to that, dear people, I have signed a bill that will allow Vaccine X25 to be given to every single man, woman, and child who lives in the lower tier Regions... for *free!*"

The eruption of the audience was so intense that the media had to cover the microphones to avoid bursting their audio equipment. Keating wiped another tear from her eye and motioned for the crowd to calm down, but their enthusiasm could not be deterred. *This is it,* she thought. *I've done it. I have taken over the world, the entire world. They love me, with absolute adoration. To them, I am now perfect. To them, I am everything. To them, I am a god. And like a god, I will smite with furious anger all those who stand opposed to my will. The streets will run red with their treacherous blood.* Keating looked up to Snitch and Scoundrel, who gave her congratulatory waves from the upper balcony. Then, she turned back to her disciples and raised her hands high into the air, absorbing their adulation like a dry sponge. All was going better than she could have ever hoped until she heard a voice over the mass of speakers.

"Tell them what happens..."

Keating's chest went cold.

"Tell them what happens to them after they take the vaccine, Ophelia," the voice demanded.

It rattled Keating from the inside-out almost forcing her to vomit. She spun to see not only Ellen, freed from her cell, but the others standing with her, strong and determined. David, now unrestricted of all control, stood in the midst of the group, glaring at her with fierce insolence. He tossed the broken bionic device at her feet.

"Wh...what are you doing here?" Keating questioned, as she stumbled around the podium. "Security!"

"There's no Security now," Carson said, as he flexed his wings triggering the audience to gasp in surprise.

"Tell them what happens when they take the vaccine!" Ellen repeated. A hush fell over the confused public. The cameras zoomed in on the strange assembly who had taken the stage.

Miles away, Ellen's mother raised a hand to her mouth in awe and moved closer to the television. "Ellen," she said as she touched her daughter's face on the screen.

"*Tell them!*" Ellen roared as Keating stumbled backward. "Or better yet, *we'll* tell them." Ellen held up BIT, who mutated into a small phonic device. The bot began to replay the exchange between Ellen and Keating directly in Keating's voice:

Tomorrow evening, in front of the entire world, I plan to pass my most significant decree yet. Vaccine X25.

Blah, blah, blah—what is Vaccine X25?

I thought you would never ask. What I hold in my hand is a breakthrough immunization for the disease Scourge—the ailment that plagues the lower Regions of the world. Years ago, when we created the Scourge virus, I had hoped it would wipe out the filthy Regions of the deprived.

Wait, you created Scourge?

Keating fell onto the stage as the audience grumbled. Debilitated by what was happening to her world, she felt her power slipping through her thin fingers.

Oh, yes...It's what inside the vaccine that really counts. In reality, it's an augmented version of the Scourge virus, one that lays dormant. This particular formulation remains inactive for approximately ninety days. Once awakened, the virus replicates at an exponential rate, killing the host in a matter of hours, leaving nothing of them but a puddle of goo.

"What the hell is this?" shouted one man.

"She's crazy!" another woman yelled.

"Get her the hell out of Parliament!" said another.

"Arrest her!"

"She ain't no *god!*"

There was no color remaining in Keating's face. She was without will. She looked up to Snitch and Scoundrel for help, her eyes pleading for them to save her, but the twins faded into the darkness of the balcony, leaving their leader to go down with the ship. She looked at Ellen and saw the smile of satisfaction on the girl's face.

Ellen glared at her and said, "And that, *Ms. President*, is how you save the world."

The Federation began to make their way back into the green room from the balcony, satisfied in the knowledge that Ophelia Keating was no more. Her reign was at an end. It would be a new world, a fresh start for the planet.

Carson turned to Hudson, who trailed behind them. "So, how did you like that?"

Hudson smiled. "Well, it was definitely…" The crowd gasped as Hudson's face contorted into a pained expression. As he fell to his knees, they saw Keating standing behind him, sweat covering the pale skin on her face that twisted into a manic pose. In place of her right hand was an android-like dagger.

Keating looked at the group with the eyes of a crazed psychopath. "I will kill you *all!*"

Before David knew what had come over him, fury and fear prompted him to strike her in the face with his new armored hand, sending her upward and back onto the floor. He stood there, waiting for her to move, yet knowing she couldn't. Ellen and Heather rushed to Hudson's side as he struggled to catch his breath.

"Hudson!" Heather cried. "Hudson, can you hear us?"

Hudson rolled over into the small puddle of blood that pooled onto the stage floor. "Help me up."

"No!" Ellen said. "Don't move. Don't move. We'll get you help." It was at that moment that Hudson fell unconscious. "Hudson?" Ellen shook his face. "Andre!"

"Oh, God…is he dead?" Carson asked, his eyes wet with tears.

Damian felt Hudson's wrist. "No…no he's not dead. But he will be if we don't…" Damian's eyes grew wide. "Mother-heifer," he muttered.

Keating rose to her feet and turned to them with a staggering stance. Her shattered jaw hung on its hinge, static and sparks from the broken appendage sizzled around the bloody fragment. The ripped flesh hung in gory clumps around the left side of her face, her red mechanical eye examined them. They were not dealing with a human. They were dealing with a functional bionic humanoid soldier. It ripped the remaining flesh from its metal face as it marched toward them. It took David by the throat, dropping him to his knees. He could feel the thing rip at his windpipe, attempting to tear through his throat.

"David!" shouted Ellen. Without thinking, Ellen jumped to her feet and threw her hands forward sending bolts of energy toward the droid. The surge connected with a blinding flash, freezing the robot in place. She felt herself connect to it, become one. Her eyes faded into milky-pale masses while the sparks rattled from the android that was helpless against Ellen's power. In her mind she heard Keating's voice: *Silly girl... you are my only weakness.* Ellen's ability to unite with the droid was the droid's weakness, its fear.

With the droid locked by Ellen's power, David used both of his bulky arms to smash the humanoid's head into fragments, ripping it from its body. The thing swung its arms and stumbled back and forth before crumbling into a heap of smoking gears and wires before them.

"The President wasn't real!" shouted someone from the audience.

"What was it?" yelled someone in the distance, as the crowd broke into loud protest.

Ellen shook the fog from her mind and attempted to steady herself.

"Ellen...are you okay?" Heather asked as she took Ellen by the hands.

"I...I think so."

Carson leaned to Ellen. "I don't know how you're feeling on the inside, but that was wicked-cool!"

David approached her, taking her into his arms. "Are you okay?"

"Yeah, yeah...I'm okay. Are you?" David nodded his head in agreement. Ellen looked to Hudson. "We have to get Dr. Hudson out of here before he bleeds to death."

"We're not getting through this crowd," Carson said, pointing to the audience that was now breaking into riot against the attending soldiers and Agents.

Heather took Ellen's hand. "That service exit…where you were."

David gently took Hudson's arm and lifted him up. "I got him. Let's get him out of here, quick!" David hoisted him over his shoulder, and they began to make their escape.

MONSTERS

The team boarded the elevator as fast as their legs could take them while the crowd outside exploded into insurrection. Damian held the scanner to the elevator's bio-print device, and Heather pressed Sub-Level 3 on the touch pad. The door slid closed.

"What…the *hell*?!" Heather said.

"That has to be the freakiest thing I have ever seen in my entire life," Carson said.

"How is Hudson?" Ellen asked.

Heather reached for Hudson's wrist. "He's alive."

"Good…good…we have to get him out of here," Ellen replied.

Damian stood there, still in shock. "The President was a robot—unequivocally a robot of the highest nature!"

Ellen was just as bewildered. "How could she be a droid? I don't understand. She was so real; she was so…so…"

"Bitchy?" Heather said.

"Right!" Ellen agreed. "How could something like that be so human?"

They exited the elevator and made their way through the shadows and the rubble toward the hidden service exit.

"Remember HANA, though, guys," Carson added. "She's real, and she doesn't even have a physical presence. Sometimes I forget she is just a hologram."

David looked back. "If Keating wasn't real, who created her?"

"What do you mean?" Damian asked.

David turned to him as they reached the exit. "Someone had to build the robot we destroyed." David pressed the button to open the heavy doors to the tunnel.

Carson paused. "Oh, hell, you're right, man. And whoever it was had to be the one running the show."

David pressed the button at the doors again. "What the hell is wrong with this thing?" he growled, as he hammered on the control panel.

Carson looked up at Ellen, alarmed. "Then...we didn't defeat Keating at all. The real Keating is still out there."

"See...and I thought you guys were dumbasses." Keating's laughter filled the space. They were immobilized by the sound of the familiar voice. A figure approached them through the shadows. It paused. "You shits have ruined everything, so I suppose congratulations are in order. I still can't believe you did it, though. Sure, I expected that you might break free, get away, come back to fight the good fight." Keating continued to walk toward them, but what stepped into the red glow of the emergency exit lights was certainly not Keating. Snitch held the tongue box of the demolished droid to her mouth, which allowed her to duplicate Keating's vocal pattern. "I didn't think that some little *wench* could demolish our new government in a matter of minutes."

"You gotta be shitting me," Carson said.

"You?" Ellen asked in bewilderment.

"No, no...not me," Snitch replied.

"Us!" shouted Scoundrel as he dropped down rom the ceiling beams.

The two began to leisurely stroll toward the group.

"But how did Keating..." Ellen began.

"Oh, the real Ophelia Keating died *years* ago. Sitting there during

326

what she thought were 'negotiations'… talking to us like she was *superior*, above us, like you *microbes* known as the human race were above the might of the Xeno species. *The people of earth will not tolerate these intrusions any longer*, she said. *Nah, nah, we can work out a compromise.* Nonsense! We Xenozians take what we wish! And so…we ripped her pretty human head off her shoulders and watched her body squirm."

"And that's when we got this great idea. The people of earth seemed to admire the annoying female," added Scoundrel. "Idolize her. So, we replicated her."

Snitch smiled. "We removed the brain of the dead human female and dichotomized it, mapped it to the perfect acumen modulation." Snitch held up the droid's dead mechanical brain, a gooey cross between the organic and synthetic. "Since we possessed the human's live neurons, we could create an altered version of her that was perfection."

"For years, the humans never knew," Scoundrel said. "*You* didn't even know!" He hooted. "We made our Keating great, powerful, a commanding leader."

"Yeah, if you say so, freak," Heather spat, causing Scoundrel to hiss at her menacingly.

"What I *say* is that our synthetic completely changed this planet," Snitch added.

"You mean, *ruined* this planet," Ellen interjected.

Snitch shrugged. "Eh…potato—potahto."

"If you two consider yourselves to be so very advanced, why create Keating to begin with?" Damian asked. "Why not just overtake the human race yourselves using your palpable aptitude and unconventional wit?"

Snitch looked at Damian. "Just the two of us? Hey, we're awesome, but we couldn't fight the whole world alone. Our people abandoned the Earth, leaving us behind."

"Smart crowd," interjected Carson.

"We needed someone who could coax society, lead them. To do it right, we had to make the droid itself believe it was a real human— which was no easy task, let me tell you. Sometimes that bitch got a little too full of itself, even for us, but we had to learn to restrain ourselves, allow her to lead completely, so not to shatter the illusion of her control. But the most important reason of all is we needed someone to shield us and…as you say…be the fall guy. Once the fake Keating had the world under control, we could decommission her and take the wheel."

David sneered. "Why not just go back to your own damn planet? Why stay here with us idiotic microbes?"

"The Federation," Scoundrel scoffed. "The strong one—he did it—he was the one who overpowered us, but not before we killed him with this." Scoundrel held up the spearhead laced with the Xenathium toxin. "They left us for dead with no ship. No Xenocraft meant no Odyssey. No Odyssey meant no Zanbar dimension."

"And no return to Xenoe," Snitch finished. "But…we found hope." She walked away from the group into the shadows at the back of the room where a massive object sat covered with a dirty brown tarp. She pulled the covering away to reveal the makeshift machine, which contained rows of silver circles centered on a control base. "In the wreckage of other Xenocrafts, we found pieces of precious Odysseys. The only thing we were missing was Xenoeon, powercells of immense energy from the mines of Xenoe. And we never thought we would find any until we saw this." Snitch held up Ellen's lost pendant.

Ellen's eyes widened. "What are you doing with that?! Give it back! That was my father's."

"Then, it wasn't his to take!" Snitch shouted.

Ellen took a confident breath and stepped forward. "Give it back, or I'll rip your arm off and take it."

Snitch laughed. She tore the pendant from the necklace and slipped it into a small aperture on the side of the Odyssey. Once she did, the machine shimmered with a bright hue outlined in strange symbols and etchings. The circles turned, spinning within each other. Faster and faster they grew until a liquid-like foundation appeared in the center of a portal that was now alive.

Scoundrel's face stretched into absolute contentment. "Yes!"

Snitch approached the Federation, but this time she pulled at the synthetic flesh that covered her scaly gray skin. "Now, we will once again destroy the mighty Federation. Then, we will return to the Zanbar dimension. We shall smite those who abandoned us, and we will gather the loyal to return to this pitiful planet to finish what we have started."

"Yes," hissed Scoundrel as he joined her, dropping clumps of his gooey skin onto the ground, exposing the alien flesh underneath it. "We will kill the humans, and those we do not destroy, we will take to enslave in the deep mines of Xenoe."

David lowered Hudson to the ground, placing him in safety. Then, he walked forward. "And how do you suppose you little guys will do all that?"

Carson smiled and joined David, spreading his wings. "Yeah, you'll have a problem there."

"There'll be a few of us to get through first," Damian said as he zipped beside the men, his body quivering with speed energy.

Heather whipped her hands forward, lighting one fist with fire, the other with ice. "You don't stand a chance."

Ellen slammed her fists together, triggering the bright blueish-white electrical sparks. "Don't forget, just one of the Federation destroyed your leader. And if one of us could kill Goliaric, imagine what all of us can do to the two of you."

As the twins ripped the last of the slimy human covering from their bodies showing their full Xenozian selves, Snitch looked to Scoundrel with a sneer. "Yes, let's show them what we can do."

With that, the twins took one another's hands. Soon, the cellular composition of their bodies amalgamated, absorbing into one another. The two beings fused together into a puddling alien mass that bubbled and pulsated, growing larger, gigantic. Two great, muscular arms stretched wide before them as the thing stood upright.

"Oh, God," David said, stepping in front of the team. There, before his eyes, stood the beast from his dream. Its large curled horns wrapped around at the sides of its head. It stood upright, towering at a full nine feet. Large tusks protruded from its strong jaws. The red eyes opened, staring straight into David's soul. "It takes both of them," David realized.

Ellen placed a hand on David's bio-metallic arm. "Goliaric," she said with dread.

They froze in place as the mighty Goliaric smiled at them. "Did you miss me?" With a quick thrust, the creature swung upward, catching David's chin, sending him spiraling upward and back into the exit doors.

"Move!" Ellen commanded as Goliaric charged like a gigantic bull. With one hand, he grabbed Ellen by her legs and tossed her effortlessly across the room.

Carson's eyes illuminated as he leapt into the air just in time to avoid Goliaric's swing. As he flew behind the creature, it swatted at him as if he were a pesky fly. Carson used his mind to boost one forklift from the back of the room, plowing it into Goliaric's spine. With a grunt, the beast tumbled onto the ground.

Grabbing a thick roll of steel cable, Damian burst into full sprint, wrapping the rope around Goliaric from his feet to his waist. Goliaric struggled to free himself from under the forklift. Damian continued to wrap the beast tightly like a mummy, but it was of no use. Goliaric shredded through the strong cables and whacked Damian with might, heaving him into the wall.

As Goliaric attempted to pull the iron cables from his body, out of nowhere threads of thick current took hold of him. He roared in pain as Ellen walked toward him, casing his body and the metal cable in thousands of watts of electricity. The monster shivered and shook under the impact. Carson soared too close, allowing Goliaric the chance to rip off the cable and throw it at him, enfolding him and his wings like an electrified lasso. Carson cried out in pain as he toppled to the floor. Goliaric rose to his feet and seized Ellen by the waist. He had lifted his other colossal fist, preparing to crush her when Heather suddenly appeared.

Fire whipped around the creature, causing him to lose control of Ellen. Ellen fell to the ground, coughing, trying to catch her breath. Heather sprinted toward the beast, pummeling him with bulky orbs of fire while he stumbled backward. He snatched her from the floor and held her with her arms stretched out before him.

"I think I shall rip you in two," he sneered. At that moment, Heather felt a fury she had never felt before rise from within her. It surged through her muscles, her veins, the atoms of her body. As he tugged at her to tear her in half, blue flames ran up her arms extending up her neck. Fire burned in her eye sockets. She shouted with a loud scream as her entire body exploded with white-hot fire, scalding the beast's hands. Goliaric fell to the ground with a thud, smoking, his flesh blistered and burnt.

As Goliaric rose from the flames to stand once again, Heather, Ellen, Damian, and Carson gathered, ready to attack him as one. It was time to take the alien down for good. They flanked him and eyed one another. Goliaric opened his arms, preparing for the attack. They were prepared to strike when they heard David shout.

"Stop!" David roared. He trudged forward, anger overpowering him. He rolled his thick neck, popping the bones, limbering up for the fight he was about to face. As he stared at the behemoth, he clinched his fists, his knuckles cracking under the pressure. The bio-metallic armor covering his right arm shimmered in the flicker of the surrounding flames. "This son-of-a-bitch belongs to me," he said.

Goliaric turned to him, welcoming the contest. "Finally...a challenge!"

"David, don't!" Ellen shouted.

David raised his hand to silence her, never breaking his eye contact from Goliaric. With guarded approach, he moved forward. "So, that's how you did it. That's how you survived being pulled apart. You were two separate halves to begin with."

"Intelligent boy," Goliaric mocked. "My people were the higher class of Xeno. Our duality gave us more power, power necessary to rule of the lesser species of our planet. I am the last of my Xeno people, the last true ruler."

"Interesting story," David said. "But you got one thing wrong."

Goliaric looked at him. "Is that so? Please, regale me with your astuteness."

"You don't *have* a damn people."

They both charged, clashing with a deafening boom. They grappled with one another, wrestling against their own might. Goliaric broke free and swung wide with great vigor. David ducked, avoiding the blow, and as he did, he shot forward, extending his silver arm and landing a great crack to Goliaric's jaw. The alien stumbled backward, amazed by David's strength. His red eyes stared at David for a moment, trying to understand.

David smiled and looked down at his new armor. "Version 2.0… go figure."

As Goliaric dashed again, David crouched and jumped high into the air. Gravity brought him down, allowing him to pile-drive his elbow into Goliaric's skull. The monster snared his ankle and slung him far across the room. David tumbled against the wall and slid down to the floor. Before he knew what had occurred, Goliaric was again on him, slamming into him repeatedly. It was almost impossible to maintain consciousness while the giant pummeled him.

Ellen ran forward. "David! Stop it!" she cried.

"No!" David muttered, falling to the floor. "Stay away!" Sweat covered David's face. The Federation could tell he was almost spent.

Ellen looked to Heather. "We have to do something!"

Goliaric laughed. "Ha! And to think, I was actually nervous for…"

Before Goliaric could finish his thought, David tackled him and heaved him into the concrete wall beyond the Odyssey. Repeatedly, David sunk his fists into Goliaric, feeling the giants thick bones crack under the impact of his blows. With one solid, steady thrust, David slammed his metal fist into Goliaric's face and ripped the tusks clean from his jaws. The alien toppled to the ground in a black, bloody heap. David stood there, waiting for the creature to rise and face him, but it only laid there, a lifeless, defeated wretch, as black liquid puddled around it. David stumbled back woozily, and then he turned to the group. "And that!" he said, "is how it's done, people."

Carson jumped with excitement. "Hell yeah!"

The group cheered David as he stepped toward them, but their celebration was impulsive.

"David! Look out!" Hudson called to him.

Goliaric had risen, armed with the Xenathium spearhead. David turned too late; Goliaric sank the spear into David's body. The creature roared in victory as it drove the weapon deeper and deeper. Ellen fell to her knees in pieces, feeling faith leave her. Heather came to her, kneeling at her side.

Carson couldn't believe his eyes. "What…what just happened?"

Damian began to pace feverishly, hands holding the top of his head.

Tears fell from Hudson's eyes. "Not again," he sobbed. "Dear God, not again. Please."

Goliaric looked down at David's pained face, waiting for the light to leave his eyes. He dropped David's wilting body to the ground and stepped over it. The group could not believe that their new friend was dead. It was inconceivable. David was their hope to establish a formidable team, complete, strong, and without him, could there even be a Federation?

Goliaric stood upright, breathing heavily. He turned to the defeated group. "I am going to offer you a choice," the creature said to them. "I will take you with me to Xenoe. Put you to work in the mines there. You'll be slaves, but you will be alive. Or, I can destroy you now."

Carson looked at the alien with intense hatred. "I'll take my chances." He flapped his wings and then spread them.

"Me, too," Damian said as the speed pulsed through his body.

Heather put her hand on Carson's shoulder. "I'll join you guys." She turned into a solid form of ice.

Ellen stood up, electricity running over her body, the rage controlling her. "I will kill you…I swear it."

Goliaric smiled and shook his head. He spat a glob of blood to the floor. "And I thought at least the new Federation would be smart. I thought…"

Both of David's fists suddenly ruptured through Goliaric's chest, covered in the alien's dark blood. The black liquid spewed from the giant's mouth, arms flailing at his sides, while David ripped the creature in two. The team could see the gooey remnants of Snitch and

333

Scoundrel fighting to hang onto one another as David continued to tear at them. With Goliaric's body separated, David reared back and threw the pieces into slimy masses on the floor. He stumbled forward and fell to his knees as the astonished group ran to him.

Ellen fell in front him, taking his face in her hands. "Oh, my God! But we saw you die! How…how did you survive?"

David dropped the crumpled spearhead in front of him with a clunk. They could see it was bent and crushed inward as if it was tinfoil. He smiled. "I guess they don't make Xenathium like they used to."

"Are you okay?" Hudson called from the corner of the room, unsteadily standing to his feet.

"Dude!" Carson called as he rounded the gooey floor and went to him. "Are *you* okay, is the question?"

Hudson threw his arm around Carson's shoulder. "I haven't bled to death, yet, if that's what you're asking." Carson led him over to where David and Ellen crouched on the ground. "Congratulations, Mr. Porter."

David smiled and held out his hand before realizing the black muck covering it. "Thanks, Doctor."

Hudson looked down at his messy digits. "You'll forgive me if I pass for the moment."

"How are you alive?" Heather asked, looking to David.

"I don't know," replied David. "I should be dead."

"Listen," Damian said as he turned his head. They could hear the turmoil above, the raging peasants storming the castle for the head of the queen. "I don't believe that is the bellow of celebration."

Ellen stood and touched Hudson's shoulder. She looked at his back and noted the damp crimson that covered it. Though it seemed as the bleeding had slowed, they still needed to get help for the good doctor. "Guys, I think we can talk on the way to the hospital."

"Right, right," Carson said.

They heard the whirring sound of the Odyssey behind them. Ellen stood and helped David to his feet. He turned to the gate. "So, what are we going to do about the remains of…" The two slimy halves of the giant crawled along the floor at the base of the gate. One half fell into the portal, making its escape. "No!" David yelled.

The remaining half of the creature hastened its escape. Heather ran toward the gooey half-form as it shrieked, scurrying to avoid the flames. Damian zipped passed her and snared it by its leg as it tried to follow its sibling into the Odyssey. Though Damian had it in his clutches for a moment, the slimy muck that covered the thing was too slippery to grip. The gelatinous mass leered at them before disappearing into the soft glow of the portal.

"Dammit!" yelled Damian as he stumbled, losing his footing in the ooze.

Heather raised her arms around her head in anger. "Shit!"

Disheartened at the escape of their foe, David trudged to the Odyssey and snatched Ellen's pendant from the device causing the portal to slow to a halt. Then, he reared back and slammed his fist through the large hinge on its side, toppling the structure to the ground. He stood there, enraged, fury consuming him.

Ellen went to his side. She placed her hand against his back, calming him. "David. Let's go. Come on. They're gone now." With that, the new Federation made their way through the exit behind them.

As they walked back toward 10th Avenue and Industrial Parkway where T.J. waited for them in the SUV, Hudson paused only once to watch Parliament burning in the bright red flames, the thick black smoke rising into the night sky of a new world.

NEW FEDERATION

Ellen sat in the passenger's seat of David's car, staring through the window at the passing traffic. She had never been inside a car like it before. While it was certainly luxurious, the sports car seemed cramped. They had said little to each other since they had left the Core. Now that the battles were over, reality was settling into their minds. It was a strange sensation, being so close to someone, yet realizing they're a stranger to you.

"You're the first girl I've ever met who didn't like a Porsche," said David, breaking the silence. He turned to her and smiled.

"It's nice," she replied. "Really."

"You don't like it."

"I don't like it," she confessed with a snicker.

David laughed. "Yeah, I may have to rethink it and get something that seats over two people."

They road along in silence for another moment. Ellen turned to him. "David?"

"Yeah."

"Do you feel…weird?"

"Most of the time."

"Seriously, you and I. It's wild to know someone…"

"And not know them all at the same time?" He turned to her. "Yeah, I get it." He focused on the road before them. "It's freaky. Maybe it's best not to over think it. But I enjoy being around you, and I hope you enjoy being around me."

Ellen smiled. "Eh…you'll do."

"Good. So, let's focus on that."

His confidence and candor comforted her. "My mom told me that there are two levels to people: the level on the surface, and the other that's deep inside. You can always get to know who someone is on the outside—that's the part they let you see—but it takes time to know who they are inside. Maybe we're just doing it in reverse."

David snickered. "That's a good point. Then we're lucky."

"What do you mean?" she inquired.

"Well…r. Hudson connected us, and he connected us on the second level, that inside level your mom told you about. Now, all we need to do is get to know each other's outside level. In a way, the doctor did the hard work for us." As they turned onto Ellen's street, David took her hand. "Ellie…who knows where this will all go? But it feels wrong not to try. Do you want to try? If you don't…"

"No, I do," she interrupted. "I do. I'm glad you feel the same way. It makes me feel better." She squeezed his wide hand. "We'll take it as it comes and see where it leads. Like you said, the hard part is done." She turned to the window and smiled. "Well, you *think* it's done. You still have all kinds of lessons to learn, like what flowers to buy me, how I like my feet rubbed, how to cook spaghetti the way I like it, how I'm always right…"

David choked with a snort. "Okay, okay…so, I have homework."

"Don't worry, honey," she said patting his hand. "It's all in the textbook."

They pulled to a stop on Waverly Road in front of Meadow Ridge apartments. Ellen looked to apartment D-416, wondering what was going on within the walls. Was Eddie being his usual charming self? Would they be lucky enough for him to be gone, drowning himself at a bar? Ellen and David walked to the front door, and Ellen placed the key in the lock. She hesitated for a moment, and then opened the lock with a click.

"Mom? Mom, you here?"

"Ellen?!" Ellen heard her mother shout as she came barreling through the living room. Her mother almost leapt over the old ottoman reaching for her. She pulled Ellen close as tears filled her eyes. "Oh, my God! Are you okay? I was so scared. And then I saw you on television last night, and I knew they had killed..."

Ellen took her mother's hands and smiled. "I'm okay, Mom. I promise."

Her mother stood back and looked at her. "You look so good, sweetheart."

"Mom," Ellen said. "This is David."

Once she noticed the tall, handsome young man was with Ellen, her mother tried to situate herself. "I am so sorry," she said to David.

"Oh, it's fine," David said. "Nice to meet you, ma'am."

"What the hell is all that noise?" yelled Eddie as he stumbled into the living room. He turned to Ellen and sneered. "*You*...you got any idea how much we've worried about you?"

"I'm sure you've been worried, Eddie," Ellen said. She turned to her mother. "Mom, listen...remember when I told you I would come back for you? Get you out of here?" Her mother's eyes glazed with emotion as she fought back tears. She nodded her head yes. "Well, that's what we've come to do, Momma. Now, I want you to go get your things and we'll take you with us. It's a nice place, very nice. We'll be safe there."

"What? The hell you say!" Eddie shouted.

"Momma," Ellen continued. "Just go get your things."

As her mother walked past Eddie to gather her things, he glared at Ellen. "What's in your head? Like I'm just gonna let you walk out of here with her and leave me here?"

"That's the plan," Ellen said.

"Well, you're full of shit! She ain't going no place! You can do whatever the hell you want. I don't care. But Dahlia stays here!"

"She doesn't belong to you, Eddie," Ellen spat.

"Oh, yes, she does! Yes, she does!" he screamed walking toward them. David moved closer to Ellen leading Eddie to scowl at him. "And what are you gonna do, tough guy? Huh? You're gonna get the hell stomped outta ya, that's what!"

Her mother walked back into the living room with her bag, her hair pinned back. As she attempted to walk past Eddie, he grabbed her angrily. "You're not going anywhere, dammit!" and with that, he slapped her, knocking her to the ground. He charged at Ellen, which prompted David to take him by the throat. Ellen's hands turned into electrical conduits, lighting up the room in blue haze, a sight that petrified Eddie.

"Momma," Ellen said, holding aim on the drunken slob. "Momma...step onto the porch, okay?" Her mother scurried past them as she held her stinging face.

"Let me go, you sonuvabitch!" Eddie choked as he fought against David, who then lifted him into the air with ease. Eddie fell silent while David lowered him back to the ground.

Ellen stepped to the slob. "If you don't mind your manners, Dave here will crush you up like one of those beer cans in the corner. Now, you may not like it, but you're going to walk over to that recliner, sit back, relax, and wait until we're gone. And if you so much as make a noise, I'm going to fry your porky ass like bacon. Got me?"

David picked Eddie up, walked to the recliner, and dropped him, breaking the side of chair. Together, he and Ellen walked to the front door and met her mother. As David closed the door behind them, he grinned and said, "*Fry your porky ass like bacon?* Really, Ellie? So, these textbooks...they talk about how *not* to piss you off, right?" With that, they started back to the Core.

"And you couldn't have just looked behind you?" HANA asked as she monitored the medical droids tending to Hudson's wounds.

He winced at the needle which ran the laser along the gash, sealing the residual bleeding. "Well, I was distracted by the thousands of people looking at us. Ow! Dammit!"

"Sorry," HANA said. She looked out into the Hub from the infirmary bay and saw the group engaged in horseplay. Triggering the intercom, she warned, "Ms. Isles, don't you dare melt that monitor. Damian, sit down and keep your hands to yourself."

Hudson chuckled as he watched Damian stick his tongue out at Heather. "Who knew we'd have children?"

"Especially five," HANA added. She moved the droid from his back. "You, sir, are as good as new. Or, at least as good as you were." She looked at Hudson as he put on his shirt and turned to her. "Now, you go on out there. It's your turn to babysit for a while."

Hudson smiled. "Yes, dear." HANA winked as she dissipated. He walked into the Hub where the group was dizzy with anxious relaxation, like the feeling one gets after landing safely on the ground after skydiving. Heather and Damian had gotten used to tormenting one another. They sat together on the long couch, waiting for the noon edition news to begin. Carson paced around the room as he waited for T.J. to arrive with Lisa and Dennis. Hudson glanced at the television and took a seat in the small armchair beside him as the news began. The screen lit up with the live coverage of what was being called the *Parliamentary Revolution*, a fitting title.

The camera focused on the Parliament building, which was smoldering in smoke. Residual smoke danced around the rubble as the fire team attempted to douse the last of the flames. The camera zoomed back to focus on a reporter standing with her hand to her ear, listening to the newsroom speak to her.

"And now to Olivia Lyson reporting live from Parliament House. Olivia, can you tell us what's happening?" asked the anchorman.

"Well, as you can see, James, things have calmed down here at the world's capitol. Last evening, during what was to be President Keating's first global address in years, she had planned to announce the release of an inoculation for the Scourge epidemic that has plagued the world for years now. It was during that announcement that a group of unknown people, people the world is now calling *heroes*, exposed the truth of what Keating had in mind."

Carson giggled. "People are calling us heroes."

"Shh," Hudson said.

Footage rolled showing Ellen addressing Keating and the dramatic events that followed. "Keating claimed Vaccine X25 was the salvation for the world. But the mysterious heroes who took the stage claimed that it was a stronger version of the virus that can kill in hours instead of months. This so-called *super-virus* was to complete an alleged secret plot designed by President Keating to remove what she considered to be problematic populations of the planet." The screen then showed Keating rise and attack Hudson in her robotic form. "But what is even more disturbing is what followed. Even more surprises came to light when the group exposed the President as a *humanoid animatron*, leading many to wonder if there had ever been an Ophelia Keating at all." The screen changed to show various members of Parliament being taken into custody, including Colonel Arklow.

"I assure the people of the world that neither I, nor any of my associates, knew of the President's intentions or of her true form," said Arklow as they led him to the Authoritan cruiser. "We will sort this out as soon…" The camera panned away.

The reporter continued. "The public outcry was an uproar of the highest magnitude, one that has taken down the mighty Parliament, and rocked the foundation of this planet. Regions have had to enact their own type of internal state-like government to maintain order and prevent looting and riots while the planet regains order."

Aundrea Normand, a local Regional Representative for Region C, appeared on the screen from an emergency press conference. "The main goal is to keep order while reorganizing our structure as soon as possible," Representative Normand said. "The primary access servers to the Global Biotic Scan Database that sat in the lower levels of the Parliament building were destroyed, causing many BSCs to become non-functional. So, the Regional governmental bodies will provide paper vouchers tomorrow for those who can use them for redemption of banked Centicoin. Your monies are safe. Since identification of citizens remains essential, Biotic Security Registration will be reviewed to provide physical identification cards for individuals using a numerical identification system. Please report to your local Regional

Resource Departments first thing in the morning to begin these processes. Visit the web address at the bottom of this screen for instructions and frequently asked questions."

The reporter appeared on the screen again. "And what of our mysterious saviors? Who are they? Where did they go? There are those who say they remember these heroes, claiming they have returned from the dead, referring to them as the *Federation*."

The team turned and looked at Hudson in amazement as he smiled. Various shots of Hudson and the team showed on the screen.

"Regardless, whoever these folks are, I feel much safer knowing they are with us as we begin once again rebuilding our lives. Back to you, James."

Heather clicked off the television. "What. The. Hell."

"People are remembering," Damian said.

"The BSCs," Hudson replied. "The database is taking them out of commission. That confirms T.J.'s theory of memory suppression. People are now remembering the forgotten Federation. Paper money, identification cards, regional governments...the past is about to return."

"Is that a good thing?" Heather asked.

Hudson smiled. "In some ways...for sure."

Damian flopped down beside Hudson. "I wonder...how was it possible that David survived Xenathium? Did he not inherit Wrath's weaknesses with his strengths? Wouldn't all of us?"

"Well, we've suspected that things would be different with you guys. You're not exact matches to your genetic counterpart. Some powers are different, like Ellen's talking to computers, Carson actually having wings. It appears that some of your weaknesses are also different," Hudson advised.

"What are our weaknesses?" Carson asked.

"I don't know," Hudson said. He sat the remote to the television on the table. "And I don't want to know."

"And what about Goliaric?" Heather asked.

Hudson deliberated for a moment. "Well, if he...or *they*...had the right pieces to make an actual Odyssey, I assume they are home on

Xenoe."

Carson raised an eyebrow. "Which makes me wonder if they'll come back, try to get Earth again."

"Oh, knowing Goliaric, I'd bet on it," Hudson said. "But that shouldn't be for a long, long time, if at all. Now that Goliaric realizes he has no idea what weakens you, he'll be more cautious about pissing you off."

"And he better, by God!" Carson said as he took a sip of his orange juice

"Calm down, Captain Asinine," Heather said, causing Carson to choke on his drink.

"Which reminds me…I want a real superhero name," Carson said.

"And I would enjoy a breathtaking superhero uniform," Damian said. "I believe Heather has very affable ideas, and suitable titles for us. Come to think of it…we still need a name for David."

"Brawn," Heather said. "I say we call him Brawn. I've been all over that. Oh!" she said as giddy as a child. "Hudson, can we go play in the Armory? I want to make some uniforms."

Hudson smiled and nodded his head. With a sigh he said, "Go on." The group took off like a shot. "And *don't* break anything! If you don't know what it is—don't touch it!"

And as the team trampled over one another trying to get to the Core Armory, Hudson got up from the chair and walked to Mainframe. But instead of accessing the extensive digital library at his disposal, he reached into the desk and retrieved a small photo album. He turned through to the pages to first photo he had taken with the team as an official member of the Federation. Not the youngsters of the present, but the friends of the past.

Soon, it would be a new world built from the ashes of time-worn principles, traditional freedoms, and old ideas—the best ideas. The inevitable dissolution of Region H would lead to the rebirth of Hudson's beloved Seventh City. It was redemption, true and pure, a rare gift given upon a chosen few, and now he could partake in its riches. What adventures lay ahead of them? The dangers? The wonders? He could only guess. And as he turned to the old photo of him and Steve Sutherland, he touched the inscription at the bottom of the photograph that read: *To my little bro, Andre: Remember, the seed of hope always grows best in the soil of destruction.*

And Hudson smiled.

VISIT THE FACTORY

Travel to
WWW.FICTIONFACTORYINC.COM
for super

FORGOTTEN

FEDERATION

merchandise and learn about the wonders of the Neither Realm.
Also be sure to FOLLOW THE FACTORY on...

Twitter @FictionFacInc
&
Facebook—https://www.facebook.com/FictionFacInc

CPSIA information can be obtained
at www.ICGtesting.com
Printed in the USA
LVOW01s1445190417

531397LV00008B/674/P